Alan Stoob: Nazi Hunter

Alan Stoob:
Nazi Hunter

*One man's continuing battle
against the Third Reich*

Alan Stoob
Britain's Premier Nazi Hunter™

A novel by Saul Wordsworth

CORONET

First published in Great Britain in 2014 by Coronet
An imprint of Hodder & Stoughton
An Hachette UK company

1

Copyright © Saul Wordsworth 2014

The right of Saul Wordsworth to be identified as the Author of the
Work has been asserted by him in accordance with the Copyright,
Designs and Patents Act 1988.

A CIP catalogue record for this title is available
from the British Library

ISBN 9781444791174
Ebook ISBN 9781444791181

Typeset in Adobe Garamond by Palimpsest Book Production Limited,
Falkirk, Stirlingshire
Printed and bound by Clays Ltd, St Ives plc

Hodder & Stoughton policy is to use papers that are natural,
renewable and recyclable products and made from wood
grown in sustainable forests. The logging and manufacturing
processes are expected to conform to the environmental
regulations of the country of origin.

Hodder & Stoughton Ltd
338 Euston Road
London NW1 3BH

www.hodder.co.uk

– For Edame Stoob

10% of all profits from this book will be donated to the
Simon Wiesenthal Centre

Alan's website: www.nazihunteralan.com
Alan's Twitter account: @nazihunteralan
Alan's fax number: Dunstable 371

Acknowledgements

I would like to express gratitude to the friends and family who have allowed me to include them in this book.

Thanks also to disgraced President Richard Nixon who inspired me to record all my conversations. Exchanges included here are accurate to the nearest syllable.

Foreword

In February of 1994 I was clearing my desk in advance of retirement. I was fifty-seven years old and had enjoyed a moderately successful career with the Bedfordshire Constabulary. As I packed away a pamphlet entitled *Known Pickpockets in the Luton Area* I reccived a phone call.

'Hello?' I said.

'Can I speak with Alan Stool?'

'Speaking – and it's Stoob.'

'Mr Stoot, this is Simon Wiesenthal – the most famous Nazi Hunter the world has ever known – speaking. Is this a good moment?'

'Not exactly,' I replied. 'I'm just packing up my things and moving to Bournemouth.'

'I know,' he replied. 'That's why I'm calling. Come to Vienna and meet me. It's important. You will find a return ticket in your jacket. Goodbye, Mr Stoop.'

I checked my breast pocket. There, nestled between a Bic biro and two glucose tablets, was a return ticket to Vienna International Airport. I dialled 1471, the last-call return service which had come into general use the year before.

'Good morning, Simon Wiesenthal's office, Simon Wiesenthal speaking, how may I help you?'

'I don't go anywhere without Edame,' I said.

'What is Edame?'

'Edame is my wife, Mr Wiesenthal.'

'Fine – I'll arrange it. See you tomorrow.'

That evening my retirement party passed me by. What did Simon Wiesenthal, the finest Nazi Hunter of all time, want from me? What could I possibly give the man who tracked down Adolf Eichmann, put the fear of god into all surviving Nazis and had an institute named in his honour? I may have helped throw the book at local recidivist George 'Eggs' Benedict but that was small beer by comparison. In the night I was sick with nerves.

The next morning we caught a cab to Luton Airport, flew to Vienna, checked into our hotel, took an afternoon nap and got ready. At 3pm we found ourselves face to face with a legend.

'Good of you to come over, Mr Stoon,' he said and embraced me. He felt thin and quite religious.

'It's Stoob – and wonderful to meet you, Mr Wiesenthal.'

'And this must be Edame,' he said before kneeling down to kiss her hand, overbalancing and crashing into a filing cabinet. Edame often has that effect on men.

'The reason I bring you here today is simple,' he said, recovering his poise. 'I am a sick man. The doctors have given me only fifteen years to live. That may seem like a long time to you. Truth be told it seems like a long time to me too, especially as I am already eighty-three. But I have so much work to do and I don't think I can cram it all in, so to speak.'

He winked at Edame.

'I have been watching you, Stoot. I have spies everywhere. Your superiors have been impressed by the expertise and insight you've shown in the areas of hiding and hunting, and the psychology of being on the run.'

He paused and scratched an elongated ear.

'I know you are planning a move to Sidmouth.'

'Bournemouth,' I interjected.

'Whatever. The point is – don't. Why waste your talent?'

'What do you propose?' I asked.

'Do you know how many Nazi war criminals there are at large in Great Britain?' he enquired.

'I don't,' I said, 'But I can find out for you if you like.'

'248!' he exclaimed. '248. Including 193 in Bedfordshire alone.'

'Bedf—'

'I need someone – the *world* needs someone – to carry out my work in the UK. Britain is the new South America, Bedfordshire its Paraguay. There are Nazis everywhere, Alan, elderly wizened ones emerging from drains and cul-de-sacs, seeking out cheap plastic surgery in Houghton Regis, integrating into the community. *You must find them.*'

We left confused. Wiesenthal himself had seemed confused, befuddled even. Were these the ramblings of a scattered mind wrung dry by obsession and kosher gin? Back home I visited the local library, principally to borrow a book about retirement activities for ex-policemen. Our daughter Tina works there. She's 6'1" and was crowned Bedfordshire Schools High Hurdles Champion in 1982. I brought up the meeting with Wiesenthal.

'It's true, Dad,' she said, towering over me. 'We did it at school. Apparently boatloads of Nazis landed in Brighton in the late sixties then caught the Thameslink to Bedford.'

'You mean the formerly-titled Bed-Pan line, so-named after the Bedford to St Pancras link?'

'Yes,' she replied. 'How's Tom?'

Tom is our son. He's forty-two and stuck in the past. More on him later.

The next time I saw Tina she handed me a folder. What I saw shocked me. She'd used A4 paper to photocopy A5 documentation. I've rarely seen such waste. But the contents were fascinating. Clearly Wiesenthal, despite seeming half-crazed and with only fifteen years to live, knew what he was talking about. I picked up the phone.

'Good morning, Simon Wiesenthal's office, Simon Wiesenthal speaking. How can I help you?'

It was him.

'You were right,' I said.

'Ah, Stooq.'

I didn't bother correcting him.

'I knew you'd come round,' he panted.

'I want the job,' I said. 'I want to be Britain's Premier Nazi Hunter.'

'I'm pleased,' he replied.

There was a long pause.

'You know that for many of us this is personal.'

I nodded. After a while I realised he would not have heard my nod so I said the word 'yes' into the receiver.

Another pause.

'Do you care enough?'

This was the elephant down the phone line. I thought hard. Was hunting Nazis a job for a goy? Could a gentile fulfil such a role with the same venom, vehemence and vigilance as a card-carrying Jew?

Unbidden I am transported back seventy-three years, to an apparently ordinary afternoon playing with my toys while my parents listen to the wireless. The regular programme is interrupted by a message from Neville Chamberlain. My father seems particularly agitated. Chamberlain ends with the words, 'I have to tell you now that no such undertaking has been received, and that consequently this country is at war with Germany.'

Fast-forward to 1941. I am stood at Leighton Buzzard Station with my mother. My small suitcase is packed. Mummy doesn't have one. I don't understand why.

'Take care, brave little Alan,' she says, stifling her tears. 'This is for your own good.'

When I return nothing is the same.

'Yes,' I told Wiesenthal. 'I do care enough. Hitler killed millions but decimated the lives of many more besides. I was evacuated during the war, the only southerner in a northern town. I won't go into detail but it wasn't pleasant. In addition I was born left-handed, am short for my age and had to wear glasses for many years. I may not be Jewish but I identify with the outsider. And like any decent person I believe what the Nazis did to be beyond dreadful.'

'Did – and are doing to this day, Stoov,' said Wiesenthal. 'I appreciate your honesty. Yours are the words of a thoughtful man. You have conscience and integrity. I wish you well in your quest. The job is yours. All I ask in return is your eternal vigilance. Any questions, call me. I'm here most days. If I'm out just leave me a message or send me a fax. Actually a fax is preferable. I love faxes, they're completely brilliant.'

Edame and I cancelled our plans to retire to Bournemouth, I converted Tina's old room into a study and embarked upon my second career – that of Britain's Premier Nazi Hunter.

I have always kept a diary. As I write this I am in my seventy-sixth year. When you reach my age it's easy to forget small details, big news and, on occasions, the names of your own children, Tina and Tom. If you add alcohol – as Edame and I have been known to do on occasion – your life can quickly descend into a haze of hogwash until one day you wake up dead. This is why I keep a diary.

Six months ago a publisher approached me and asked if I wanted to write a book about Nazi Hunting.

'No,' I said. 'I'm too busy looking for them. Plus I could die any moment and the book would be left unfinished.'

'OK,' they said and went away.

Then they came back.

'Alan?' they asked.

'Yes,' I replied.

'Do you keep a diary?'

'Yes.'

'Could we publish one of your diaries instead?'

'OK.'

'Thanks, Alan. What about the one from last year?

'That's a good one. Lots happened. Knock yourself out.'

Alan Stoob, January 2013

Who's Who in Stoob's World

Edame Stoob	Wife
Tom Stoob	Son
Tina Conti	Daughter
Marco Conti	Son-in-law
Haden Conti	Grandson
Houdini Conti	Granddaughter
Bob Scalp	Neighbour
Nigel Hitchin	CEO, British Nazi Hunting Association
Interpol Steve	Steve (works for Interpol)
Heinrich Snuff	Bad Nazi
Felix Pump	Bad Nazi
Stefan Cuntz	Good Nazi
Dr Moshe Grossmark	Physician
Detective Constable Mike Moomin	Bedfordshire policeman
Potato George	Edame's ex-boyfriend
George Michael	Popular singer
The Griffin	Nazi Nemesis

– The history of man is the history of crimes, and history can repeat

(Simon Wiesenthal)

– The past is the future

(Gary Lineker)

January

Wake with a mouth like Hitler's bunker. Edame and I drank an entire bottle of Sainsbury's Basics port to usher in the New Year. Not sure I like port. It was, after all, Hitler's tipple of choice. While Edame sleeps it off I give the study a clear-out. There are Post-Its everywhere, newspaper cuttings and endless printouts of Nazi sightings. I make two piles: one of possible leads and one for Monday's recycling. As I do I come across my last-ever letter from Wiesenthal, congratulating me on ensnaring Boris Boot, the Prannock of Potsdam, back in 2005.

> You have undoubtedly blossomed into Britain's finest Nazi huntsman.

It says.

> Until last year I would have put Arthur Pob ahead of you but since your audacious swoop on evil Boris Boot in Flitwick Town Hall you are now firmly entrenched in the number-one spot. Who could have known that Nazi hunting would so quickly establish itself as the career of choice for ex-policemen in the UK.
> How glad I am that you and Edame are back on track. It is vital you have stability in your personal life. This is of

course true of any job but in particular the emotionally demanding role of Nazi Hunter. You are a credit to the industry, Alan. Stay vigilant and stay in touch. Send me a letter or even better a fax. Have I ever told you how much I enjoy receiving faxes? They're incredible.

Inspired anew by Si's words I sit at my desk and create a fresh document in Word for Windows entitled *Alan Stoob's Key Targets for 2012 by Alan Stoob*. Using the bullet point tool I list my top three most wanted: Heinrich Snuff (The Truncheon of München), Silas Pilsner (The Schweinhund of Schleswig) and The Nibble Sisters, Myra and Valerie. I print off the list and circle Snuff, who according to the latest Interpol intel was spotted only last Thursday strangling a cat outside Biggleswade Station.

I then slip on the weighted pants Edame bought me for Christmas and start the year as I mean to go on by speed walking round the block. What it says on the box is true; once removed you feel as light as anything. I experience some mild chafing but the instructions state this should pass. After applying nappy rash cream I return to my desk to find an email from local business, Pete's Hams.

Dear Alan

It is with great regret that I must inform you we are unable to continue sponsorship of your vital work tracking down Britain's surviving Nazi war criminals in the Bedfordshire region. Our business has fallen dramatically in the past year, principally because people keep buying sausages online. You may have noticed we've had to slash our prices to compete with the likes of Amazon, Walmart and eBay.

All of us at Pete's Hams hope we can still count on your business.

Wishing you every success for 2012.
Regards from Pete of Pete's Hams

PS Love to Edame.

I didn't expect that from Pete, we've always bought our chops there. I pull up my sponsorship spreadsheet and amend accordingly. Deep down I know why Pete has withdrawn his support. I suspect it's the same reason Radio Rentals, Somerfield, Café Gnob, NATO and the UN have done the same: the Whipsnade Incident. Briefly I feel despondent until Edame enters on the dot of eleven with a kiss on the cheek and a hot Ribena in my Britain's Premier Nazi Hunter™ mug.

'I hope you're not frettings too much about Whipsnade,' she says.

'Course not,' I reply. 'Onwards and upwards, my love. 2012 is going to be Alan's year.'

'You are the loveliest, most handsome Nazi Hunter I know!'

'More handsome even than Arthur Pob?'

'Don't be the silly billies!'

I look deep into her pale Dutch eyes.

'Listen, Edame, about last ni—'

She puts a finger to my lips.

'There is more than one ways to be a man, Alan Stoob.'

Heartened, I dedicate the afternoon to researching Wolfgang Schnitzel, the Helmet of Hanover. Sources claim he is hiding out in the rabbit holes of Luton Hoo, though this remains unconfirmed. It is sickening to learn he once broke his daughter's arm so she would fit in a suitcase. Therefore I am glad for the distraction of a phone call on the office line. It's our son Tom.

He arrives ten minutes later plugged into his Sony Walkman and heads straight for his old room. Emerging shortly after clutching a bag of cassettes and the life-sized ET given to him by his ex-girlfriend Susan back in 1987, he hops on his Grifter and is gone. One of the tyres is completely flat. He looks terribly out of condition. His increasingly unpredictable behaviour is troubling all of us. In light of the withdrawal of Pete's Hams we may not be able to keep his Toddington flat on for much longer.

Spend the rest of the afternoon brainstorming fundraising ideas by myself. Following the failure of last year's T-shirt campaign ('Nazis – they're not for everyone') I am drawn to the idea of a calendar. I jot down the word 'Alan-dar' before breaking off for a small sherry with Edame. She has taken Tom's fleeting appearance badly. To cheer us up I unwrap the *Bergerac* video box set she bought me for Christmas. John Nettles is clearly the finest actor of his generation, though Edame refuses to believe he dyes his hair.

Before retiring I print off mugshots of my three principal targets for the year and pin them to the wall.

Edame and I end the evening with an intimate massage. She asks if she can call me John. I don't reply.

*   *   *

Last night I dreamt I cornered Jurgen Moof, the Plasterer of Paris, and was throttling him with my bare hands. I awake clutching a filled sock. I don't tell Edame, she would only make a quip about Derek Boone, Britain's least successful Nazi Hunter of the past decade.

I leave my shapely wife reading her large print copy of *Fifty Shades of Grey* and prepare myself a kosher breakfast of gefilte fish and scrambled egg with matzah. Despite my gentile status I find orthodox Jewish fare helps focus the mind.

In the study the red message light flashes urgently.

Alan. Nigel here from the British Nazi Hunting Association. Hope all is well, old chap. This is merely a courtesy call to remind you that the position of Britain's Premier Nazi Hunter is up for renewal later in the summer. This means putting in a solid performance in the first half of the year. No time to live off past glories or get hung up on failures. In other words, let's not dwell on Whipsnade. At 74 you're entering your prime as a hunter. Remember, Wiesenthal did some of his finest work in his early 80s, notably securing the arrest of evil Truma Smung. All of us here at the BNHA are rooting for you. Frankly none of us want Herb Derb in the position.

Thanks, Alan. Oh, and love to Edame.

If Whipsnade taught me anything it is never to run low on my blue inhaler. With that in mind I dig out my repeat prescription chit and circle Ventalin (asthma), Clopidogrel (angina), Naprosyn (arthritis) Magnesium Hydroxide (constipation) Loperamide (diarrhoea) and Citalopram (anxiety and clinical depression).

At the surgery they greet me warmly, particularly Dr Grossmark who bounds out of his consultancy room and implores me to 'nail that Jerry bastard'.

On the 62 bus home a woman tells her friend she has broken a nail. 'It's like the worst thing in history,' she says. I lean forward and politely remind her of the Holocaust.

Back home I find a note lying on the mat. Could be my first big lead of 2012.

TESCO'S LEAGRAVE THURSDAY 11AM

PETFOOD AISLE

COME ALONE

A FRIEND

I ask Edame if she saw anyone come to the house but she claims she was too engrossed in her book to notice. I study the handwriting. It is written with the precision of expression and the kind of efficiency one would normally associate with a German or (at a stretch) an Austrian. The Rs lean backwards indicating sociopathology or a strong wind. The ink is blue meaning the scribe is a man. The nib is a fountain, ergo the messenger is over fifty, wealthy or pompous. The paper is of high quality and smells like the beaches of Aberystwyth. I dust the letterbox for fingerprints but all I find are traces of saliva left by Goebbels, our Labrador, who died suddenly in 2007.

I suggest to Edame we visit Tesco's later in the week. She is a creature of habit. I could have anticipated the response.

'But you know we always shop at the Sainsbury.'

'What if we get there and I can't find a banana?'

'Anyway it say "come alone".'

I handle all of Edame's objections but the truth of the matter is I want her there for moral support. My supermarket agoraphobia has worsened considerably since Whipsnade. Dr Grossmark says I should have her with me whenever possible ('The world doesn't need a Nazi Hunter with panic attacks, Alan').

After dinner I take the note to local handwriting specialist Edgar Mopp. Edgar isn't in but his wife Maud has a look and says she believes it to be 'the work of a man – or a woman'. Something of a wasted journey.

Edame and I pass the evening watching two more episodes of *Bergerac*. I remain transfixed by Nettles' effortless charisma, which is so much more pronounced than during his *Midsomer Murders* era. It must be the confidence of youth. A profound sadness washes over me. Nettles is Edame's sex-in-a-lift crush – i.e., if they ever get trapped in a lift together they have my blessing to make love. Considering changing mine from seventies daytime television doyenne Mavis Nicholson to Denise Welch off *Loose Women*. Not that I could do much about it even if we were stuck between floors for a month.

Bob from next-door pops round. He says he's come to feed the cat while we're away. We tell him we've never had a cat and we're not going anywhere. He looks confused and extremely tired. I invite him in and he snoozes on the sofa. We let him out at midnight, just like we would the cat we've never owned.

*   *   *

Wake in surprisingly good mood. Today is Tuesday. Hermann Goering died on a Tuesday.

Begin the day with stretching routine in Tom's old room. Midway through a lunge my hip pops out. Thankfully I am able to force it back in by ramming it against the hostess trolley, just in time for my 9am conference call with Interpol.

I am faced as ever with the rigmarole of their phone system ('If you've captured an internationally-renowned serial killer press one; if you're on the run for a crime you did not commit press two . . .'). Truly the whole organisation is a shower, yet whenever I try to complain they shut down their customer service department. Last Friday the whole of Interpol took the afternoon off to go ten-pin bowling.

The conversation begins with the news that one of their

agents has tracked Hitler's missing testicle to a leisure park outside Boulogne. It's hard to tell whether they're pulling my leg so I play along. After the usual sexual badinage it's down to business.

I learn that:

1. Mathias Wengl's new name is Roderick Smoof and he runs a gastropub in Caddington.

2. Evil Alois Purlang, the Muppet of Mannheim, was recently spotted scavenging for leftovers at the rear of Pizza Express, Bedford Town Centre.

3. Boots of Harlington has reported that Hertz van Rental, the Badger of Bottrop, purchased a Foley all-silicone catheter last Tuesday.

They end by telling me an especially foul joke about a hamster. I force myself to laugh but truly they revolt me. Plus they insist on rhyming Edame with 'arm' and not 'army'. If it wasn't for local Nazi leads I would sever all contact with them in a heartbeat.

No sooner am I off the phone to Interpol than my former colleague Detective Constable Mike Moomin appears at the door. I ask him about the Pinkerton case ('Too early to call but we're pretty sure we know who threw shit at the mayor') and we engage in small talk. When I ask him in he tells me his isn't a social call.

Instantly my brain switches to overdrive.

What does he mean?

Has something happened?

Is it Edame?

'I'm sorry to have to tell you, Alan, that at 1400 local time we apprehended a Mr Thomas Stoob shoplifting a plastic sword from the 99p shop. We arrested him and are letting him off with a caution. I know you could do without this, especially after Whipsnade.'

I pick Tom up at Dunstable police station. Poor lad looks glummer than Rudolf Hess at a bar mitzvah so I administer a Werther's Original. I know they're German but so was Johnny Weissmuller and he is our favourite Tarzan. In the car I ask him what he wanted the sword for. He claims he 'just felt angry', is 'very sorry' and 'could I come and stay for a few days?' I tell him it would be lovely to have him around.

Once home Tom goes straight to his old room and locks the door. The deafening sound of what Edame identifies as The Thompson Twins is accompanied by the sweet aroma of marijuana. As the former self-proclaimed Constable of Dunstable I cannot condone the inhalation of class B drugs but it's his only solace.

Dinner in silence. Tom sits there with his Walkman on, chasing potato waffles round the plate. Edame barely touches her salad. A solitary tear rolls down her porcelain Dutch cheek. She dabs it with a radish before draining her wine. I feel like I've failed our boy. Perhaps I was too busy with the force when he was young. We both place a hand on his formless shoulder as he struggles with the Ice Magic.

The mood is lightened when our grandson Haden pops round. He's wearing his trousers so low I can see his pants (thankfully they're clean). Haden and I leave Edame and Tom to re-runs of *Tales Of The Unexpected* and retire upstairs to

Stoob HQ. Haden shows me the Nazi hunting website he's constructed at my behest. It includes a short history of National Socialism, an updated list of the five most wanted Nazis in Bedfordshire and a contact page with my phone and fax details. The site even has music, though I'm not sure the theme from *Jaws* is an appropriate choice.

I offer to pay him. He says he doesn't want money (a relief), announcing instead he would like to accompany me on my next Nazi hunt. I'm a little shocked by this and tell him that at the grand old age of fifteen his vigilance levels are unlikely to be fully developed. He reminds me he will be sixteen in two weeks' time and that at 6'4" and 132 pounds he is more than capable of looking after himself. His height is definitely an advantage though his lack of bulk remains a concern. He looks like Peter Crouch on a grapefruit diet. Before leaving he changes the tune on the website from *Jaws* to the theme from *Schindler's List*.

The day ends with the sad news that Ludvig Froop, Belgium's foremost Nazi Hunter, has died after a long battle with the local council. The Gent of Ghent will be sorely missed.

*   *   *

Feel so vigilant today I wake before five. Must be the prospect of meeting my mystery informant. Only visited the bathroom three times in the night. The last time that happened Michael Foot was leader of the Labour Party.

We start the day by lighting a candle and observing a minute's silence in memory of our dog Goebbels, who died five years ago to the day. Tom joins us. He and Goebby were very close. Tom is inconsolable. I breakfast alone.

After the washing up, during which Edame insists on

humming the theme to *Bergerac*, we leave Tom to arrange his collection of *Whizzer and Chips* in chronological order and head to Tesco's and my 11am appointment.

We arrive early. Early is reassuring, as is the presence of a blue inhaler in my pocket. We load up on a few staples before I leave Edame by the prunes and head off to meet the stranger.

The aisle is empty. I stroll cautiously towards the pet food section and wait. A few lonely-looking ladies stoop to pick up huge bags of cat litter but otherwise there is little activity. To kill time I run through the top ten Nazis I've hunted. I've read that reminding oneself of past successes boosts confidence. Just as I reach Edith Tongue, the Harlot of Hamburg, I notice a message scrawled in bold letters on a jumbo pack of animal bedding.

I SAID **ALONE**

FLITWICK BOWLS CLUB MONDAY 10AM

NO EDAME THIS TIME

A FRIEND

I tell Edame the mystery informant was a no show and we finish our shop. It is only when we return home that I reveal the truth. Rapidly she spirals into one of her Dutch furies, calling me a 'bloody idiots' and shrieking abuse. At one point she even suggests we get plastic surgery ('just like Nazis!') to avoid detection. I understand where she is coming from, though I don't see why she needs breast augmentation – or me a penis extension. When I challenge her she hurls the Britain's Premier Nazi Hunter™ mug at my head. I duck just in time. China fragments litter the floor. It's like Kristallnacht. Tom comes downstairs in tears and asks if we're going to get a divorce.

I should never have taken Edame along. It was a mistake. But since Whipsnade my confidence has been fragile, my self-belief shot to pieces as if by a trained SS assassin. We sweep up the mess and Edame apologises. She rarely gets angry but when she does it's over in a flash. We hug and she massages my bunions before starting dinner.

My daughter Tina and her husband Marco arrive for a summit meeting. Tina is wearing heels which allied to her coat-hanger shoulders means she blocks out most of the light. She towers over the rest of us including Marco, who is whippet thin and alert, endlessly checking his phone.

The four of us discuss Tom, who remains upstairs listening to Bananarama. Marco says he is happy to go and knock some sense into him. We all agree this is a bad idea. Edame pulls out Tom's psychiatric notes and reads.

Thomas Douglas Bader Stoob is a 42-year-old man suffering from an acute case of arrested development triggered after his ex-girlfriend Susan Clawfoot broke off their relationship in 1988. Tom is suspended in the past and unable to face up to the reality of his current situation. His symptoms include petulance in the presence of adults, on-off regression and remaining in his room compiling miscellaneous tapes of '80s music then sending them to Susan.

'They were so good together,' says Tina. 'It's just a shame she moved to New Zealand in 1991, got married and had four children.'

Midway through our conversation Tom appears in his *Metal Mickey* pyjamas and asks if anyone has a spare TDK D90 he can borrow.

After dinner I retire to my study to write a letter to David Baddiel because I read he was once voted Britain's sixth Sexiest Jew.

Bob shows up at 11 and tells me how sorry he is to hear about the death of my brother, Horace. I inform him that I have never had a brother and was born an only child. He says he feels faint and asks if he can have a glass of water. We show him to the spare room. Before we can fetch a blanket he's spark out.

Woken at 3am by the phone. Wagner plays down the line. Soon a whispering Germanic voice sings strange words to the strains of 'Close To You' by The Carpenters.

Why do Nazis suddenly appear/
Every time you are near/
Just like Mengele/
They wish to stay/
Close to you.

My home-made phone tracer suggests these calls are coming from the Houghton Regis area. It has all the hallmarks of my nemesis, The Griffin, but for now I have no proof.

*   *   *

Wake with a sore throat and an erection. The latter passes in no time, the former lingers. Forced to gargle with warm brine. Not the best start to the day.

Bob is still fast asleep. I greet him with a cup of tea. He looks confused and asks whether it's true the president has been shot. Prior to Gladys's death he was as energetic and bright an eighty-six-year-old as you were likely to meet. Bereavement has knocked him sideways. Apparently this kind of fatigue-amnesia is common after the death of a spouse. I just hope Edame and I go at the same time, ideally on a luxury cruise round the Caribbean, all drinks included.

Over breakfast Edame reveals she is lunching with her old boyfriend, Potato George. She always tells me on the day of their meeting, perhaps to spare me weeks of fretting. Although they broke up in 1959 he's always on the scene, waiting for me to slip up. I feign indifference but inside I'm dying. This is made worse when Edame hums the music to 'Private Dancer' by Tina Turner throughout the morning. If George were a real potato I'd mash him.

The moment she leaves I am seized by a terrible fear. I recognise it instantly as separation anxiety triggered by my evacuation to the Yorkshire Dales in 1940 and the dreadful events that ensued. Seventy years on and the psychic wound is still gaping. Even though I understand why I feel this way, when it comes there's almost nothing I can do to stop it.

In an attempt to distract myself I switch on *Escape To The Country*. Aled Jones has certainly filled out since his choirboy days. He must be at least a B-cup. I wonder whether Simon Wiesenthal ever sought comfort in daytime television. Perhaps he'd become engrossed by the big game between Haifa Tel Aviv and Eilat FC or dip into *Old Jews Tell Jokes*, though I doubt it. Perhaps all it takes for evil to flourish is that good men watch daytime TV.

Then a thought strikes me: Wiesenthal would *never* be diverted from the pursuit of Nazis, whether his delinquent son had stolen a plastic sword or his wife was out with her ex, because for him it was personal. He was a Jewish man on a mission born of personal experience. What am I? Just a goy. Si carved out a unique career chiselled from hatred, passion and the overwhelming desire to right a wrong. I'm just an old man who made a fool of himself at a safari park.

How much do I hate Nazis? On a scale of 1–10 I'd say a 9.

Many are utterly despicable but some, for instance Albert Speer, have redeeming qualities. Even Hitler liked dogs, though he did shoot his German Shepherd, Blondi, before taking his own life. Assuming that he's dead of course. A recent sighting places him living rough in the Ampthill area, though this is unconfirmed.

It's not that I don't like Jews. I admire them immensely: Jackie Mason, Sasha Distel, Benjamin Netanyahu, Albert Einstein, George Cohen, Woody Allen (especially his early stuff), Golda Meir, Peter Falk, my former colleague Detective Sergeant Eli Goldman, Simon and Garfunkel, Sacha Baron Cohen, Stephen Spielberg . . .

Where the hell is Edame?

By now I know the signs. I'm slipping into a full psychological meltdown. There's nothing else for it. I call Beryl.

'You've reached the voicemail of Beryl Tant, psychotherapist and masseuse. Please leave your message after the tone.'

'Hi Beryl!' I say, self-consciously upbeat. 'Alan here, hunter of Nazis. Sorry to call but I've got myself into a bit of a state. I know it's not our appointment day but I was wondering if we could have a quick chat? I'm feeling pretty wretched, actually. Tom's got himself into trouble, people keep mentioning Whipsnade, Edame's out with Potato George and apart from everything else I haven't been able to get it u—'

'Alan,' a voice interrupts, 'this is Beryl.'

'Beryl!' I blurt. 'I was just leaving you a message. Hope you don't mind me call—'

'I heard your message, Alan. I'm sorry you've been experiencing some challenges today but as you know this is my rest day. Let's explore these issues during our next session.'

'OK Beryl,' I reply. 'I suppose all I wanted was a few words of reassur—'

She hangs up.

I pop my head round Tom's door to see if he fancies a chat but he's solemnly reading an old copy of *Look-In* so I exit. Downstairs I flick through *Cycling Weekly* but am unable to concentrate so I slip on the weighted pants and head for the door.

The gentle rhythm of my step helps ('exercise improves your mood by releasing endolphins' according to Edame) as does the fresh Dunstable air, though the chafing is worse this time. It seems I'm oversensitive to both small slights and slight smalls.

After half an hour I am calm enough to seize hold of my thoughts. How can it be that after so much time, so many pills and talking cures, I remain prone to such anxiety? I'd like to blame Hitler for ripping me from the family teat and depositing me with cruel and sadistic strangers, as well as for the seismic loss I faced upon my return. But if Beryl has taught me one thing it is to assume responsibility for one's own troubles. Still: fuck you, Adolf.

When I return Edame is home. I ask how Potato George was. She says he's depressed because he has to wait nineteen months for a new hip. This cheers me up. An afternoon nap followed by three chapters of *Feel The Fear And Do It Anyway* by Susan Jeffers and the cloud has almost lifted, though after today I realise I am not yet ready to come off the anti-depressants.

Having lost most of the day to my mood I work through dinner. As ever I am sidetracked by nonsense from the general public ('Is Cher a Nazi? At no point during "If I Could Turn Back Time" does she mention killing Hitler.') There is also a message offering a no-win-no-fee for Nazi Hunters injured in the line of duty.

We end the evening watching a film called *Trading Places*.

Janet Leigh's daughter, Jamie Lee Curtis, is very fetching. The bit where she removes her bra is completely exciting.

In bed I asked Edame if I can call her Jamie Lee. She doesn't reply.

*   *   *

The day I am supposed to meet my mystery informant at the bowls club and the ground is thick with snow. My attempts to reverse the car out of the drive end in failure. Bob comes out to help but slips and cracks his knee on the bumper. Edame takes him in and gives him a hot Ribena. He falls asleep immediately. I hope the mystery informant understands the weather is preventing me from making it out to see him. Assuming of course it's a him. It could yet be a trap from the evil daughter of Heinrich Slaughter.

By late-afternoon the snow is thawing and the roads clearing so I take the Stoobmobile for its annual MOT. With money tight I decide not to bother with a full service. I wonder what Si would make of such a choice. It's hard to believe the great man would have compromised on the reliability of his primary method of transport. On reflection I shrug this off. I doubt he would think it was worth servicing a P-reg Vauxhall Omega. Besides, his elevated profile meant he received more funding than I could ever dream of. Rumours abounded of him paying for lap dances with petty cash.

Outside the garage I call Edame to see how Tom is. She says he seems OK and is upstairs playing *Buckaroo*. Mid-call my phone beeps. It's a text message from a secured number.

DON'T WORRY ABOUT THIS MORNING, WEATHER WAS JUST AWFUL, WASN'T IT? I DON'T SUPPOSE YOU'RE FREE NOW,

ARE YOU? IT'S JUST I'VE GOT THE DOCTOR'S TOMORROW
AND DIALYSIS ON WEDNESDAY.

SAME PLACE?

TO REITERATE COME ALONE.

THE SAME FRIEND AS BEFORE.

I text Steve at Interpol to see if he'll cover a cab. He agrees so I flag down a people carrier on Dunstable High Street. Ten minutes later the driver drops me outside the front entrance of Flitwick's premier bowling association.

The gate is padlocked, the road cloaked in silence, the late afternoon cold and misty. I wish I'd worn an extra pair of cotton trousers. I hear a distant cough. In the dusk all I can see is smoke pouring forth from the chimneys. I hug myself for greater warmth. Another cough, this time louder. I make out the silhouette of a man walking unhurriedly towards me. He is wearing a homburg. Panicking, I fumble for my blue inhaler but it slips through the pocket lining. Before I can withdraw it the man is standing before me. He looks well over a hundred.

'Who are you?' I ask.

'A friend.'

His cut-glass accent and impeccable manner reminded me of the late Sir Alec Guinness. Was it possible he was a Nazi imitating an Englishman?

'Are you a Nazi imitating an Englishman?' I ask.

'Do I look like a Nazi?' he replies.

'Bit,' I say.

'That'll be mother. She was born in Nuneaton.'

He removes his hat, exposing a thick thatch of white hair, slightly off centre. A wig, perhaps.

'I need to know more if I am to trust you,' I tell him.

He looks down at his shoes, a pair of expensive Grenson Derbys.

'Very well, Mr Stoob,' he says, eventually. 'I am what is known as an independent agent. I sit between Interpol, Mossad, MI5, the Bundestag, the FBI, NATO, the UN, the EU, the Red Cross, the Belarusians and Dunstable Downs. I am not affiliated to any one of these organisations. I am everywhere and I am nowhere. I am a floater, if you will.'

'A floater?'

'If you will, Mr Stoob. Nobody knows my identity, my past, my present, my political leanings or my proclivity for strong cheese and cold sausages, and that is how it shall remain. I have contacts both high and low, names and faces you would recognise, yet none would recognise me. I have access to intelligence the likes of which you could only dream. I have seen files you didn't know existed on computers you couldn't envision from countries that dare not whisper their own name.'

'Oh,' I say, both impressed and bemused.

'I am happy to provide you with certain data, Mr Stoob. I have watched you from afar and am suitably impressed, particularly within the context of your waistline. But please don't ask who I am or I will lose patience and our arrangement shall be terminated.'

My waistline?

'You look very old, if you don't mind me saying.'

'I have seen combat, Mr Stoob. Both wars.' He gazes off into the distance. 'Thankfully I have been blessed with longevity.'

I looked down at his shoes once more and catch my own reflection. He set his eyes on me.

'I have information that could help you in your quest.'

'What sort of information?'

'Nazi information.'

'Ooh, that could be handy.'

'Mr Stoob, are you aware that your life is in danger?'

'Of course it is. I'm seventy-four.'

'I do not appear to be making myself clear. There are men out there who are, shall we say, out to terminate you.'

'They want me dead?'

'I can see you are not Britain's Premier Nazi Hunter for nothing. Take this.'

'What is it?'

'It's an aspirin. Helps thin the blood. In fact take one a day. They are ideal at your age. Also take this.'

'What is it?'

'The address of evil Heinrich Snuff, The Truncheon of München.'

I examine the piece of paper.

'This address – it says Harpenden. But that's . . . in Hertfordshire. I don't understand.'

'It is true that a great number of Britain's Nazis are resident in Bedfordshire, Mr Stoob. But not all. Those with the grandest ideas have been known to move outside of the mother county. Catch Snuff and he may lead you to The Griffin.'

'Catch The Griffin and I could . . .'

'Discover the location of the ratline that continues to bring surviving Nazi war criminals from Germany to the Chilterns?'

'Exactly. Hold on, I thought the Nazis arrived in Brighton by boat then caught the Thameslink up to Bedford?'

'They used to, Mr Stoob, but the ticket inspectors wised up. Now there is a state-of-the-art underground passage linking Bremen with Biggleswade.'

'I see.'

'Crafty bunch, the Nazis.'

'So I hear. How do you know all of this?'

'Like I say, I'm a floater.'

'A floater.'

'Like I say. Now I leave.'

'So soon?'

'I need a wee, Mr Stoob. At my age when you need to go there's no messing around.'

'Thank you so much, Mr Informant.'

'Vorsprung Durch Technic.'

The elderly man nodded in acknowledgement, turned and hobbled off into the night. Within seconds he had disappeared from view.

I stared back at the piece of paper.

20 Park Mount, Harpenden, Herts.

For now merely an address, in time perhaps my salvation. I memorise the data before swallowing it. It doesn't go down smoothly and I suffer instant heartburn. As ever I am thankful for pocket Gaviscon.

On the bus home I text Haden excitedly to tell him of the meeting. He replies 'BOOK'. When I ask what 'BOOK' means he says it's the predictive text version of 'COOL'. 'Yes BOOK', I write. He texts 'ROFL'. I reply 'Harris?' but never hear back.

Edame claims she's 'over a moon' when I tell her my news but she barely looks up from her new book, *Riders* by Jilly Cooper. Her face is flushed and her slacks partially unbuttoned.

I knock on Tom's door. He says he is pleased for me ('well

done, Dad, especially after Whipsnade') though his smile doesn't reach his eyes. He adds that he wishes he could assist in hunting down Bedfordshire's surviving Nazi war criminals. I reassure him that such a day will come but for now we need to concentrate on getting him better. He tells me he's written a song on the guitar and asks if he can play it to me. The song is called 'I Don't Like Change', has one chord and only four words ('I don't like change'). After five minutes I make my excuses and leave.

Confused by the earlier ROLF and BOOK conversations I find something online called the Senior Citizen Texting Code. It includes BFF (Best Friend Fell), BYOT (Bring Your Own Teeth) and LMDO (Laughing My Dentures Out). I print it out and stick it on the monitor.

Haden pops over after rugby practice. Shockingly his trousers are lower than last time. He also appears to have grown an inch and lost a stone. I give him an in-depth account of my mysterious meeting. He is fascinated and reminds me of his request to join the next hunt. He also helps me create a Twitter account. I send my first tweet ('Hello everyone. Stay vigilant. Regards Alan') but nothing happens. Immediately I follow some of my favourite people including Bradley Wiggins, Sir Alan Sugar and Stella Rimmington. I also follow David Baddiel and with Haden's help ask him whether he received my letter. He doesn't reply.

* * *

Today I slide effortlessly into my seventy-sixth year. To celebrate Edame gives me a foot massage and a state-of-the-art lumbar support for the car. I would happily have forgone the fancy cushion and doubled-up on the massage. That said, *Which?*

magazine claims the one she got me is the best in the price range.

Fun card from the Simon Wiesenthal Centre that moos when you turn it upside down. Classy one from the Kinnocks featuring a portrait of Aneurin Bevan. Nothing again from Boutros-Boutros Ghali. Still no idea what I've done to upset the man.

Morning spent in the study. Edame keeps popping in to plant small kisses on my cheek. She's so kind and loving but in the end I am forced to padlock the door. The price of hunting Nazis is constant vigilance and a strong work ethic.

I check my emails. Along with the usual timewasters ('I work by myself and suspect that I might be a Nazi, should I invade Poland?'), there are a handful of messages which independently place evil Heinrich Snuff in the nearby town of Harpenden, tallying with the tip-off I received from my mystery informant. I open my Britain's Premier Nazi Hunter™ leather-bound diary, mark next Saturday with a circled 'H' for hunt and add 'Haden?' in the margin.

My plan to spend a quiet evening watching *World At War* has been hijacked by Edame, who has arranged a family gathering. The gang arrives in a whirl of noise and gifts. My daughter Tina gives me *The Best of Lord Haw-Haw* on tape and a pair of foot alignment socks; her husband Marco hands over a crate of grappa (I don't drink grappa); Haden and his younger sister Houdini buy me a Gripmate Dexterity Aid and some angled chiropody scissors. Tom comes downstairs and says he would have got me something special but he's not allowed in the 99p shop anymore. He looks plump, balding and woebegone.

It's a typically boisterous Stoob family evening. Houdini

bosses everyone around using her pink wand and puts a spell on her brother Haden to keep his bedroom tidy. He fishes in his pocket, only to remove two fingers which he waves in her face. Houdini responds by punching him in the thigh with an impressive upper-cut. He winces. Houdini smiles, innocently twirling her dark curls.

Edame has prepared a lavish Dutch spread of bitterballen, stroopwafels and patat. The wine flows, most of it straight into Marco's mouth.

'Why don you just-ah get a job Tum, uh?' he says.

'Marco – leave it,' says Tina.

'Just asking a question, innit. You donna mind, do you, Tum?'

Tom shakes his head.

'Cos-ah you know the longer this-ah going on the more-ah you a burden on your mama anna papa?'

'Fuck's sake, Marco!' says Tina, rising to her impressive full height. She removes her glasses as if preparing for fisticuffs.

'Listen, baby,' says Marco, now lower in his seat, 'this ah-boy he-ah forty-two, he need to ah-know the problem he ah-causing to this-ah family.'

Tina remains standing.

'Why don't you have some olliebollen, Marco?' says Edame.

'When I was-ah your age Tum I already father of-ah two anna successful carpet fitter innit.'

'JUST LEAVE ME ALONE!' shrieks Tom before upsetting his plate of alphabetti spaghetti and fleeing. Tina gives Marco a hard stare ('Whah I do?') before hurrying after Tom. The party breaks up early, though not before Houdini eats an entire tube of English mustard. She's a tough little number and quite the character.

Tom takes a long bath with his comics then comes downstairs in his Luton Town FC dressing gown and asks if I'll read the first chapter of *Stig Of The Dump* to him in bed. I do this with a heavy heart. Edame takes over as I begin to flag and gives him two spoons of Phenergan to help him sleep. Not sure I approve but it seems to relax him. We used to administer it when he was a child. Perhaps it reminds him of happier times. There certainly aren't many of those at the moment. He appears to be regressing.

Bob pops by with a drawing he has done of a mouse in a top hat. He plonks himself on the sofa and falls straight to sleep. We throw a blanket over his feet and one over his face before turning out the light.

At midnight Edame perches on the end of our bed and brushes her still-glorious auburn hair.

'What can we doing about our son?' she says. 'If only he could find some ways to get over that silly Susan. Human being is like a fish. If it doesn't move forward it died.'

'I know, my love,' I say. 'We have to keep taking him to the psychiatrist, keep making him take his pills and hope for the best.'

We end the night with a short session of mutual masturbation. I remain flaccid but enjoy the camaraderie.

* * *

The day begins badly, with Edame calling out in her sleep for the late Henry Cooper. I spend the morning holding in my resentment until it spills over with the arrival of a tepid Ribena. Edame spins off into one of her Dutch tempers, berating me for holding something against her that happened nearly fifty years ago. 'And besides, it wasn't as if you didn't got your own back with the Deborah Meaden!' She knows full well I would never have gone biblical with Meaden if I hadn't found her on the bunk beds with Cooper.

The image of Our 'Enry 'splashing it all over' is still too much to bear. Up until today I hadn't thought of him in weeks. I sit slumped in Stoob HQ, staring at the marks on the wall where we measured Tina and Tom growing up. Tina's surprising height – 5'10" aged 12 – still makes me question whether I am truly her father, and Haden's current spurt is a kick in the teeth. Not to mention Houdini's punching ability. Since Cooper's death there's no one to ask except Edame and she always avoids the subject. I have considered a midnight DNA swoop on her toothbrush but remain petrified of the results.

Lunch with Bob at the Dog and Nincompoop. I try talking to him about the late Henry Cooper but all he does is show me a doctor's note that describes his ingrowing toenails as 'inoperable'. After half a spicy tomato juice he excuses himself. Twenty minutes later there's still no sign of him. Following a fruitless search of the gents and the garden I leave the pub and knock at his door. He answers in a Beefeater outfit. Once more he has left mid-drink and, confused, headed home. I boil him an egg and put him to bed.

Back in the study I feel wretched. I cold-call a couple of local businesses in an effort to find new sponsors but my heart isn't in it. Both hang up on me mid-sales pitch.

I measure my heart rate using the finger pulse oximeter issued to me by Dr Grossmark. At 176 bpm I am perilously close to the 180 threshold beyond which I must call Grossmark's private line. I close my eyes but all I can see are Cooper's thrusting buttocks, trousers down by the knees.

Edame knocks lightly and enters. She seems remorseful for

her sleep-utterance and perches on my lap. My back goes into spasm but this passes. I discuss my anxieties over her relationship with Cooper. She is tender and patient; she knew what she was doing was wrong, she says, but reminds me I was away a lot and she became caught up in the glamour, especially after Cooper floored Ali in the fourth at Wembley Stadium in 1963. We kiss passionately. I move her gently over to the daybed I have in the study for afternoon naps. Slowly we undress and I slip off my underpants.

Nothing moves down there, not even a twitch.

These days it's impossible to tell whether this is the natural passage of time, a lack of trust or my youthful obsession with cycling that culminated in my fourth place at the 1965 Milk Race but cost me a fully functioning wilbur. Edame does her best not to take it personally. As we lie there her face is silhouetted by the streetlight as it streams in through the window: she looks brave, handsome, resigned. Eventually she falls asleep. I remain awake, pondering whether it's me she really wants to be with.

While Edame dozes I send my second-ever tweet ('Hello. I am Alan Stoob, Britain's Premier Nazi Hunter'). Still nothing. Not sure it's working properly. I decide to follow dear old Bob Holness, only to hear he died that morning. Everyone keeps telling me Twitter will help put me in touch with the online community and aid me in my search for surviving Nazis in the Bedfordshire area. Let's hope this is correct because I'm having to wade through a lot of rubbish, especially from Michael Winner.

Tom seems a little better and over dinner wants to discuss the 1981 Test series between England and Australia. He shows genuine excitement when I talk him through Botham's astonishing spell of five for one from twenty-eight balls at Trent Bridge. Edame smiles throughout but I feel insecure. It's all I can do not to call Beryl.

In the study I pick up an email from the BBC.

Thank you for your letter regarding your proposal, The Nazi Hunter's Apprentice starring Karren Brady and yourself. This message is to inform you that we will consider your programme idea before turning it down.

Still nothing from Baddiel.

* * *

In the night I dream about my wedding day. Edame and I seem very happy, but when I turn round it's not me at all – it's the late Henry Cooper, kitted out in full red-flannelled tracksuit. As the vicar reads the vows I challenge the partnership. Cooper strides over, winds up a punch with a windmill-like swirl and sends me hurtling through the roof. I wake with a bang to the headboard.

My mood improves with the arrival of a letter of support from Fatima Whitbread, plus £25 in cash.

After penning a thank-you letter to the former javelin champion I log on to my Twitter account. My plan to have more followers than Hitler did by 1927 is fast becoming a pipe dream. I write, 'Today is the 67th anniversary of the liberation of Auschwitz lol'. Haden recommends the insertion of 'lol' after every message. Apparently it means Laugh Out Loud. Not sure why Laughing Out Loud is deemed an appropriate sign-off motif, especially in this context. I won't be doing it again.

To the surgery for my flu jab. Hoping very much I don't

go the same way as our neighbour Ifor, who died last March with the needle in his arm. The nurse is patient with me, though I am desperately tense. Dr Grossmark emerges from his consultancy room and asks me to rate my mood out of five. 'Two' I tell him. He punches me playfully on the shoulder, right on the newly-applied plaster. I'm tempted to bring up the fact that my underpants are a demilitarised zone but I don't have the heart, especially in front of the attractive receptionist.

En route back from Grossmark I visit my rented office space at the local business centre on Sponge Close. On days like today I appreciate having somewhere to sit that doesn't remind me of boxers from the East End with a reputation for cutting easily. As ever the staff greet me warmly, though clearly they think I am a doddery old gent who only comes in for the heat, the free coffee and the truly excellent toilet facilities.

I sit in the lounge and plan out my MO for next Saturday. The more I consider it the clearer it is I need an extra body for the task. I'd ask Nigel but I know government cuts mean the British Nazi Hunting Association has lost twenty-five per cent of its staff in the past year (i.e. Joyce from human resources). On the way out the girl on reception asks whether it's hard to hold in a fart at my age.

Tina, Marco, Haden and Houdini arrive for Haden's sixteenth birthday dinner. He is such an impressive young man, with an understanding of information computers that is truly beyond me, though I worry about his lack of burliness. Edame and I give him a £5 record voucher plus the book he requested (*Nazi Nutters: The Worst of the Worst*). I inscribe it with THE FIGHT NEVER ENDS, Edame adds kisses. So that Houdini doesn't feel left out we give her a Barbie doll.

Marco jokes it should have been a Klaus Barbie doll. I laugh, though no one else does.

Once Tina has had a couple of glasses of wine I broach the subject of Haden accompanying me on a Nazi Hunt.

'He's still a boy, Dad,' she says, cleaning her glasses on the tablecloth.

'Let the boy-ah do what he want, uh?' says Marco.

'Is it what you want, Hade?' asks Tina, staring hard at Marco. Haden nods.

'I WANNA GO ON A NAZI HUNT!' screams Houdini.

'You're too young, princess.'

Houdini folds her arms and starts muttering.

'What if one of them's got a fucking walking stick that's also a fucking gun?' says Tina.

'That's only in *The Day Of The Jackal*.'

'If I let you go – and it's a big "if" at the moment, young man,' says Tina, 'will you promise to look after yourself and do everything Granddad asks you to?'

'Defo,' says Haden.

Tina becomes emotional and Edame comforts her. This gives Marco the opportunity to slip Haden something under the table.

'You a man now, uh?' he says, slapping Haden on the back. Haden coughs.

'DADDY GAVE HADEN CONDOMS!' shouts Houdini, before performing five one-armed press-ups.

This is all too much for Tom, who leaves the table and can be heard upstairs playing 'Heaven Knows I'm Miserable Now' by The Smiths. Coming of age stories are clearly too close to the bone for someone who has remained perched perilously on the threshold of adulthood since 1988.

Was I there for him enough as a child? Did I put my needs over his? Was he unduly affected by my short-lived but intense love affair with TV's Deborah Meaden? I hope he understands the affair with Meaden only took place in the long dark shadow cast by Cooper.

Edame turns in early. I sit in the study and google adverts for Brut 33. Cooper looks muscular, relaxed, happy. No wonder Edame fell for him. Women couldn't resist the smell of Brut 33. I bet he had boxes of the stuff, with the promise of 'Enry's 'Ammer at the end of it.

Before I turn in I text Haden to confirm we are all systems go for Saturday. He replies 'PHAT'. I presume this is a mistake and turn off my phone.

Still nothing from Baddiel.

February

Woken by a text message at 5.54am.

We have been trying to contact you regarding your accident.
We now know how much you are owed. Just reply CLAIM.

I don't recall having an accident, but who knows? Perhaps I had
one and lost my memory as a result. If that's the case how could
I know I'd had one? This is one of the many problems associated
with growing old. I reply 'LEAVE ME ALONE I AM 75'.

As I lie in bed the memory of inserting a banana into the
exhaust of Cooper's TR7 comes to me, unbidden. I giggle and,
cheered, rise early. I even find myself whistling the theme to
Bonanza in the shower. Edame joins me there briefly, though
only to look for an earring.

After a Jewish breakfast and a hot Ribena it's time for the
weekly call with Interpol. They regale me with an especially
vulgar joke about Heinrich Himmler before 'revealing' that
Lord Lucan died in 1982 after choking on a pork scratching
in a pub in Hull.

Unperturbed I pass on the address given to me by the
mystery informant. They place me on hold for thirty-four
minutes before confirming that it corresponds with their own
intel. They agree with my hunt MO and recommend I move
fast ('Ideally in an electric wheelchair!').

First face-to-face session of the year with Beryl. I tell her of my anxieties about taking Haden on his inaugural Nazi hunt. She says he's an adult and can decide such matters for himself. I also bring up my jealous thoughts about Edame's affair with the late Henry Cooper. Beryl tells me time is up and that I should bring these matters to our next session. Each time we meet it feels like she puts the clocks forward and the fees up.

Home to an email from Haden entitled 'NAZIS':

'Will they speak like in the films?'
'If one touches me do I become evil?'
'Is it true they keep hating Jews for three days after their death?'
'Can you ward them off with garlic?'
'If you cut a Nazi's hand off does another one grow back?'

Sometimes I forget the boy is only sixteen. I do my best to allay his fears, most of which he must have picked up from the playground, or Marco.

Edame comes up behind me in the study and nibbles my ear. When I turn round I notice she is naked from the waist down. For a woman of sixty-seven she can still turn heads. Frustratingly I find it painful to turn mine. I place an order with C&A for a swivel chair and hit the hay.

*   *   *

Dreamt that someone nibbled my ear. When I turn round I find Klaus von Ribbentrop, naked from the waist down. I wake and promptly dry heave.

Breakfast with Tom. He cuts a sorry figure, rolling cigarettes and drinking black coffee in his tatty *Incredible Hulk* T-shirt. The stubble on his chin is mostly grey.

'How are you feeling today, old son?' I ask. He finishes preparing his DIY ciggie, inserting a makeshift filter in the end.

'Do you think I'll ever get back with Susan?' he asks. He is clearly serious so I give it some thought.

'That's a difficult one because I'm not Susan,' I tell him. 'But from what I understand she lives in New Zealand and has a family. Perhaps what's more important is focussing on your own life and looking forward.'

'I know that's what I'm supposed to do but I can't,' he replies. 'How would you cope if Mum left?'

The boy had a point.

'Some of us are born strong and robust, but we all of us have weaknesses in our character,' I tell him. 'You are an enormously talented boy who is bright and sensitive to other people's needs and moods. Your oversensitivity is a gift but it means you get hurt easily. I'm the same, your mother less so. I was evacuated as a child and it left its mark. It's why I hunt Nazis. It's probably also why like you I'm fragile and prone to periods of despair and self-doubt. Perhaps the rockiness between your mother and me left its imprint on you. Maybe that's why you felt an undue attachment to Susan and why it felt so painful when that bond was broken. What's important to remember is that we loved you very much when you were growing up and we continue to love you and will do whatever it takes to make you happy again.'

He looks at me optimistically.

'In that case can I have a return ticket to Auckland please?'

'That's not quite what I meant.'

'Forget it then,' he says angrily and exits to smoke. I sit defeated for a while before heading upstairs to Stoob HQ and writing an email to Interpol Steve, stating clearly that if standards do not improve I shall register a complaint with the EU. Steve replies within an hour, promising to put his 'troops in order'. For some reason he feels the need to tell me that Interpol Brian has got his hands on an old Enigma machine and did I know my name was an anagram of 'Anal Boost'?

Visit Tina's house to discuss the POA with Haden. He seems pleased to see me, though I remain troubled by his trousers. Houdini says hello briefly then goes back to playing Terrorists and Hostages with her dolls, one of which is already headless.

Tina cooks me dinner while she grills me about Saturday. She wants me to guarantee Haden's safety. I confess I am unable to do this and brace myself. She shouts something about 'throwing our only fucking son to uncle Fritz' and makes me so nervous I have to use the bathroom. When I return I explain that Nazis used to be an exceptionally dangerous breed but today even the youngest German war criminal is a minimum of ninety-eight. What is more, science has shown that their testosterone levels will have plummeted to such a degree that the notion of fighting is alien to them (I make this up). I tell her about the stab-proof vest I will be issuing Haden. She seems placated by this, which is a relief. It means I will have to do without.

After dinner Tina and Marco go to the cinema to see *Bridge Over The River Kwai* 3-D. Marco jokes that they got 'two for the price of Hun'.

I stay behind with the kids. Haden and I go over the finer details of Saturday's hunt while Houdini plaits my hair. I hand over Haden's hunting outfit: a British Gas uniform that will enable us to enter the targeted residence.

'What's your hunt called, Granddad?' says Houdini, nibbling on a jalapeño. 'It has to have a name like Operation Eagle or Bigfoot or Barnacle or something.'

We decide to name it after her favourite soft toy. She is thrilled.

When I return home the smell of marijuana fills the upstairs landing. Personally I don't see the appeal of drugs. The only time I took pot I spent five hours hoovering: a useful after-effect but far from pleasurable.

After her louche behaviour on tonight's *Celebrity Big Brother* I inform Edame that Denise Welch is no longer my lift sex celebrity of choice and Mavis Nicholson is back in.

* * *

Put final plans in place for Operation Shitface.

Spend morning going over the plan but my hip doesn't feel right. I try stretching to ease the discomfort but it's no good. I ask Edame to help. Eventually after some manipulation it pops back into place with a terrific snap. Shirley from next-door thinks she's heard gunfire and calls 999. Five police cars pull up, plus the armed response unit. The situation is highly embarrassing, especially for Shirley who receives a caution for wasting police time.

After a Dutch lunch of Edam and chips I forgo my afternoon nap and drive to Kilburn in north London to visit the Spy Shop. It has been three years since I was last there and parking restrictions on the High Road have changed. As a non-permit holder I am unable to park up anywhere close by. In the end I am forced to drive back to Luton and catch a train into London.

Howard offers me a warm welcome. He has had the shop since 1985 when his father, former double-agent Herbert Pickle, died after being stabbed in the leg on Waterloo Bridge by a Russian orphan, who then disappeared.

'Nazi hunt in the offing, Al?' he enquires. I nod. 'A word to the wise: forget Whipsnade, remember Biggleswade!'

I purchase a new butterfly net, camera pen and skeleton key, and try on a couple of the bullet-proof vests. They feel robust but are far too expensive, especially in light of my sorry sponsorship spreadsheet. As I am about to leave my eyes are drawn to the Kinsey Shoe Bug™. Normal price £200. Today: £80.

'Get yourself one of those, Alan,' says Howard, 'and I'll bung in a Maple Home Lie-Detector Test™ for an Ayrton.'

Twenty minutes later I am walking along the Kilburn High Road, my goods stashed in an old Woolworth's bag for camouflage.

Instead of heading straight home I visit Bedfordshire's premier rented office-space provider, on Sponge Close. The office manager bows before me in a patronising fashion then tells me his grandparents have recently moved into an astonishingly comfortable retirement home, that I appear to be of similar age and would I like the number? I humour him and change the subject. He shows interest in my experiences of riding alongside the Belgian great, Eddie Merckx, and asks whether it's true all cyclists took amphetamines 'back in the day'. I tap my nose, make use of the superb toilet facilities and move through to the business lounge.

Email from Haden. Seems he's 'forgotten' to tell me he's got rugby at the weekend vs Leighton Buzzard Boys School.

Last year I got proper mashed up by my opposite number at inside centre, granddad. As I have yet to truly fill out I am placing myself in a position of considerable danger every time I step out onto the field. By coming with you instead of playing rugby I am likely to avoid the kind of ritualistic humiliation that could have a profound effect on my confidence in later years.

The boy doesn't half lay it on thick, though I sympathise. My experience of rugby at school-level often meant facing boys who started puberty in the late 1940s. I on the other hand didn't display any grass on the wicket until well after the Coronation.

I log onto Twitter and tweet that tomorrow I will be embarking upon a Nazi Hunt in the Harpenden region. I get one response, from the singer George Michael:

'Stay vigilant, Alan. Regards George.'

Edame has prepared my pre-hunt dinner: brown rice, white fish, a bread roll and two pickled eggs. A week has passed since the Cooper dream and I am feeling a lot better about things. We chat freely and I mention my exchange with George Michael. Edame becomes excitable and immediately rings Tom, handing me the phone.

'I can't BELIEVE you chatted to half of Wham! Dad!' he says, before reeling off a litany of their hit records from the 1980s.

I explain he too could interact with George Michael – all he needs do is borrow my laptop. There's a long silence, then he hangs up. That my son refuses to go near modern technology or anything that post-dates the departure of Susan is an ongoing sadness. Perhaps the promise of a Twitter message from a fellow pot smoker will in time nudge him in the right direction.

After dinner I excuse myself from the washing up and begin my pre-hunt ritual. This involves laying out all items required, checking them off on the inventory, packing them into a high-vis rucksack, removing them, laying them out again, checking them off again, then re-packing them. Some people, e.g. Beryl, would label this an OCD. I don't see it that way, though recent failures are undoubtedly playing on my mind. Items I pay particular attention to include handcuffs, German phrasebook, pocket Gaviscon, angina pills, replica gun, warm socks x 2 and dubbin. I also pack two blue inhalers for peace of mind.

Edame suggests an early night. It must be my hobnobbing with the former lead singer of Wham! I pre-heat the bedroom and put on *The Best of Del Shannon* but it's no good. We say goodnight and Edame flicks on LBC.

I wake at three, haunted by Whipsnade. Scenes from the reptile house flash before me: the stumble, the fall, the asthma attack, the unflattering headlines, the telegram of condolence from the Simon Wiesenthal Foundation.

To distract myself I search online to see whether it is possible to purchase Viagra on the internet. Seems it is, though it is unclear whether it can be used in conjunction with beta blockers.

In a final effort to get back to sleep I count Hitler moustaches. Not even that works. In the end I get up and check my bag.

*   *   *

The big day – Operation Shithead. Edame rises early and prepares my usual pre-Nazi hunt breakfast: Hot Bovril, porridge and prunes. The prune is the epitome of the anti-Nazi fruit. I fasten the cufflinks she gave me for our fortieth wedding anniversary. They are a source of strength, plus they have a secret compartment for poison.

I'm certain Edame is feeling as anxious as me but she remains in high spirits, all fluttery brightness and brushing of collars ('I must add the Head 'n' Shoulders to next shopping list,' she says). Tom comes downstairs for a late breakfast and wishes me well. He looks unkempt and his mouth is sad. I give him a hug and tell him I'll see him later with a boisterous certainty that makes us all nervous.

Drive round to Tina's to pick up Haden. She wheels him out like it's his first day at school. His trousers are at less than half-mast, their lowest altitude to date. Without speaking he opens the door and sits in the passenger seat. He looks pale, tense and thinner than ever.

'I'm fucking not fucking happy about this, Dad,' says Tina.

'It'll be fine,' I say. 'I'll look after my Reich-hand man.'

'As long as it's not a repeat of, you know . . .' she says, trailing off.

'If there's a problem we'll call.'

She leans into the car and kisses Haden, telling him she loves him.

'What about me?' I enquire. Sometimes I am embarrassed by my own insecurity.

From Dunstable it is approximately a twenty-minute drive to Harpenden.

'You OK, Hade?' I ask as we pass Luton Hoo on the A1081. 'You don't look yourself.'

'I'm fine, Gramps,' he replies. 'Truth is I had my first wet dream last night and I'm trying to process it.'

We sit in silence for a further five minutes.

'You are going to tweet this, right?' he says, breaking the hush.

'What do you mean?'

'I don't think anyone's ever live-tweeted a Nazi hunt before, Granddad. People will be interested, you'll collect followers and might even gather a few new leads.'

I pull over and hand Haden my Nokia 3210. While he does his twizzling I measure my heart rate using the flashing digital car clock. 116 bpm. Good. Well below the Grossmark threshold. Haden hands the phone back.

'Write what you think here and press send. Just don't go above 140 characters.'

'You're a character,' I tell him.

'In telecommunications terminology characters are a unit of information, Granddad.'

'Oh,' I say – and we're off.

- Hello I am Ala

- Hell

- Good morning everyone. Today I shall be live tweeting the capture of a WWII Nazi in Hertfordshire. I hope you're ready.

- All due diligence is complete and I can tell you that the Nazi in question is evil Heinrich Snuff, Truncheon of München.

- He's hiding out in North Harpenden, Herts. And I'm off to hunt him.

- I know what you're thinking – 'Hertfordshire, Alan?' – but lest we forget not all Nazis settle in Beds. Anyway Harpenden is only just over the county border.

- Currently sat in the Stoobmobile (P-reg Vauxhall Omega made locally in Luton). We are two miles from the address.

- My grandson, Haden, is alongside me for backup. He's just turned sixteen and is brilliant at computers and plugs.

- Though I do worry about his lack of Eva (brawn). Not a lot of meat on those tall bones.

- My wife Edame is back home, no doubt clearing up breakfast. This hunt is for her and the support she's given me since Whipsnade.

- Thanks Edame.

- Don't know why I mentioned Whipsnade. How do you delete a twitter?

- Feeling a bit low now. Give me a minute.

- OK, better now. We're ready to go.

- And we're off! Haden is doing the gears and the steering while I write this. He says it's good practice (he'll be learning to drive soon).

- Much is riding on this hunt. If I am able to capture Snuff he may lead me to The Griffin.

- I'm sure you've heard of The Griffin. If you haven't, google him on the internet. I warn you though, it won't make for pleasant reading.

- Latest intel suggests he resides in Houghton Regis but hasn't been photographed since 1986.

- He may have undergone plastic surgery – and not for cosmetic purposes.

- Just passed a TR7, an unwelcome reminder of the late Henry Cooper.

- As is Haden's height.

- Nearing the secret location address area. I'm excited and nervous in equal measure. Regards Alan.

- Thanks also to my daughter Tina for letting Haden accompany me. I'll keep him safe (he's got a stab-proof vest which is more than I have).

- We are now parked up on Park Mount opposite the house of Heinrich Snuff. It's a chilling thought. Feeling a little short of breath. Must be anxiety.

- I don't believe this. I've forgotten my blue inhaler. I have no idea how this is possible. I packed two.

- Wheezing. Timeline put back twenty minutes.

- Anyone in the Harpenden region with a spare one please contact me.

- Sucking on a mint. Helping.

- Annoying thing is I have the brown inhaler with me but it's useless during an acute bout. Brown = long-term treatment. Blue = immediate.

- So strange. Checked my bag twice. Nazi conspiracy?

- Meanwhile no movement from the house. Once my breathing has settled we can press on with our MO (from the Latin 'Modus Operandi').

- Haden is erecting a workman's tent outside the Nazi's house. I secured two British Gas uniforms for us. We shall don them in there.

- ENTERING THE WORKMAN'S TENT.

- Seems we got the uniforms muddled up. Haden has mine on and vice versa. He's 6'4" and I'm 5'7". We need to change. Back soon. Regards Alan.

- That's better. I've got a clipboard and shall do the talking. WE ARE ABOUT TO KNOCK ON THE DOOR.

- A woman answered. My guess is it's Snuff's daughter. We are now inside the house of a Nazi.

- Her father is at the shops, she says. We are free to read the meter. She has offered us tea. YES is the answer. Stay cool, Alan.

- The Führer drank camomile, Rudolf Hess a workman's brew (milky, three sugars). Let's see what kind of tea she provides.

- 'Where are you from?' I ask. 'Deutschl . . . I mean France,' she says. Very suspicious. There is a signed photo of Himmler in the bathroom.

- This has to be the house.

- Mid-winter yet no heating? Inhumane. Hurry up with the tea, Nazi lady.

- Finding this tension unbearable. Have asked where the electricity meter is, she says her dad knows, he'll be back soon . . .

- HER DAD IS EVIL HEINRICH SNUFF, THE TRUNCHEON MUNCHEN.

- In my excitement I forgot to put the word 'OF' in between 'TRUNCHEON' and 'MUNCHEN'. Apologies. Alan.

- I bet if Hitler was on Twitter he'd write EVERYTHING IN CAPITALS.

- Tea has arrived. Tastes like ordinary tea. A clever ruse. But the way that she served it up. So efficient.

- The daughter seems pleasant. Feel guilty I'm about to shop her ageing father. Stay strong, Alan. He's a bad Nazi.

- Haven't been this close to a National Socialist since last summer when I paid a visit to Betty Schwartz, the Rotter of Rostock.

- Haden is acting nervously. He's talking too much. The daughter is looking suspicious. I don't like it, don't like it at all.

- RELAX, Haden, for God's sake. Snuff will be back soon. I've done a tiny piece of wee in my trousers. This can happen when under stress at my age.

- 'Can't you come back?' she says. 'Busy schedule' I reply.

- Asking for more milk. An old stalling trick Arthur Pob taught me.

- Haden's leg is vibrating and he's spilt some of his tea onto the saucer. It's a giveaway. The daughter looks increasingly anxious.

- She asks to see our ID. Haden shows her his.

- 'It has here you're fifty-six,' she says to Haden. He doesn't reply. 'Clerical error,' I blurt. I fear she's onto us.

- 'I have to make a call,' she says. 'It's OK we'll come back,' I tell her but she's already left the room. We've blown it.

- Nothing else for it. Have to abandon. We head for hallway. 'Goodbye!' I call out. No response.

- As we approach the front door I see a figure through the frosted glass. A phone rings – it's coming from outside.

- Snuff must be outside. He was about to come in. WE'VE GOT TO GET HIM!

- Oh god I

- Disaster. The moment we opened the door evil Heinrich Snuff, the Truncheon of München, threw a net over us.

- We've only just struggled free and have no idea which way he went. I'm heading down the road, Haden is heading up.

- Perhaps we can head him off in a pincer-like movement as favoured by Erwin Rommel, the Desert Fox.

- Have stumbled across a bag full of groceries, most likely abandoned by Snuff. Cursory examination (bratwurst and Liebfraumilch) suggests so.

- My gut feeling is Snuff will aim for the disused railway known as the 'Nicky Line'. Plenty of trees and shrubbery for cover.

- At times like these I ask, 'What would Simon Wiesenthal do?'

- The answer is always 'NEVER GIVE UP'. I just wish I had my blue inhaler.

- Haden has texted. He has indeed spotted Snuff on the 'Nicky Line' running over the Luton Road (A1081).

- I've told him to wait for me close to Roundwood School.

- Have reached Haden. Haden says Snuff disappeared from view five minutes ago. We have time to make up.

- Haden sets the pace. He's a strong walker. But I'm strong too. I was fourth in the 1965 Milk Race, Britain's Premier cycling race.

- Then again I didn't have asthma back then.

- No sign of Snuff. He's fleet of foot for an ageing Nazi, I'll give him that.

- THERE HE IS! He's taking a breather, leaning up against a fence.

- He's seen us and has started up once more. He's labouring, no question.

- We're closing in on him. He's on the bridge, high above the Luton Road (A1081). He looks about 105 and extremely evil.

- 'I've got an idea,' says Haden. He disappears into the undergrowth and down one side of the bank. No idea what he's up to.

- Brilliant! Haden has popped up the other side of Snuff. There is nowhere for Snuff to go. He's surrounded.

- He's raising his hands. 'Ich bin nicht who du think ich bin,' he is saying. He's pleading. Let him plead, I say. What a shit.

- (Apologies for the swearing, I'm a bit het up.)

- He's approaching Haden. Why is he doing that? I don't like it. Come to me, Snuff.

- He's talking to Haden. Haden seems distressed and is looking to me for assistance. I've broken into a trot.

- 'What has he said to you, Haden?' I shout. 'He says I'll never make a Nazi Hunter, Granddad.' How could Snuff say such a thing to one so young?

- Christ, I hate this Nazi. I'm going to throttle him.

- Oh no he

- This is terrible, just terrible

- I went for Snuff but out of nowhere he karate kicked me in the chest. I hit the ground hard. I swear I've broken my bottom.

- Then he leapt from the bridge onto a passing lorry. Just like James Bond or Coburn.

- He's got away. I repeat got away.

- I can't get up. Haden is inconsolable. He's never been so close to a Nazi before.

- The whole thing's a farce. I should never have got out of bed.

- I would like to apologise for today's mess. Clearly there are some operational issues to be addressed. I hope you can forgive me.

- More especially I hope Tina can.

- I could murder a whisky right now.

- Or a Nazi.

- This is Alan Stoob, Britain's Premier Nazi Hunter™, signing off. Stay vigilant. Regards, Alan.

I shuffle back to the car, Haden supporting me. His feelings have been hurt by Snuff. It's not even true he won't make a decent Nazi Hunter. He's green but he'll learn.

As we dismantle the gas tent I see Snuff's daughter through the window, arms folded, smiling. She draws her finger slowly across her throat before closing the curtains.

I drop Haden outside his house and speed off. I daren't face Tina, she might wallop me.

As I pull into the drive Edame is waiting out front. She always judges a hunt by my expression. Today she must think someone has died, which of course they nearly have in a way.

I offer her a weak smile and keep walking, through the front door, up the stairs, shoes off and into the study where I unlock the desk drawer, remove a half-bottle of Sainsbury's Basics whisky and crawl fully-clothed into my day bed.

What was I thinking asking Haden to accompany me on such a dangerous mission? I must be losing my judgement. A Nazi Hunter without judgement is no better than a vigilante or crazed squirrel.

Arthur Pob, former hunter and author of *Goose Steps and Goose Bumps*, has always maintained that Nazi Hunting is a young man's game. Perhaps I have had my day. I wouldn't be the first public figure to outstay their welcome. Muhammed Ali didn't know when to stand aside and in the twilight of his career was pummelled by Larry Holmes; Winston Churchill's second tenure as Prime Minister saw him merely preside over the break up of the British Empire; Brian Clough held on too long, bottle in hand; Bruce Forsyth is withering on the vine.

Yet age did not diminish Wiesenthal. Quite the opposite. Si continued hunting well into his nineties. His track record as a nonagenarian makes me look like a mere stripling. But things were different then. Back when Si was in the game a few failed hunts were considered part of a steep learning curve. Si made some massive cock-ups in his early days, notably his arrest of the wrong Adolf Eichmann and the botched attempt to entice Rudolf Hess's vegetarian wife Hilde with a hot sausage.

Nazi huntsmanship has moved from the amateur pursuit of gentlemen to a professional enterprise, complete with targets, commission and whiteboards. Today it's a results-driven business, with greater pressure to deliver from sponsors and the Jewish lobby. People don't understand that to succeed you also need to fail. 'Fail again, fail better' said Samuel Beckett, who I'm certain would himself have made a notable hunter had the pull of the written word not proved too strong.

There was no getting away from it, I'm a Nazi Hunter on a losing streak. I glug from the bottle, kidding myself that it's for the pain in my buttocks and anus. Right now I cannot live with the guilt of embroiling my own flesh and blood in this afternoon's sorry charade. I am old and I am ashamed.

A light tap at the door ('Visitor, Alan?') and Edame ushers Bob into the room. I'm pleased to see his scrunched-up face, though I'd be amazed if he knows what has happened. This he underlines by asking whether I think the Russian linesman got it right with Hurst's second. Before long he is curled up at the end of the bed and snoring like a congested piglet. I leave him to it and head downstairs.

In the kitchen Edame is nursing a cup of tea. She stands, engulfs me in a bosomy cuddle and walks me through to the sitting room where she settles me on the sofa. She then rises, poised as if to speak.

'Boris Boot April 2005, Arnold Schoom July 2009, Bruno Snatch January 2011. You have striking rate on a par with Wiesenthal in his heydays,' she says. 'Perhaps you shouldn't have taken our grandson with you today. That was your calling, be it far from me to question you, Alan. My only concerning since 1994 has been your well-be. I want you safe and happy in the face. If either of these matters are under assault it is time to ask the important questions. Whatever you decide I will always be in your sides, preparing stamppot, ironing your undercover disguises and rubbing your bunions or alternatively basking in deck-side sunshines on our way to luxury cruising of a lifetime off the beautiful shores of the Coral Reefer, half price in October for over-seventies.'

She pecks me on the cheek and pours us both gargantuan G&Ts.

With each kind word and measure of spirit memories of the day ebb. I still hate myself and feel like I want to lie low in Great Barford but for a few hours these feelings are held in abeyance. It is the two of us, laughing, crying, watching *Lovejoy* on the Yesterday channel, being as one. Edame and I may have our ups and downs (e.g. Cooper and Meaden) but I don't know what I'd do without her.

Actually that's not true: I'd probably continue to Britain's Premier Nazi Hunter, I'd just be really depressed.

* * *

Wake with a thick head and a furry gullet. Getting tipsy after a Nazi hunt – especially a foiled one – is a habit I've never grown out of. I had vowed to give up all binge-drinking activities beyond the age of seventy but it seems I can't resist getting out of it when the hunting goes bad. The booze may have taken the edge off last night's agonies but today I feel doubly wretched.

I flounder at the bedside table, seeking water. There is none. Instead I find my phone and a text message from Tina. It reads 'SEE ME'. I have been summoned. Edame is half off the bed, bucket on the floor, dead to the world.

The doorbell goes. I struggle out of bed and put on Edame's dressing gown. It's Bob. He must have slipped out in the night. I explain now is not a good time and could he come back later. He agrees. Five minutes later the door goes again. It's Bob again. He's clearly forgotten so I let him in. He heads straight for the downstairs toilet and dozes off leaning up against the towel rack.

I call round at Tina's in a state of high anxiety. She is furious, vacillating between anger and indigestion. Marco tries to calm her but she's not having it. Haden appears and says he's fine though clearly he's not. He claims he's old enough to make his own decisions, it was his idea and he forced me into it. She bellows that he's grounded for a month. 'IT'S NOT FAIR!' he screams before bursting into tears and running back upstairs. I should never have let him come.

After half an hour Tina calms down enough not to shout every sentence.

'No more fucking hunting fucking Nazis with my son, you elderly fuck,' she says.

'Of course,' I reply.

'And tomorrow you write a fucking letter to the fucking school explaining why he fucking didn't turn up to fucking rugby on fucking Saturday. Now fuck off.'

Back home Edame is up and dressed, sipping tea from the oversized cup reserved for hangover days. She must sense I've been the recipient of a dressing down. Without uttering a word she removes my socks and administers a foot massage. To do this when you're feeling as pale as she looks is a charitable gesture and I'm grateful. She ends with what she refers to as her 'happy finish' (a kiss on the arch). Seconds after there's a knock at the door. I presume it's Bob, but when I open it Marco is standing there in a cowboy hat.

'Listen Al,' he says. 'I personally donnah mind if-ah Hade go on-ah de Nazi hunting with you. Tina do mind though.

You wanna do this again, you come-ah see-ah me-ah first, uh?'

I'm surprised by his attitude, but grateful.

Wiesenthal was no bacon man but we allow ourselves the odd rasher, especially on mornings like this. I fire up the ring and tune into BBC Radio Bedfordshire. Edame comes hurtling in and switches it off, claiming her head is too tender for the noise.

My five-rasher butty goes a long way to settling my hangover. Edame leaves her crusts, dons dark glasses and heads to the library to pick up her reserved copy of *Lady Chatterley's Lover*.

It dawns on me that I haven't spoken to Tom since my botched hunt. I labour up the stairs and knock at his door. He's in bed, his Doc Martins protruding from the end of the duvet. He is watching an old episode of *Neighbours*.

'It's the one where Jim Robinson is involved in a car accident outside Lassiters,' he says. 'I was looking for my *Wurzel Gummidge* tape and came across it. I remember watching it with Susan. It's very moving.'

I sit on my son's bed and watch twenty minutes of television that no one remembers, wondering how he feels about his contemporaries who at this moment are most likely engaged in important board meetings or summing up high-profile cases before packed courtrooms.

'I let you down yesterday,' I say to him over the closing credits. He looks at me in a puzzled fashion.

'You never let me down, Dad,' he says. 'Not since Meaden, anyway. It's me who lets you down, on a daily basis.'

I place a hand on what through the duvet I guestimate to be his knee.

'You're doing OK, son. It's all about pigeon steps. Would you like to try and send a tweet to George Michael today?'

'Not today, Dad,' he replies. 'That episode of *Neighbours* has brought back too many painful memories. I feel worn out. Think I'll sleep for a bit.'

I head downstairs.

Edame appears to have disconnected the radio from the wall. I don't have the energy to plug it back in so I make myself a cup of decaffeinated Earl Grey and take it through to the living room. I pick up *Feel The Fear And Do It Anyway* but the image of Heinrich Snuff using my chest as a springboard assails me, breaking my concentration. I measure my heart rate against the flashing video clock. 156 beats per minute. High.

I rise to rearrange the cushions on the sofa. Beneath them are today's newspapers, each with its own unflattering headline.

BUMBLING STOOB FLOPS AGAIN
The Bedfordshire Advertiser

SHADES OF WHIPSNADE AS STOOB FALTERS
The Flitwick & District Observer

STOOBY DOOBY DON'T
The Sun

AGEING STOB COMES CLOSE IN NAZI CUNT
The Guardian

NAZI HUNTER 'ENCOURAGING IMMIGRATION'
Daily Mail

Edame must have popped out for the papers when I was at Tina's. This was why she didn't want me tuning in to Radio Bedfordshire. She was trying to protect me.

'My backside is so very sore,' I convince myself, moving over to the drinks cabinet and half-filling a tumbler of whisky.

'Hair of the dog.' The first sip is warm to the taste. With the second all thoughts of yesterday are banished.

I peek through the curtains. A small group of photographers has gathered outside. Were they there before? I didn't notice. Instantly I am snapped, glass in hand. Nice work, Alan. Tomorrow's images will no doubt serve to stoke the fires of discontent. What an idiot I am.

I pour the whisky down the sink and head back to bed. Edame joins me later in the afternoon. We spoon into the darkness until the oblivion of sleep finally comes.

*   *   *

Dear Headmaster Hoare,

I am very sorry your pupil (and my grandson) Haden Conti accompanied me last Saturday on a Nazi Hunt in Bedfordshire, when in fact he should have been playing inside centre for the second XV against Richard Hale School.

As you may know I am Britain's Premier Nazi Hunter™. As such I pride myself on my abilities in the Nazi-hunting field and also in my choice of sidekicks. I believe it reflects well on Haden that I selected him to be my cohort for the day (even though his flustered state blew our cover). This is both a credit to him as an individual and to you as a school collective. You have clearly helped shape him into the impressive young man he is today.

It was wrong of me however to take Haden out of school for what could have been and nearly was a dangerous escapade. You have my word this will not happen. At my age I should know better (I was seventy-five last week).

Stay vigilant,

Alan Stoob (seven 'O' levels)

57

I spend most of the morning avoiding work looking at animal clips on the internet. Some of them are hilarious, especially Nora the Piano Cat. When I finally log in I find a succession of grammatically-incorrect missives.

'Alan your shit!'
'Try and Nab nick Griffin hes fat and so probably slow?'
'HUNT YOURSELF YOU CNUT!'
'Less Verbals more goebbels'
'ballbag-g'

I call Beryl. She agrees to see me at short notice.

I discuss my feelings of inadequacy over the failed Nazi hunt. She says such feelings stem from the fractured bond I experienced with my mother as a result of my evacuation. I counter this by citing the headlines in the newspapers. She remarks that some of the wordplay was quite clever. I ask her which ones. She reels off three I hadn't seen, none complimentary. I enquire why she feels the need to share this with me. She says she's the therapist and why don't I shut up. I apologise and tell her I am in the doghouse with my daughter for taking Haden with me. At this point she breaks wind. This puts me off my stride. The last ten minutes are spent in silence. As I leave she calls me Adam.

Dinner at Tina's. Her mood is hostile. Every remark I make, however innocent or well-meaning, is instantly discredited. I feel extremely uncomfortable, not least following an afternoon session with the weighted pants.

It is Edame who steps in, pointing out that I've apologised and shouldn't we all try and move on. Tina's jibes become less frequent, though she still refers to me as an 'ass-hat'. Haden seems better, his trousers higher than previously. Houdini takes me to one side and says she feels the failure of the hunt is down to her insisting we come up with a name for the operation. I plant a kiss on her black curly mop and tell her not to be silly. She promptly bursts into tears and runs to her mum, complaining that I said she was silly. Tina looks angry again but the moment passes.

Each time Tina raises the foiled hunt Marco backs her up. Yet each time she looks away he gives me a wink. I feel uncomfortable with this collusion. Eventually Tina catches him. He says he has something in his eye. 'Good,' she replies, 'because I don't want you coming onto Dad like you did Uncle Thomas.' An entire boiled egg rolls out of Edame's mouth.

As we leave, Tina, by now quite tiddly, hugs me while resting her chin on the top of my head. She says she's sorry for giving me a hard time and hopes I understand why. Of course I do, I say, and apologise again. She squeezes harder and as she does my troublesome sixth vertebra clicks back into place. What began an inauspicious evening turns out to be one of both emotional and orthopaedic resolution. I only hope she didn't inherit her strength from the late Henry Cooper.

Back home I tweet 'Sorry everyone'. Nothing happens. I then try 'Sorry lol' and receive a number of supportive messages back, including one from Rabbi Lionel Blue.

*   *   *

After a few days of hard work, no booze and a letter of support from Sir Clive Sinclair I am beginning to feel more myself. This new-found strength is invaluable as I prepare for my weekly call with Interpol. Thankfully it's a short one involving only brief teasing and a moderately rude joke about a hog roast. Perhaps the message has got through.

Bob pops round mid-morning. 'Hard luck the other day,' he says. 'No one likes coming fourth but there's always next year. How's the bike holding up?' He begins another sentence but drifts off midstream. I remove his monocle and place a rug over his feet.

After a lunch of Jerusalem artichokes and kosher tomatoes I return to Harpenden and the scene of last week's debacle – this time alone.

Parking up outside the property I take my replica .44 Magnum from the glove compartment. I feel surprisingly nervous. It must be the recollection of failure multiplied by the potential for violence. As I open the car door my mobile phone buzzes with a text from Edame ('OK if I watch the extras on the *Bergerac* box set without you?'). I ignore it.

The house looks quiet. I approach the door with trepidation and give a gentle nudge – it opens.

Inside it is almost unrecognisable from the house we so patiently sat in awaiting the return of evil Heinrich Snuff. All tables, chairs, books, pictures and busts of the Führer have been removed. The carpets have been torn up and the light bulbs are missing. I open a tiny battered fridge: two German sausages and a half-empty can of WD40. I pocket the lubricant and head upstairs.

The first room is huge but empty. The second has a chest-of-drawers positioned in front of an enormous bay window. I open each drawer in turn. Save for the *Der Spiegel* lining paper there is nothing to see, but something is not right. I take a step back. From the outside the bottom drawer looks deeper than the others, yet when open is the shallowest. I pull it out and tap: like Doris from number seventy-two it appears to have a false bottom. I feel around until I locate a tiny catch. On releasing it an extra level is exposed.

Before me is a treasure-trove of letters, photographs, diaries, Swastika ink stamps and false noses. An impromptu erection appears. I ignore it and remove a handful of material.

I am staggered at the information before me: passports under assorted names, a signed copy of Mein Kampf, NHS correspondence relating to what looks like a long-standing coccyx problem. There are up-to-date photographs of known Nazis from across the Bedfordshire region. Alarmingly there are also images of me in a clinch with Deborah Meaden.

An old-fashioned telephone rings.

I look around. There is no sign of a phone. I scour the room, trying to locate the sound, before I realise it is coming from under the floorboards. Frantically I slide to one side a threadbare Nuremberg rug. One of the boards is loose. I force it from its groove, lower my arm into the darkness and pick up the receiver.

Silence at the other end.

'Guten tag?' I proffer.

More silence.

'Ich heisse Heinrich Snuff,' I say. 'Ich bin ein Nazi.'

'FOR GOTT'S SAKE STOP SPRECHING GERMAN HEINRICH, YOU'LL GET US ALL KILLED!' bellows a voice.

'Sorry,' I say.

'Ich thought you'd already fled?'

'Nearly done, just taking out all ze light bulbs,' I say.

'You got se new address sen?'

'Erm . . . ich think so.'

'Ve sink north London ist se perfect location fur du,' says the voice. 'Right under sare noses.'

'Yes,' I say, 'right under sare noses.'

'You're OK mit verking in a kosher bakery sen?'

'Why wouldn't ich be?' I reply, trying not to sound surprised.

'It's se perfect double bluff,' says the voice. 'Fye fud anyfun sink sat ein former Nazi war criminal mit ein history of unspeakable crimes against Juden fud open a kosher bakery in se heart of Golders Green?'

'Vell quite,' I reply.

'Foteva you do don't furry. Se only person after us ist zat fatty Stoobs and fe all know he's a scheissing joke.'

'Now hang on just a secon-'

'You've got mein number – call me if du need anysing.'

'Er, actually, can I check your number, just to be sure? You know what I'm like!'

'Sorry – got to go – Lebensraum meeting in twenty minuten.'

The line goes dead. I gather up all the documentation and leave. Outside night has fallen. Every bush, tree or elderly man with a claw for a hand sets me on edge. In the car I text Haden telling him of my find. I receive an instant reply:

'Tina here. Don't involve the boy. Now fuck off.'

*　　*　　*

I have now spent three days and nights fine-tooth combing the material I found at Heinrich Snuff's former abode. During that time I learnt:

• Snuff made his way from Berlin to Bedford via boat and Thameslink in 1948.

- In 1949 Snuff changed his name to Harold Chum and ran Harold Chum's Medicaments on Leagrave High Street until his retirement in 1981.

- Since 1981 Snuff has split his time between working as a life model at Luton College of Art, holidaying in the Seychelles and raising funds for the Nazi Party.

- Together with evil Nazi architect Albert 'Build it Here' Speer, Snuff was instrumental in designing the Bremen-to-Biggleswade underground ratline that opened for service in 1989.

- Snuff is in contact with surviving Nazis through a central organisation known as the Nazis of Bedfordshire (NOB). NOB members congregate on a monthly basis, though it is unclear where.

- Snuff's wife Gertie moved to England in 1951. She died in what appears to be a revenge killing amid rumours she slept with Martin Bormann and Edith Hitler on the same afternoon.

- Snuff is partial to pornography of the feet.

For the first time I have proof of a central network overseeing Nazi war criminals in Britain. This means funding, administration, a paper trail and a large group of people who have to keep schtum. If somehow I am able to penetrate this network I may be able to clear up the country's Nazi infestation in one fell swoop.

I also find £28 in cash, which will come in handy.

Over a lunch of pickled herrings and kosher ham I tell Edame for the first time about my Nazi cache. She seems genuinely pleased, while at the same time reminding me we are a family in turmoil, that I mustn't neglect my forty-two-year-old son who remains suspended between childhood and adulthood and with that in mind would I please drive us all to family therapy with Dr Hamish O'Davies at the Bedford General this afternoon.

Edame takes up her customary position in the front seat. Tom sits in the back repeatedly completing then undoing his Rubik's Cube. Both seem agitated. The atmosphere isn't helped when I run over an owl.

Dr O'Davies kicks matters off by asking Tom to describe the colour that's in his head. Tom replies 'green'. O'Davies then asks what colour he'd like it to be. 'Green' says Tom, 'with Susan in it'. O'Davies makes notes for ten minutes before dragging over a hat stand and asking what Tom would say to the hat stand if it were Susan.

'You look nice,' says Tom to the hat stand.

'Anything else?' asks O'Davies.

'Did you get that Depeche Mode mix I sent?'

O'Davies adjusts his toupée and stares at Tom.

'Why do you think your life has ground to a halt since your girlfriend left?'

'Suze is the only one who understands me,' declares Tom, chewing at his collar.

'Are you aware twenty-four years have passed since she left?' asks O'Davies.

'DON'T CARE WANT SUZE,' blurts Tom. He pulls out a picture. 'Look,' he says. 'Bathe in her beauty.'

O'Davies examines the photograph.

'She's pretty,' he says. 'But I've heard she's on the other side of the world and has a family.'

'Don't care,' says Tom. 'Want Suze.'

'How do you think your mother and father can help?'

'Not have any more affairs,' he says. Edame and I glance at each other.

'Son,' I say. 'What happened was a long time ago. I give you my word it will never happen again.'

'Dad had it off with Deborah Meaden,' says Tom.

'Who's Deborah Meaden?' asks the doctor.

On the way back we pass the owl lying mashed in the gutter.

'I am that owl,' says Tom. 'Flattened by the wheels of fate.'

Back home Tom locks himself in his room. Edame, drained by the meeting and distressed by the owly remains, takes a snooze. In the study I receive an email asking me to 'like' the SS on Facebook. I'm not even on Facebook. There's also a joke from Nigel at the BNHA ('Knock Knock' 'Who's there?' 'The Gestapo') but it doesn't make me laugh, especially after I check my bank balance.

'Hello, this is Alan Stoob, Britain's Premier Nazi Hunter™,' I tweet. 'Could someone send me some sponsorship money please? Help the aged and stay vigilant. Alan.'

The only response I receive is from George Michael. 'You've got to have faith, Stoob,' he says. 'Don't beg – stand proud.'

I attempt to put this approach into operation tonight with Edame. Without doubt there is greater rigidity on display than of late. Recalling the tumescence of the Nazi cache seems to help, though not enough for full-scale 'take-off'.

*   *   *

Awake with a sticky foot. Seems Edame hid a bag of toffees at the end of the bed. No doubt she's seeking sweet comfort in the absence of hard sex. Not the kind of reminder I need on a day when I must hunt for Nazis in London's Jewish quarter.

After breakfast I root through my box of disguises. I briefly consider dressing up as Shimon Peres before plumping for the Hasidic look (big hat, big beard, black garb, ringlets, serious face). In the full get-up I stare back at myself in the mirror. I look Jewish, but do I *seem* Jewish? There's something in my gait that I fear betrays my gentile status. Despite everything Jews have confidence, self-belief, chutzpah. Woody Allen may pretend he doesn't but you don't step out with Diane Keaton if you're a nebbish.

I try out my Yiddish accent (aka my Jackie Mason impression). Edame enters and is so startled she whacks me with an umbrella. This is a good sign.

Shortly after she wishes me good luck and departs for her tennis lesson. Tom is out at drama therapy. With a couple of hours to kill I wander aimlessly through the house and end up in the garage. As ever my beautiful bike, celeste blue, the colour of the Italian Bianchi brand, takes my breath away. The smell of chain oil and metal transports me back to the day I was in the breakaway during stage six of the 1965 Milk Race. Jimmy Savile, himself a highly accomplished cyclist, was also in the group though for some reason he slowed as we approached a school, leaving me and three others to battle it out to the finish in Blackpool. With two miles left I was on the brink of victory, only to accidentally ride into the sea.

I pass my hand over the contours of the saddle. Could they be the reason for my penile dementia? Has my increased softness affected my self-confidence and impacted my hunting abilities? Is it the other way round? Will I ever come to terms with the horrors of my evacuation and more especially what followed?

I return to the house, my head plagued by all kinds of anxious thoughts. After twenty minutes of relaxation exercises I feel more 'anchored', as Beryl would say. Following a light lunch of gefilte fish and Hebrew cheese I change into my dark disguise and drive the thirty miles to Golders Green, the famous Jewish suburb of North London. I park up off the world-renowned Finchley Road, check myself one last time in the wing mirror and stroll into the Yiddish quarter.

There are Jews everywhere, going about their business, chastising their wives, haggling over the price of second-hand Volvos and generally adding gaiety to the locale. I slip into Hebron's, the first traditional Jewish bakery I see. There serving I find an older man and a younger woman, a replica of the dynamic that has served news anchors so successfully over the past fifty years, most recently BBC *Breakfast* starring Susanna Reid and Bill Turnbull.

No sign of Snuff. So as not to arouse suspicion I order a hot salt-beef sandwich with gherkin and extra mustard. Heaven knows why hot salt beef is regarded primarily as a Jewish dish. It blows any Christian or Muslim meal clean out of the water.

I leave a generous tip and head to the next place, renowned Semitic bagel emporium Oy Vey! Again no Snuff. An elderly woman behind the counter serves me. I ask for a traditional Jewish loaf. She says there's no such thing so I buy a doughnut. While she's sorting the change I notice a signed photograph of Simon Wiesenthal next to the wall-mounted Torah.

In the third and final bakery on the Golders Green Road

I strike Nazi gold. Inside Talmud, laughing and joking with the customers, I find evil Heinrich Snuff, complete with orthodox Jewish curls, Yiddish asides and characteristic shrugs.

'Fot can I get you, sir?' he asks in a mixture of German and faux-Israeli.

'Two plain bagels plus one of those Nazis,' I say.

He freezes.

'Sorry sir, please repeat?'

'I said two plain bagels plus one of those pasties.'

His shoulders relax once more.

'Of course, sir,' he says and bags them up. '£3.20 please.'

I give him a fiver. He short-changes me.

'Excuse me, you're 50p short,' I say.

'I sink not, sir. Good day to you.'

I glance at my watch. It's 3.38pm. And it's Friday. According to the *Jewish Chronicle* local shops shut at 3.45pm on the Sabbath. In seven minutes' time Snuff will close for the day and head home. I hurry to the Stoobmobile, start her up and drive back to the bakery. I arrive to find Snuff chewing on a raisin bagel and locking up. He tries the door a final time before climbing into his Mercedes. No Jew worth his salt would drive a German car, least of all one with the licence plate H8 JUE. He starts the engine, I do the same and keeping my distance I follow him.

Slunk below my steering wheel I observe Snuff removing his curly sideburns with disdain. He drives like a madman and I struggle to hold his tail, despite the Omega's 2.2 litre multipoint fuel injection. Eventually he draws up outside a grand semi-detached property on Kings Avenue in Muswell Hill. In my effort to keep up I nearly knock down Ray Davies of The Kinks, who it appears still lives locally.

Snuff leaves the Jewish paraphernalia in his car and enters the house. I hear three Chubb locks and a metal bolt securing him into his private space. 'Good,' I say to no one in particular. 'I've got him ruffled.'

I note down the full address and text Haden.

'I want in,' he replies.

'No,' I say. 'Not after last time.'

'Yes,' he says.

'No,' I say.

'YES.'

'NO.'

'TBC.'

*　*　*

Wake with the semblance of an erection. Unfortunate then that Edame has chosen this morning to visit Enid in Milton Keynes.

After final consideration I write an email to Haden listing the reasons why he cannot come hunting with me ('You're grounded'; 'Tina will murder me'; 'You weren't exactly helpful last time'). I linger over the message before hitting 'send' and head to Bob's.

Bob is on sparkling form, i.e. he's awake. After a cup of tea I ask him if he'll accompany me on my hunt to capture evil Heinrich Snuff as I'm old and could do with the extra manpower. He nods although it's difficult to tell whether he's up to it, especially when he takes a sip from the goldfish bowl. If funding wasn't an issue I would get someone from the agency. Now I have to hope the hunt coincides with one of Bob's better days.

Back home Tom slopes downstairs late-morning. He looks worse than ever. I make him a hot Ribena and prepare a small plate of biscuits, cheese and sliced apple. To keep him company I mix myself a strawberry-flavoured glass of bulk-forming Fibrogel.

He burns his top lip on the Ribena and his eyes fill with tears. 'It's so hard,' he says. We take our drinks out into the garden. It's a glorious day. Tom says it only makes him feel worse as it reminds him of the time he and Susan sat in this very spot listening to 'The Queen is Dead' by The Smiths before pledging to spend the rest of their lives together until she dumped him, moved to New Zealand, got married and had four children.

'Dad, why do things have to change?' he asks.

'Because that's life,' I reply.

'In that case I don't like life.'

I ask him if there is anything that he'd like to do besides go back out with Susan. He replies that he'd like to speak with George Michael. I explain he is but a click away and that to connect with him all he need do is borrow a computer. There is a half-hour silence.

'OK,' he says.

We go back inside and I fish out my old IBM ThinkPad that has been collecting dust since 2002.

'What's this?' he asks.

'It's a computer.'

I take him through the basics but he complains it's too complicated and can't he connect with George Michael through his scientific calculator. I tell him this isn't possible and that he should take the computer to his room and have a fiddle ('I haven't had a fiddle since Susan left,' he says). I give him a hug before heading for the surgery and my midday appointment.

It's always reassuring to see Dr Grossmark, especially prior to a hunt. He likes to give me a medical and a pep talk. I hunt Nazis on behalf of people like him: kind, clever and Jewish.

Grossmark takes my blood pressure ('Lower than 2011'), measures my bunions ('About the same') and asks me to score my mood out of five (three-and-a-half). The ECG goes OK, though he recommends a pet for lowering my heart rate ('Or a pacemaker if you have allergies'). He tests my reflexes by looking one way then throwing a cricket ball the other. I catch it one-handed. When it comes to measuring my lung capacity he proffers the usual toilet roll contraption and asks me to blow. I'm all puffed out after a couple of seconds but the sound of distant mewing continues to emanate from my chest for a further twenty.

'You have the lungs of a ninety-seven-year-old,' he declares. 'Regular intake of spring onions is definitely helping.' He finishes by asking me to name the current Prime Minister. I'm a little offended at this but answer dutifully.

'Are we ready to reduce your dose of anti-depressants?' he asks as I button up my shirt. 'Whipsnade was quite some time ago now.'

'Maybe, but Harpenden was only three weeks.'

'The fallout wasn't nearly as severe. Stay positive, Alan. Shall we try half a pill a day, see how you go?'

I agree. While Grossmark writes out a new prescription I notice a poster on his wall: 'Starve a fever, run off a coronary'.

'Hunt on the horizon I take it?'

I nod.

'Anyone I might have heard of?'

'Doubt it,' I say. 'Pretty unsavoury character though.'

'Aren't they all,' he says before removing his spectacles and massaging his brow.

'Alan, as we know I have a particular interest in your over-coming the Nazi scourge but as both doctor and friend I advise you not to overdo it. Please remember your blue inhaler and do not place too much strain on your heart. We all know about your cycling heroics but that was forty-five years ago. By rights seventy-four-year-olds shouldn't be tracking Nazis across Bedfordshire.'

'I'm seventy-five now,' I say. 'And this one's in London.'

'It's your life, Alan, but think of Edame.'

'Always, doc.'

'Remember – at this age what doesn't kill you makes you weaker. Stay off the coffee.'

Keen to get off this awkward subject I ask Grossmark whether it is possible to receive the penis-stiffening wonder drug Viagra on the NHS.

'Of course,' he replies. 'But it's not a free prescription. You have to pay full whack. You can find Viagra online for peanuts but you never know what you're getting; sugar pills, aspirin or something to make your willy go hard.'

I request a prescription for ten Viagra and tell Grossmark I'll cash it in if there's no sign of a stiffy by spring.

Edame and I catch two episodes of *Bergerac* before bed. Whenever Nettles is on screen her hands are nowhere to be seen. I don't blame her; where Nettles is youthful and vibrant, I'm elderly and anxious.

In bed I glance out of the window. The moon looks like Hitler. Next door Tom strums the same minor chord until eventually I dissolve into sleep.

M❖rch

Dream I make an appearance on the television programme *Room 101*. In the dream I ask to put the whole of Nazi Germany into Orwell's infamous chamber. The presenter, comedian Frank Skinner, denies me my request. I grow so angry I shoot him in the shoulder before turning the gun on the audience. One to discuss with Beryl.

With the hunt for Heinrich Snuff only twenty-four hours away I split my day into bite-size chunks, a technique first cited in an academic paper by top hunter-turned-psychologist, Arthur Pob. It was devised to help reduce pre-hunt anxiety through the accounting of every hour in the day, e.g.:

1–2pm: LUNCH + SHORT SNOOZE.

4–5pm: EIGHT PRESS UPS. CONFERENCE CALL WITH INTERPOL. DON'T TAKE ANY SHIT.

6–7pm: STAY VIGILANT.

8–9pm: ONE EPISODE: *BERGERAC*.

9–9.30pm: ONE EPISODE: *THE GOOD LIFE*.

Edame spends the morning cleaning, clear evidence of her own apprehension. This latest Nazi pursuit must be getting to her. Her manner is rather too breezy, her whistling too upbeat, the tune (the theme from *The Great Escape*) somewhat crass. It unsettles me so I shut and padlock the study door.

Following a short call with Nigel at the British Nazi Hunting Association I scan my 'Fundraising Ideas' document and call

Dunstable Public Halls to ask how much it would cost to organise a one-day workshop entitled 'All You Ever Wanted To Know About Nazi Hunting But Were Afraid To Ask'. They reply saying I can have the smaller of the two halls at the reduced daily rate of £225 on account of my age and ongoing fight against National Socialism. I tweet about the workshop. The first reply I receive is from George Michael.

'Might be interested, Alan,' he says. 'Is lunch included?'

Edame makes a variation of my pre-hunt dinner. It's delicious, though I skip the prawns for fear of a repeat of the stomach issues that sabotaged my pursuit of Tomas Joop back in 1997. Tom, Walkman on and flicking through the pages of an old copy of *Smash Hits*, tucks into his potato waffles. He seems contented enough.

In bed Edame offers me a Dutch massage. As she works my shoulders what I presume to be tears cascade onto my back. I immediately tell her to stop – once she's done my thighs.

As she lies in my arms she says she loves me so much it hurts her heart. This time it is I with the misty eye.

Once she starts snoring I conjure up possible scenarios that could befall me tomorrow:

Evil Heinrich Snuff is not in.

Evil Heinrich Snuff recognises me and runs off.

Evil Heinrich Snuff is armed and kills me.

Evil Heinrich Snuff is armed and kills Bob.

Evil Heinrich Snuff is armed and kills us both.

I capture Evil Heinrich Snuff and become a hero.

Evil Heinrich Snuff captures me and becomes a Nazi hero.

Evil Heinrich Snuff is such a nice person I let him go (unlikely).

Evil Heinrich Snuff has moved house.

I oversleep and don't make the hunt.

I double check the alarm and nod off. Three hours later I wake in a pool of sweat. Has someone shouted 'Whipsnade' in my ear? Must be a bad dream.

* * *

The big day: eight per cent excited, eighty-five per cent nervous, the rest a mixture of heartburn, constipation and uncertainty about Bob's suitability for the task.

For breakfast Edame has managed to import some Weetabix from Israel. It's a loving touch. As we part she hides her face, saying she has something in both eyes. I hold her in my arms and jest that if I'm not back by five she can start internet dating.

I hoot for Bob, who emerges in a dinner jacket.

'I do love a wedding,' he says, climbing into the back seat and dozing off. As I drive down the cul-de-sac I think I see Amon Hels, the Cruncher of Cologne, performing a Nazi salute, before realising it's just Neal pointing at the guttering. Clearly I'm on edge.

The drive to north London is a familiar one. I had wanted to go through the plan with Bob but better he sleep now than inside the house of a Nazi. At least time in the car is time to think.

How many times can one flop before the people say 'No more'? It depends how full your inner tube of goodwill. Back in 2010 my tube was pumped to 140psi, the wheel rock solid. Now I have a slow puncture. If today goes to plan that puncture will self-inflate. If it doesn't the mechanics of fate may be called out. They may even consign the tube to the rubbish and remove the wheel.

I check my pocket. At least I have the correct inhaler. Bob leans forward from the back.

'Are we at Wembley yet?'

'Nearly,' I tell him. 'Just relax. I'll let you know.'

'Thanks, Mark,' he says. 'Now back to Gary in the studio.'

The M1 has been a friend to Nazi Hunters since she was built in 1961. I pull off at junction two, travel briefly along the A1 before swinging left and heading for East Finchley. We arrive on Kings Avenue in Muswell Hill at 11.05am. I wake Bob. He stretches out, then goes back to sleep. I climb into the back and lightly slap his face.

'I love you, Gladys,' he says. I give him a stare. He gets the message and exits the car.

In our dark suits we undoubtedly resemble Jehovah's Witnesses, though Bob's dinner jacket is a somewhat unnecessary flourish. I collect my copies of *Watchtower* from the boot. To secure them I had to invite two Jehovahs into my home, claim to be a fan of 'good news' and purchase ten magazines. Since then I've not been able to shake them off. Three times a day they've come knocking, requesting I join their church. The only way I could get shot of them was explain I was a transsexual Islamic Buddhist who preferred men. Even then one kept returning, I think for his own reasons.

Kings Avenue is a typical north London street of imposing Edwardian buildings mostly converted into flats. I doubt people know each other from one house to the next. War brings people together, affluence drives them apart. I'm not in favour of war, but London makes me sad.

Before we reach the house I straighten Bob's tie and wipe the jam, Marmite and butter from his chin. I explain his job: smile, stand behind me and repeat everything I say about God until we're inside. By the way his eyes narrow he seems to understand.

We approach 25 Kings Avenue. The blinds are down. I check Bob is awake, clear my throat and knock.

I stand back and look up at the house. I feel dizzy and my neck clicks so I concentrate on the door.

Nothing.

I knock again.

Down the road a mother stands with her child, handing out leaflets promoting the benefits of high-intensity exercise in a middle-class environment.

Still no reply.

Bending down, I flick open the letterbox. The signed photo of Himmler from the previous house hangs above a hallway phone, a small bust of Hitler next to it. Dead flowers, a regular fixture in a Nazi household, adorn the table.

I had assumed Heinrich Snuff would be in. If old people aren't in it usually means they're dead or at a funeral. Bob yanks violently at the tail of my jacket. I ignore him, but he does it again so I turn round. He is indicating towards the alleyway, where evil Heinrich Snuff has emerged on his bike. Before I can speak the renowned National Socialist blithely pedals off. He rides up to the junction and stops. He hasn't noticed us. I consider chasing him down on foot but there is a break in the traffic and he's gone. I grab Bob's arm and lead him back to the Stoobmobile.

As we speed-walk towards the Omega I explain the plan: follow Snuff in the car at a safe distance, then when he dismounts we nab the Nazi. Bob giggles at the alliteration and clambers into the back seat.

We have some distance to make up on Snuff and only reach him at Muswell Hill roundabout. He pelts down the other side. We clock him at 38 mph. For a centenarian that's some pace. At the bottom he turns right and heads towards Crouch End.

'Perhaps he's meeting *EastEnders* actor Steve McFadden for a coffee,' says Bob, out of nowhere.

The problem at the bottom is we don't turn right. Nor do we turn left. We don't turn at all because the Stoobmobile has ground to a halt. The engine is silent. Not even a polite phut. It's dead, as dead as Hitler (allegedly) or Rudolf Hess (confirmed). I knew I should have gone for the full service.

I tell Bob to remain in the vehicle. He slaps his thigh and screams excitedly. I leap out and flag down the first man I see on a bike, explain I'm chasing a Nazi and flash my membership of the British Nazi Hunting Association. The first thing I notice is how incredibly light the bike is compared to the wrought-iron vehicle I rode in the 1965 Milk Race. The second is the pain from the saddle, which travels to the tip of Little Alan and remains there.

It takes me time to pick up pace, at least according to the speedometer. Normally I'd be happy with 8 mph but Snuff is still a long way off. As I enter Crouch End I warm to my task and gain on him. He appears to be flagging. I'm not surprised; he is 106.

With only 100 yards between us he dismounts outside Budgens, chains his bike up and enters the supermarket. I do likewise.

I spot Snuff in the soft drinks aisle, though am briefly distracted by the sandwiches which are already reduced. I grab a prawn mayonnaise at only 39p and head towards the miscreant. To see him up close reminds me of our meeting on the bridge. His eyes are like tiny slits of evil, surrounded by the puffy bags of Satan. But it's busy in here, hard to get close and Snuff is fast, all jerky movements and unexpected darts. I try to grab him by the plums but he fizzes off.

Briefly I lose him in the crowd. If only I could have found someone from the agency. I get stuck behind a small group of north Londoners fighting over the last pot of guacamole. As they disperse I spot Snuff at the fast check-out. He's paying and leaving.

To my chagrin I am forced to drop the sandwich and follow him out. He's already unlocked his bike and is heading onwards towards Crouch Hill. I unlock and pursue. The hill is steep at the bottom and grows steeper. I tap into the anguish that saw me blow my big chance of a stage win during the 1965 Milk Race.

I gain on Snuff.

Thirty yards . . .

Twenty yards . . .

Fifteen . . .

Ten . . .

Twelve . . . (I slow down a bit)

Ten again . . .

Eight . . .

Five . . .

Five yards from a Nazi.

'Hello Heinrich,' I say, my breathing fast but controlled. 'Need a hand?'

He looks round and, panicking, pedals harder. In desperation he flings first the fruit and veg then the garlic sausage from his basket. It makes no difference. Snuff is showing his age. I close the gap to three yards, two yards, one yard – then BANG. I knock him off his bike.

He lies flailing in the road.

'I've got one!' I bellow. 'I've got a Nazi!'

He lies there muttering in German. It's an unfortunate language on the ear, though the problem is mainly one of association. I remove my Taser and study the instructions.

79

Snuff continues to mumble. He looks at me, then his weasel-like eyes register huge alarm and he points over my shoulder; I turn. There is nothing there. I look back, only to see Snuff's legs disappear down a manhole, the cover still revolving on the tarmac. Snuff is in the sewers.

If I wasn't so angry at myself for falling for such a hackneyed trick I'd think how a sewer was wildly appropriate. I remove my utility belt and ease myself down the hole.

Only I don't get very far. Half-way to be precise. My legs make it but my forty-inch waist prevents me from venturing further and chasing the Nazi. Not only can I not enter the hole, I cannot pull myself out either. I'm lodged. I call for help but no one is interested. All they do is film me on their camera phones. Typical Londoners.

It is then I feel a tugging at my left foot. Someone – presumably Snuff – is removing my shoes. After that the socks – a gift from Edame's mother Edamame – come off. Please dear god, don't tickle me.

Snuff tickles me. Sporadically at first as an hors d'oeuvre, then a full-on assault. It is unbearable. My attempts to wriggle from his clutches come to nothing. The only mercy is that he concentrates on the less ticklish of my two feet.

After ten minutes the hell ends and evil Heinrich Snuff is lost to the north London sewage system. An ambulance arrives. Then the fire brigade. It takes three men and a full tub of salted butter to lever me out of the hole. They give me a once-over and find me to be in good health. None of them will lend me any socks. I am forced to ride back to the car barefoot. I climb into the driver's seat and call the AA. They tell me three hours.

'So?' says Bob appearing in my rearview mirror. 'Was it a goal or not?'

Five hours later I park up in the driveway. Bob is asleep in the passenger seat, mouth opening and closing like a guppy. Leaving him there I force my way through a horde of journalists, enter the house via the kitchen, lock the door behind me, lower the blinds, put on a pair of sturdy shoes and kick the fridge. Twice.

I call out for Edame but there is no response. In the kitchen I find a note from Tom ('Gone to the roller disco'). I fish two Penguin biscuits from the sweet tin and put the kettle on.

It seems I am becoming accustomed to humiliation. Welcome to old age, perhaps. How much more of this my reputation can take I have no idea. Where is Edame? She's always here for me after a hunt.

I take my tea through to the sitting room. What I see sends a blitzkrieg of shock through my system.

Edame is slumped forward in her chair, her hair trailing over her knees, empty bottle of port beside one ankle, full ashtray next to the other. Handheld footage of my manhole disgrace is playing on the BBC news channel.

I try to rouse her; she comes to with an almighty hiccup. Taking no chances I rush her to the downstairs bathroom and hold her still-beautiful auburn hair back from her face as she yacks up Dutch vomit. Between heaves she berates me in her mother tongue. 'Staakt u bloedige huunts!' she says. 'Stop your bloody hunting!'

I wipe her mouth with the spare flannel and with some difficulty carry her upstairs. It reminds me vividly of the last time she got drunk like this, in December. I place her in the recovery position, stroke her cheek and head back downstairs in search of a bucket. The television is showing close-up footage of my anguished red face.

I let Bob out of the car. He looks rested, winks and heads

off in the wrong direction. The pool of journalists remains, including Audrey Shaw of *The Bedford & Flitwick Express*. She covered my inaugural hunt, that of Alvin Yapp, and is the only one who wrote a supportive piece following the Whipsnade Incident. I beckon her in, promising hot Ribena and half an omelette. I do not wish to be alone.

'Delicious,' she says, removing shell from her teeth and sniffing the air. 'Have you started smoking?'

'That's Edame,' I reply. 'She got drunk, did smoking and vomited down the toilet. She's alright though.'

'Sorry today didn't work out for you, Alan,' she says. 'How are you, in yourself?'

'Bit down, but I'll live. Not for long mind. I'm seventy-five.'

'Wiesenthal made it to ninety-three.'

'Perhaps, but he was driven by hatred and the pursuit of justice.'

'Not doubting yourself I hope, Alan. You're the best we've got.'

'We all have moments of self-doubt, Audrey. It's what makes us human.'

Looking at Audrey I feel a twitch in my nethers. There was always a chemistry between us. I picture us making love in the wheelbarrow position before squeezing my eyes shut to extinguish the thought.

'Do you have a message for our readers?' she asks.

'That they remain vigilant,' I say. 'The danger looms large but the deepest darkness is always before the dawn. I shall not be deterred.'

Audrey takes my photograph and despite myself I assume my usual thumbs up pose. As she sits back down she spills hot Ribena on the armchair. She is deeply apologetic and dabs the wet patch with her scarf. I tell her to stop but she insists, lifting the cushion and wiping down the side of the leather.

'Oh,' she says, stopping in her tracks.

'What is it?' I ask.

'Nothing,' she replies, turning her back to me.

'Audrey?'

Reluctantly she hands me the item.

'Sorry,' she says. 'It was just there.'

It takes my eyes time to absorb the horror of what is before me, but the image is unmistakable: a photograph of the late Henry Cooper, advertising Brut.

I flip it over.

To my darling Eds. Let's hope our summer of sex never ends.

Love – your 'Enry xxx

'I didn't—'

'It's OK,' I say. 'One of the grandchildren put it there. You can see yourself out.'

Audrey picks up her coat in a sheepish fashion and turns to me.

'Sorry, Alan,' she says. Seconds later the front door slams shut.

I toy with the idea of faxing Deborah Meaden before taking to the spare room.

* * *

I rise early and pass the master bedroom. Pausing I tap lightly at the door. All I hear is snoring so continue downstairs. It's a beautiful day. What a shame my heart is dark, heavy and full of sorrow.

In the kitchen I kick the fridge once more, this time quietly so as not to disturb Edame or alarm Shirley next door.

The weighted pants are airing over the banister. In search of something to lift my spirits I remove my cotton slacks and my usual lightweight pants and pull on the weighted ones. I then re-trouser and check under the stairs for my comfy trainers with the orthopaedic inserts. As I do there is a *rat-tat-tat* at the front door. I hobble into the hallway. An envelope inscribed 'Mr Stoob' sits squarely on the mat. I open the door, only to see a blur of black cloak disappearing from view.

With no time to waste I slip on my moccasins and head off in pursuit.

The cloaked figure makes slow progress but so do I, labouring in my heavy underwear. I am able to keep pace with him but my breaths are becoming shorter and more constricted in the cool air.

The figure crosses over to Greggs on Dunstable High Street and hails a bus. I am gaining on him but as I get close he climbs onto the 37 towards Woburn, which quickly disappears from view.

Beaten, I lean up against the bus shelter. My lungs are burning and my undercarriage sore. Chasing down strangers in my slippers? I must be mad. The 321 to St Albans pulls up but I wave the driver on. He looks annoyed. As my breathing gradually returns to normal I read the letter.

OH DEAR

NOT HAVING TOO MUCH LUCK ARE WE

MEET ME OUTSIDE ARGOS LEAGRAVE

TOMORROW IOAM

COME ALONE

A FRIEND

(OBVIOUSLY THE SAME FRIEND AS BEFORE)

Why the mystery informant needed to flee I have no idea, though I guess mystery informants have their reasons. If anyone is entitled to be a law unto themselves it's mystery informants. This one hasn't let me down yet. Perhaps he can provide the next piece in the Nazi jigsaw of destiny. After the shame of yesterday I could do with a little help.

I slink into the bus shelter and remove my undergarments, the cold air acting as balm to the soreness. Gingerly I make my way home, heavy pants slung over one shoulder.

The house is basking in a fragrant aroma. There are fresh flowers from the garden and the French windows are wide open. I have been gone longer than I thought. Edame appears, angelic and braless, in a white flowing dress, her hair wet from the shower. She throws her arms around me, her smile uncertain. I nestle into the crook of her shoulder and inhale the aroma: sick, port and Channel No 5.

'I love you so much I couldn't bear you having another dishonour so I got totally boozed up,' she says in my ear. 'Can you never forgive me? I haven't done a sick in weeks.'

I want to know how much she misses Henry Cooper, find out which of us was the better lover, learn who had the thicker penis. I want to ask whether she was looking at the photograph yesterday and whether she touched herself while she did so. I want to know if she was there when Cooper knocked down Jack Blodwell in 1965 to win the Commonwealth title and whether she gave him a rubdown after the fight. I want to ask so many questions but the moment is slipping away and I realise all that matters right now is that Henry Cooper is no more and I love my wife.

As we embrace Tom enters and asks if either of us has seen his 'Frankie Says Relax' T-shirt. Edame says she's been using it as a general kitchen cloth and he storms out. I wonder to myself whether an 'Alan Says Relax' T-shirt would sell.

The afternoon is spent snuggled up on the sofa watching *The World's Strongest Man*, which I recorded at Christmas. It's one of our favourite programmes and perfect for a day when TV, radio and newspapers are off-limits. As we settle into the penultimate round – the Atlas stones – I receive a text.

'Still good for four, Alan? We'll call you just before, then link you in. Peter.'

In the hustle bustle of the past 24 hours I had clean forgotten about my appearance on *The Geoff Lime Show*. The timing is awful but it's bad form to pull out and Geoff is known for his depth of knowledge and intelligent approach.

I pause *The World's Strongest Man*. Edame gives me a peck and leaves the room. I compose myself then make the call. Peter the producer is encouraging and puts me at my ease before patching me through to Geoff, who is direct and to the point ('No swearing'; 'Silence is dead air'; 'Remember I'm the star'). Before I know it we're underway.

Geoff: That was Fine Young Cannibals with 'She Drives Me Crazy'. This is Geoff Lime and you're listening to Chiltern Radio 97.6, the only radio station for Herts, Beds and Bucks with a no-nonsense guarantee. Now it's time for our series, *Bedfordshire's Most Famous Residents*. Today we shall speak to the man sandwiched

– so to speak – between singer Paul Young and cricketer Monty Panesar. It gives me great pleasure to welcome Bedfordshire's fourth most famous resident and Britain's Premier Nazi Hunter, Alan Stoob. Alan, are you with us?

Alan: In a manner of speaking, Geoff.

G: Huge pleasure speaking with you, Alan. What are you up to this afternoon?

A: Just watching *The World's Strongest Man* on video. Other than that not much. Had a bit of a disagreement with my wife earlier so we've been spending some much-needed time together.

G: Sounds like a plan, Alan. I'm sure by now you know how this works: I ask you as many questions as I can think of in sixty seconds. You ready to play?

A: I suppose so.

G: OK. Alan, time starts . . . now: Alan, why did you become a Nazi Hunter?

A: Because Simon Wiesenthal asked me to.

G: Who is Simon Wiesenthal?

A: He was the world's most famous and successful Nazi Hunter.

G: Never heard of him.

A: Yes, well.

G: Isn't seventy-five a bit old to be hunting Nazis?

A: No.

G: Alan, can you turn your radio down in the background please?

A: Sorry . . . better?

G: Much. Dog or cat?

A: Dog.

G: Tea or coffee?

A: Tea – no coffee for me – doctor's orders.

G: Kiss or cuddle?

A: Both.

G: How did you meet your wife?

A: Across a crowded newsagents.

G: What does she think about your exploits?

A: It makes her nervous. For instance last night she got drunk and was sick all down the toilet.

G: I read on Twitter that yesterday's hunt didn't go so well.

A: Yes, well.

G: In fact I heard—

A: Can we change the subject please, Geoff?

G: Sure thing! Have you ever travelled under a pseudonym?

A: When on Nazi business I always check into hotels as Michael Throat, if that helps.

G: How many times has your life been put in danger?

A: Seventeen.

G: Dream dinner party?

A: Hitler, Himmler, Goebbels, Von Ribbentrop and Joseph Mengele – then excuse myself and blow the room up.

G: Describe an average day in the life of Alan Stoob.

A: For security reasons I am unable to do that.

G: What is the best weapon against Nazis?

A: The truth.

G: I read your favourite song is the theme from *Schindler's List*.

A: Not true. I prefer 'Miss Eleanor Rigby' by The Beatles.

G: What are you up to tomorrow?

A: Meeting a mystery informant who will hopefully lead me to the heart of Bedfordshire's Nazi operation.

G: Thank you, Alan, for playing *Bedfordshire's Most Fa—*

A: I have a message for your listeners, Geoff. Stay vigilant, people. Remember to keep an eye out for Nazis in your local neighbourhood. Telltale signs include a heavy German accent, long steps and general nastiness.

G: Alan, thank you fo—

A: Also if you're interested in sponsoring my efforts to hunt down National Socialists in the generalised Bedfordshire zone please visit the website my grandson Haden has set up and find out how to donate.

G: Thanks, Ala—

A: Help the aged and please give genero—

G: Alan, enjoy your evening! Alan Stoob there, Britain's Premier Nazi Hunter. What an interesting man. It's five to five which can only mean one thing: time for Kraftwerk!

After the call I make my feelings known to Peter regarding the superficial nature of the questioning. He apologises. At least I was able to insert something about funding without anyone noticing.

'You were brilliant!' says Edame as I enter the kitchen. She's cooking egg curry, with Angel Delight for afters. I sit at the table. In front of me is a brochure of foreign cruises. It falls open at a page headed 'Six-month trips round the Cape of Good Hope'. In red are circled the words, 'Half-price for the over-seventy-fives'. I do love Edame but she is as far from subtle as Bonn is from Biddenham.

Tom comes down for dinner, my ancient laptop tucked under his arm. He has questions about the internet; when it began, who invented it, what it's made of. Edame and I hold hands under the table, pleased that our son finally appears to be embracing modern technology.

'My favourite web page so far is Alta Vista,' he declares.

'Have you heard of the Facebook?' says Edame. 'It's a brilliant new link on the world's wide web that allows you to say what you're doing and look at other people on holiday. Potato George showed me his Facebook the other week.'

'You went to your old boyfriend's house?' I ask, suddenly flushed.

'Don't be silly, Alan. He showed me on his smartyphone.'

Tom removes a notebook from his back pocket and writes 'the face book' on the first page.

'What other links are good?' he says. 'Sounds like you know a lot.'

'The BBC is very useful,' says Edame.

'The BBC?' says Tom. 'I thought that was just TV.'

'Everyone is at it these day,' she replies. 'Even Dad has got a web.'

'NO WAY!' says Tom. 'What's the number?'

'The easiest way to find it is to look up my name,' I say. 'Have you tried googling?'

'Susan wouldn't let me.'

'It's like an online encyclopedia,' I tell him. 'You visit Google. com and type in anything you want to know.'

Tom writes 'google dot com' on his pad, balances his bowl of Angel Delight on his laptop and heads back upstairs.

Before bed I pop my head round the study door. The emergency phone is flashing, intermittently bathing the walls in orange. Leaving the lights off I move towards the desk and press MESSAGES.

Alan, Nigel here from the British Nazi Hunting Association.

Please call me about yesterday as a matter of considerable urgency.

* * *

Awake much of the night worrying about the voicemail from Nigel. When I do finally get off I dream that the late Henry Cooper picks up Edame in his TR7 and drives her to Tring for a sex weekend. When they arrive his twin brother George is waiting in his dressing gown.

Thankfully my mood is lifted by a kind email from Ralph McTell. While I am in the office the emergency phone rings three times. Three times I lift the receiver and three times I hang up. I can't speak with Nigel, not until I've met with the mystery informant.

This bitterly cold spring day brings with it the sad news that Neil Jarlsberg, Cumberland's leading Nazi Hunter for the past twenty years, has died after choking on someone else's vomit. It's always distressing to hear of the death of a fellow huntsman. I email his wife with my condolences, though I know their relationship became strained after photos from a Gestapo-themed S&M party came to light.

With two bowls of porridge and a kiwi fruit inside me I head off to meet the informant. Outside it's minus two. Lucky I'm wearing a pair of Edame's tights. She doesn't mind. In fact she quite likes it. They certainly add a layer of snugness, though my life wouldn't be worth living if Interpol found out.

I stand outside Argos, shifting from one foot to the other in an effort to keep warm. A huge blacked-out people-carrier rolls to a stop beside me. The door opens and a be-gloved index finger beckons me in. I enter, my hand clasped around the blue inhaler in my pocket.

Inside the car is pitch black. I cannot see a thing. I hear faint wheezing and the vague clicking of arthritic joints. A voice emerges from the darkness.

'Not exactly in the clover are we, Mr Stoob?'

'Had a bit of bad luck,' I say. 'That's all.'

'You think it's down to luck?' he asks while eating an apple. At least I think it's an apple. It's pitch black. Perhaps he's snacking on a crab.

'I have two pieces of advice for you,' he says, his voice strong and precise.

'Who are you?' I ask.

'Surely we have no need to go through this rigmarole again, Mr Stoob?' he says, a sigh in his voice. 'I am a floater. I float. Like a butterfly, Mr Stoob. I know everything and I know everyone. I sit betwixt yet remain hidden. My knowledge in the field of espionage, in the arena of the unknown, is unprecedented, unsurpassed and unpossible.'

'Unpossible?'

'I am the cat that got the cream, the nail in the coffin, the water under the bridge and the all-seeing eye. I see everything, Mr Stoob. Including you.'

'Then tell me your name.'

'I told you last time, I'm a friend.'

'I usually know my friends' names.'

'Then call me Jimmy.'

'Is that your name?'

'No, my real name is . . . ARE YOU TRYING TO TRICK ME, MR STOOB?'

He lets my name hang heavy in the air.

'You know something but you do not know everything. Like a disorientated dog you are barking up the wrong treehouse. The answers to your questions are closer than you imagine but you must act fast. Plans are in place to change the very fabric of British life towards, shall we say, a more Teutonic way of being.'

I asked him to explain. A long silence ensues, during which I plan dinner.

'Hunt down The Griffin, Mr Stoob. You may imagine he sits in the background, unseen and rarely heard, but this is a man psychotically driven on by a thirst for power and the necessity to control. He runs the entire operation, from the ratline and the schedule of new Nazi arrivals to the Beasts of Bedfordshire annual award scheme. He is the key but remains the greatest danger. Catch him and everything falls into place.'

An arm reaches across me and opens the door.

'Goodbye, Mr Stoob.'

'But you only told me one piece of information, Jimmy,' I say.

'No I didn't, I told you two.'

'Definitely only one.'

'Am sure it was two.'

I address the car.

'Didn't he only tell me one?'

'He's right,' says a low voice from the front. 'Tell him the other one.'

'Really? Very well. To the east of Bedford lies Priory Country Park, a pleasant municipal strolling arena. Enter the park from the south side and count the trees. At the seventeenth tree point yourself right. You will come upon a small clearing. There you will find a birch with a root in an unusual shape. Climb the tree. Find the hollow. Look inside. Goodnight, Mr Stoob – and as they say in Baden-Baden, guten glück.'

I find myself on the pavement once more. The car accelerates the wrong way down a one-way street and off into the freezing fog. I remain in the chilly air having once more encountered the mystery man with no name unless it really is Jimmy and he's double-bluffing.

Back home I call Nigel.

'Where the shit have you been?'

'Hello, Nigel.'

'We were worried sick, Alan.'

'I needed some time to work on a lead.'

'I thought something dreadful had happened.'

'Sometimes I need space to work.'

'Listen, Alan, you know how much we appreciate what you've done for the British Nazi Hunting Association . . .'

'I don't like your use of the past tense, Nigel.'

'I didn't mean it like that. You're the Sir Alex Ferguson or Arsène Wenger of the Nazi Hunting world.'

'Meaning?'

'You and you alone will choose the timing of your departure. After all you have done in tracking down Nazis across the whole of Bedfordshire.'

'And beyond . . .'

'And beyond,' he concurs. 'The timing is yours. But I have to make this call or I wouldn't be fulfilling my role as Director of the BNHA. I must tell you that the other day – and indeed events in recent months – haven't looked good or reflected well on you, or us, or anyone in the Nazi-hunting business. You know how much we rely on the US lobby for funding. Fiascos like the manhole incident and Whipsnade cost us dear.'

'Fiascos now, is it?'

'We've known each other long enough to be straight, Alan.

I hope you know that here at the Association you are held in the very highest esteem. If there was a Nazi Hunting Hall of Fame you'd be in it, straight off. You are often spoken of in the same tones as Si.'

'Don't bullshit me, Nige.'

'It's true. I simply want to see you happy and going out in a manner befitting a champion, whenever that is. Herb Derb is champing at the bit to take over the title of Britain's Premier Nazi Hunter, but he can wait.'

'He certainly can.'

'What's all this about a lead anyway?'

'Not sure yet. Will let you know if it comes to pass.'

'OK, Alan. Hope I haven't hurt your feelings. Love to Edame.'

I take to my bed for a couple of hours in the afternoon, pondering just how the 'very fabric of British life' could be under threat.

When I wake the weather is foul. I tweet:

It's raining
It's pouring
Let's catch
Hermann Goering.

No one replies.

Two episodes of *Butterflies* before bed. I ask Edame if I can swap Mavis Nicholson for Wendy Craig in the lift. She doesn't answer.

*　　*　　*

Another of the clan has passed. That's two in a week. According to reports, Handel Pimm, Wales' foremost huntsman, has died after swallowing someone else's tongue. He will be greatly missed, not least for his sense of humour and oversized hand.

I call Pimm's widow, Animal Rachel, to pass on my condolences. She asks me to give the eulogy at Pimm's funeral in the small village of Llanrhaeadr-ym-Mochnant, Powys, and says there is something she needs to discuss with me face to face. I agree, pending a discussion with Edame (Edame hates Animal Rachel as she once tried to seduce me before a live studio audience).

My day to visit Beryl. She seems in good spirits and welcomes me with a peck on the cheek. My problems are merely 'minor setbacks' and everything, she claims, is surmountable. I've never seen her like this. Midway through the session it dawns on me that she's drunk. When I bring up Edame she splutters, 'Fuck Edame!' Later in the session she insists on telling me how promiscuous she was in her twenties. As I leave she asks for a light.

From there it's to Bedford in the Stoobmobile.

Drizzle turns to rain as I enter Priory Country Park. Somewhat grudgingly I unfurl my Pete's Hams miniature umbrella. Once the pathway begins I count the trees. An exceptionally attractive woman walks towards me smiling and makes me lose count so I am forced to begin again. This involves walking back to the start, thereby making it seem as if I am following the lady. After a while she looks behind and starts running. There is nothing I can do about this so I simply keep walking until I am close enough to the first tree to recommence counting. This time I am determined not to lose the tally. Another pretty lady approaches but I shield my eyes to her charms. Eventually I reach tree seventeen.

I look right and, as foretold, see a clearing. I walk purposefully towards it, wondering whether Simon Wiesenthal ever had an appointment with a birch.

The area is covered in condoms and loose pages of pornographic magazines. This surprises me. From what I understand young people's pornography needs are today met by the internet. Eventually I locate the tree. Now I understand what 'Jimmy' meant. Its roots are in the shape of a swastika. A truly horrific freak of nature and one that *That's Life* would most certainly have dined out on had it still been in production.

In an effort not to ruin my suit I remove my jacket, trousers and shirt before slipping my shoes back on and shinning up the trunk. Ten feet up there is a hollow. I push my hand inside and to the right. Nothing. I change my angle and force it left. Still nothing. Clinging on with my left hand I adjust my angle one more time and force my fist upwards into the body of the tree.

My fingers experience a cool metal surface. A couple more prods and I am able to dislodge the box. On the outside in faded lettering it reads 'Messerschmitt Cigars'.

Excitedly I lower myself back down to earth, clasping the box between my still-excellent teeth. Inside I find fifty euros in cash, a phone number and a message:

PLEASE TAKE ZE MONEY BUT LEAVE ZE PHONE NUMBER
IN ZE BOX. DANKE SCHON.

Once more an exciting discovery diverts the blood from my head into my previously-lifeless penis. I pocket the cash, input the number into my phone and shin back up the tree to replace the box.

As I lower myself back down I see the smiley woman

approaching the tree pointing in my direction, two male police officers in her wake.

* * *

Edame teases me all morning about the incident with the police. I play along, omitting to mention the erection. She might think I'm more interested in Nazis than her (I'm not).

After a lunch of crisps and smoked salmon I type yesterday's phone number into Google. Nothing comes up. I ring Interpol, only to find they have diverted their phones through to NATO.

Time to call someone I know I can rely on.

'Hello?' says a quivering voice.

'Tony – it's Stooby!'

'Stooby?'

'You know – Stooby!'

'Stooby?'

'STOOBY!'

'Oh . . . STOOBY!'

Tony Perkinson, friend and former head of recidivism with the Bedfordshire Police.

'How's life?' I ask.

'Good thanks, Alan.'

'And Penelope?'

'Oh, she died.'

'I'm very sorry to hear that.'

'It's OK, I met someone new.'

'Well that's great!'

'Not exactly – she died too.'

'Oh Tony.'

'It's OK – then I got a dog.'

'Listen, Tony. I know you're retired but could you check a number for me?'

'Is it Nazi business?'

'Of course.'

'Big fish?'

'Could be.'

Twenty minutes later he calls back.

'The number is ex-directory and encrypted. I asked Laker, Bedfordshire's foremost codebreaker, to decipher the encryption. All he could tell me was the combination points to the German quarter of Biggleswade, possibly to the house of a little-known but highly dangerous and sophisticated Nazi war criminal named Felix Pump who moved there after the unexplained death of the previous owner in 1986. That's what Laker the Codebreaker said anyway.'

I thank him and hang up. Tom enters with the laptop.

'Watch this, Dad,' he says before showing me a clip of a small baby called Charlie biting the finger of his elder brother. 'I found this amazing world web page called Your Tube. The internet's quite exciting, isn't it?' He exits. I feel emotional.

Felix Pump? Not a name I recognise and nothing in the files. Sometimes only the library will do. The first person I see there is Tina, who is working today. I approach warily but she stoops to give me a peck, waives Edame's fine for the late return of *Fanny Hill* and directs me to the microfiche section.

I locate the *Bedfordshire & District Examiner* box and remove the film for 1986. It is a laborious process. Most of the head-lines relate to the pedestrianisation of Bedford City Centre and the controversy surrounding the plastic pitch at Luton FC. One news item sticks out, however.

Local Man Bludgeoned To Death In Nazi-Style Killing

Flitwick is today in shock after local man Andrew Puppy was murdered to death in what appears to be a ritualistic killing with the hallmarks of the Third Reich, writes Sally Bijou.

Puppy, 47, was said to be walking down the high street 'eating a BigMac and minding his own business' when the murder took place. Witnesses spoke of a tank pulling up alongside Puppy, who was chased down the street by an SS chief then shot 96 times in the back.

Then three weeks later.

Murder Victim's Home 'Bought By German'

The home formerly belonging to local murder victim Andrew Puppy has been sold at auction to Felix Pump, an elderly German man from Alsace-Lorraine, Mark Stirrup writes.

The house, which is very large and has a really massive garden, was the most sought after item at yesterday's Biggleswade auction. Locals believe that Pump, 82, will be an asset to the community unless crossed.

This is what I am up against: a cold-blooded killer who will murder for a panoramic view. Unless there was another reason he wanted that house.

'Hope you found what you were looking for, Dad,' says Tina. 'Come for dinner later. Houdini's making spicy Black Forest Gateau.'

Back outside the Stoobmobile fails to start. That's the second time in a couple of weeks. I leave a note in the window ('Broken down – apols, Alan') and walk reluctantly to the bus stop, pondering whether somehow there is a correlation between the engine in my car and the penis in my pants.

'The Stoobmeister!'

My heart hits the floor. It's the last person on earth I want to bump into. It's Potato George.

'Hello George,' I say.

'I had no idea you were reduced to waiting for buses these days, Alan. The Jag is parked close by, fancy a lift?'

George has always been a topper, always tries to top everything I do. He must be cock-a-hoop to find me waiting for the 316 to Dunstable Church Street.

'Thanks, George, but today I choose to travel by bus.'

'Remember what Thatch said about people and buses, Alan! Of course I understand, a man of your limited means. Despite being only sixty-four I too qualify for free travel, though frankly I prefer the Jag. Fewer plebs!'

I hate him.

'And how are the kids?'

'Very well, thanks,' I reply.

'Such a shame about poor Tom. I did try and guide Edame towards private education for the boy. I would happily have paid, Alan. Anything to see my Edame smile again.'

The rage inside me grows. I feel close to a panic attack.

'If it's all very well with you, George, I'd rather wait on my own.'

'Suit yourself,' he replies. 'Please send my love to Edame and tell her to call me.'

I mumble incoherently.

'Oh, and Alan?'

'What?'

'Cheer up!'

He walks off, his expensive Italian shoes clicking ostentatiously and incongruously on the Bedfordshire paving. Three minutes later he flies past in his soft-top Jaguar XJ8, hooting and, so it seems, aiming for a puddle in the gutter. To avoid a soaking I scuttle backwards only to topple head first over a bush and into somebody's garden.

On the bus home I work on Handel Pimm's eulogy but I'm distracted by the nettle stings to my neck and by my encounter with Potato George. I liken my position of Edame's husband to that of an incumbent government. All the weight of expectation and responsibility lies with me. It's far easier being in opposition, dropping in unannounced to highlight inadequacies, cutting a swathe, unfettered by accountability. This is a role Potato George plays with ease, all easy charm in the absence of the daily grind. Sadly it says rather a lot for Ed Miliband that while George can pull off this performance with aplomb, the leader of the opposition cannot.

Back home I complain to Edame about PG.

'He's such a bloody topper,' I say.

'I know,' she replies. 'And he looks fool doing it.'

'Do you love him?' I ask, shocked by my own uncertainty.

'He's an old friend, that's all. We had something once but I was teenage back then. He means nothing to me. I've only ever had eyes for the Premier Nazi Hunter.'

'Herb Derb?' I joke.

'No!' she says, smiling hugely.

'Even with my tatty suits and my car that doesn't work?'

She kisses me tenderly on the elbow and we head upstairs for a siesta.

You can't beat an afternoon snooze, it's like a reset button. Matters that weigh heavy at two seem mere trifles by four. I wake in an excellent mood and head to the study with renewed zest, only to suffer terrible cramp in my right calf, a situation later made worse when I follow through during *Look East*. I am forced to take a shower. Thankfully Edame is in the garden throughout.

At seven Tom saunters downstairs carrying a Fine Fare bag containing my laptop. These days he never goes anywhere without it. He looks smart in his Peter Gabriel sweatshirt. Edame is a picture in her yellow spring dress. I drive the three of us to Tina's.

When we arrive Houdini is on the sofa reading the Ladybird *Book of Nazis* we gave her last Christmas. She leaps up, hugs me and announces she's got the hardest punch in the infants'.

Haden is on the kitchen table playing a keyboard ('Hey, Granddad, it's a Nazi synthesizer!'). Tina looks harassed. Marco is notable by his absence. Tom leads the kids upstairs with his computer. Thirty seconds later the words 'Charlie bit my finger!' ring out to great laughter.

'Tom's the best he's been in ages,' says Tina, opening a second bottle of red.

'That's the internet for you,' I reply.

'Sorry to hear about the fudged hunt, Dad. Time to call it a day?'

I look to Edame. She winks back.

'Still some important work to do,' I tell Tina. 'Wouldn't have thought I'll be at it in five years' time though. Where's Marco this evening?'

'Gone back to his old ways.'

'What do you mean?' asks Edame.

'Rough trade,' says Tina, between gulps of wine. 'And the rest.'

Back home I email Interpol to see if they know anything of Felix Pump, only to receive an automated response telling me the entire organisation is on an extended team-building exercise in Las Vegas.

* * *

Last night I dreamt the national anthem had been changed to 'Lady In Red' by Chris de Burgh. Or did I? The confusion lies in Edame's penchant for keeping the radio on throughout the night. Sometimes I can't tell whether something is real or imagined, e.g. the sinking of the *Belgrano*.

While Edame drowses I slip out of bed and into the garden. I sit with my coffee and sachet of bran supplement. It's a beautiful morning.

I remove my phone and stare at the number for Felix Pump that I found in a tree. I click 'edit', 'edit number' then add '141' before the '0', thereby hiding my identity from the recipient. A crow stares at me curiously from Bob's roof. I dial. It rings five times. The crow flies off. Then an answer.

Heavy breathing. Nothing else. Then . . .

'Eez eet safe?'

I am frozen, unable to speak. Seconds elapse. They feel like hours, days or even weekends.

'EEZ EET SAFE?'

'Ja,' I reply finally, 'eet eez sehr safe.'

'About fucking time.'

'Sorry, Herr Komrade,' I say trembling. 'There is a delay on ze line.'

'So, you found ze tree.'

'Ja.'

'Which means you must be pretty desperate, ja?'

'Oh, ja.'

'Vot is your namm?'

I pause momentarily as I conjure a believable German pseudonym.

'Rod von Hull,' I reply.

'Vhy are you coming up as "number vithheld", Herr Hull?'

'I have ein funny phone.'

'I see. Your current situation please?'

'I am married.'

'NOT ZAT SITUATION DUMBKOPF!' the voice shrieks back at me. 'DEINE SITUATION IN A NAZI SENSE.'

'Sorry,' I reply. 'Meine situation is zat I fear mein cover may be blown, Herr Komrade.'

'Voz it a Jew?'

'Erm, no, it was actually a communis—'

'The Jews are such shits, are zey not?'

'Much verse zan ze Christians.'

'Votever. Ve need to get du neu papers. But first ich must ask du some questions to be certain du are who du say du ist. Fur ziss du vill come to mein haus. 71 Gallstone Drive, Biggleswade. Tomorrow 10am sharp. Tell no one or ich vill have du killed.'

Tomorrow? I need more time than that.

'Can vee make it later in ze week?'

There is a pause.

'Ich thought du said du ver desperate?'

'Oh, ich am, Herr Komrade – sehr sehr desperate – but ich verk on ze vegetable counter at Asda in Hockliffe and ich have a number of shifts approaching. If ich miss these ich bin likely to arouse suspicion.'

'Gut sinking, Herr Hull. Sechts days time enough?'

Six days gives me time to put a plan in place, request back-up from Interpol and attend Handel Pimm's funeral.

'Zat would be perfect, Herr Komrade.'

'OK, see you then. Auf wiedersehen and Heil Hitler!'

'Heil Hitler for sure!'

I hang up and crawl back into bed, resuming the previous spooning.

Dare I masquerade as a German? What if they recognise me? Am I being set up?

I am woken by Edame, who is stood at the foot of the bed. I glance at the clock. It's gone eleven. My wife looks suspicious, as if she knows about the dream I've just had starring Debbie Reynolds and Janet Leigh.

'Package for Alan,' she says, throwing it onto the duvet. 'All the way from China.'

I wait until she leaves before opening it. I am not disappointed: twenty-five shiny blue tablets, with the word Viagra emblazoned on the thin metal strips. I'm tempted to pop one straight off but decide that with the funeral tomorrow I must finish Handel Pimm's eulogy first.

It's not hard to think of generous things to say about Handel. This, after all, was the man who singlehandedly ensnared six Nazis inside Cardiff Arms Park. The difficulty comes when writing of a friend whose partner has been consistently unfaithful to them over four decades. They don't call her Animal Rachel for nothing.

At 2pm we set off for Llanrhaeadr-ym-Mochnant. In an uncharacteristic display of kindness Interpol have promised to cover my petrol. They draw a line at the M6 toll, however, so I stick to the main route.

We check into the Wynnstay Arms before taking a stroll through the village. It's a quaint place; leather-faced men with pipes loitering outside newsagents; old ladies running small shops; a river running through it. Llanrhaeadr is a parish that time forgot. Nevertheless I get the feeling we are being watched.

'This is where they filmed *The Englishman Who Went Up A Hill And Came Down A Mountain*,' I say.

'I remember that films. Starring Hugh Grant?' replies Edame.

'The very same. Grant was in *Paper Moon*, directed by Roman Polanski. Polanski escaped from the Kraków Ghetto in 1943. In the end everything comes back to the Nazis.'

Edame squeezes my arm. I firm my bicep to remind her of better times.

'Are you nervous about tomorrow?' she asks.

'Only about you feeling funny around Animal Rachel. You know I have to talk to her?'

'I do,' she says. 'It's OK, I know she won't try anything.'

'Last time she asked to see my willy,' I remind her.

'I don't blame her,' she replies. 'You've got a lovely little willy.'

I thank her with a handshake, which turns into a kiss. I fish around in my pocket until I find what I'm looking for and surreptitiously pop it in my mouth.

'Look!' I say to Edame before sticking out my tongue to reveal a small blue pill.

'What is it?' she asks.

'What is it? Why it's Viagra!' I exclaim before swallowing it down in an exaggerated fashion. 'Care to accompany me back to the hotel, miss?' I proffer my arm.

'It would be my pleasures,' she replies, giggling like an Amsterdam schoolgirl.

I guess Dr Grossmark was right. You don't know what you're getting online. Perhaps this batch is sugar pills. Next time I'll go through the official channels.

April

Edame fixes my tie, brushes my shoulders clear of dandruff and tells me I look as handsome as the day I married her. This is clearly a massive lie but I appreciate the sentiment. She doesn't look nearly as good as she did back then, though she's still what my grandson would call 'fit' for sixty-seven-and-a-third.

While Edame is downstairs having coffee with Julie Moole, Britain's sole lady hunter, I check in with Interpol.

'Alan, you old cunt!' says Steve.

'Good time in Vegas?'

'What goes on tour stays on tour, Alan. Sad news about Pimm.'

'I'll be delivering his eulogy in an hour,' I tell him.

'That Animal Rachel is a hot piece of ass. Did you know she flashed Lance outside Nando's?'

I profess not to doubt it.

'Still, four in two weeks is dreadfully unlucky.'

'What do you mean?' I ask.

'Pimm, Jarlsberg, Heddleston and Hinton,' he replies. 'Five if you count Negative Graham.' Five Nazi Hunters? I only knew about Pimm and Jarlsberg.

'No reason to believe there's foul play involved,' he says. 'Just rotten luck.'

I feel panicky. The bran flakes threaten to drop out of my stomach.

'If it's not inappropriate get me Mrs Handel's digits, will you?'

I remain seated on the bed. Five of my colleagues snuffed out in fourteen days. Rotten luck my bottom, this smacks of an organised assault on the clan.

'Are you OK, Alan?' asks Edame as she returns to the room. 'You look as if you've seen a ghost, or a Nazi.'

'I'm OK,' I tell her.

'Don't worry about giving the eulogy, you'll be fine. Just focus on a spots in the middle distance and think of Si.'

The chapel where Handel is being buried is a ten-minute taxi ride up into the hills of the Tanat Valley. We travel with Harold E. Biscuit, a leading huntsman from North Yorkshire, and his wife Betty. While Betty and Edame exchange gossipy stories about Animal Rachel, Harold regales me with tales of Handel's generosity, his strike rate as a Nazi Hunter and his famous oversized hand.

'His wrist, it were like a calf,' he says, 'and that hand, it were like a neck.'

I smile back but my thoughts are elsewhere.

The chapel concourse is a veritable who's who of Nazi Hunters: Charlie Horowitz, Peter Crab, Jim the Tooth, Titus Anatschev, Abraham Goldmann; all have made the effort to ensure Handel receives the send-off he so richly deserves. I nod at Nigel from the British Nazi Hunting Association who remains deep in discussion with Herb Derb, my would-be-successor. Animal Rachel strolls over with her daughter Meg.

'I'm so sorry for your loss,' I tell her.

'Don't worry about that, show us your wilbur.'

I wish I could say she was crazed with grief but I've never seen a widow look quite so consolable, nor a daughter come to that. I offer them both a Werther's Original and move on, sidling up to one of France's leading hunters of the last ten years, Jean-Claude le Ping.

'Any bites recently?' I ask. 'Non,' he replies. 'I ate zees jub.' Not quite the attitude I would expect on a day like today. I look past le Ping and towards the cars parked up on the far side of the road. Amongst the many Volvos, Saabs and other vehicles manufactured by neutral countries stands a solitary Mercedes-Benz. Leaning up against it are two heavy-set men, each with dark glasses, each holding an umbrella. There is no sign of rain. A voice whispers in my ear.

'Could be us next.' It's Peter Crab.

'What do you mean?' I ask.

'Come off it, Alan, you of all people know exactly what I'm talking about.'

'I take it you've heard about the others then,' I say.

'I know about Pimm, Jarlsberg, Hinton and Mumford.'

'Mumford?'

'On the radio this morning. Shot himself in the face with a bicycle pump.'

'How can you sh—'

'That's what I thought. Something's going on. I've already spoken to Nigel but the Association is trying to play it down. I'm checking out, Alan. Judith is sick of me never being around. She didn't even want me to come today, though that's more to do with Animal Rachel. Look at us all, gathered in one place like this. We're sitting ducks. I can't believe there's no security. If you want my database, just let me know.'

A sharp pain fills my skull. Stress headache. I haven't had one of these since Whipsnade. I ask Edame for paracetamol but she doesn't have any. I dig in my pocket where the lining has perished and get lucky. I swallow it down.

'The funeral will commence in two minutes,' says Rabbi Bloombergstein. 'Everyone please take their seats.'

I walk round to the back of the chapel past a small group of orthodox hunters kissing a photograph of Simon Wiesenthal and find the bathroom. Breathing deeply in through my nose and out through my mouth I steady myself for the eulogy. Despite having spoken in public for over sixty years it still makes me very nervous. I unzip my fly and let nature take its course. Suddenly the end of my nose is being sprayed with a jet of yellowy liquid. I look down in time to receive an eyeful. My penis is pointing skyward.

I have taken a Viagra by mistake.

With some difficulty I squeeze Little Alan away, wash my face and hands, enter the chapel and take up my position in the front row between Animal Rachel and her daughter, Meg. Both smile at me and each places a hand on my knee, not helping matters. Animal Rachel leans over.

'I knew you were pleased to see me, Alan Stoob,' she whispers.

Rabbi Bloombergstein introduces himself and says a few kind words about Handel before asking us to rise for Psalm 121, 'Levavi Oculos'. I hold the hymn book over my groin in an effort to disguise the swelling. Meg looks down, winks at me and licked her lips. If the Viagra doesn't wear off soon I will be forced to give the eulogy while in possession of a massive erection. I try picturing a naked, gambolling Himmler but nothing seems to shift it.

I remove my phone and text Peter Crab.

'Stage fright. Please read eulogy on my behalf? Alan.'

A quick response.

'Would but forgotten glasses. Peter.'

'Yet you can read this?'

'Got it set on extra big font.'

'OK – borrow Harold's specs.'

'Where's he sitting?'

I turn round.

'Next to you.'

'OK.'

When it was time for the eulogy I told the rabbi that I was too stiff with sadness to read and that Peter would take my place. This had the effect of inducing sympathy from the ladies flanking me, which once again was the last thing required.

Pete does an excellent job and adds a little flourish of his own ('Ashes to ashes, dust to dust, if Alan don't get you then Handel Pimm must'). By the time we filter out the greatest tumescence has passed.

'Alan, I need to talk to you,' says Animal Rachel, taking my arm.

'Look, Rachel, I think you're nice looking for your age range but I'm married to Edame and she possesses a killer karate chop.'

'Not that, silly. It's about Handel's death.'

'I know. It's a tragedy, to die swallowing someone else's tongue.'

'That's not what happened. There's a cover-up. I have it on good authority that Handel was pierced by a javelin thrown from a moving bus belonging to the Berlin Athletics Club.'

At first I didn't even register the noise as gunfire. I imagined the sound to be a scarecrow and as I looked towards the field beyond the road I saw a flock of starlings soaring into the

Powys sky. It was then I happened to notice the burly men using the roof of the Mercedes to steady their umbrellas, which had converted into automatic weapons.

As the second wave of gunfire filled the air I hit the ground and looked round for Edame. I could see her foot sticking out from beneath Roger Yeoman, the recently retired Nazi professor. Animal Rachel was next to me, begging me to lie on top of her. A cry went up from Harold E. Biscuit – 'I've been hit!' He staggered, grasping his shoulder.

Suddenly Handel's daughter Meg emerges from behind a gravestone holding an Uzi in each hand, and walks towards the assailants, unloading both weapons in their direction. The bullets bounce off the windows and side panels. The marksmen dive into the Mercedes. Both nearside tyres are punctured as Meg continues her fearless assault. The driver starts the car and speeds off, though not before one of the Nazis emerges from the sunroof to unload a final volley of shots into the melee.

Hesitantly, the cream of Britain's Nazi Hunters clamber to their feet.

'Other than Harold, is everyone alright?' I shout.

Harold stands clutching his shoulder, drenched in blood.

'Someone call an ambulance,' I say before hurrying over to Edame. She is standing next to Ephraim Spielbaum, shaking. I take her in my arms. She must be in shock and seems unable to speak. I consider slapping her, so am surprised when she wriggles free from my clutches, withdraws her right arm and delivers the most ferocious whack to my left cheek.

'Over here,' shouts Peter Crab. We move towards the opening of where Handel was to be interred. There, next to the coffin and clutching an order of service, lies Rabbi

Bloombergstein, a tiny hole in his forehead and a thin trickle of blood threading its way towards the open grave.

Edame and I drive home in silence. Despite the cost I take the M6 toll road. Once we are home Edame heads straight upstairs. I make her a cup of tea and take it up. We meet on the landing. In her hand is a suitcase.

'I'm going to the Eindhoven to visit mother,' she says, her face hard, expressionless.

'Why?'

'After the peril you put us in today, do I have to do the explains?'

'Can I come?'

'No.'

'It's late.'

'I am staying at a hotels inside the Luton Airport.'

'Can I have a kiss?'

'No.'

She leaves, closing the door behind her. Outside I hear the wheel spin of a taxi on the gravelled driveway.

More than seventy years since the war was won and still the Nazis are ruining lives.

*   *   *

Barely slept. Kept reaching over for Edame only to find an empty space. It's been years since we spent a night apart. We are known as the Paul and Linda of the Nazi hunting community (though few of them know about Cooper or Meaden).

My instincts told me something was afoot in Llanrhaeadr. I should have read the warning signs. Ninety-three per cent of my job is to act on my instincts, to trust them. Arthur Pob was right, this is a young man's game. I call Tina.

'Have you heard from your mother?' I ask, doing my best to sound nonchalant.

'No,' she says. 'Everything alright?'

'Not exactly. We had a bit of an argument after nearly getting killed at a funeral in Wales. I think she blames me for putting us both in extreme danger.'

'That's not good. I'm sure she'll come round, Dad. Can we chat later? Marco brought a man in a distressed leather t-shirt back to the house in the early hours and I need to have it out with them.'

How could I be so casual about the safety of my wife? I may throw caution to the wind when it comes to my own well-being but I must never neglect Edame. She deserves better.

The study phone goes. I dash upstairs to pick it up.

'Our internet connection is down and I just can't cope.'

It's Tom. He's phoning from his bedroom. I can hear the echo.

'You've only been online three weeks,' I reply impatiently.

'So what? The internet is a basic human right!'

I hang up. The house seems eerily quiet without Edame. I open the desk drawer. Behind the Copydex and my collection of ration books lies a half bottle of Babycham. I stare at it before closing the drawer. I reboot the wi-fi and turn on my computer. The internet is fine. I find temporary reprieve in a video featuring a baby monkey riding backwards on a pig but soon enough I feel the panic rising. I call Beryl. She agrees to an emergency session, double rates.

I arrive all wobbly. She beckons me in and offers me a gin and tonic. I accept.

I tell her Edame has left to visit her mother in the Netherlands and I'm desperate. She says she suspected all along Edame was sexually involved with her mother. I try to remain open-minded but am surprised by this analysis. She hands me some paper and a pen and asks me to draw my feelings. Without anything hard to lean on my picture of a lonely pigeon in the Luton Arndale Centre could be anything but Beryl spends quarter of an hour analysing it. When I describe the blackness Edame's absence brings she cites my experience of evacuation and asks when I last emptied my bowels as this could hold the key. I refuse to answer the question. As I leave she hands me a bill for £950.

Sitting in the car outside I call Edame but it goes straight through to voicemail. I try another fourteen times before stopping for a breather. It is then that my own phone beeps. It's a text message, from Deborah Meaden.

'Fancy some company? I'm not wearing a petticoat xxx'

Almost unbeknownst to myself I turn the ignition and head in the general direction of the Oxfordshire countryside. My heart is thudding in my chest, my head woozy, thick with unthought. I have no idea what I am doing. My body is pointing itself towards what promises to be the loving touch of human kindness and to hell with what Edame and I have built up together over the past forty-five years.

As I switch from the M1 to the M25 anti-clockwise the traffic thickens. Tears stream down my dappled cheeks but I continue on my path, impelled to betray my loving wife. I know this is simply a repetition of the abandonment I experienced in 1940 when I was evacuated to Grassington in North Yorkshire and forced to live with the loathsome Meekers but I feel powerless to curb my impulse. I crank up Chris Rea to deafen my conscience.

My phone beeps again. I activate my hazard lights and pull over onto the hard shoulder.

'Arrived safely. Home in a few day. Just needed some spaces. Here's the kiss you didn't get yesterday. Edame x'.

Deactivating the hazard lights I pull away from the hard shoulder, continue for a mile, come off at the next junction, drive round the roundabout and head home.

As I arrive back at the house it is strangely reassuring to see Bob leaning up against the garage, drowsing. I could so easily have returned an adulterer. As it is, nothing happened and nothing has changed. An enormous sense of relief washes over me. Although she is away, knowing Edame sends her love makes all the difference. I feel 'centred' again, to use Beryl's parlance.

I let Bob in. He's brought his own sleeping bag and heads for the kitchen, making himself comfortable in Goebbels' old basket which Tom insists we keep. While he snoozes I brew myself a strong pot of decaffeinated Earl Grey and head for the study.

I open Google and type in 'Niall Heddleston + obituary'.

Niall Heddleston, who has died after pouring sulphuric acid into his bath and drinking it all, will best be remembered for his pursuit and capture of Phyllis Garnt, the Matron of Munich.

I do the same for Mumford:

If ever there was a man cut out for the pursuit of Nazis in Cornwall it was Tony Mumford, who has died after being slaughtered by accident and converted into sausages during a routine visit to his local abattoir.

Hinton . . .

The death of Richard Hinton following a freak yawning mishap draws to a close a career that reached its apotheosis with the capture of Heinrich Himmler's cat, Mr Muffles.

And finally Jarlsberg:

The untimely demise of Neil Jarlsberg after inadvertently choking on someone else's vomit brings the curtains down prematurely on what promised to be a successful career as Scunthorpe's leading Nazi Hunter.

Heddleston, Mumford, Hinton, Jarlsberg. Pimm makes five, Negative Graham six. All dressed up as accidents.

The office phone rings. It's Interpol Steve.

'Hi, Alan,' says Interpol Steve. 'Everything alright, is it?'

Filthy jokes and teasing are notable by their absence.

'Alright-ish,' I reply. 'Just in my study doing some research online.'

'Good,' he says. 'The internet is where it's at.'

A long pause.

'Has anyone tried to kill you in the last day or two?'

'Kind of,' I say. 'Why?'

'Oh no reason,' he says. 'Just routine inquiry.'

'Routine, you say?'

'Yes. New Interpol policy. Make people like yourself feel more secure.'

'Secure?'

'Yes.'

'Come off it, Steve.'

'Nothing doing,' he says. 'Like I say, just routine.'

'You know those other Nazi Hunters were murdered, don't you?'

'Good lord, you do have a vivid imagination, Alan.'

'Am I in danger?'

'Of course not.'

'Is that so?'

'Yes, though it has just occurred to me you might want to undergo extensive facial surgery and move to Argentina.'

'Argentina?'

'Yeah. Only if you fancy it. No pressure.'

'So basically you want me to behave like a Nazi?'

'When in Rome, as we say at Interpol. Got to dash. I'll email you contact details of our man in Woburn, the one who did Herb's nose.'

I open my diary. Three blank days, then a trip to the house of evil Nazi war criminal Felix Pump. I text Edame.

'Thank you, my love. I too am going away for a few days but I'll be back soon. Here's a kiss for now x and one for later x. Stay vigilant.'

I dial a number I haven't used in over ten years. I let it ring three times before hanging up. That will be enough to alert them. I head downstairs to let Bob out before my departure. He must have squeezed through the dogflap we had built for Goebby. I leave £20 for Tom, and set off.

Driving time is thinking time and the journey across Bedfordshire to the fenlands of Cambridgeshire is certainly one that orthodox Jews might term a 'fair schlep.' Is this the right move? My life is clearly in danger, my wife sick of my constant hunting and my judgement of late questionable. On the flipside for the first time in my second career I have the chance to infiltrate the Nazi network, worm my way into their secret world, capture The Griffin, shut down the flow of National Socialists into the Bedfordshire region and retire, universally admired.

I stop at a petrol station and fill up. There's a text from Interpol Steve.

'just checkin ur still alive lol'

I ignore it. That should put the frighteners up them.

I arrive in the small village of Grantchester, park opposite the house and remove my overnight bag. I lock the car and stare up at the vast intimidating structure, set back from the road with two lion statues defending it. A lone light shines out from the front window. As I ascend the grand steps a shadow shifts behind the net curtains. I ring the doorbell seven times. The light flicks on and off twice. I hold the buzzer for a further eight seconds. One by one the locks on the door are unbolted, the chains released.

'Mein freund,' says the diminutive German standing in the doorway.

'Stefan Cuntz, well I'll be damned!' I say. We embrace.

'I got your coded phone message. Ich am impressed you remembered. You vere not followed?'

'No.'

He checks over my shoulder before beckoning me inside.

'For such ein special occasion ich shall mach traditional German dinner of bier, sausages und bier,' he says, showing me to my room. 'But first ve must verk.'

It is ten years since I last saw Stefan. The ensuing years have not been kind. He was always small, perhaps 5'4". He now stands 4'10" at best. His hands are shaky and when seated his legs bounce up and down. Hiding out from the Third Reich as a known traitor has clearly taken its toll.

I throw my overnight bag onto my bed. Plumes of dust shoot off in all directions. Who last stayed here? Perhaps it was me, back in 2001. The wall has pictures of Stefan's wife and family. He won't have seen any of them in over a decade.

In the kitchen a cup of tea is waiting. I raise the cup to Stefan and take a sip. It's cold. Stefan tends to the open fire.

'Drop your trousers,' he says, raising the poker. 'Bite down on ziss vooden block.'

Soon the air is filled with my screams and with what smells like frying bacon, which seems ironic. Afterwards, as I bathe my buttock in a tray of cold water, Stefan informs me that all Waffen-SS have a swastika branded on their right cheek.

'Ich didn't press hard so it should fade vithin funf weeks,' he says. Once I stop whimpering he takes me through a short history of the SS. I make notes. Seeing this, Stefan grows livid and throws my jottings on the fire, insisting I retain all information in my head.

'Ziss ist fur your own safety,' he says. We move onto my new identity. He drums the details into me, getting me to repeat each fact over and over until it becomes second nature.

'Vot ist your name?'

'Rod Boris Klaus von Hull.'

'Vare vere du born?'

'In ze tiny village of Umlaut on ze Belgian border.'

'Vot are the names of your siblings?'

'Jens, Jörg and Jurgen.'

'Vot woz ze name of your first pet?'

'Professor Wolfgang.'

'Vot kind of student vere du?'

'Very conscienschluss.'

'Vot did du do during ze vor?'

'I vas Hauptsturmführer with ze Waffen-SS 1940-45.'

Finally we stop work at 11pm. He hands me a Holsten Pils.

'To a verld free von Nazism,' he says. We clink bottles. Mine froths over.

During dinner we update one another on our lives. I tell Stefan about the Nazis I've hunted, the humiliation of Whipsnade and my ongoing concern over Edame's relationship with the late Henry Cooper. He in turn fills me in on the troubling tale of how he left his wife Birgit in Rumbelows one Tuesday and how she never came home, how he didn't report it for fear of drawing attention to himself and his fugitive status, how he hasn't seen his children in ten years and how all he can do is hide out, make Airfix models and watch war programmes on the History channel.

'They took Birgit in broad daylight,' he says as he attempts to uncork the bottle of Riesling I brought. 'I should never have taken the path I did.'

'I will get onto Interpol about Birgit the moment I leave but you must not condemn yourself,' I say, taking over the uncorking duties. 'You did as you did because you are a good man. Without your help I would never have tracked down Fiena Nibble, easily the most evil of the three Nibble sisters.'

'Ich know zat,' he says wearily. 'But ich miss Birgit and ich miss ze kids. Even though Silke and Ulrich are only in Colchester ich dare not contact zem. If somehow zay are linked to me zay vill be viped out by ze Nazis tyranny, no qvestion.'

'You gave up so much to work for the British Nazi Hunting Association,' I say, resting my hand on his bird-like shoulder.

'Yes,' he says. 'Und now ich bin just ein lonely old mensch zat kinder make fun of.'

'Maybe. But by preparing me for my interrogation with evil Felix Pump you are an essential component in my effort to overthrow the Nazis. And besides, you are my friend.'

'Und du mine,' he says.

We retire to our rooms. I hear Stefan quadruple lock his

door and cock his pistol. It can't be much fun living with a death sentence hanging over you. His circumstances remind me of Salman Rushdie so I tweet the acclaimed author of *Midnight's Children*. He doesn't reply. Some of these so-called celebrities are right up their own fundaments.

*   *   *

After a hearty breakfast of assorted cold meats Stefan teaches me party songs instilled in him as a Hitler Youth back in Bochum. The first is sung to the theme from *Robin Hood*, the second to 'Deutschland Über Alles'.

> Rudolf Hess, Rudolf Hess, driving to Berlin
> Rudolf Hess, Rudolf Hess, drinking Gordon's gin
> His suit is a treat
> His hair nice and neat
> Rudolf Hess,
> Rudolf Hess,
> Rudolf Hess.
>
> Grab a fraulein by the skirt
> Lift it up and have a flirt
> German ladies love it dirty
> 'specially when they're over 30
> HEY!

Next he shows me the Nazi handshake, which entails tickling the palm of your fellow shaker with your little finger while raising your left leg off the ground and keeping the right eye clamped shut.

During our mid-morning break I call Tom.

'How is everything?' I ask.

'Good thanks, Dad,' he says, sounding upbeat. 'Have you heard of planking? It's when people lie down like a plank in unusual places and take photos of themselves. There are some hilarious pictures of people doing it on the world's internet. I also found googles and looked you up. Your web pages are really excellent. Did Haden do that?'

'He did,' I reply.

'I wonder if he could do a page for me about Susan.'

After our break Stefan teaches me how to goose step, for which he stretches my hamstrings. He shows me how to concoct a German omelette, how to tie a Hanover knot and regales me with eight German sex jokes, three of which I barely understand. Next it's role-play. I am von Hull and Stefan plays my German interrogator, Felix Pump. It is highly realistic, right down to the inspection of my buttocks.

'The key,' he says as we unwind with a Kia-Ora and a packet of Scampi Fries, 'is to remain calm und efficient. Deutschland is built on efficiency. Have you ever seen Germany fail in ein penalty shoot-out? Ze German people have ein unflappable quality zat has served zem vell, especially in the areas of sport und vorfare. Your accent und diction are fine, but if you panic und get alles svetty zey vill know you are ein fake.'

After a modest lunch of sour bread and pickles we say our farewells.

'Ein pleasure to see du again, Alan,' says Stefan, his eyes watery with emotion. 'Promise you'll call Interpol about mein wife?'

'I'm on it,' I tell him.

'Macht sure you check unter ze car, ze bonnet, ze steering column und ze passenger seat before you set off.' We embrace before he retreats once more into his castle.

I check warily along the road before crossing to the Stoobmobile. Outwardly there is no sign of any interference. I lift the bonnet, check under the seats and use my mirror-on-a-stick to examine the vehicle's undercarriage. It seems safe. I start up the Omega and slip out of Cambridgeshire, apparently unnoticed.

The A428 is an excellent road in the middle of the day and as I approach St Neots I relax into the drive. It is then I notice a jet black BMW five series on my tail. The number plate is German. It could be a coincidence. I drive on, checking the mirror. When I slow it chooses not to overtake. When I accelerate it keeps pace. I indicate left, it does the same.

I am sweating. I call Interpol Steve and ask him to put a trace on the number plate but he says Julian in IT is having a duvet day. White flashes of panic assail my stomach. I find Beryl's number. As I am about to call it I remember Stefan's words:

Remain calm. Unflappable.

I continue on the road, breathing deeply through my right nostril – the left remains blocked after a blow from Sacha Tamler, the Freak of Freiberg – and try to devise a plan. Eventually it comes to me.

I approach the intersection for Elstow at speed. I indicate left, then at the last possible moment swing right. The BMW is unable to respond in time and slides left before trying to correct itself and gets caught up in the oncoming traffic.

I press my foot hard to the floor and feel a surge of adrenaline, like a Spitfire pilot outfoxing a Messerschmitt over Manchester. I drive the rest of the way home singing along loudly to *The Best Of Tennessee Ernie Ford*. There is no better feeling than getting one over a Nazi, especially at my age.

As I round the final corner into our cul-de-sac, The Keswick, I observe a hefty German people carrier. I park in the drive and collect my things, including the replica .44 Magnum from the glove compartment. I approach the house. The front door is ajar.

Using the end of the barrel I push gently at the door. It creeks open, the lock intact. I step into the hallway and close the door behind me. Silence. Holding the gun before me I enter first the sitting room then the kitchen. A half-eaten apple rests on the table. I approach with caution, nudging it with the end of my gun. The exposed flesh has yet to turn brown.

I climb the stairs, mindful of my clicking limbs. The door to the master bedroom is wide open. I enter. The unmistakable aroma of broken wind hangs in the air. The smell is unfamiliar.

I switch my phone to silent and cross the landing to Tom's bedroom. Across the floor are strewn LPs by Yazoo, Depeche Mode, Wham!, Kim Wilde and Howard Jones, plus a copy of *Now That's What I Call Music 6*. Next to his bed an ashtray, a copy of *Internet for Dummies* and a framed picture of Susan circa 1986.

I move back across the landing and creep silently into the study, grateful that this is a modern property with no creaky floorboards.

Someone has been at my desk. Papers that were orderly when I left are now disordered. Someone is looking for something.

Silently I leave the study and stand outside the bathroom. The only closed door in the house.

'Tom?' I say, quietly. 'You in there?' There is no reply.

I move gently to the far side of the hallway. Pausing briefly to collect myself I charge at the door and kick it open with my good leg – only to find myself pointing a fake gun at the forehead of an attractive sixty-something lady hovering over the toilet seat.

'JESUS FUCKS ALAN WHAT THE SHIT ARE YOU DOING?'

It takes Edame a long time to calm down. I make her three cups of tea and a hot Bovril before she will even look at me, and then only to glare. Eventually she dozes off in the chair by the window.

When she awakes it is dark.

'Put on your socks,' she says. 'We're going out for dinner.'

The drive to the Farmer's Boy on Common Road is a silent one. Edame is still angry with me for threatening her with a gun when she was on the toilet, not to mention the damage to the door. I ask how her mother was ('Fine'), how Eindhoven was ('Fine') and how the food was ('Fine'). When I enquire about the flight ('Just bloody drive will you!') I get the message. This wasn't the time to inform her that 'mother-in-law' is an anagram of 'woman Hitler'.

I order our drinks at the bar (half a lager for Edame, ginger beer for the driver) and bring over a packet of cheese and onion crisps for placatory purposes. After the waitress leaves with our dinner order Edame takes a sip of her beer, places a hand on my arm and speaks.

'I want you to stands down.'

Although there was perhaps an inevitability to her words, I had never heard them spoken before. I nibble a crisp before responding.

'I understand where you are coming from, my dearest, but you have no idea how close I am to capturing evi—'

'Please, Alan,' she interjects. 'If you retire tomorrow you'll be remembering as the finest Nazi Hunter this country has

ever produce. Keep going and you'll turn into even more of
. . . you'll become the figure of fun. Go now, keep your integrities. Don't weather on the vine.'

I offer Edame a go on my ginger beer. She declines.

'You are in the danger of ruining your legacies,' she continues. 'You can't keep going like Si did. Back then there was no competition. Today there are Nazi Hunters all over the world, not only trying to hunt the you-knows but competing against one and other. I want you to enjoy your retirements, for us to enjoy it in togetherness.'

The scar where I was stabbed in the Luton Arndale Centre by Klaus Barbie begins to agitate.

'Stop the huntings, Alan,' she says. 'For me.'

I don't regard myself as a selfish person. I could see her side of the argument. I just need a little more time to put the Nazi house in order.

'If I stop hunting now they will have won,' I tell her. 'I don't need a long time but I do need longer. I am on the cusp of something huge, something that could solve the National Socialist problem in Dunstable and beyond. This is the real deal, Eds. Surely you can see I cannot shirk my responsibilities. You know what a proud man I am.'

'Yes, Alan, and we all know that pride comes before the falling.'

'The phrase is "pride comes bef—"'

'Oh yes,' she says interrupting, 'pick up on the little Dutch girl's poor commandment of the English. What about me, Alan? I gave up so much when you became Britain's Premier Nazi Hunter. We were nearly killed to death in Wales. I've had enough. ENOUGH!!'

The whole bar looks round. I apologise and say my wife

has lost an earring. This is counterproductive. Edame's face hardens.

'Since 1994 I've faithfully stood by your sides,' she says, whispering now, but with purpose. 'When I agreed to go along with your plan to hunt the Nazis I felt I owed you after the sad I caused over the late Henry Cooper. I made all your meals, including your special pre-hunt dinners and breakfasts. I ironed your disguises, waited up night after night. I even acted as bait to Andreas the Unpleasant. But I'm finished, Alan. Finished with the wait and the worry and the phone calls in the centre of the night, with Robert Wagner in the background. We have a son who refuses to listen to a single pieces of music recorded after 1988. I want to dessicate some time to him, not spend the rest of my lives worrying about you. The funeral of Handel Pimm was the last straw that broke the camel's bed. If you want to keep pursuing Nazis into your eighties you can do it on your toddy.'

With that she rose, tossed her shawl over her shoulder and strode to the car – only to return seconds later and sit back down, remembering she cannot drive.

We sit in silence. Our food arrives but we pick at it. Edame's mention of Tom is the killer blow. It is difficult to come back from that, distasteful even. But I try.

'I appreciate everything you say, my love, and as always you're right on every count – but please hear me out. Without question I owe you an enormous debt of gratitude. You have dedicated the last eighteen years to supporting me in my quest. I loved you so much before, and I love you even more for indulging my passion for Nazi Hunting, something I was clearly born to do. I know that our son is in danger of permanent stagnation. I see signs of improvement but it's not enough and I worry that much of it is down to me. Once I hang up my butterfly net I will dedicate what's left of my life to making up the time and attention this is owed, both to you and our dear son.

'But I cannot go out on a whimper. My life is in danger, yes, but my reputation and legacy will be decimated – *decimated* – if I leave now. It will smack of cowardice. I can fix all of this if I have one more chance. And for that I need time. Not a lot, as Paul Daniels used to say when he was still on the telly, but enough to meet with evil Felix Pump. I have an appointment with him the day after tomorrow. Through Pump I can get to The Griffin. Get to The Griffin and I could bring down what remains of the Third Reich. If I do that we'll be set up for life.'

Edame chews on an onion ring, unmoved.

'You think I haven't seen those "one more jobs" gangster movies?' she says. '*The Sexy Beast* starring Ray Winsome, *Carlito's Way* with Al Pakino. I've seen them all and you know what, it never work out.'

'This isn't cinema,' I tell her. 'This is real life starring me, Alan Stoob.'

'And if you fail?'

'Then I fail. At least I will have given it my best shot.'

I suggest one pudding, two spoons. Edame says no. I pay the bill. We drive home wordless. I make us both tea, leave Edame's in the kitchen and retire to my study.

At midnight she appears in the doorway.

'One month, that's it.'

I pump my fist – a little like Tim Henman, only with more passion.

* * *

In the night I dream about my new identity as Rod von Hull. I wake with Edame staring at me, propped up in bed, arms folded. Apparently I have been talking in my sleep, in German.

Over breakfast she lays out a few ground rules for the coming weeks.

1. improve security on the house

2. do not use impending deadline as excuse to escape domestic chores
3. give thought to our retirement plans

4. spend quality time with Tom

5. purchase authentic Viagra from chemist

'Most of all I want you to be careful,' she says. 'Twenty-eight days is plenty of the time to come the cropper.'

'I thought you said a month?'

'Twenty-eight days IS a month.'

Clearly we were going to have problems.

I spend the morning working on Edame's security request. This includes removing the spare key from under the mat, purchasing net curtains for all downstairs windows and boarding up the dogflap. A full alarm system is great in theory but would be stretching things financially. In the garage I find the box the microwave came in. I paint it white, write ADS Security on the bottom and attach it to the front wall of the house.

After lunch I visit Tom in his room. His smile of the past few weeks has slipped. He looks desolate and unkempt. I kneel next to him. Both knees crack in protest.

'It's the Twitters,' he says, mournfully. 'I've been doing so well recently, I know I have, but I just can't get to grips with the Twitters. It's all tache-hags and funny A's with a circle round them. What is a retwitter? What is at-ing? It's another language. I've tried writing stuff like "hello" and "who remembers Flock of Seagulls?" but nothing happens. How can I approach the likes of George Michael, Kim Wilde or Bonnie Langford if I don't know what I'm doing? I'm floundering, Dad. I feel like an idiot.'

The elation he experienced after making the step of borrowing my laptop was wearing off. I'd seen him like this before, like the time he went to the hairdresser's with the intention of getting shorn of his curtains, only to back out at the last minute and remain in a funk for months.

'This is only a minor setback,' I tell him, resting a hand on his heavy shoulder. 'Besides, you only needed to ask about Twitter. Haden or I can give you a lesson any time. We are all in this together.'

'Isn't that what George Osborne says?'

He was right. I apologised and left him to it.

After lunch I sat in the study and ran through possible questions Felix Pump might throw at me tomorrow. Name. Date of birth. Which football team I supported. How I feel about the Jews.

I flick through the hunter's bible – Arthur Pob's *Goosebumps and Goosesteps* – for last-minute tips.

Chapter Six: Let The Mask Becometh the Man

During face-to-face scenarios with real Nazis confidence is crucial to the façade of personal Nazism. Look strong. Maintain eye contact. Offer a firm Nazi handshake. If you are required to perform the Nazi salute shoot out a purposeful arm. Shout 'Heil Hitler'. Remember to use your right arm and NOT your left.

By three my brain is foggy. I head to the garage and remove my bike. I pump up the tyres, tuck my trousers into my socks and don my Eddie Merckx cap.

At the end of the cul-de-sac I point the bike eastward and head out of Dunstable towards Houghton Regis. The wind is behind me and I pick up speed. At one point I am level with a Volvo. A Jewish baby smiles back at me from its child seat.

The bike feels great, so much better than the old Nuremberg Raleigh I had in the early seventies. I pedal up Houghton Road, past the Trawlerman fish café, under the bridge and up past the house that Hitler earmarked as his English country retreat had things turned out differently.

The road pitches up then dips right and what begins as a gentle climb turns into a descent. I lower my head and assume the racing position. Instantly I am transported back to stage six of the Milk Race, breaking away from the peloton and in hot pursuit of Jimmy Savile.

The sheer exhilaration thrills me as I hit maximum speed. After thirty seconds of high excitement I reach the bottom and apply the brakes. Nothing. It's as if I have no brakes. I try to use my feet to slow myself down but it's no good. I career straight across the junction, missing by inches a lorry transporting Nazi memorabilia to a local auction house.

Some flat then another fast descent. I narrowly avoid a 1983 Talbot Samba. A bump in the road bounces me off the saddle. I land again, crushing Little Alan. The gradient flattens but my speed is still great. I flash through a no-entry sign. The road has become one-way. Suddenly I am being propelled into a stream of oncoming traffic. There is nowhere for me to go.

At the last second I spot a dropped kerb and mount the pavement. Pedestrians scatter, flinging 99p shopping bags hither and thither. Taking a hard left I weave through the barriers and hit a short patch of grass. I am heading for the river. Again I try my feet, again with no luck. As I hurtle towards the water my life flashes before me: evacuation, loss, Edame, the kids, Cooper, Meaden, Wiesenthal, Whipsnade, my brain frantically plundering itself for an experience that can save me.

Ten yards from the water's edge I spot a tree. I take my feet off the pedals, stand on the bike frame and step onto the saddle. I stand tall long enough to grab onto the thickest branch. As I swing I see the bike disappear at speed down the bank and into the river.

I release my grip and come crashing onto the grass, landing squarely on my coccyx.

A young mother approaches.

'You alright, granddad?' she says.

Very slowly I raise myself up, clutching my upper bottom. 'I think so,' I say. 'Spot of bike trouble.'

'Let's have a look,' she says. 'I work part-time at Mr Bell's bicycle shop on West Street.'

We walk over to the river and together rescue my beloved Bianchi from the water. The frame is bent back on itself, the front wheel mangled.

'Your problem is your frame is bent back on itself and your front wheel's mangled,' she says.

'That just happened,' I explain. 'It was my brakes. They didn't work.'

She takes a closer look.

'I'm not surprised,' she says. 'The cables have been cut.'

'Eventful,' I tell Edame when she asks how my ride was.

'That's nice,' she says. 'Do the washing-up, will you? There's a building-up from the breakfasts.'

After my chores I email Interpol Steve.

Hi Steve.

Please may I have a bodyguard please?

Regards,

Alan.

Next I call the British Nazi Hunting hotline. They promise to send someone within half an hour. Eight minutes later Mike Trottman pulls up on his scooter eating a smoked salmon and cream-cheese bagel. Systematically he checks the house, inspecting everything for booby traps.

'You've got a problem with the radio in the kitchen,' he says. 'It's wired up to detonate when you tune into the World Service.'

Outside he gives the Stoobmobile the twice over. He departs with the bike and the radio. I keep this from Edame.

In the study there's a response from Steve:

Dear Alan,

Sorry, Alan, Herb Derb took the last bodyguard.

Any further thoughts re the Argentina/plastic surgery option?

As a Nazi Hunter one is always under potential threat. Rarely does this translate into a full blow assassination attempt. To tamper with a man's brakes is contemptible, as is fiddling with his radio. Not even Himmler would have signed that off.

After dinner I lay out my uniform for tomorrow's meeting with Felix Pump: black jacket complete with swastika insignia, peaked cap with SS eagle and skull and crossbones, starched white shirt, jackboots, breeches. Will it draw attention? I doubt it, not in a Nazi heartland such as Biggleswade – not unless they know who I am and I'm walking into a trap. I buff up my Totenkopf and slip a blue inhaler into the breast pocket.

In bed Edame tells me the story of how she came to live in England. I've heard it many times before but find its familiarity soothing, especially the part about her night in a Bayswater hostel with eighteen other Dutch girls. All the while the idea that someone wants to kill me plays on my mind. Which I feel is not unreasonable on my part.

*　　*　　*

I wake nervous in the mouth and nearly do a sick. Edame rises and offers to make me my hunter's breakfast on the promise I spend part of the morning researching longboat holidays in Norfolk.

I print out the best Norfolk, Suffolk and Spalding have to offer before changing into my SS outfit and heading downstairs.

'I was just about to bringing you a hot Ribe . . . good lord, Alan, you startles me,' she says. 'You look so . . . German. As a finished touching you might want to slip out of those moccasins.'

I head back upstairs to collect my jackboots.

'What if they ask you some of the things you don't know?' she says.

'I'll wing it,' I tell her, pulling on the boots.

'Just be careful. I don't think I could bearing it if something happening to you, not with only twenty-one days left as a hunter.'

'I thought it was twenty-five.'

'Oh no it's definitely twenty-one.'

'You're doing it again!' I tell her.

'Doing what?'

Edame and I embrace in the hallway. There are tears in her eyes. There never used to be. She can sense my vulnerability. I hope the same is not true of Felix Pump.

I catch the 132 bus from in front of what used to be Dunstable Building Society and flash my travel pass for Biggleswade Town Centre. Once on board I draw puzzled looks from my fellow passengers. One boy asks if I'm a Morris Dancer. I tell him no, in a German accent. He starts crying. The Teutonic tongue instils fear in even the youngest traveller.

After alighting and walking for ten minutes I am standing at the end of the snaking driveway that leads to Pump's mansion. My watch tells me I am nearly an hour early. I feel panicky – haven't been this nervous since the morning of my wedding. On that occasion the best man plied me with snifters until I relaxed. I walk back into the village and find a pub.

'Guten morgen,' I say to the barman. 'Eine kleine whisky, bitte.'

'You local?' he asks.

'Nein,' I say. 'Ich bin von Umlaut. In Deutschland.'

'Oh right,' he says. '£1.86.'

I place myself in a dark recess of the bar. The clock reads 11.15. A man wearing an old Nazi uniform catches my eye. He raises his glass. 'To ze Führer,' he says and downs two-thirds of his pint in one gulp.

I consider running home into the arms of my wife and announcing my retirement on the spot. Then once more I remember the words.

Remain calm. Unflappable.

I don't need alcohol to relax. I abandon my drink and exit the pub. As I pass the window I witness my fellow 'countryman' staggering over to the table I have just vacated and taking advantage of a free whisky. I walk back towards the house, breathing in through my good nostril and out through the mouth. A sense of calm washes over me. Five hundred yards from the address I hide my phone and my car keys under a hedge. A Vauxhall key ring would be a giveaway, as would Interpol on speed dial.

The door of Pump's abode is tall, black, imposing. A German flag flutters in the gentle breeze. An ornate bell is next to the house sign ('Lebensraum'). I press it. 'Ride of the Valkyries' by Wagner plays. Two minutes later the door opens.

'Eez eet safe?' croaks a bowed elderly figure with scar tissue where once a left eye had been.

'Oh ja – very safe,' I say, before stretching out my hand and doing the special squinty one-legged Nazi handshake. The unsightly German gentleman beckons me forth.

The hallway is huge. A cough from the ancient butler echoes up the twisting marble stairwell. The ceiling displays a thirty-foot depiction of the Führer, a chandelier hanging from each ear. A further six portraits of Hitler's henchmen adorn the walls, plus a novelty clock. The space is a homage to the Third Reich.

I pass through the library, its shelves filled with a plethora of Nazi tomes. I spy a copy of the bestseller *Why Germany Will Rule The World Again* by Annie Krankenhaus, which I happen to know is a pseudonym used by Angela Merkel. The aroma of sizzling bratwurst fills the air.

The wizened figure leads me through into a huge-windowed study, offers me a chair and leans up against the wall, staring. There is no sign of Pump. He is making me wait, just like the Führer at Nuremberg.

At first distant, almost inaudible, then louder, comes the clicking of heels along the wooden floor of the empty hall. Click, click, CLICK CLICK then WHAM, the doors fly open to reveal a squat man with shaven head and pug-like face. 'HEIL HITLER!' booms a shockingly harsh voice. He shoots out an arm. I rise quickly and do the same. He stares at me, unflinching.

'So du think eet eez acceptable to salute our Führer MIT YOUR LEFT HAND, DO YOU, HERR VON HULL?'

Shit it.

'My sincerest apologies, Herr Komrade, it hast been a long time and ich bin in a state of grosse distress.'

What a dreadful Nazi faux-pas and a terrible way to begin the meeting. Pump circles me, his stride slow and exaggerated, all the while tapping his cane gently against a highly polished leather boot. He looks 110 and smells of meat and eau de cologne. Moving towards his desk he opens a drawer and removes a pair of callipers. These he places on my forehead, measuring the distance to my nose. I've seen this before, on propaganda films made by Josef Goebbels.

'Vee cannot be too careful,' he says, jotting notes on a clipboard.

I tell him the story he wants to hear, that I was spotted by Jews who recognised me from the war. I flesh this out by describing the Jews and the weather on the day. He asks me at great length about my wartime placement, what I did, who my colleagues were, the name of my first pet, whether I enjoy being a Nazi and how I feel about my mother ('Ein boy's best friend ist his mutter').

Suddenly he stops.

'Vot year ver you born?'

'1914,' I tell him.

'Du do not look 98 jahres alt,' he says, circling me once more.

'Ich have always looked jung for mein age,' I say. He examines my hands for liver spots.

'Pull down your trousers!'

I do as he requests, exposing my newly-acquired tattoo. He licks his thumb and rubs at the tattoo. Stefan clearly did a good job.

'Du have a sehr muscular behind for a mensch of your age. Are du ein homosexual?'

'Nein, just ein keen cyclist,' I explain. 'I even rode in the 1965 Milk Ra—, the Tour of Germany, during which I came fo—'

'SILENCE! How many times do you visit the badenroom in der nacht?'

'Anywhere between eight und twelve times,' I reply.

'And ven did you last have ein erection?'

'1982, Herr Komandant. Excluding Viagra use.'

The tapping ceases. Pump stands before me, his face jutting aggressively into mine. The stench of salami is overpowering.

'Do du know vot we do to those who try to infiltrate our gang, Rod von Hull?' he whispers.

'Nein, Herr Komrade.'

'Nor do ich actually,' he says strolling over to his desk and perching on the end. 'ONLY JOKING! I hand them over to Big Klaus over zere.'

He gestures towards the hideous Nazi leaning against the wall.

'By ze time he's finished with zem zey are nothing more zan dog food.'

Big Klaus cackles, then hiccups.

Pump approaches once more. He appears to be mapping my forehead, peering closely as if studying for an exam. He removes a sheet of blotting paper from his lederhosen and dabs at my temple. He walks to the window and examines it before turning, staring madly.

'Gut news!' he screams. 'Zare ist no sveat. Vich means du are indeed ein Nazi. Heil Hitler!' He sticks out his arm and performs a small German jig. I salute with my correct arm and attempt a similar dance. Big Klaus returns with two glasses of brandy and cigars fatter than my wrists.

'I apologise for zat little show, Herr Komrade,' he says, lighting up. 'Ich am sure du realise how important it ist zat ve interrogate all zat come through here, in case ve have a mole in our hole. Ha! Ich like zat, it rhymes!'

I nod politely and light my cigar, coughing immediately. I haven't smoked since 1953.

'Do du vant us to dispose of ze Juden zat recognised du?'

I try to hide my horror and suggest instead that such a move could be counterproductive.

'Ich bin happy with ein identity overhaul, Herr Komrade.'

'Ziss ve can arrange fur du, kein problem.'

'Herr Komrade,' I say, 'I feel already that ve are friends, yet ve have not been formally introduced.'

He leans across the desk and extends a hand. Once more

I close one eye while lifting a leg and waggling my little finger into his palm.

'Ich heisse Felix Pump but du can call me Pumpi,' he said, smiling. 'Kopf von Laundry, 1941–45.'

'It is indeed ein pleasure to meet someone of such high standing vithin our organisation.'

He sits back down, opens his desk drawer and removes a remote control.

'Vood you care to vatch some violent pornography vith me?' he enquires.

'Actually du are alright,' I reply. 'I vatched some earlier.'

'As du vish, Herr von Hull.'

He glances at his watch before draining his brandy glass and stubbing out his cigar.

'Vell if zare ist nothing more ich should be getting on vith my tag. Big Klaus vill give du your neu identity on ze vay out.'

'Actually zare ist one sing,' I reply. 'Ich vould very much like to get to know a few Nazis in ze local area. Since ich moved to Bedfordshire ich have rather kept meinself to meinself. Do du have any gatherings round this vay?'

'But of course!' he replies, throwing his arms up in the air. 'Montag nachts, Biggleswade Town Hall, 8pm. Ve are all zare, come rain oder shine. Next one next veek.'

'Vill your boss be zare?'

His eyes narrow.

'Mein boss, Herr Hull?'

A threatening tone.

'Ich bin nicht sure of his namen, Gribbin oder Griffin oder zumthing. Ich vood liebe to meet him.'

'Du may vell vish to meet him, Herr von Hull,' he replies, fixing me with his thyroid eyes, 'but du must know zat ze person of vich du speak ist ein sehr busy mensch. He spends much of his time easing ze passage for neu komrades to make zare vay over von Deutschland to Bedfordshire via our specially constructed but highly secret ratline. He ist rarely seen in public. He ist unlikely to vant to meet someone like du, mit all due respect. Ich vood be grateful if du didn't mention his name to me again. If du want to bring him up, write it down on ein piece of paper.'

'Of course, Pumpi,' I reply and rise from my chair.

'Ich hope ve vill see du next week at ze town hall?'

'Sehr likely, Herr Komrade.'

Once more Pump shoots an arm out in the form of a Nazi salute.

'Heil Hitler!' I belt, feeling sick.

'Ditto,' he replies.

As I exit Big Klaus hands me a cheap satchel similar to the one I received at the Dunstable Police conference of 1986. On the side it reads: *The Third Reich: 1923 to date.* Inside I find a passport, driving licence, German identity card and library card for central Bedfordshire, all in the name of Gippa Leipzig, my new Nazi identity.

After departing I return to the hedge where I hid my phone and car keys. Both reek of dogs' urine. I catch the 132 back to Dunstable. Outside the house I notice that my makeshift ADS Security box has fallen off the wall.

When I open the front door Edame bursts into tears and flings her arms around me.

'I'm so glad you're back safe,' she says. 'I can hardly bearing it. These last nineteen days are going to kill me!'

Nineteen now, is it?

I take a shower and wash Pump's sausagey spittle off my

face before donning my Britain's Premier Nazi Hunter™ dressing gown and heading back downstairs for dinner.

Over kosher mushrooms Edame talks fifteen to the dozen about barge trips, holidays in Barbados, cruises around the Scillies, bridge weekends, group Callanetics, even trying for another baby ('There's only very slim chancing, but why not?'). One minute she's teary, the next it's future plans. She's up and down like a Nazi knicker.

Like all men, I have mastered the face of the listener, responding to the inflections in the voice and nodding when required. The truth is I am lost in thought, thoughts of Felix Pump, of Monday's meeting with the Nazis, of The Griffin. He is key. Get to him and I can dismantle this entire organisation. But there isn't long. Nineteen days, apparently.

I ask Edame if I may leave the table. She says yes on the condition that I clear it and do the washing up. I do as requested, though I doubt the pans would stand up to close inspection.

Once upstairs I stare at my timeline spreadsheet. Today is Thursday. Monday is the Nazi get-together. Somehow over the next two-and-a-half weeks I must catch The Griffin and take down the entire Nazi infrastructure, while still making myself available for household chores and a possible long weekend in Chichester.

m✠y

Wake to a text message from Deborah Meaden.

The wrinkles on your thumb are ribbed for my pleasure.

I delete the message and remove Meaden's number once and for all.

After a breakfast of Yiddish kippers I head to the chemist with my prescription for Viagra.

'Sorry, Alan, we're fresh out,' says Mr Salaman. 'Had a run on the stuff. It's the elderly. Did you know that VD is up 470% in the over-eighties? New shipment in a couple of days.'

Twitter lesson for Tom. Three times he tries sending a message to Toyah Willcox and three times he sends it to himself. But he is embracing new technology and that is all that counts.

After a brief lunch and a short snooze I pay a visit to the architects Herbert, Chapman & Grumble of Harlington. I'd noticed their letterhead on an item of correspondence in Felix Pump's study. Flashing my old constabulary badge I claim to be a policeman following up an old lead in a hurry.

'We did indeed carry out some work for Mr Pump,' says Mr Herbert.

'He wanted an underground tunnel built,' says Mr Chapman.

'It was quite an undertaking,' says Mr Grumble.

I ask to see the drawings. They refuse – until I show them

my search warrant, which is in fact my outstanding Viagra prescription.

'As you can see the tunnel begins in Bremen,' says Mr Herbert.

'And comes out in Mr Pump's back garden in Biggleswade,' says Mr Chapman.

'It was quite an undertaking,' says Mr Grumble.

It seems the work began in 1986, the year Pump murdered the previous owner and moved in. Clearly he'd found the perfect spot for the end of the ratline so he removed all known obstacles. What a total bastard.

I head home and indulge in back-to-back siestas. Edame has raised the head of the bedstead by ten inches to counter her hiatus hernia. It doesn't affect my sleeping, though on waking from the second snooze I do find myself at the foot of the bed.

Dinner at Tina's. There is considerable frost between Tina and Marco, who is sporting a black eye. It's unclear whether he received this from his wife or the homosexual underworld. The kids however are on good form, as is Tom who clearly received a fillip from this afternoon's Twitter session and does impressions of everyone in the family. It's great to see him in high spirits though.I find his mimicking of Edame kissing the late Henry Cooper ('Oh 'Enry, those 'ans, they so beeg!') somewhat unsettling.

'So what's the latest then, Al?' enquires Marco, mouth full of meat loaf, glancing anxiously at Tina.

'A few bits and bobs,' I say. Edame reaches under the table and squeezes my fingers. I hope she's not disappointed by their modest girth.

'Alan has given himself another few days then he standings down,' says Edame.

The whole family stops eating and looks up.

'Actually it's more like two weeks,' I add.

'Bloody hell's titties!' says Marco.

Tina stares at Marco. He bows his head like a chastised dog.

'Apologies for my husband's vulgar outburst,' she says. 'When did this happen?'

'Not long ago,' I say. 'Things have been getting a bit hairy of late, especially after the incident at the funeral in Llanrhaeadr when the vicar got shot to death.'

'Never had you down as a quitter,' mutters Haden.

'Nobody's quitting,' I reply, trying to remain calm. 'I'm retiring. I'm seventy-five in case you hadn't noticed, young man. And pull your trousers up please. Some of us are trying to eat.'

'Simon Wiesenthal never quit,' he counters. 'He remained vigilant to his dying day.'

'Don't be so fucking rude and impertinent,' says Tina. 'Carry on, Dad.'

'Anyway,' I continue, 'it's not as if I don't have important work to do before I call it a day. I'd hate to speak too soon but I could be on the brink of something huge.'

'So why are you quitting, then?' says Haden. 'It doesn't make sense.'

'You are too young to remember but your grandmother gave up her retirement in Bournemouth to support me and assist with all my hunting requirements. I owe her some peace and quiet.'

'How long have you got left?'

Edame and I speak at the same time. She says nine days, I make it thirteen.

'Nine days,' she reiterates.

'And if you don't crack this big case?'

'I'm confident I will.'

'Yes, but if you don't?'

'Then I'll hand the information over to Herb Derb.'

Houdini looks up.

'You can't let Herb Derb drive the investigation,' she says, her button nose scrunching up. 'Mummy says he's a shitbag.'

'We don't use language like that at the dinner table, young lady,' says Tina. 'Go and sit on the Nazi step.'

Houdini slumps off, clearly used to this charade.

'And you,' Tina says to Marco.

Marco points questioningly at himself. Tina nods. Reluctantly he joins Houdini at the foot of the stairs.

'What's the next move?' asks Haden.

'Tomorrow I shall be attending a meeting of senior Nazis dressed up as one,' I say. 'By this method I hope to track down The Griffin and shut off the flow of Nazi war criminals into our beloved county.'

'All that in nine days?'

'I think it's possible.'

'POSSIBLE?' says Haden. 'You've been hunting Nazis for 18 years and suddenly you hope to wrap the whole thing up inside two weeks?'

'Unfortunately my wife isn't very flexible on this matter.'

Edame lets go of my hand.

'You used to be my hero,' says Haden.

Another silent car journey. I'm getting used to them. Once home it's straight to bed, lights out.

'I've always supported you both publicly and in the privates,' says Edame from her side of the bed. 'I put up with a lot of the rubbish from you, Alan. The least you could do is back me up when we're together.'

Aggressively she turns her back to me and breaks wind. I wish Tina hadn't served scotch eggs.

*   *   *

Dreamt I drove to Henry Cooper's house in East Ham to have it out with him. He wasn't in.

Decide to stay out of Edame's way, locking myself in the study and practising relaxation techniques in advance of this evening's Nazi gig. Is it possible The Griffin will show? What about the Führer himself? Interpol remains cagey on that one. Maybe instead there will be a guest speaker from the National Socialist pantheon of evil, or a well-known racist from the world of entertainment.

At lunchtime I head downstairs. On the kitchen table is a note from Edame.

Gone to see Potato George. Back later. Good luck.

I know I shouldn't have performed an act of public disunity yesterday but did I deserve this? I felt the panic rise up from my belly. Deep breaths through the nose. Then I remembered with relief: today was a Beryl day.

'We are changing things around a bit this afternoon, Alan,' she said. I noticed she was wearing a shorter skirt than normal. 'None of this lying back and thinking of England. I want you to sit opposite me.'

The chairs were a couple of yards apart. Beryl had a glass of wine next to hers. I sat.

'Tell me about your childhood,' she said, taking a sip. 'I'm all ears.'

'You're not wrong,' I thought, observing her left one in particular which stuck out like a wind sock.

'I think we've done my childhood,' I said. 'I was born happy, got evacuated, had a terrible time, came home to find my family in ruins and have struggled to come to terms with the experience ever since.'

'Tell me again,' she said, opening a packet of peanuts. 'Therapy is all about repetition.'

'You said that last time,' I remind her, 'and the time before.'

'Do it, Alan – for me.'

I regale Beryl with the story of my early years. She seemed captivated, nodding repeatedly and doing her sad face at appropriate moments.

'Alan, your story moves me,' she says. She was sat uncomfortably close. My *lebensraum* was being invaded. Her legs were crossed. She made to uncross them. Edame and I had recently watched *Basic Instinct* on ITV4. I averted my eyes.

'Sorry, have to go,' I told her in a panic, staring at the Mark Rothko print on the wall. 'Just remembered – got to try on my uniform for tonight.'

'But I thought you said you'd already done that?'

'Nazi Hunting,' I said, 'it's all about repetition!' I ran out.

Back home I steadied myself and recalled the words of Arthur Pob and chapter 7 of *Goosebumps and Goosesteps*:

We all have butterflies, but some of us have learnt to fly them in formation like the Red Arrows.

I dress up in my SS uniform and order a cab to Biggleswade.

The grey municipal building looked as shapeless and anonymous as ever. What marked the scene out as unusual was the steady stream of high-spec German vehicles pulling up and dropping off extremely elderly men and women in expensively tailored suits.

The board in the foyer displayed the list of events taking place, the lettering arranged neatly by hand.

HALL ONE: WOMEN'S INSTITUTE

HALL TWO: BEDFORDSHIRE ONION SOCIETY (BI-ANNUAL)

HALL THREE: NOB

NOB: the secret acronym for **N**azis **O**f **B**edfordshire.

I approached the entrance to hall three. The door was guarded by a broad-shouldered man with a strong resemblance to Max Schmelling, the former German heavyweight boxer who once knocked out Joe Louis but ended his life a Nazi puppet.

'Namen?' it said, staring down at me.

'Rod von Hull,' I replied, sticking out a hand. He shook it so I wiggled my little finger, keeping my right eye shut.

'Go through, komrade,' it said, parting the thickly veiled maroon curtains while looking the other way.

I was presented with a scene apparently lifted straight from the pages of a fictional book about Nazi hunting. Two hundred elderly ladies and gentlemen drinking wine, chatting animatedly in German, singing party songs, playfully slapping their own and each other's thighs, doing impressions of Hitler and generally having a high old time.

I recognised almost every last one of them.

Whether it was Rudolf Bumble, Helga the Difficult, Josef Schalke or evil Hans Muncher, I had spent the previous two decades trying to track down most of those present. Now they were chuntering away, seemingly without a care in the world.

'Komrade von Hull! Or should I say Gippa Leipzig! Gut of du to join us!'

It was Felix Pump.

'Danke schon, Herr Pump,' I said. 'Heil Hitler.'

'Fuck all that, ve are here for ein gut time nicht ein long time!' he replied. For the first time I sensed the Führer really was dead. Pump rummaged in his blazer and pulled out a cigar.

'Hope du are getting used to your neu identity,' he said, lighting me up. 'Have the Juden given du any more problems?'

'Nein,' I replied, sucking and coughing.

'Gut, gut. Comme mit me, zare ist somevun ich vood like du to meet.'

Pump grabbed me tightly by the wrist and led me through the rogue's gallery. I averted my eyes, hoping not to be recognised. When I glanced up I felt Bloater Stench, the Dunce of Darmstadt, staring back at me. How on earth did he survive the plunge through the frozen River Lea back in 1997? Does he recognise me? He looks away, apparently uninterested, and continues his conversation.

'Herr von Hull,' says Pump, 'Meet Komrade Tobias Warble, the Tit of Tessen. Ich believe du two are from ze same town von Umlaut. Now if du vill excuse me ich must go und mingle like Mengele!'

Warble stubs his cigarette out in a nearby ashtray and breaks into a smile.

'Any freund of Pumpi ist ein freund von mine!'

He embraces me. I hug him back, holding on longer than is necessary to fix my story.

'Du been back to ze old place since ze war?' he asks, collecting two drinks from a passing waitress.

'Umlaut?' I reply. 'Nein. Ich like to let sleeping hunds lie. Und du?'

'Every Christmacht!' he replies, chuckling to himself for no obvious reason. 'Meine mutter ist still zare. Ich sneak over using the underground passage from Bremen to Biggleswade zen catch ein tram.'

'This ist ze age of ze tram,' I say.

'Vich schule didst du attend, Herr Komrade?' he asks.

'Ich vas schuled at home by mein parents,' I reply, a pearl of sweat trickling down my back.

'Und vhere wast das, exactly – in ze north oder in ze south?'

'Oh ze south,' I reply. 'Ze north ist for losers.'

I had taken a risk. He looks searchingly into my eyes, before breaking into a hearty laugh.

'Ve have ein scoundrel in our midst!' he says, slapping me across the shoulder so vigorously my spine clicks satisfyingly into place. 'Ich suspect ve are around ze same age. Who vere your freunds in ze village?'

I pretend not to hear, forcing him to repeat his question while my brain whirrs some more.

'Ich voz very close to Karl-Heinz Marx, Ludwig von Garbo and Heidi Herzog, ze fräulein mit ze big befundles,' I tell him.

'Ja,' he says. 'Ich still see Ludwig. Ich vill send him your best.'

'Please do,' I reply. 'Does he still have skin like Rudolf Hess and ze breath of a romany?'

'Nein,' he replies. 'His skin ist fine und his breath no vurse zan yours. Perhaps ve are talking at cross purposes.'

I'd clearly gone too far and change the subject.

'Tell me, Herr Warble, hast du ever met . . . ze Griffin?'

Warble looks down, seemingly examining his shoes then up

again, bear hug and spine-correcting wallop notable by their absence.

'Zhere are some people,' he says in a hushed tone, 'even *ve* must nicht speak of.'

A gong sounds.

'Ladies und gentlemensch!' says Pump atop a raised platform. Many of the throng lift their drinks. Bloater Stench raises a bread stick. 'It ist sehr gut to see so many of du here again today. Alles of us at ze party feel zese netvorking events are vital to keep ze movement und ze fight going. Ich vanted to bring your attention to ze fact zat ve have a neu party of freunds arriving via ze secret unterground tunnel tomorrow. If du see any of zem in ze local area please mach zem feel velcome. Zay vill be feeling lost, zumthing ich am sure vee can all relate to ven vee ourselves moved von Deutschland into ze Bedfordshire region.'

Murmurs of agreement.

'It ist vital zat ve retain our security at threat level orange for now,' he continued. 'Ve know zat local idiot Alan Stoob ist still on our trail, but ve also know he ist ein incompetent shrew und his tags are numbered!'

A ripple of laughter, some mild applause.

'On ein entirely separate note, ich vould like to velcome Rod von Hull. Herr von Hull ist vun of us und must be treated accordinglich. Rod, please identify yourself.'

I raise my hand in acknowledgement.

'Von Hull has been on ze receiving end of ein hard time from some Juden and has been forced to change his namme to Gippa Leipzig. Please support him and offer him ein kind verd.'

A couple of old Germans pat me on the back. Briefly I am

reminded that everyone, whoever he may be, is capable of normal human responses.

'There ist ein final piece of informatzion that ich vanted to fill du in on. Before ich do ich cannot stress enough ze top secret nature of vot ich am about to tell du.'

The room falls silent.

'Ein grosse plot to overthrow ze coalition government ist currently being hatched by ein assembly of senior Nazis. Ze details are ein bischen sketchy but ich thought du would like to know zat exciting plans are afoot.'

Perhaps this was what 'Jimmy' was referring to in the cab. A wave of excitement spreads through the room.

'Fen fill fe know more, Herr Komandant?' asks a man of 120 dressed in full Nazi regalia.

'Ven ich hear, du vill alles be ze first to know,' says Pump. 'Alles ich can say mit certainty ist zat ve live in revolutionary times und great change ist afoot.'

A smattering of Heil Hitlers passes through the crowd.

'Ze Englische may haf stopped us funce but know ziss: unterestimate us at your peril, Englische. Now unless zare ist anything else ich vood like to vish du all ein enjoyable abend. Trink up und long live ze Nazis!'

The battle cry of 'Long live ze Nazis' rings out through the hall and, I would imagine, straight into the Women's Institute next door.

A plot to overthrow the government? This sounded like fiction. How would it transpire? One thing I did know: The Griffin would be at the centre of it.

I do my best to look at ease but my fear of being unmasked compounds the strain. I collect a whisky from a Nazi dwarf waiter and throw it back, repeating the process twice more.

'Du look familiar,' says an elderly lady, sidling up. 'Perhaps ve have met before. Ich heisse Monika Weis. Ich bin ein hundert und neun.'

We certainly have met before, Monika Weis. I successfully hunted you in 2001, only for Interpol to assert that the Chinese burn I inflicted upon your person was torture. My defence – that I mistook your wrist for a jar of pickles – was thrown out and you walked free.

'Ich haf one of those faces,' I say, shaking her withered hand.

'Du are ein handsome man, Herr von Hull,' she says. 'Forgive mein directness but at mein age vun does nicht have ze time to linger uber pleasantries.'

'Ich know vot you mean,' I reply.

'Gut. In zat case vood du like to come back to the funf bedroomed haus ich bought mit Jewish geld and do some sexing? Ich haf plenty of Viagras.'

I do my best to hide my revulsion.

'Ich vood love to,' I tell her, 'but alas ich bin married to mein beautiful German vife, Hasse.'

'Ziss ist ein shame, Herr von Hull. Ich could have done mit ein mensch like du, alles grosse und charismary.'

'If things don't verk out ich know vare to come,' I say. Feeling emboldened by the whisky I spoke again. 'Before ve part could du possibly help me vith zumthing?' I say.

'Zat depends,' she says.

'Ich am very keen to meet ze Griffin.'

She pauses and adjusts the brakes on her wheelchair.

'Ich only know of ze Griffin,' she says. 'Ich doubt he vill vant to speak mit du.'

'Ich am sure he von't,' I reply. 'Ich just vont to know how to make contact vith him.'

'OK, Herr von Hull, I vill help du in your qvest to find ze Griffin. But it vill cost.'

'How much?' I asked.

'Ein snog.'

The whisky in my mouth shot out, spraying all Nazis within five feet.

'Enschuldigen!' I say to the assembled. They give me icy stares before continuing their conversations.

'Ein snog fur infomatzion, Herr von Hull,' she repeats and reverses away. I intercept the waiter once more, take a further whisky and throw it down my throat.

I find the old lady outside, lighting up. I pull up a chair, take the cigarette from her hand and plunge my tongue deep into her mouth. Her mouth is rough and dry, like fresh sandpaper. The taste of tobacco is revolting. She bites my lip. I recoil.

'Vasn't so bad now, vas it?' she says, retrieving her cigarette from me.

'Ich enjoyed it very much,' I reply.

'Liar.'

'So, The Griffin . . . ?'

'Ah, ja. Ich cannot help du mit ze Griffin, no vun can,' she replies. 'No vun knows vhere he lives, vhere he sleeps, vot he does mit his time.'

'But du said du vood tell me how to contact him in exchange for ein snog.'

'Ich say lots of things, Herr von Hull!' she replies, cackling like a cancerous drain.

I rise and slope off, furious I'd been duped into a minor infidelity by the oldest National Socialist I'd ever met.

'Ich have heard he checks ze personal ads of *The Bedfordshire*

& District Examiner,' she says as I leave the veranda. 'If he feels like responding, he vill. Don't forget to write it in code. Ve can't be too explicit viz our messages.'

As I left the hall my shoulders relaxed, my breathing slowed, my hands grew less clammy. I wiped my mouth and spat. A sense of surreality swept over me. Had I really been witness to a meeting of NOB? Were there two hundred war criminals on the other side of the curtain? Did I frenchie a 109-year-old?

I walked back out onto the street, weaving my way through the plethora of German cars parked outside. Many were manned by drivers leaning up against their bonnets, smoking cigarettes, exchanging German small-talk. One was wearing a 'Keep Calm and Invade Poland' T-shirt.

'You will not *believe* what I've seen this evening!' I said to Edame as I came through the back door.

'That's great, Alan, but the Kinnocks are coming for the lunch tomorrow so I need you to mop the kitchen floor and cleaning the bathing room.'

'This second?'

'Please.'

'Why the hell have you invited the Kinnocks?'

'I didn't *invite* them, Alan. Neil said they were passings through. May I remind you the world does not revolving around you and your foolish hunts!'

'"Foolish" is it now?'

'I don't ask much – just a bit of cleanings and entertain-ups. You've still got five days to do all the hunting you need.'

'IT'S TWELVE!'

Up in the study I find myself doodling a caricature of The Griffin. He was die großer käse, the big cheese. Knobble him and I can penetrate the network and locate every living Nazi on this planet, if I'm lucky.

I draft a message to *The Bedfordshire & District Examiner* before checking the submission details. The advertising rates are £2 per word. I edit my message down from 315 words to eight:

Griffin? Rod von Hull. Nazi. WLTM. ASAP. RSVP.

Before bed I watch Bayern Munich lose the Champions League final to Chelsea on penalties. Not so unflappable now, are we?

*   *   *

The Kinnocks never came. I imagine it was another ruse to distract me from the matter in hand. Just as well they didn't show, we had carrots.

It's been two days since my ad went in the paper. I head to the local shop and buy a copy of *The Bedfordshire & District Examiner.*

'Morning, Alan, any new huntings?' says Geoff the newsagent.

'Maybe.'

'Valerie says you should knock it on the head.'

'You can tell Valerie I'll knock her on the head.'

'79p please.'

I check the personals. Nothing from The Griffin.

The *Examiner* is published bi-weekly. If The Griffin replies in the next issue that might be cutting things too fine, especially if he suggests a rendezvous the following week. If he doesn't reply in the next one that takes me beyond Edame's cut-off date.

Over scrambled gefilte fish Edame assails me with retirement plans. I smile but my thoughts are elsewhere. It is only when I stand to leave that I discover I have provisionally agreed to the purchase of a luxury mobile home.

I head to the study and ring the *Examiner*.

'Hello, advertising sales – for that vital ad in these times of austerity – Simon Simeon speaking. How may I help?'

Simon Simeon. One of Tom's old friends from school. Jewish too. How serendipitous.

'Simon. It's Alan Stoob here, Tom's father.'

'Good lord, Alan, how nice to hear you. How are you – and how's Tom?'

'I'm fine thanks, Simon. Tom is stuck in the 1980s but we're working on that.'

'Please send him my best.'

'Will do. Simon, perhaps you can help. I placed an ad in the personals the other day and wondered whether you'd received a response?'

'If we have it will make its way into the paper, Alan.'

'Of course. I was simply wondering whether since going to press you have had a response to my message, from someone called The Griffin. If you could read it to me down the line it would save a great deal of time.'

'Hold on,' he says.

'Popcorn' by Hot Butter plays briefly in my ear.

'We may have received one, Alan,' says Simon, 'but unfortunately I cannot reveal its contents. How do I know you are who you say you are?'

'But you've just called me Alan,' I reply. 'Surely that shows you know it's me.'

'Perhaps, but I can't be sure it was you who placed the ad.

It is better all round if these things take their natural course. The next issue will be in all good newsagents from Friday.'

'But I need that message before then.'

'Sorry Alan, rules is rules, especially at *The Bedfordshire & District Examiner*.'

'Come on, Simon, can't you bend the system for an old hunter?'

Silence.

'What if I was to offer you a little sweetener to lubricate the channels of communication?'

'Are you trying to bribe me, Alan?'

'Yes.'

'How much?'

I pull up my sponsorship spreadsheet and calculate the maximum I can offer Simon.

'£74.20?'

'Throw in an evening with your lovely daughter Tina and it's a deal.'

I pause.

'Let's just call it £80.'

'Done. Shame about Tina. What's your fax number there?'

Five minutes later the personals page of a yet-unpublished issue of *The Bedfordshire & District Examiner* arrives.

I scan the ads but nothing jumps out at me. The only one that seems to bear any resemblance to what I'm looking for reads thus:

Zoe says 'Hi'. See you at the caravan.

I text Haden, who I happen to know has been studying codes for GCSE maths. He arrives looking like Mick Jagger after a forty-day fast. We stare at the page together.

'Does the word "caravan" mean anything to you, Granddad?' he asks.

I draw a blank. He scratches his head before asking if he can use the bathroom as sometimes it helps him think. While he does I stretch out my hamstrings. My knee cracks nosily. Shirley hammers on the wall.

'Granddad!' exclaims Haden from inside the bathroom. 'It's not the caravan one, it's the one underneath!'

The chain flushes. Seconds later my grandson flings open the door and bounds into the room.

'Look!' he says, his low-slung trousers still undone. He points at the page.

Herr von Hull: it would be ein pleasure.
How about Friday, 1pm, The White Horse, Letchworth?
Regards, The Griffin.

How we had missed such an obvious message was now academic. I had a date: a date with destiny, a date with a Nazi, a date with death, perhaps. A date three days from now. That meant three days left as Britain's Premier Nazi Hunter; three days to save the world from the tyranny of National Socialism; three days to shift this chesty cough.

I thank Haden for his help and hand him 50p. He seems nonplussed. I then fire off an email to Steve at Interpol.

Dear Interpol Steve,

How are the piles?

Big news: I have tracked down the head of Bedfordshire's

Nazis. He goes by the epithet 'The Griffin' and I will be meeting him on Friday at 1pm in a local pub (this is not a social occasion, I shall be in disguise).

More big news: I have it on good authority that the Nazis are hatching a plan to overthrow the UK government. This could be some kind of big joke but I doubt it. The Germans are not known for their sense of humour.

Not only is this a chance to capture Britain's leading Nazi war criminal, it is an opportunity to locate and shut down the ratline, intercept all other Nazis, tap into their network and prevent an assault on Westminster.

We must seize The Griffin, of that there is no doubt. To ensure this happens I wish to call upon your assistance. I know that I have let you down in the past, with particular reference to a local zoo. That said the level of professionalism at Interpol has been severely found wanting these past few months. Frankly you've been something of a shower. This is an opportunity to balance the books on both sides. Either way on Friday evening, come success or failure, I shall be retiring to spend more time with my Edame.

RSVP and stay vigilant,

Alan Stoob
Britain's Premier Nazi Hunter™

In my eighteen years as a Nazi Hunter I have subsisted for the most part on scraps, tidbits, crumbs and conjecture; a person who knows someone in Woburn who remembers a friend in Leighton Buzzard who once saw a man goose stepping across Leagrave Community Park. Such people sap the time and energy of the hunter.

This was the real deal.

I knock on Tom's door.

'I got a tweet from George Michael!' he declares, clearly delighted.

'That's great, son!'

'He said it was a pleasure to receive a message from the son of Britain's Premier Nazi Hunter. How kind is that?'

'It's a compliment to both of us,' I tell him. 'I've also got some news. Friday will be my last ever hunt. After that my focus will be you and Mum. You have my word.'

'Thanks, Dad. And I'm on the Facebook!'

'Brilliant, son.'

Edame is in the kitchen, topping and tailing carrots while perusing a magazine about short breaks in Venezuela. I approach her from behind and wrap my arms around her, burying my face in her freshly-washed hair.

'Griffin Friday,' I tell her.

'But Alan,' she says, turning, 'your last day as huntsman is Thursday.'

'Come on, Eds,' I say. 'Friday The Griffin. Then that's it.'

She sighs and kisses my hand.

'OK,' she says. 'Friday then no more.'

'No more.'

'The Griffin is a big prize.'

'I know,' I reply.

'Finger him and you go down in the history.'

'I know.'

Although I was excited, in no way had I planned to go out like this. Secretly I assumed I would continue hunting Nazis until I died, or got hunted back.

I didn't want to stand down. I'd never been good at embracing change, particularly when it was forced upon me. It took me a good year to bed down as a Nazi Hunter and that included a full six months chasing a communist by mistake. But the bitter pill of retirement would be eternally sweetened by success on Friday.

I sit in the study, lights off. The walls are moonlit, the book spines reflecting back their titles: *Nazi Doctors*, *Nazis in Lincolnshire*, *Nazi Pets*, *Edith's Hitler's Favourite Recipes*, *At Home with the Himmlers*. I pull down a fictional account of what Luton might have been like had the Nazis won the war, signed by the author.

Stay vigilant, Alan, Bedfordshire needs you – Frederick Forsyth

My computer pings.

Hiya Alan,

Piles much better thanks. Anusol really is a life saver.

I read your message with interest and a fresh pot of coffee. As you will know, Interpol has been forced to make a number of cutbacks in recent months as a result of the credit crunch, which I used as a front to remove people who have made unnecessary comments about my weight. We have, however, retained a pot for Special Ops.

We know little of The Griffin, save that he is the man at

the apex of Bedfordshire's underworld network. We have never been able to get close to him. You have gone one better. Fine work, Alan, especially at your age.

Sorry we've let you down of late. There are no excuses – though we have had a leak in the roof since March.

Let us put the incident inside the reptile house behind us and join forces in what will be your last hurrah. I shall dispatch three of my top men forthwith and can guarantee they will be on their best behaviour. Let me know if there is anything else to ensure you go out at the top.

Love to Edame.

Interpol Steve
Head of Operations™

J☸ne

5.18am: a hammering at the front door.

I grabbed Edame's short pink dressing gown and hurried downstairs, my knees and ankles going off like indoor fireworks. On my way down I collected the blunderbuss from the wall.

The shadows suggested more than one. There was shouting in foreign tongues. Nazis? Surely not, though I know how early one rises as one gets older. What happens when you reach 110? I puffed out my chest, unfastened the locks and opened the door.

Before me stood three suited men in their thirties, each carrying a rucksack and a sleeping bag.

'Hi, Alan. Hope you don't mind we're early, we travel all night from Belgium,' said one as he barged his way past me. 'Nice gown.'

'Who in hell's name are you?' I belted out.

'Interpol,' said another. 'OK if we stay? Steve said you wouldn't mind. It's the cuts.'

They stank of cheap booze. It didn't take a hunter to surmise they had been drinking on the Eurostar, or the ferry. Edame appeared at the top of the stairs, wearing one of my shirts.

'Alan, you randy old dog!'

'Check out the MILF!'

'This, gentlemen – and I use the word advisedly – happens

to be my wife!' I said, barely concealing my fury. 'We were in bed – ASLEEP. I would rather gouge my own eyes out than have you stay here. There's a tent in the garage. Come back at one and you can erect it.'

They snigger.

'In the meantime get out of my house!'

'What shall we do for the next seven hours?'

'I don't give a damn.'

'Mind if we leave our bags here?'

'OUT!'

Back in bed I punched the pillow until I was short of breath. Edame handed me my inhaler.

'Come on, Alan,' she said, 'they're not so bad.'

I think she fancied the one with the big shoulders.

I draft an angry email to Interpol Steve, then delete it. At least it was extra manpower. I only hoped Edame wasn't planning on getting any of it.

I lay there, not able to sleep, still livid. In the end I couldn't help myself. I texted Steve.

They arrived drunk

He replied immediately *got to see funny side lol!!*

I rose and prepared breakfast. At least the men had made themselves scarce, no sign of them in the garden.

'I won't miss Interpol one bit,' I told Edame.

'Come on, Al,' she said. 'They're only doing their best.'

'By turning up drunk?'

'You probably intimidated them with your tracks record.'

After elevenses I tell Edame I'm heading out for a recce of the White Horse in Letchworth.

'Let me come,' she says. 'I'll just pop a bra on.'

The drive takes twenty minutes. As ever I let Edame do the

gears. It's the nearest she gets to driving and she loves it, save for second-to-third which she has yet to master. Once there I leave her in the car and check round the grounds, making notes and drawing up a rough map. I then enter the pub, order a small ginger beer, have a gawp and exit.

Back in the Stoobmobile I place my notes in the glove compartment, take out a tissue and clear my good nostril.

'I know how much you love to chase the bad Nazis,' says Edame, 'but I look forward to having you to myself by the end of tomorrow.'

I place the tissue in my pocket, take her hand in mine and offer a smile.

'Thank you, my love,' I say. 'Either way we're nearly there.'

'Sorry I've been shortening up your hunting time and nagging you about holidays,' she says. 'Here is a little small something for the luck and to say sorry.'

She hands me a box. I open it. Inside is a silver Cross pen. Inscribed along the shaft a message:

You will always be Britain's Premier Nazi Hunter™ in my hart.

It seems petty to point out the small error so I give her a cuddle, which she thoroughly enjoys.

'How will you recognise The Griffin?' she asks, coming up for air.

'The man is a 107-year-old Nazi war crimimal,' I say. 'Something tells me I just will.'

Back home I drag the tent from the garage and deposit it in the garden. No sign of the Interpol Three. Thirty minutes later I am woken from my nap by singing. It's them, back no doubt from further lubrication courtesy of a handful of Dunstable hostelries.

From the study I see them struggling to erect the tent before giving up and dozing off in the sunshine. The sound of their snoring prevents me from getting back to sleep so I play the tape of jungle noises I bought from the *Reader's Digest* in an effort to win their prize draw of £250,000 (I didn't win).

At five I fling open the study window.

'Dinner at eight!'

To a man they wake with a start and swiftly stand up. Two of them assume a karate pose.

'Oi!' I shout. They look up. I give them two fingers and close the window.

At 8.01pm there is a knock at the back door and the three of them sheepishly shuffle in. Somehow each is wearing a crisply ironed shirt. The one with the curly hair is holding a small bunch of fresh flowers.

'Alan,' he says, eyes cast downwards, 'I hope you will receive these chrysanthemums we picked from your garden in the manner in which they are intended. We are deeply sorry about the whole turning-up-drunk-then-drinking-some-more incident. If we could turn back the clock we would have shown you more respect. Truth is we're all rather in awe of you and our nerves got the better of us. Please accept our humblest apologies.'

They bow in unison. Edame winks at me. When they raise their heads the small one has tears in his eyes.

'I accept your apology,' I say.

'Phew!' replies Shoulders. 'Now, what we having?'

Over dinner I run through the MO for tomorrow. It couldn't be simpler, I tell them: Curly enters the bar half an hour before me and behaves as an ordinary patron; Tiny stays out front; Shoulders covers the rear entrance (I'm impressed there are no sniggers at this). I enter the establishment ten minutes after the arranged time to show The Griffin I am not unduly nervous. I introduce myself as Rod von Hull and buy the Nazi a drink. We sit at the table and I ask him a series of pre-prepared, legally-binding questions. As ever I shall be recording the conversation. When I feel I have enough information to guarantee a conviction I will indicate I am ready for Interpol intervention by announcing loudly, 'I don't know about you The Griffin but I'm Hank Marvin' – the Shadows being a popular beat combo in Germany in the early sixties. Curly will alert the other two by walkie-talkie. They will then enter the building and the four of us shall overpower and arrest The Griffin. He's bound to have some back-up but we four should be strong enough to prevail, and besides, I'm still pretty strong for my height (5'7").

'To Alan's plan,' says Shoulders, raising his can of lager.

'Alan's plan,' say the others and clink glasses.

Edame winks at me again. At least I think it's at me.

'So Alan,' says Shoulders, 'what is it like to be Britain's Premier Nazi Hunter?'

And with that the floodgates open:

'Did Hitler really only have one ball?'

'Do you think Jewish Nazi Hunters are more determined than gentile ones?'

'Is it true Goebbels slept with his mum?'

'Do Nazis really keep hating Jews for three days after their death?'

'Where's the bathroom?'

They were eager listeners. I told them about Si, about how

he had approached me back in '94. And I told them about how much Edame had given up to allow me a free hunting reign.

During pudding Tom came downstairs to ask if either of us had heard of a website called Wikipedia. Shyly he said hello to the Interpol boys. They greeted him back. He looked timid.

'Do you think you'd like to take over your dad's mantle as Britain's Premier Nazi Hunter?' asked Curly.

'Maybe, once I get Susan back,' he said before retreating back upstairs.

At around ten the boys excused themselves, citing the long day ahead. Each in turn shook my hand and gave Edame a peck on the cheek.

Once they had left, Tom snuck back down. The three of us sat in the kitchen, listening to rain batter the windows. Edame suggested we ask the boys if they wanted to sleep inside. I told her no way.

'You know it's Dad's last day tomorrow,' Edame said, cradling her Horlicks and double cream.

'I know, he said,' Tom replied. 'Besides, I read it on the Twitters.'

'Eh?' I said.

'George Michael posted a link from the Interpol website: "Stoob to stand down at end of week, says Interpol".'

'Even I haven't seen that!' I declared. Tom continued reciting from memory:

'"Sources inside Interpol claim that Alan Stoob, Britain's Premier Nazi Hunter, is to hang up his hunting net by the end of this week, much to the relief of Nazi war criminals everywhere . . ."'

'That's great!' said Edame.

'You're making excellent progress, son,' I said, placing my hand on his flabby forearm.

'Anyway, got to go,' said Tom, rising. 'I promised Tina I'd Skype her at eleven.'

'Skype now, is it?' I replied, the pride flushing my cheeks.

Edame and I remain at the table listening to the deluge for a further thirty minutes, comfortable in our silence. I picture myself on *Newsnight*, being warmly congratulated by Jeremy Paxman. I feel happy, content and ready.

* * *

Awoken by Edame with a tray of food: eggs Benjamin, Frosties and falafel. One of my favourite pre-hunt breakfasts. She climbs back into bed and plants a kiss on the small of my back.

'What was that for?' I ask.

'For making this day your last.'

'I love you,' I tell her.

At 10.30am the Interpol three bundle through the back door. Each is dressed in a black suit and dark sunglasses, each has an earpiece. I send them back out with the instruction not to dress like the FBI. They return in an assortment of attire, notably Curly who is wearing a harlequin costume. Although unusual perhaps it was a stroke of genius. What kind of spy dresses like a jester?

They depart by taxi at 11.30, leaving me to follow. I climb into my lederhosen and stand before the mirror.

'Ich bin Rod von Hull,' I say, 'Ich bin ein former member of ze SS danke schon.'

I look at my Twitter account. A couple of messages from Henry Blofeld but nothing of great import. Then something grips me; pride, insecurity perhaps, or the desire to be noticed. I hammer out a tweet to Jon Snow of *Channel Four News*:

'Hi, Jon. White Horse Letchworth 1pm. May have a world exclusive for you. Regards, Alan.'

My taxi arrives early. I ask the driver to wait.

'Well, my dearest,' I say, approaching Edame.

'Please don't, Alan,' she replies, backing up. 'I'll break downs. Just come back safe. That's all I ask.'

In the taxi my breathing is shallow, my back sodden with sweat. 'Unflappable,' I say to myself, chanting these four syllables, two with the in-breath, two with the out, until we arrive in the pub car park.

The fare is £8. I hand the driver a £20 note and tell him he can keep the change if he writes me a receipt for the full amount. I notice a gargantuan BMW. As ever the windows are blacked out. A thick-necked man stands next to it, smoking two cigarettes at once.

I exit the cab and walk towards the pub. Shoulders is standing outside the back entrance.

'Hi, Alan!' he says, excitedly. I can hardly believe it. What kind of idiot exposes his own man in such a fashion. I purposefully avert my gaze and walk by.

'Sorry – I mean Herr von Hull,' he says, pointedly. 'How are you, Rod? Have you seen Alan recently?'

The pub is crowded. I force my way through the bodies with repeated requests of 'entschuldigen' until I pierce the throng and am standing in a clearing beyond the bar. Curly is in the corner. He waves.

Sitting alone reading a copy of *Die Welt* is a thick-set man who I would estimate to be in his 110s.

'Entschuldigen sie bitte,' I say over the man's paper. 'Bist du . . . Ze Griffin?'

I do not believe in the notion of innate evil but never before had I encountered an aura hinting so clearly at the darkest possible deeds. The figure does not move, indicating instead, using only its eyes, that I should sit.

'Ich heisse Rod von Hull,' I say and offer my hand, conjuring the special shake.

The Griffin flicks his paper abruptly, his piercing cool eyes revealing their impatience.

'Du seem sehr keen for me to see du know ze Nazi hand-shake, Herr von Hull,' he says. 'Vee are in Engerlande now, vee do as zee Englishe.'

'Jawohl!' I say excitedly. 'Of course.'

I have lost my poise, am gabbling, talking too much. Un-flap-uh-bul. Un-flap-uh-bul.

'Vell?' says the imposing figure opposite. 'Are du going to offer me ein trinken or do du expect me to die von thirst?'

'OF COURSE, HERR GRIFFIN!' I boom. The entire bar looks round.

'Bist du nervous, Herr von Hull?' he enquires, eyes to his paper once more.

'Nein, mein herr,' I reply. 'Just excited.'

'Vell burn off some of zat fucking excitement by ordering us both ein fucking gin und tonic there's a gut mensch.'

'Of course, mein herr.'

I excuse myself and head towards the bar. On my way I pass Curly.

'How's it going, Al?' he mutters. I ignore him and plough on.

Lunchtime ordering must have been at its peak. Fifteen

minutes in I still hadn't been served. I force my way back through the masses and made my way to The Griffin.

'Eet eez taking me ein bischen longer than I thought, Herr Griffin. Shall ich order lunch vile I'm zare?'

'ZWEI GIN UND TONIC!' he bellows.

I nod nervously and reverse up, backing into the fray.

Twenty-five minutes later I return with the drinks. He sips his then places it back on the glass table.

'Ich do not sink ich speak out of turn,' he says, fixing me with an icy gaze, 'ven ich say du lack any semblance of bar presence votsoever.'

'Ich am not usually this bad!' I reply, hastily. 'Ich once got served straight off ze bat at Ze Old Cock in Flitwick!'

'SILENCE!' he says, leaning forward in his chair. 'So vot eez eet du vant to see me about zat is so *important*, Herr von Hull?'

His face is extraordinary, like latex. What is left of his hair is brilliant white. Each ear is nearly a foot long, gravity having taken its toll. There is something familiar about his eyes.

'Ich bin neu to ze neighbourhood,' I say, gripping desperately at the underside of the table. 'Ich had heard zo much about du ich thought it vood be gut to meet.'

'*Gut*, du say?'

'Ja, gut.'

'Und du came over von Deutschland via ze ratline, ja?'

'Ja, herr Griffin.'

He looked at his watch. Tag Heuer.

'Vich vun?'

'Beg pardon, Herr Griffin?'

'Ich said vich vun.'

'Vich vun vot?'

'VICH RATLINE, DUMKOPF!'

Which ratline? I thought there was only one, from Bremen to Biggleswade? Perhaps there were many: Berlin-Bedford, Luton-Laatzen, Hanover-Herrings Green, who knew? My grip on the table increased until there was a small splintering sound.

'Ze usual ratline, mein herr,' I reply without confidence.

He clicks his neck and suggests we order. Here is my cue to shout 'Ich don't know about du but ich bin Hank Marvin' but I'm not ready. The Griffin hasn't said enough. I need to continue my questioning.

'Ich vood love to hear about your vor,' I say. 'Vare du were stationed, vot du got up to, how many mensch du killed, how ze Serd Reich shall rise again.'

The Griffin takes a long draw on his gin and tonic and finishes the lot, ice and lemon included.

'Ich bet du vood,' he replies, spitting a succession of lemon pips into his glass. 'In fact, *Herr Stoob*, ich bin certain du vood like to know everysing zare is to know about me.'

My head swam. I couldn't feel my trousers. Desperately I looked for Curly but he wasn't there. I fumbled in my pocket for my mobile and my inhaler. Both gone.

'Relax, Herr Stoob,' he said, grinning. 'Cast your eyes at three o'clock. . .' I did. A huge Aryan man waggled a phone at me. The inhaler was in his mouth.

'Don't worry about your freunds. Zay are safe. Unconscious but safe.'

We sat there in silence, The Griffin revelling in my obvious discomfort.

'Here ist ze plan,' he said eventually. 'Soon our food vill arrive. Ich bin hungrig like ze volf und zat takes priority. Ich took ze liberty of orderling fur du. After zat ve vill go for eine

kleine valk, just du und I. Oh, und don't try anything, Herr
Stoob. Zare are three guns trained on du as ve sprechen,
including one of mein own.'

I looked down at my high polished jackboot. Reflected
in the toecap was a Walther PPK, aimed at my ineffective
genitals.

I had come close to death before at the hands of a Nazi. I
would never forget the day Klaus Barbie stabbed me in the
Luton Arndale Centre, nor the time Franz Stangl pushed me
out of a moving Intercity 125. I was lucky to land on a horse.
Today there were no horses, metaphorical or otherwise.

'So Herr Stoob, tell me vot eez it like to face certain death?'

The Griffin tucked into his plate of sausages like a savage.
I toyed with my battered cod and chips, flipping the fish over
and over. He wiped his mouth with the back of his hand
and demanded one of his henchman order us both another
'G und T'.

'You'll never get away with this!' I said, though the threat
had a hollow ring. 'I've got Channel Four outside; Interpol are
tracking the whereabouts of their men; I've got back-up com—'

'How ist your lovely wife zese days? Edame, isn't it?'

The words cut straight through me.

'Do whatever you like with me but leave Edame out of
this.'

'Such an elegant ankle for an older lady,' he continued.
'In Nazi Germany great store is held by a strong ankle.
Does she do special foot-rolling exercises to maintain ze
trimness? Perhaps she learnt ze technique from ze late Henry
Cooper . . .'

He let the words trail off. How could he know about
Cooper? I was nearly sick in my mouth.

'Must have been difficult not to compare yourself sexually with ein mensch who nearly beat the negro Ali in 1963.'

'Cassius Clay,' I replied, defiantly. 'That was his name in 1963. He changed it in 1964 after joining the Nation of Islam. Ali is a black man. You don't like black men very much, do you?'

'Du are somevot unvise to challenge me in our current situation, Herr Stoob. Du may have forgotten zat ich hold all ze karten, leaving du merely vith ze jokers.'

The Griffin was revelling in my helplessness and ordered a pudding. I was sweating profusely and beginning to dehydrate. And then I remembered.

The cufflinks.

The anniversary cufflinks Edame bought me to celebrate 40 years of togetherness contained a special compartment within which was hidden a dose of deadly nightshade.

Beneath the table I felt carefully at the right cuff and fumbled my way to the tiny catch beneath the head. Using the last remaining nail on my left hand I forced the mechanism. It sprung open. I tipped the powder into my left hand, closed the compartment and rested my hands once more on the table.

'You have got me surrounded, you bastard,' I said. 'I suppose that man over your shoulder is one of yours too?'

The Griffin very slowly craned his corpulent neck to look. As he did I lunged forward and tipped the powder from my palm into his drink. As he turned back round I lurched back once more. His Victoria and Albert sponge arrived.

'Ich don't know zat person,' he replied. 'Zo seeing as ziss ist Bedfordshire zare remains ein gut chance zay are ein Nazi. Are du sure du wouldn't care for a pudding? Zay only use organic produce here, no sveeteners.'

I couldn't be sure whether any of Griffin's henchmen had observed my sleight-of-hand but none stepped forward to warn him. The elderly Nazi before me ate his pudding, picking up the bowl and licking it clean before blowing his nose on the napkin and laying it down.

'Wunderbra,' he said, belching.

'All that eating must be thirsty work,' I said, staring at his glass.

'Oh ja,' he replied. I crossed my fingers under the table and thought of Edame.

'It ist vital to quench vun's thirst at ze end of ein long meal,' he said before picking up the glass, motioning as if to drink from it then hurling its contents straight past his ear and in the direction of a dog sitting at the feet of its owner. 'Unfortunately as du can see ich have ein drinking problem,' he continued, laughing to himself. 'Du disappoint me, Herr Stoob. Surely du didn't sink ich vood fall fur ze oldest trick in ze buchwald?'

I glanced over at the dog. It lapped feverishly at the floor.

'Ich am growing bored of ziss,' said The Griffin. He placed a £50 note on the table and removed a single glove from his jacket, slipping it clinically over the fingers of his right hand. I looked once more at the dog. It completed three back flips before collapsing in a heap.

'Follow me out through ze cellar or ich vill murder du in a bad vay,' he said before winding up his arm and smashing his fist into the fire alarm on the wall, breaking the glass and triggering a deafening klaxon.

Beer splashed the ceiling. Some people ran, others remained rooted to the spot, screaming helplessly. The man with the dog dragged the limp mutt towards the exit. Using his gun

Griffin gestured for me to rise. He jammed the barrel into the small of my back and forced me through the melee, through a gap at the side of the bar and down into the cellar. At the rear of the cellar was a door. I went first and found myself climbing a step ladder. Two minutes later we were outdoors in glorious sunshine, next to a footpath.

We walked, The Griffin holding the gun in my side. When people approached he jabbed it hard into my ribs, warning me not to do anything 'untovord'. I greeted each passing rambler with a polite 'Hullo'.

After twenty minutes we reached Letchworth Lake, one of the eight wonders of Bedfordshire. The sun shimmered off its surface. I couldn't help but notice the beauty of our surroundings. I'd always recognised the region as Britain's best for scenic vistas.

I tried to conjure a solution out of my hopeless corner but nothing came. I looked once more at the lake, wondering if it was to be my last view.

'Ich bin sorry it hast come to ziss, Herr Stoob, but zat ist ze life,' said The Griffin. 'Sadly ze Serd Reich ist more important zan ze existence of vun silly little man von Dunstable. Ich read on ze internet zat ziss voz to be your last day as ein Nazi Hunter. Zay vere not wrong. Put ziss on.'

The Griffin handed me a blindfold. On each eye was glued a swastika. I hesitated but he aimed the gun at me, cocked the barrel and shot past my ear. I took one last look at the sky and slipped the blindfold over my head.

'Your clothes,' he said. 'Give zem to me.'

I asked for some final decency but he refused, insisting I strip right down to the wilbur.

'At least let me keep my watch,' I said. 'It was a gift

from Edame. Please let me die with her aura encircling my wrist.'

'*Everysing*,' he said.

I removed the watch and dropped it at my feet. The sun was warm on my buttocks. I stood there, waiting for the shot. The knowledge of death brought with it an unexpected calm. There was nothing I could do. I was resigned.

I thought of Edame and of Tina and Tom. I prayed they would survive without me. Would Edame marry again? Jealously I hoped she wouldn't, that she would never recover from the gruesome event about to ensue. Another part of me wished her only happiness and if that meant settling down with another man – as long as it wasn't Potato George – then I wouldn't begrudge her. I'd be dead, after all.

The seconds passed, turning into minutes. I addressed The Griffin, demanding that he put this particular dog out of its misery. He was playing with me, refusing to answer. I could feel the sun dipping. My bottom was starting to get chilly, my back too. The certainty of death was ebbing. I was becoming anxious again.

'SHOOT ME, YOU BLOODY BASTARD!' I screamed. Nothing. Was this a test, him still stood there, the gun pointed at my temple?

'OK, YOU SHIT!' I shouted. There was nothing to lose. I reached for my blindfold and ripped it off.

My clothes were gone, but so was The Griffin. I was alive. Naked, but alive. I looked at the lake I thought I would never glimpse again and collapsed in a heap on a hillock.

Eventually I headed back up the path. En route I bumped into ramblers. I nodded while covering my modesty. All were too polite to mention my nude penis. Instead they offered a friendly 'Good day!' or 'Lovely weather' as we passed, though one little girl ran away screaming.

Why had The Griffin spared my life?

Was I still in danger?

Was Edame?

I picked up my pace and hastened towards The White Horse. As I neared its rear I saw a TV van, complete with satellite dish on the roof. Next to it stood a tall thin man with grey hair and a ridiculous tie. Jon Snow.

'There he is!' a voice went up. Everyone turned to look at me. Instinctively I raised my hands in a 'surrender' poise, exposing my manhood. Snow ran over holding a microphone, a cameraman following behind.

'Alan – I got your tweet – what happened – did you nab a Nazi?'

Suddenly I was surrounded by journalists and bystanders, all filming me. I had no idea what to do or where to put my hands. A middle-aged man asked for an autograph. Not wishing to be impolite I granted him one but exposed myself in the process. Eventually someone passed me a shawl which I wrapped round my waist.

Ten minutes later I was sat in the Channel Four van drinking tea with Jon Snow and Zeinab Badawi.

'What happened out there was TV gold,' said Snow offering me a Hobnob.

'Please tell me you're not going to put this out,' I begged.

'It's already gone,' he said. 'We were live. Don't worry though, Alan, we did our best to ensure your cock was pixilated out.'

I asked to use a phone. Kate Adie, who was chatting to Krishnan Guru-Murthy, handed me hers.

'Dunstable 371?' came a familiar voice.

'Edame, it's me!'

'Alan! Are you OK? I just saw your willy on the telly!'

'I'm fine. The Griffin threatened to kill me, but didn't.'

'I'm so glad you're OK! He got away?'

'Yes.'

'Oh Alan.'

'I know.'

'Never mind. Come back home to where everyone is in love with you.'

'Lock yourself in a cupboard until I'm back, will you? Just a precaution.'

I feel a tap on the shoulder.

'Cut it short, would you?' said Adie. 'I've already exceeded my minutes for the month.'

Badawi dropped me off outside the house. Once more the road was swarming with reporters. I offered no comment. My keys had been in my trousers. I rang the bell. No answer so I opened the letter box and shouted, 'YOU CAN COME OUT OF THE CUPBOARD NOW, IT'S ALAN!' Seconds later Edame flung open the door, pulled me inside and held me tight for what felt like minutes. My shawl fell off.

'He stole the watch you gave me,' I said, eventually.

'I don't give a monkey nut about that,' she said, her cheeks damp. 'Thanks god you're home. I am never, ever, letting you out of my slight again!'

Tom appeared from upstairs and, unphased by my nudity, joined the hug.

'So sorry you didn't ensnare The Griffin,' he said. 'I was following it on Twitter. There's load of footage of your willy. Some angles are better than others but I wouldn't watch it if I were you.'

Edame and I ordered an Indian takeaway from our favourite Indian restaurant, Dr Indian. We ate in the kitchen, blinds down, ignoring the constant knocking at the door. We shared a small bottle of Kingfisher lager and held hands.

'I guess this is the end of your life as Britain's Premier Nazi Hunter,' said Edame.

'I guess it is,' I replied. 'It's just not how I had hoped to bow out.'

*　　*　　*

Every news channel remained awash with footage of my naked surrender. YouTube had over a thousand clips of my penis, including one with Hitler's face on the end of it. The newspaper front pages made their feelings clear.

NAKED NAZI HUNTER CALLS IT A DAY
The Telegraph
RUDE STOOB STANDS DOWN
The Sun
NUDE STOOB'S LAST BOOB
The Mirror
NAKED PENSIONER FOOTAGE 'TRAUMATISES TODDLERS'
Daily Mail
'NAKED FEELS AS NATURAL AS CLOTHED,' CLAIMS TOP NAZI HUNTER
The Nudist

'It is said that all great political careers end in failure,' wrote Deborah Orr in *The Guardian*. 'From hereon perhaps all Nazi hunting careers will culminate in abject humiliation.'

Edame had pulled the phone out of the wall but the doorbell remained under constant siege. An envelope with a blank cheque from *The Sun* arrived. I pulled back the net curtains and caught a glimpse of Audrey Shaw from *The Bedford Observer*. She waved tentatively. I offered a half smile before withdrawing.

Channel Five cobbled together a documentary about my career as an excuse to show the footage of my nudgie, which hadn't been pixelated out. They repeated the clip seven times in the first five minutes after which I switched it off and ran a bath. Too embarrassed to stare at my naked body, I bathed in my underpants.

I lay there in a daze, overheating. For nearly twenty years I had been defined by my occupation. Who was I now? Just an elderly man who didn't know when to quit. I was no longer Britain's Premier Nazi Hunter. As of today I was plain old Alan Logan Stoob of 14 The Keswick, Dunstable.

What would get me up in the morning? Not Little Alan, that's for sure. What was my purpose? To see out my days, crumbling into irrelevance, my memory faltering? Am I not surrendering the very thing that keeps me alive, that gives me purpose? Images of retirement flashed before my eyes: doddery men in polyester slacks sharing silent pub lunches with their wives; naps that span whole afternoons; abandoned rounds of pitch and putt; grab rails; meaningless drives to places of no beauty; death in the afternoon.

I felt peculiar and lay down on the bed. Edame joined me, resting my head in her lap and rhythmically stroking my brow.

When I awoke it was dark. I was alone. The commotion from outside had abated. I swung my legs off the bed and unsteadily made my way downstairs. Laughter was emanating from the sitting room. At the front door I noticed an umbrella and a pair of highly polished tan brogues.

As I entered the sitting room I clapped eyes on Nigel from the British Nazi Hunting Association.

'Alan!' he said, leaping up from the sofa. 'So good to see you! Edame's been telling me all about your retirement plans. World cruise!'

'That's not definite,' I replied, pointedly.

'Sorry to spring this on you so soon, Alan, but the BNHA needs to appoint a successor ASAP. As you know, the previous incumbent nominates the new man.'

'I don't feel it's appropriate for me to do so standing here in the nude,' I said. 'Let me go and put some clothes on.'

Barely twenty-four hours had passed and I was already being cleared out, moved on, shelved. I was an instant irrelevance, like an actress over forty or an open sandwich dropped on the pavement.

I made a point of dressing up in my smartest M&S suit and re-entered the room. Nigel and Edame were sipping sherry.

'I don't believe any one of them is my "rightful heir" as Britain's Premier Nazi Hunter,' I barked, startling them both. 'Too many of my fellow hunters are in it for the fame, the groupies and the extra £60 a week. I also know if I don't provide a name, you'll nominate someone anyway. The best I can come up with is Herb Derb, the man behind the near-capture of Magda Baum, the Menace of Meinhoff. I don't trust him, he doesn't have much of a pedigree and he's not even fifty, but I can't think of anyone else.'

'Despite our own reservations we agree that Herb is the

most natural choice,' said Nigel. 'Thank you. Nice suit by the way. I remember it from the awards dinner back in '98.'

Nigel and Edame continued chatting about sun-kissed holidays in the Pyrenees. I sat there contemplating my new life of cushioned toilet seats and flexible magnifier lamps.

'Lovely to catch up,' said Nigel eventually. He stood in the doorway, raised his collar and opened his umbrella. 'If you could divert your emails to Herb's account that would be great. Ciao!'

Edame went into the kitchen to make dinner. I hauled myself wearily up the stairs and into the study. I turned on the computer. It revved up at a snail's pace, giving me more time to ponder the hunter-shaped hole in my life.

My inbox was overflowing with messages: negative, positive and spam. Novelist Hilary Mantel ('Hard cheese, Alan'), fifth Beatle George Martin ('You have done this country a great service for many years') and comedian Freddie Starr ('Nice knob') counted amongst the positive. Martin Amis and Duncan Goodhew were far from complimentary.

As I tried to work out how to forward my account an email pinged into my inbox.

Wotcha Alan,

George Michael from Wham! here.

Bloody hell, Alan, what an awful way to bring down the curtain on your career, waggling your cock like that. I can only imagine the public backlash if I ended my final performance with a full frontal. Some might like it, but many would be disturbed.

That's why I'm writing. Don't knock it on the head.
You're too good at this hunting lark. Stick with it. Just a
little longer.

If you need help, a getaway driver, a spot of pot to take the
edge off those arthritic joints, whatever, I'm around and I'm
quite left wing. We could fit it in around tour dates.

Let me know.

George xxxxxxxxxxxxxxxxxxxxxxxxxxx

I pressed delete and logged out.

Six o'clock. The earliest acceptable time to open a bottle of
wine. Today I need a place to hide, or at the very least a
window between myself and reality. Perhaps from hereon in
I will sleep through the day and drink into the evening. That
way my retirement will be manageable, albeit wished away.

Two episodes of *Bergerac* after dinner. My dark mood renders
it a joyless experience. In bed Edame is out like a light. Each
time I close my eyes it feels like I'm falling.

July

In my dream Herb Derb is interviewed by Michael Parkinson and makes a joke about my penis. The laughter from the studio audience is so loud Norris McWhirter is called in. He verifies Herb's remark as the funniest of all time.

I doze until ten before I am finally woken by Edame, who is Hoovering the duvet. I sense she wants our new life to begin. I'd prefer a slow day with plenty of time for melancholy self-reflection.

Edame grows increasingly impatient until she can wait no longer and announces she's off to get her hair done at Natural Born Curlers, followed by lunch with Joan. She says she'll be home by four, kisses me on the forehead and is gone.

I sit on the sofa eating cereal from the box, inert and bedressing-gowned. With no idea what to do I turn on the telly and flick between *The Wright Stuff*, *Homes Under The Hammer*, *Location Location Location*, *Antiques Roadshow* and a *3–2–1* starring Dusty Bin. Footage of me running naked, tiny penis embedded in my scrotum, plays on ITV2. I switch off and shuffle into the kitchen. There's a note from Tom.

Gone to Citizens Advice Bureau. Back later.

Through the house I wander, stopping off in every room. In each I straighten the pictures. Some of the frames I find myself moving off centre simply to readjust them. A small task. Creating work for myself. I am my own enclave of communist Russia.

In the back bedroom I find a box of Alan Stoob fridge magnets. We only sold three. I wonder what they would fetch on eBay. Less than the mugs, I imagine.

In the bathroom mirror I stare back at myself until my face makes no sense. Using Edame's hairbrush I sweep what remains of my grey lustrous locks into the different styles I've had down the years: Denis Compton grease back, Teddy boy, Elvis quiff, side-parting, other side-parting, Bobby Charlton-near-the-ear. I locate Edame's curlers and insert eight in an effort to recreate my perm of 1985.

When the door goes I find I am sat on the landing chair, staring up at a photograph of my late mother, recalling the moment I returned home in May 1945 to discover she had been killed during an air raid. The fact that all that time she had kept from me my father's death at Dunkirk in 1940 only compounded matters. With no parents I was sent straight back to Yorkshire and to the living hell that was The Meekers.

'Mr Stoob?' asks an overalled man, two others behind him. 'Sign here please.'

The crest on his blue boiler suit – a swastika with a thumbs down superimposed over the top – is that of the British Nazi Hunting Association.

'Show us where you keep the computer and books and we'll do the rest.'

'What do you mean?' I say, but they bundle past. One of them winks knowingly at me while sticking his finger through his fly.

'In here,' shouts a voice. I chase them as best I can up the stairs and into my study, where they are already disconnecting the monitor.

'WHAT ARE YOU DOING?' I bellow, catching my breath. 'The computer is the property of the BNHA.'

'I need these files for my memoirs!' I exclaim. 'You can't do this!'

'It is our understanding these books were purchased with BNHA money. We'll need to take them too.'

'No you won't!' I scream. 'Many of these I bought myself.'

'Sorry, Mr Stoob, but we have been requested to commandeer all hardware, information and data related to the hunting of Nazis. If you have any queries I suggest you contact customer services once we've left.'

'Remind me where this is going, guv?' says one.

'Mark all the boxes for the attention of Herb Derb.'

'This is outrageous,' I tell them. 'I'll be speaking with Nigel about this.'

They don't look up.

'I want you to know that my neighbour sometimes comes over to use my computer. If you find any compromising images of Diana Dors on there that will be him.'

Five minutes later the room is hollow, barren. Save for a few photographs the shelves are bare, the desk displaying a light patch where the computer once sat. The front door slams shut. The sound of a lorry starting up and driving off, then silence.

I sit in the swivel chair behind my desk and open the top drawer. Inside I find my signed copy of *Justice Not Vengeance* by Simon Wiesenthal. At least they didn't swipe that.

My dear Alan,
it says on the inside front cover . . .
You have earned the right to be Britain's Premier Nazi Hunter –
today, tomorrow and forever.
Your friend,
Si
I press the book's cover to my cheek, trying to discern meaning in its coolness. Did anything mean anything anymore? Who was I? Who am I? How are you supposed to start again at seventy-five?

I put Si's book back and dig out my small black Filofax. I dial.

'Can I speak with Mark Eddison please?' I ask.

'Sorry madam,' a voice comes back. 'Mr Eddison died in 2003 from complications.'

'Complications from what?'

'Yes, I'm afraid so. Sorry I couldn't help.'

I call Mark Shirt. His wife tells me he had his legs removed three days after retiring from the Bedfordshire Constabulary and can't come to the phone; Simon Fletcher's wife says Simon is in hospital with scurvy; Peter Hurp has moved and left no forwarding address; Stuart Scrivens is unobtainable; Steven Hilditch doesn't remember me; Rupert Reeve claims he is in a lift and can't talk: Tony Duckett and Martin Chump are both on world cruises and won't be back until 2014. Of the other eight I try, seven are dead.

Peter Yerby is the only one in. We have a short chat as he is off to bowls but he says he'd love to meet up for lunch and how is my diary looking for early next year.

Early next year?

I tell him I am busy then and hang up.

'Coo-eeee!'

Edame is home and full of chatter: fancy hairdos, news about Joan, Carol's getting Botox, so much to report. I had a different story to pedal.

'Since you left all I've done is find out half of my old friends are dead and the other half live rich lives punctuated by activity and variety. I on the other hand have been so far up my own fundament hunting Nazis I've not kept in touch with any of them or developed any interests and as a result I have no one or nothing and am an empty shell of a man.'

'Nonsense,' she says. 'You've got me – and Bob next door. Plus you've got my curlers in your hair.'

Hurriedly I yank them from my barnet.

'Your hair looks nice,' she says. 'Good job, I'm taking you out for a pub supper to cheering you up.'

I drive the two of us to the Ferret & Amanda on Flitwick High Street. It's Thursday: two-for-one on starters and a third off all puddings.

Edame asks for a white wine spritzer. For me a tomato juice, extra spicy. Alcohol might depress me further. I insist on crisps.

'To our retirings,' says Edame, forcing a clinking of glasses. She pushes a brown paper bag across the table. I put my hand in and pull out *The Guardian Quick Crossword Volume Seven*.

'I thought we could start doings them together,' she says with an expectant smile. 'It will help improving my English and is a thing we can do between meals or in the evening. Part of our new routine.'

I open it.

'One across,' I say. 'Four letters. Depressed ex Nazi Hunter, currently sat in a pub just off the A5.'

'Good lord, what an odd clue,' says Edame, confused. 'Does it really say that?'

'Of course it bloody doesn't!' I tell her. 'It's a made up clue. I made it up.'

'Well what's the answer?'

'Alan.'

'OK,' she says. 'Write it in then.'

I sip my juice. Edame opens the crisps and tears the packet wide open. I hate it when she does that.

'Something else,' she says. This time the package is gift-wrapped.

'What is it?' I ask.

'Open it, you bloody idiots!' she replies. I do. It's gardening gloves. Another step closer to the grave.

'Tomorrow I thought we can go outwards into the back garden,' said Edame. 'It's very therapeuticing.'

I look down at the gloves. Their greenness depresses me.

'I don't want therapy,' I say, 'I want to hunt Nazis.'

Edame is quiet, but I can feel a volcano brewing. She throws a crisp at me. It glances off my cheek.

'Don't schijting starts that again!' she hisses. It's always bad news when she swears in Dutch. 'I've bought you schijting gardening gloves! Tomorrow we schijting garden!'

I bend down to pick up the crisp, and eat it. Edame visits the bathroom. When she returns she has recovered her poise.

'I just want us to be happy,' she says. 'You did amazing jobs hunting a Nazi all those years. You were Britain's best. But all good things must come to the finish. We must move onto the next phase of our lives. Together.'

A man walks up behind me, taps me on the shoulder and

says 'Hi, granddad, nice cock' before walking off and collecting money from his two friends, presumably for a bet.

'Did you get the Viagra like I ask?' says Edame.

'They were fresh out,' I tell her.

'When was this?'

'Last week.'

'Go again then.'

'Was Henry Cooper better in bed than me?'

There is a long pause.

'Yes.'

Another pause.

'And no.'

* * *

Dreamt Himmler had me in a headlock. I escape, but leave my head behind.

Breakfast outside. The birds are chirruping, the sun warming. Tom joins us for coffee and tells us about a website he has discovered called Chat Roulette. I laugh along, determined to put a brave face on things but the hot weather and forced bonhomie only serve to accentuate my misery.

After the washing-up Edame hands me a shoulder bag containing my new green gardening gloves, a trowel and a number of small packets. I open one of them, only for the contents to litter the kitchen floor.

'Oh Alan,' she says. 'You've spilt your seed.' This embarrasses both of us. I head upstairs and don my tracksuit.

Edame is project-managing the morning's activities. While she tackles the rhododendrons I have been instructed to root out the weeds which threaten to overrun the gnomes at the end of the garden. After that I am to prepare the soil for planting before sowing the seeds. Edame suggests I imagine that 'each weed is Nazi that needs to be obliterating'. I appreciate the joke, her first of the year.

The weeding itself is mildly enjoyable. There is a certain pleasure in ensuring each plant is yanked out, roots and all. I assign every weed a Nazi name. Firstly I dispense with Heinrich Himmler. He is swiftly followed by Franz Stangl, Josef Goebbels, Adolf Hitler, Magda Goebbels and Myra Nibble. I tug hard at The Griffin but the roots remain solid in the ground.

After half an hour I have at least fifty of the world's most notorious Nazi war criminals stuffed into a Sainsbury's bag. I saunter down to see Edame. She is sweaty about the nose. I wipe the outsides of her nostrils with my sleeve and report on my progress. She plants a moist kiss on my lips whilst raising a leg and suggests it's time to prepare the soil.

I enjoyed the weeding, viewing each as the enemy and acting accordingly, with extreme violence. Sticking a trowel in the earth on the other hand doesn't do it for me. I try to see the entire bed as a Nazi – or Nazi Germany – or even the Third Reich – but the space is simply too formless, the notion too nebulous, to make sense. I complete the job joylessly. Edame appears at my side, resting her arm on my shoulder.

'Very good,' she says. 'Next the seeds. Like hunting Nazis, planting seeds is all about preparation. Do the work now and you are rewarding further down the lines.' I appreciate her effort in drawing a comparison between gardening and Nazi hunting but frankly I am beginning to feel a bit embarrassed for her.

There is mild satisfaction to be gained from ensuring the distance between each plot is uniform, just as there was with flattening the soil, but I am still fundamentally bored. You can't win the Nobel Peace Prize for bringing on a few azaleas.

I was about to point this out to Edame when I twisted to pick up my trowel and felt the small of my back tighten like a corkscrew. I attempted to stand upright but the tightness doubled, leaving me fixed at a ninety-degree angle. I was immobilised.

'SHITTING JESUS ON TOAST – GET ME A FUCKING AMBULANCE!'

Edame returned a minute later with two ibuprofen, a glass of water and a chair for me to lean against until the ambulance arrived. The tiniest movement and my back grew tighter. I was in genuine agony. All I could think about was the many cases I had read of people buying the farm within days of their retirement. If I were still hunting this would never have happened.

Ten minutes later a paramedic arrived brandishing gas and air.

'This should be enough to get you inside, Mr Stoop,' he said. 'After that we can get you to a hospital.'

'Shit off you will!' I shouted. 'No hospital. You go in well and come out dead. I'm not ready to die. Five days ago I was Britain's Premier Nazi Hunter!'

Two minutes later I was completely mashed up out of my head on the gas and air, like I'd had four pints of mild but without the need to urinate. Flanked by Edame and the paramedic I made it to the sitting room sofa where I was laid out flat, my wellied feet jutting off the end.

'The back will take a few days to settle, especially at your age,' he said. 'You'll probably need an osteopath to give you exercises. And you're going to want plenty of painkillers. I recommend eight paracetamol and eight ibuprofen a day. Don't go over though or you'll know about it.'

Edame saw the man out and returned, hands on hips.

'I can't help feelings that in some way you slabotaged today for me, Alan,' she said, a mixture of anger and disappointment etched on her face. 'You've made this happen. I know what you're like. You knew how importants this was to me.'

'Bloody hell, love, I'm in agony here,' I said. 'I didn't plan this, how could I? Please may I have a cup of tea and five paracetamol?'

For some reason I got an erection. A big one. Edame must have noticed for she threw the rug at my lap and left the room. I could hear her footsteps on the stairs followed by the slamming of our bedroom door. No tea then.

I tried to lie still, every movement firing pain down my legs. Eventually I got to sleep, only to be woken by the phone. Three rings, four, five, six. Cursing I reached behind, feeling for the receiver. Sciatica shot down my right thigh. I winced, then picked up.

'What?' I said, impatient.

'_____.'

'Hello?'

'_____.'

'LISTEN, THIS IS NOT A GOOD TIME TO PLAY SILLY BUGGERS.'

'Don't be like zat, Alan,' said a familiar voice. 'Vhy be rude to somevun who spared your life?'

A fear gripped me, tensing my back anew.

'What do you want, The Griffin?' I asked.

'To see how du are, old freund,' he replied. 'Ich voz vurried about du.'

'I forbid you to think about me,' I said. 'Think about Herb Derb instead.'

There was a long pause.

'But Alan,' said the voice. 'Derb ist nothing to me. He ist but eine kleine Nazi Hunter. As far as I'm concerned zare vill only ever be vun premier hunter von Grosse Britain.'

'I am retired, Griffin. You know that. You brought my career to an end you big cunt.'

'Now Alan, no need to use such language.'

'I disagree,' I said, trying to improve the pillow arrangement on the sofa. 'If you've rung to taunt me you've caught me at a bad moment. I could do without an extended chat.'

'OK zen, Alan, ich vill leave du to your own business . . . Oh hold on, zare vos vun thing. Now vot voz it. Ah yes. Ich thought du should know zat plans are sehr much afoot to overthrow ze coalition government. Ein few veeks und dein country vill never be ze same again. Zat's vot it voz. Of course. Nice to chat. Auf wiedersehen, Alan.'

'Wait! What do you mean? You can't just say something like that then hang up. That's not how it works.'

'Ich didn't know zare ver rules.'

'There are. Anyway you're talking out of your German behind. You have to go through the correct channels to create a government. The people of Britain will never have you.'

'Vee have vays, Alan.'

'Vot vays – I mean what ways?'

'Just vays.'

'And why are you telling me this?'

'Ich thought du might like to be kept in ze loop.'

The Griffin was right. I did want to be kept in 'ze loop'.

'Why did you spare me my life by Letchworth Lake?'

'Because, Alan, ich enjoy playing kat und mouse mit du.'

'But you knew I was set to retire that day, regardless of the outcome of my efforts to bring you to justice.'

'Pah,' he replied. 'Zare ist no such sing as retirement, Herr Stoob.'

'Of course there is.'

'Says who – your vife?'

'How dare y—'

'If du vant to live your life according to ze vishes of a mere *voman* zen of course your days as Britain's Premier Nazi Hunter are truly over. Ich merely vanted to tell du ich miss du.'

He hung up.

I badly needed a pee.

Two hours later Edame reappeared. She did her best to remain civil but the hostility remained. I thanked her for the tea, the pills and the empty bottle of Shiraz to wee in. Later I noticed a little red halo on Little Alan's head.

'I know this probably isn't the best time to say this as I'm laid up and you're being really kind to me,' I told her, 'but what would you say if I told you I refused to retire?'

She stood there and broke into a smile.

'It's very simple, darling,' she replied. 'I would wish you all the very best in your futures and you would never see me again.'

'Just wondered,' I said.

She drew the curtains and closed the door.

'Goodnight,' she said from the hallway. It was 5pm.

*   *   *

Woke up in agony. Or at least I thought I did. Turned out I dreamt I awoke in agony. When I woke up for real ten minutes later I was also in agony. Two hours spent trying to reach the remote control last night can't have helped.

Edame has played nurse perfectly adequately these past few days but there was little warmth in her manner. Painkillers were forced into my mouth, water sloshed in the general direction of my face. I contented myself with the notion she would probably fit right into the NHS. She was still cross.

After a lunch of Jewish soup I asked Edame to sit with me.

'I'm so sorry,' I told her. 'About the back thing and the asking-to-still-hunt-Nazis thing. I'm taking some time to readjust to my new life, that's all.'

'I know, Als,' she said. 'But I'm sure you can also see it from my points of hugh. It's like I'm not getting any of the good times after putting up with the Nazi times, you know?'

'I do. Listen, I'm bound to be laid up for a few more days. Why don't we get Tina and the gang round for dinner? Lighten things up a bit.'

'And I suppose you expect me to cook, do you, mister?' she said, punching my arm hard enough to know she meant it.

'Actually I thought I would shout us a takeaway,' I said. 'How about the Dutch place called The Dutch Place?'

'Sorry, but I don't rate their stroopwafels. Let's go Indian.'

'I'll call Tina.'

I dozed for most of the afternoon whilst doing my best to hold in a motion. I figured another day or so and I'd be able to get to the bathroom myself. There seemed no need to submit either of us to that particular indignity.

I also had a plan for the evening.

Tina and Marco arrived around seven, Haden and Houdini in tow. Everyone gathered around me on the sofa. As ever I appreciated the attention.

'I want a fahl,' said Houdini.

'You don't want a fucking fahl,' replied Tina. 'It'll be so fucking hot you'll commit suicide.'

'Tina!' said Edame.

'Can I have a bottle of Kingfisher?' asked Haden.

'I donna see-ah why-ah not,' said Marco. 'Might help-ah to bulk-ah you up a beet.'

'Mutton vindaloo and a garlic nan for me,' I said. 'Anyone mind if I put on the telly?'

Houdini made it her duty to seek out the remote control. She definitely had the hunter in her. Her biceps were beginning to show through her cardigan.

'Good lord,' I said, feigning surprise. 'It's the inauguration of Britain's brand new Premier Nazi Hunter, Herb Derb, live this very second on BBC2.'

Edame gave me The Look.

'Grandma, PLEASE can we watch this?' said Haden.

'Yeah, Grandma, PLEASE can we watch this?' said Houdini.

'OK,' said Edame reluctantly, 'but it goes off the jiffies our food arrives.'

The ceremony was a far more lavish affair than the one I'd been sworn into back in 1997. I never had the likes of Rachel Riley from *Countdown* pinning the upside down thumb on *my* lapel. Robert Robinson did his best all those years ago but it was hardly a photogenic moment. Today's commentary by David Dimbleby seemed unnecessarily genuflectuary. Maybe I was just bitter.

'Thank you, all of you,' said Derb. He had a new suit and a sun-bed tan. 'To be honoured as Britain's Premier Nazi Hunter is to tread the footsteps of some great men, from Eric Thumble in the fifties and Christopher True in the seventies, right through to totemic figures such as Norman Chillyboy, Garold Hermaine and . . .'

Go on. . .

'. . . of course . . .'

Yes?

'. . . Kenneth Horsepen.'

Bastard.

'I shall of course bring my own style to the role,' he continued. 'That is imperative. Not that I shall be purposefully distancing myself from certain previous regimes – but put it this way, I doubt you'll be seeing my willy any time soon!'

Uproarious laughter.

'Herb's a Herbert,' said Haden.

'He's stupid and a dum-dum,' said Houdini.

'If,' he continues, 'I ever have what could best be described as a "Whipsnade Moment" you have permission to shoot me in the street!'

'Sod him, Dad,' said Tom, getting up. 'He's a lightweight candidate. He's the last person to have Britain's Nazis quaking in their boots.'

'That's what I'm afraid of, son,' I replied.

My mutton was chewier than usual. Edame generously donated a third of her chicken tikka. Haden got drunk. Houdini made short shrift of her fahl.

'So, Al, we was all-ah thinking about-ah going away,' said Marco. He was sporting a new black eye, this time on the other side.

'Long weekend on a barge,' said Tina.

'In Norfolk,' chimed Edame.

'I can see I've been set up,' I said. 'When though? My back is completely fu—ruined.'

'Three days' time,' said Edame. 'Nurofen and Cabernet will getting you through.'

'Do I have a choice?'

'Come, Granddad!' said Houdini. 'We can make jokes about Derb the Herb.'

That night Edame made up a bed on the floor next to me in the lounge. We held hands until she fell asleep around midnight. I remained awake, a mixture of neuralgia and indigestion. As I was looking up Norfolk weather on teletext a message appeared on my phone.

WHO'S THE DADDY NOW?

I did not recognise the number so I rang it, ensuring to insert the prefix 141 so as to come up withheld. It went straight through to voicemail.

'You've reached the voicemail of Herb Derb, Britain's Premier Nazi Hunter. Please leave a message after the tone or I'll hunt you down . . .'

August

At 9am a horn sounds. Edame and I look up from our Coco Pops to see Tina, Tony, Haden and Houdini outside in the car. Houdini is sporting a big floppy Spanish hat; Haden has shaved his head; Tina is wearing a beautiful white sundress; Marco an especially tight-looking t-shirt.

'Granddad!' shrieks Houdini. 'We're going on our lolidays!'

'You nearly-ah ready, old-ah man?' says Marco.

'Not exactly,' I tell him. 'I'm seventy-five and have the most terrible bad back. We'll follow on in half an hour.'

'Nonsense!' he says. 'We drive in-ah the convey, uh?'

Midway through our packing Tom enters the bedroom.

'Not sure I'm going to come,' he says. 'I just tweeted Carol Decker from T'Pau and I don't want to miss her response.'

'Don't be the silly billies!' says Edame. 'You'll only spend the time here mooning away over that Susan.'

'I don't want to talk about Susan,' he replies, somewhat surprisingly.

'They're bound to have 3G,' I tell him. '3G is like oxygen, it's everywhere. Come, son. We want you there.'

We set off. Edame rests her right hand on my left thigh throughout the journey – except when I ask her to change gear.

'This is real power,' she says, sliding from third to fourth near Royston, the place where she lost my virginity.

At a roundabout near Stokesby my phone rings. The number

is withheld. There is a gap in the traffic but I pause, considering whether to answer.

With an almighty thud we are thrust forward, shunted from a standing start by a huge force at the rear. Marco has driven into the back of the Stoobmobile, inflicting mild whiplash on Edame and fixing my back.

'Old man, did-ah you not-ah see-ah the gap in-ah the traffic?' he asks, clutching his groin, which has apparently collided with the steering wheel.

'You like a bit of rear-ending, don't you, Dad?' says Haden.

I apologise profusely. Both cars are driveable. We agree to split any excess and limp to our boat mooring at Ludham by mid-afternoon. The narrow boat – named *Infidelity* – didn't look especially narrow to me.

We chose our rooms, cast ourselves off from the mooring, handed round individual cans of gin and tonic for the adults and Coke for the kids, and pushed ourselves clear of the siding. I offered to take the helm for the first hour. This gave me the chance to listen to my voicemail.

Guten tag, Herr Stoob, ziss ist Ze Griffin spreching. Ich hope du ist nicht habing ein gut holiday! How do ich know du are on holiday? Ich see everyzing, Herr Stoob.

Anyvay ich vanted to give du ein sneak preview of vot du can expect to see over ze coming veeks.

Soon, und vithout varning, ze policies of ziss government vill begin to lurch to ze right. At first ziss vill be subtle, but gradually und over time vill become more obvious until it ist quite clear zare ist ein Nazi government in place. How ve pull off ze crime von ze century ist very much mein secret. Und ich do liebe ein gut secret, Herr Stoob.

Just thought ich vood keep du abreast. Du bist mein favourite adversary; ve are like Carl Hanratty und Frank Abagnale in ze

Hollyvood blockbusten Catch Me If Du Can. *Love to Edame. Tschuss.*

As I listened again to the message I ploughed straight through a paddling of ducks. Haden emerged from the cabin, his jeans at a disconcertingly low ebb.

'What are the others up to?' I asked.

'Not much,' he said, gargling a G&T. He must have swapped it for a Coke.

'I need to tell you something and you must swear not to repeat it.'

'It's in the vault, Gramps.'

'The Griffin has left me a voicemail saying he is planning to replace the current government with a Nazi one.'

'How's he going to do that?'

'No idea,' I told him. 'All I know is this is his plan and I have little reason to disbelieve him.'

'Shit the bed, Gramps.'

'Exactly.'

I pulled up Nigel on speed dial, but something stopped me. Whether it was ego, pride, lack of trust or concern over my daytime tariff I couldn't say. All I knew was for now I preferred to keep the information to myself.

'If Grandma really will leave you if you start hunting Nazis again,' said Haden, 'perhaps the best thing is to do it on the downlow.'

He tapped the side of his nose and returned to the bowels of the boat.

Hunt Nazis on the quiet? Talk about a high-risk strategy.

Edame appeared clutching two mini bottles of Sancerre and a grab-bag of pork scratchings. She never used to eat pork scratchings when I hunted Nazis.

'You OK, love?' she said. 'You look deep in the thoughts.'

'Fine thanks,' I said and wrapped my arms around her. How could I hide anything from this woman? She would never do anything to hurt me.

And then I remembered: the late Henry Cooper.

Edame hummed the theme from *Randall and Hopkirk (Deceased)* all night in her sleep. Barely caught a wink.

At breakfast Haden accuses his dad of having camp wrists.

'Better a camp wrist than a camp commandant,' says Houdini. Silence ensues.

A plan is hatched for a pub lunch at the Three Bells up the water in Farthing. Tom takes the helm for most of the morning while lamenting the lack of 3G. I sit on deck with Edame, enjoying the sun, thinking and dozing. Three hours later we docked and locked up the boat. I told everyone to go on, that I'd join them shortly.

I was tricking myself into justifying my next move. The memory of Cooper was the only way I could convince myself to go behind Edame's back. I removed my phone and dialled.

'You've reached Interpol. If you think you've spotted Lord Lucan press one . . .'

I hit five.

'Steve, it's Alan.'

There was a long silence.

'I can't talk to you, Alan,' came the eventual reply.

'Why not?'

'Just can't.'

'But WHY?'

Another pause.

'Edame told me not to.'

'She did WHAT?'

Yet another pause. The longest so far.

'She was worried you'd try and start up operations again,' he said. 'She told me to blank you if you ever called.'

'I don't care what Edame told you to do or not do,' I said. 'There's something I need. It's small but I expect you to give it to me. We go back, Steve.'

Another pause. This call was costing me a fortune.

'Sorry, Alan. I just can't.'

'Ah well, that's a shame,' I said. 'How is Susie by the way? It's ages since I last saw her. Perhaps we could go out as a foursome, now that I have more time on my elderly, quivering hands. By the way, did you ever tell her about your affair with Hot Pattie? Perhaps you didn't. Of course she doesn't need to know about that. It would ruin her. I'll have to remember not to send her an anonymous postcard on the matter.'

This time the pause lasted 40 seconds. I know because I timed it.

'What do you want, Alan?'

'A phone number.'

'Whose?'

'The Griffin's.'

'That's not going to be easy.'

'I'll be patient.'

'Well, I . . .'

'Just find it.'

I hung up and joined the others.

We passed a jovial afternoon. Haden got drunk on Guinness after I told him that's what Bryan Robson drank at West Bromwich Albion to build himself up. Marco disappeared for an hour. We all ordered scampi save for Houdini, who entertained us by eating whole chillis. Tom went outside intermittently in the vain quest for 3G. Everyone was having such a good time we remained in our seats and ordered the same meals for dinner.

Yet despite the revelry I felt detached. I harboured a guilty secret. What's worse, I felt excited about it, almost sexually, which in turn intensified both the guilt and the excitement. I was drunk on my clandestine inner world, and two-and-a-half pints of Scrumpy.

'You've not been with us today, Alan,' said Edame as we finally left the pub. I felt myself flush.

'I'm tired,' I replied. 'Must be finally winding down after 18 years as Britain's Premier Nazi Hunter!'

My boisterous bonhomie wasn't washing. She stared back at me, narrowing her eyes until it was barely conceivable she could see.

'As longs as that's all it is, Alan . . .'

All the adults helped put a tiddly Haden to bed. He muttered something about The Griffin so I turned him over and asked Edame to fetch a bucket.

As the night grew dark I sat on deck with a small port and checked my phone. Nothing back from Steve at Interpol, just a mocking text from Herb Derb who'd obviously seen the Diana Dors images on my commandeered desktop. I didn't feel good about what I was doing. What was more, I could feel a cold coming on. A guilty conscience weakens the immune system.

*   *   *

I awoke at 5.30am to find Edame sitting upright in bed. Her arms were folded.

'You just mumble something about waiting for The Griffin's telephone numbers,' she said, staring straight ahead. 'If I find out that's what you are up to Alan I'll leave you quicker than you can say "anschluss".'

'It was a dream!' I told her. 'None of us are responsible for what happens in our dreams.'

'You also said something about taking me up the precinct.'

'See – it's all a nonsense.'

'I'm watching you, Alan – like I was a Nazi.'

I shook with nerves during my strip wash.

After breakfast it was time for the family ramble. Haden looked terrible and was sick at the base of the first tree we passed. Tom lurked at the back of the group, fiddling with his phone, his mouth sad. Houdini made a walking stick from a branch and stuck it in every cowpat we passed.

The countryside looked stunning as we crossed the fields. I kept my distance from Edame and walked with Marco. He talked a little about his childhood in Italy and the shadow of Mussolini. I was about to ask him about the country's fascist legacy and his interest in men when my phone beeped. I apologised and dropped back from the group.

Here's your number: 01462 303 639. Please don't tell Susie. Steve.

We returned to the boat around two. Edame and I went to our quarters and lay down. I felt tired but fought it. I could sense Edame fighting it too. She was clearly suspicious – but within ten minutes she was asleep, eased into oblivion by the rise and fall of the boat and by my gentle massage of her earlobes.

I slipped carefully out of the room and made my way up onto deck. The clouds hung low overhead. Rain was threatening. I dialled up the number, cupping my hand over the phone.

'Flitwick 639?'

'Greetings, Griffin,' I say.

Handel's Messiah was playing in the background.

'Who ist ziss?' the voice replied.

'Stoob,' I said. 'Hunter of Nazis.'

'How did du get ziss number?'

'Ve haff vays,' I told him.

There was a short pause, during which I heard a needle dragged across a gramophone record. The music ceased.

'Vot do du vant?'

'To meet,' I reply.

'Ich thought du vere retired?'

'Let's call it a comeback.'

'Comeback?'

'OK, more like friends reunited.'

'Herr Stoob, ich alvays haf time fur du – but vot is it du vant to see me about? Forgive mein uncertainty but vot vith me being Bedfordshire's Premier Nazi und do being ein retired hunter ich thought it only proper to check.'

'It's a bit embarrassing really,' I said. 'Basically my therapist says I need to make peace with the man responsible for my naked humiliation on national television.'

'Und by zat ich suppose du mean me.'

'It would mean a lot, Griffin.'

'Ferry vell, Herr Stoob. Since it's du.'

A pause.

'Herr Stoob, vye are du talking so quietly?'

'I'm not.'

'Edame doesn't know about ziss, does she? Oh ziss ist marvellous! She vood have your guts fur garters if she knew du vere meeting ein Nazi. Vot a naughty Stoob!'

'When and where, Griffin?' I said, pointedly.

'Ziss veek ist quite gut.'

'Tomorrow lunchtime?'

'Zame place?'

'Perfect.'

'See du zen.'

'Have a nice day, Griffin.'

'Thanks, Herr Stoob,' he said. 'Oh, und Herr Stoob? Ich spared your life vunce. If du try anything ziss time ich shall haf no alternative but to dispense mit du in ein gruesome fashion. Auf.'

'Terrible news,' I announce over dinner.

Summoning all my youthful acting skills that at their peak saw me shine as Samuel Pepys at the Dunstable Youth Theatre, I tell them a sorry story: Bob from next door called, I say. He was in a terrible state. He thought I was Gladys, his late wife who died after choking on a cat's tail back in 1987. I'm worried he'll get so confused he'll eat himself, I say, or think he's a leg of lamb and climb into the freezer. He has no one else, I tell them. It is my duty to return and check up on him.

Houdini sidled over and held my hand, looking up at me with sad eyes, French mustard all over her face.

'Does this mean you're going home, Granddad?'

I looked down at her tiny face. Her bottom lip was quivering.

'I'm sorry,' I said. 'You know I'd stay if I could. But it's Bob from across the road. He doesn't have a mummy and a daddy like you and he's all alone. Plus he's got early onset dementia. You wouldn't want him to be sad would you, sweetheart?'

'I wouldn't want anyone to be sad, Granddad,' she said, hugging my leg. 'Especially you.'

Tricking little kids now, is it, Alan? Admirable behaviour.

'I'm coming with you, Dad,' said Tom. 'I can't get 3G for love nor money out here.'

Edame stared at me for what felt like an everlasting moment before asking who was for pudding and clearing the plates.

I spent the rest of the evening teaching Haden and Houdini how to play Nazi Yahtzee. Edame's eyes remained on me throughout. She hardly spoke. She just stared.

'Shall we turn in, my love?' I said, around ten.

'I'll be in later,' she replied coldly.

I sat up in bed reading *The Hitler Diaries*. Despite being proven a fake they remain a rollicking good read, but I was struggling to concentrate. When I looked up Edame was stood in the doorway. I had no idea how long she had been there. She was backlit by the moon, her hair wild from the breeze, her nostrils flared. Still facing me she closed the doors behind her.

'You're hiding some of the things from me, you, you klootzak!' she said, hovering menacingly at the foot of the bed. 'Tell me what it is!'

'I'm not!' I cried, feebly.

'Nonsense!' she replied. 'Tina lent me a book on neuro-linguine programming. It's about reading people's body languages, Alan. Your mouth is saying one things but your body another.'

'Thanks very much!' I said jokily, but the confidence was draining from me.

'Which is it – Meaden or Nazis?' she demanded.

'Bloody hell, Eds, I'm too old for either these days.'

'What's all this bloody bollock about Bob? He's been like that for year. Why should it make any difference today?'

'Bob is like the brother I never had,' I tell her, hoping to elicit sympathy from my only-child status. 'When Bob's sad, I'm sad. When he's down, I'm down. When he thinks his best friend is actually his wife, it's my duty to visit him. My heart tells me it's the right thing to do.'

Edame stared at me again, checking my face for a weak spot.

'Yes, well,' she replied. 'Sort your bloody body languages out. It's all over the place like a kipper.'

We read together in bed. Edame starts with her NLP manual but quickly moves onto *Woman's Own*. Lights out at 11.

I am woken in the pitch black. I light up the screen on my Casio A164WA-1Q classic digital watch. It's 3.15am.

'Alan? Are you awaking?' whispers Edame.

'Yes, my dearest,' I tell her. She takes my hand.

'We've been through so much. I don't think I could take another sock.'

* * *

Dreamt Edame cut off my testicles and fed them to genetically modified dogs. I am clearly not cut out for this subterfuge but I cannot stop now. I have to see it through, starting with my lunch appointment with The Griffin.

Edame, Tina, Marco, Haden and Houdini come to wave us off.

'Do send our love to Bob,' says Tina. 'Hope he's OK.'

'I'm sure he'll be fine,' I say. 'Just needs a familiar face to snap him back into reality.'

'Good luck, Alan,' says a rather formal Haden while sipping a protein shake.

'Drive careful,' says Edame, blowing me a kiss through the window. I make to catch and eat it. I am a fraud.

Despite its recent shunt the Omega ran fine, chugging us smoothly along the M11 past Duxford. Tom played with the radio. His face looked sad.

'Nearly home,' I tell him. 'Then you can go online.'

'I was supposed to speak to someone yesterday. Because of the poor connection not only did I miss them, I couldn't even tell them I was out of range.'

'Who was this person?' I asked.

Tom stared out at the fields.

'Now they'll think I don't care.'

Back home Tom went straight upstairs and shut his bedroom door. I changed out of my shellsuit and into smart-casual attire suitable for a pub-grub luncheon. Things were moving fast; I hardly had time to get nervous. I picked up my blue inhaler. I also remembered the small high-tech item that would act as a centrepiece for the meeting.

As I was leaving, Tom appeared on the landing.

'Why are you dressed so smartly – I thought you were going to visit Bob?'

'When Bob is in a state it's best to visit him in clothes he associates with the past,' I replied, thinking on my bunioned feet.

'OK. Send him my best.'

So as not to arouse suspicion I decide to visit Bob quickly before my rendezvous with The Griffin.

Bob opens the door in a Hawaiian skirt and offers me a cup of tea, leading me through to the sitting room. When he returns, instead of tea he presents me with a brick wrapped up in a flannel. He himself has a block of butter, which he eats out of a bowl.

I look at Bob with his butter meal and feel great

compassion. I also saw that here was my one chance to unburden myself. With so much guilt locked inside I knew I couldn't hold on for much longer without something seeping out. My conscience was close to erupting.

'Bob,' I said. 'I wish I didn't have to have this conversation with you but it's come to that. I'm afraid I've used you as a front for returning early from our holiday. I hope somewhere in that addled brain of yours you can find a way to forgive me. I know that you of all people understand how important gainful employment is. It was your position on the board at ICI that kept you going for so many years after Gladys suffocated on a cat's tail. What Edame doesn't understand is that if I leave things the way they are Nazi-wise I will never know whether I could have stopped The Griffin. He is threatening the very fabric of society via a mysterious plot to replace the current government with a fascist regime. So I apologise to you and I apologise to Edame, whom I have not been able to explain this to. She wants a holiday in the Caribbean. I on the other hand wish to fulfil my destiny and save the world. I'm not saying that one is a more honourable intention than the other. OK, I am really. I just wish she could understand that I am the only one who can save us. That's not ego, that's a fact. Thanks for listening, Bob. I hope that somewhere deep down you can hear me.'

Bob looked back at me blankly then placed his bowl of butter on the table. His right hand began to tremble; at first gently like an alcoholic who'd missed a round, then more vigorously like a tulip in a cross wind. Soon his whole upper body was shaking. He was trying to speak, dry mouthing his words, but no sound came. Then a breakthrough: animal-like noises, a cuckoo, a hen, a horse. Then silence.

'Let's get this out of the way,' he said suddenly, clear as day. 'You need to be very careful, Alan. I understand how important your work is but you seem to have forgotten what you've put Edame through. Day after day she would come round here when Gladys was still alive and cry her eyes out, worried about your whereabouts and asking how much danger we thought you were in on a scale of one to ten. We all know she erred with the late Henry Cooper but you didn't have to punish her with Meaden. You of all people should know that an eye for an eye is no way to right a wrong, Alan. You've both done your time. I strongly advise you to leave things as they are. Let The Griffin do what he's doing. Interpol will see to him, or the British Nazi Hunting Association. Take Edame away. Give Tom some attention. Knock the hunting on the head. You're seventy-five for fuck's sake.'

I sat there, mouth agape. I hadn't heard so many sentient thoughts from Bob since . . . well, ever.

He began shaking again, hard and fast at first, before slowing down to a gentle rhythm, a tremulous hand, then nothing.

'Gladys?' he said. 'Is that really you?'

I placed Bob's favourite checked rug over his legs and turned down the Sex Pistols, which had been playing in the background. I took the bowl of butter into the kitchen. When I returned he was out cold, respiring like a hog.

I realised I'd forgotten my spare inhaler so I returned to the house. The hall was filled with an unusual sound, not one our walls had heard for over twenty-five years. A strange sound, a happy sound. It was the sound of Tom laughing. Not just laughing either: chuckling his fortysomething teenage head off.

I crept upstairs and found his bedroom door wide open. I

stood to the side and listened. He was talking to someone, though I couldn't hear their side of the conversation. My heart filled with joy.

I took a peek round the door. Tom's face was lit up by the laptop screen. He was smiling broadly.

He saw me.

'FUCK'S SAKE, DAD!' he shouted. 'CAN'T ANYONE GET ANY PRIVACY ROUND HERE!' He rose, headphones attached to the laptop, and headed towards me. As he reached the door his earphones detached from the computer. I heard a woman's voice. Then the door slammed in my face.

I looked at my watch. I was late for The Griffin.

I reversed out of the driveway, scattering tiny pebbles. The chaffinches in Bob's willow took flight. The wheels of the Stoobmobile spun. Harold at number thirty gave me a withering look before continuing his watering. Wasn't there a hosepipe ban on?

I was hurtling towards one of the most evil minds of the twentieth and twenty-first centuries yet I felt little fear, more an exhilaration. Edame was away; the BNHA and Interpol knew nothing of my movements, nor Beryl for that matter. I felt a rush of freedom. I located Classic FM on the dial and hummed aggressively along to Greensleeves.

At the pub I handbrake-turned my way into a small space, inciting curious stares from The Griffin's henchmen who were once more assembled outside, puffing away. Henchmen-sorts must all die young, I thought to myself as I central-locked the car behind me and hurried to the entrance. One of them spoke into his sleeve.

I burst into the pub, the double-doors swinging shut behind me. The patrons stopped to stare. One-third must have been German. A man of six foot eight with a shock of blond hair pointed me in the direction of The Griffin. I hastened over. There he was, same chair, same clothes, same newspaper, different headline. The aura of menace remained unmistakable.

'Du sink it ist politik, Herr Stoob,' he said, 'to keep ein evil mastermeind such as meinself, somevun vith ein history von sickening crimes against humanity, vaiting in such ein fashion?'

'Sorry I'm late, Griff,' I replied. 'Traffic was a bitch.'

Slowly he lifted his head from the newspaper and set his eyes on me. He stared for a count of ten before speaking.

'Ich pardon du, Herr Stoob,' he said, extending his hand. I stared as it gently oscillated, the liver spots a-blur.

'I am grateful to you for not finishing me off,' I said, 'but I cannot condone a fascist regime, albeit one whose best days are long passed. Ergo, I cannot shake your hand.'

'Du snub ze Griffin?' he said, withdrawing his hand and cracking his knuckles.

'To spare my life you had to be in a position to kill me in the first place. Which means you're not a very nice person.'

'Du have hurt my feelings, Herr Stoob,' he said. 'Not zat du are correct about our regime being past its best. Vot ve have planned for ze coming veeks vill rock ziss country to its very foundations. And ich do nicht use ze verd "foundations" lightlich.'

The Griffin snapped his fingers. A waiter scuttled over.

'Zwei visky,' he said. The waiter ran back to the bar, banging his knee when he got there. The Griffin looked at me. I looked at him. Then he looked at me again.

'It eez a little, shall vee say, awkvard, is it nicht, zat your wife does nicht know about our kleine meeting?'

'She knows all right,' I said. 'I told her.' I could feel the red seeping into my cheeks. The Griffin laughed hard, a speck of spittle coming to rest on my nose.

'Clearly ich have du . . . vot ist ze English phrase . . . over ein barrel.'

'I thought you were a man of honour.'

'Oh, ich am,' he replied. 'Ein hunderdt percent. I'd just hate to see du unhappy.'

'I'm not here to discuss my wife, Griffin. I want to know more about your plan.'

The Griffin smiled.

'So du are nicht here to make peace vith your past after alles, Herr Stoob.'

'I would never make peace with a low-life Nazi scuzzbucket like yourself,' I said. 'Tell me the plan.'

'Vunce ein hunter, alvays ein hunter!' He placed his hands behind his head and pushed himself backwards on his chair, further and further, until his spine cracked with a sickening snap, like gunfire.

'Vell Stoob, it ist like ziss,' he said, pausing for effect. 'None of dein business!'

I felt in my pocket. The device was still there.

'Damn you, Griffin,' I said. 'If you don't tell me, how can I alert Herb Derb and the British government of your evil intentions?'

'If du thought ich vas simply going to unveil our plans to du,' he replied, 'zen perhaps du really did retire at ze right time. Zay say Ronald von Reagan voz senile for ze last two yahrs of his presidency. Ich believe ze test fur ze Alzheimers is very straightforward. Ich can put du in touch mit ein top specialist if du like.'

Gently I began working my fingernail, which I had filed to a point, at the material, fashioning a tiny hole in the right pocket of my tan slacks.

'I hoped I could trick you,' I said.

'Trick me?' he responded. 'Ha! Du are funny, Stoob. Du should go on ze stage. Tell me, do du have any pictures of ze lovely Edame? Perhaps ich vill arrange for vun of mein people to take some shots . . .'

Finally the hole was big enough.

'Leave my wife out of this, Griff,' I uttered defiantly. 'I insist you tell me what's going on.'

'Ist ziss vot ist known as English fair play?' he said. 'It ist ein nonsense. Since du haf clearly come here to waste mein time, Herr Stoob, ich shall haf to be on mein way. Unless du fancy another naked trip along ze pathway, ziss time culminating in certain death?'

The Griffin rose ponderously from his seat. As he did I forced the device through the hole in my pocket. I felt its coldness brush the side of my thigh as it slipped down the inside of my trouser, glanced off the rim of my shoe and lay motionless on the floor, its sharp pin pointing skyward.

'Are du nicht going to rise and greet me like ein gentlemensch?' he said.

I stood. The Griffin tottered towards me. I glanced down and saw that on his current path he would miss the small metallic tablet by a few inches. I moved slightly to the right and stuck out a hand. Almost imperceptibly he changed direction. His foot covered the device.

'Ich wish du ein swift recovery from your very obvious dementia, though zat ist most unlikely.'

I shook his hand. It felt like paper. He moved past me, his shoulder brushing mine.

When I looked down the device was gone.

The waiter arrived with two whiskies. I drained one of them and removed a pair of earphones from my pocket, plugging them into my Nokia 3310. I located the app entitled Kinsey Shoe Bug. The sound cut in and out; a rhythmic crunching, the slamming of a car door, an engine starting.

I sipped the second whisky. 'Won't be long now,' I said to myself.

A fuzzing. The sound of a precision-engineered car almost imperceptibly changing gear. Then they began.

'Stoob voz such ein idiot!' said an unmistakable voice in my ear: The Griffin. 'Ich cannot believe he thought ich vood spill ze beans about our monumental plan!'

'Ja!' said another voice. 'As if ve vood tell him about our top secret scheme just because he vants to hear it!'

'Be careful,' said a third, more considered voice. 'Herr Stoob is cleverer than du think. He may appear to have fallen into senility but that could have been ein act. Ve must all remain vigilant until the deed is done. Ja?'

A chorus of 'ja's' followed.

I'd done it. I'd managed singlehandedly to establish a line into the highest echelons of Bedfordshire Nazism. I felt so pleased with myself I downed the second whisky. It was then I realised I was now over the limit, so remained seated at my table for a further forty-five minutes before exiting the hostelry. I drove home smiling, one ear plugged into the Third Reich.

I parked in front of the garage and let myself in. Edame was standing in the hall, headscarf wrapped around her face.

'You look pleasing with yourself,' she said, removing her overcoat.

'I didn't expect you back until tomorrow,' I said, the shock and guilt no doubt imprinted on my features.

'You don't seem happy to see me, Alan.'

'Of course I am,' I say. 'Just surprised.'

'How is Bob?'

'Not so good,' I told her. 'But I think my presence helped a little.'

'What's with the headphones?'

'Debussy,' I say. 'I've really been getting into Debussy.'

Edame stared at me before tilting her head, exposing her lovely pink neck.

'Well, aren't you going to give your wife-wife a kiss-kiss?'

It seemed Marco had gone looking for rough trade soon after I'd left, only to get beaten up in a nearby wood and have his wallet stolen. On his return he had tearfully confessed to enjoying the company of both men and women.

'As you can imagine that set the cat among the people so we called it a day,' said Edame.

'I hope Haden is OK,' I said. 'I'll give him a call later.'

'Good idea,' she said. 'Nap?'

I carried Edame's suitcase upstairs and removed my shoes, trousers and cardigan. She followed, taking off her high heels, skirt and navy blue pullover. Her stockinged legs looked admirable. Summer warmth poured in through the bedroom window. No need to get under the covers.

Edame lay next to me, her head resting on my shoulder. I pinched my thigh in an effort to stay awake. After a couple of minutes she fell asleep. I gently wriggled down the bed and, using my feet, lifted my trousers from the footstool. My hip cracked like a whip but Edame did not stir. I fished in the pocket for my phone and hooked myself up to the audio, listening with my left ear which was hidden from view from Edame, who remained to my right.

The Nazis were watching German football. I have always admired the pure efficiency of the Bundesliga. It has often surprised me that more English players do not sample the strict pleasures of the Germanic first division. Kevin Keegan did it all at Hamburg but that was thirty years ago.

Suddenly I came to. I had dozed off. Edame was not in the room. I threw on my trousers and dashed downstairs. I found her in the sitting room, on the phone. She saw me, whispered something into the receiver and hung up.

'Who was that?' I asked, feigning a casual air.

'No one,' she replied. 'Which movement by Debussy moved you, Alan?'

'All of them really,' I said. 'Especially the third movement – the one they use in the Yakult advert.'

'Very moving that movement,' she said, smiling. She rose and walked towards me. She kissed me once on the cheek. I remain rooted to the spot.

'Glass of wine?' she said from the kitchen.

'Please!' I shouted and followed her in, puppy-like.

Edame prepared my favourite dinner: toad-in-the-hole Dutch style, complete with broccoli and a garnish of plain crisps. Normally I only get this at the anniversary of D-Day. Pudding was Baked Alaska and waffles. We opened a second bottle of wine, something of a rarity these days.

After dinner I called Haden. He sounded confused about his father's behaviour and was worried it meant he had what he called the 'bummer gene'. I told him this was unlikely and that 'bummer' was not acceptable talk for a Stoob.

'I met with The Griffin,' I said quietly.

'How exciting, Alan!'

In the last few days he had taken to calling me Alan.

'What did he say?'

'Not much,' I told him. 'He didn't need to. I've bugged him. Now I can work out what his plans are vis-à-vis over-throwing the coalition government.'

'That's great, Alan. Can I be involved?'

'Too dangerous,' I said, 'but I'll keep you in the loop. The most important thing is not to tell Grandma.'

'I'm not an idiot, Alan.'

Edame insisted we watch the first three episodes of *Bergerac* ever made. I was surprised at this as we'd seen them only a few months previously but my guilty state made me acquiesce.

During the first episode Edame held my hand, by the second her head was against my shoulder and by the third – the classic where Charlie Hungerford, played by the peerless Terence Alexander, loses his cigar down a well – she was holding me round the midriff and barely looking at the screen.

Upstairs she watched as I brushed my teeth. In bed she cuddled up from behind, her arms wrapped round my chest. The wine takes hold and I fall asleep quickly.

At 2am I am woken by the sound of crying.

'What is it, my love?' I ask.

'I want you to know that you are the love of my lives, always have been and always will be. Forget Henry Cooper. Forget Potato George. Forget Geoffrey Moore,' she said, sobbing into my chest.

'Who is Geoffrey Moore?' I ask.

'You have made me so happy and super over the years,' she continued. 'I need you to know how I feel about you. I need you to hear such things now.'

'My love, I feel precisely the same as you,' I tell her. 'I am nothing without you. You mean the universe to me. You are everything.'

'Please don't say these words, Alan,' she said and sobbed harder, the intensity unnerving me.

'These are good things to say, are they not?'

'Yes and no,' she replied.

We lay there in silence, her head on my chest. After ten minutes the numbness in my right arm required adjustment.

'I don't want this moments to end,' she said, but her voice was drowsy.

'There's always tomorrow, and the next day and next week and next month and next year and if we're lucky next decade.'

'Goodnight,' she said. She kissed my lips, sucking hard on the bottom one. 'I love you so much.'

'And me you.'

'Hold my hand, Alan.'

I did and slowly we drifted off.

*   *   *

Even before I opened my eyes I knew Edame was gone. Perhaps it was the strange silence, the absence of warm breath on my neck, the lack of appetising aromas emanating from downstairs. Or perhaps it was a feeling, something about the night before. I felt a terror rush through me, though I couldn't be sure of anything yet.

I got up and sought out my dressing gown from the back of the door. Normally both our gowns hang there. Today there was only mine. My panic intensified. A strange sensation; I see myself from above.

I headed downstairs and, swallowing hard, entered the sitting room. I hoped to see Edame clad in her pink number sat in front of *Bergerac*, episode four. The room was empty.

The video box set was gone.

A voice in my head told me to avoid the kitchen. Kitchens are where personal letters in envelopes are left, propped up on kitchen tables. I headed back upstairs to the bedroom and opened Edame's wardrobe: it was bare. The suitcases under the bed: gone. The toiletries on the table remained, but the decorative porcelain hand where she kept her rings was ringless. I became aware of the silence in the house and began humming. Briefly I glimpse myself in an empty house, clutching a half-empty bottle of whisky, unshaved and wretched.

I can't put it off any longer and head for the kitchen. I flick on the kettle and avoid looking at the table. I make two cups of tea, one for Edame, though I know she's gone. I turn. There on the table is a letter with my name on it. I feel a death dread in my stomach. I open the letter.

My dearest Alan,

It with the heaviest of harts I write this.

Trusts between a couple are everything. Without trust they have not a thing. I broke that trust when I first felated and later made the love to late Henry Cooper. That was in 1965, the years you was fourth in the Milking Race. I know how much it hurt you. I was sorry then and I'm sorry now.

I had broken down our trust and I new that one of the days you would find a way to break my trust on the return journey. So when it came, with leading businesswoman

Deborah Meaden, it hurt like a hell but I expected it, even welcomed it. We were all the squares.

And that is how it remained throughout the years, right up until the last few days when you began acting strange like a weirdo.

I checked on an internet web site. de Bussy did not write music for a Yakult advert. That's a lie Alan. That made me think you were not being straight, like a bad ruler.

You thought I was a sleep yesterday afternoon but I wasn't. It was your mistake to doze away. I found you were listening in to Nazi chatter.

It broke my hart to hear those voices – not because of the content of the conversations all though that was quite strange – but because the last straw between us had been broken. Snapsville.

I call Steve at Interpol. Don't blame Steve – and don't blackmail him over him doing it with Hot Pattie. He told me you'd been after The Griffins number. You were hunting the Nazis again. You said you had re tired, but you had gone back on your words and gone back to work.

There are three people in this relationship Alan. You, me and the Nazis.

I never loved you more than during your times as Britain's Premier Nazi Hunter: the command you respected, the cups we printed together, our after-hunt drink ups. It's been a wonderful life but you lied to me like I was a Dutch idiot. You lied to your wife about why you had to come home early from holiday. You lied about listening to de Bussy. You lied into my face Alan.

Into my face.

No one lies into my face Alan.

The trust is broken. I'm too old (67) to have to deal with this. I'm worth more.

When I found out you were hunting the Nazis again I called Potato George. He's taking me in. When you read this I'll be inside his tastefully decorations house, my suitcases in the hall, sipping away on a cup of expensive tea. Later I imagine we may have some of the wine and watch a telly. Part of the deal is that I share George's bed. Tonight I suppose we shall make love. George is a man enough to pay for full Viagra prescription on the NHS. That's right Alan, George has got it going on.

You've put me in a position I never expected. I love you Alan but you betrayed me. I gave my hart and in return you gave me hell. That's what Tears for Fears say and they was right. I never thought it was possible to love another human being as much as I loved you Alan but it's over, finished on toast.

I have no idea what you are going to do. Perhaps you will go on fighting the Nazis until your dead. I hope that is sustaining you. Or perhaps as you age your abilities will egg and you will be hunted down and murdered to death. I truly hope that is not the case.

Please do not attempt to contact me.

I will continue to see our children and grandchildren but you mustn't come. If I get wind. That you are close by I shall disappear once more to George's home.

There is nothing more to say except I left my mobile in the drawer upstairs. Is better that way. It still has £7 on it, feel free to use it.

Incidentally I found this quote on line. It's by Nietzsche who I believe is a German. It's about you.

'He who fights with monsters should be careful lest he thereby become a monster. And if thou gaze long into an abyss, the abyss will also gaze into thee.'

See?

Take care,

Edame

Calmly I walk through to the sitting room, pick out the fullest bottle of whisky and lie down on the sofa.

S✡ptember

'I'm going to make us chicken soup, Dad.'

A voice. Tom's, I think.

My day is a haze of tears, alcohol and surfing the internet for images of 1950s Hollywood starlets.

'Please butter the bread on both sides,' I say vaguely. 'It's what mother does.'

Curtains opened. Curtains drawn. Hot cocoa.

'No doctor,' I say. 'It's my fault. Bring me the earpiece.'

Memories of my evacuation. The brown paper. The scullery. A beating for wetting the bed. The train home. Mummy and Daddy dead. Back we go. More loneliness than a child can bear.

'Herb Derb wants to know whether he can have your car.'

Sleep.

*　　*　　*

I am walking through a poppy field in high summer with Edame. The sky is clear, the day still. We are holding hands. Every now and then she breaks off to dance and twirl. But I look down. The poppies have transformed themselves into potatoes. Edame kneels and digs up a single spud. She brushes the mud from its surface and starts kissing it, at first gently then passionately, before sticking it up her skirt.

I wake in a cold sweat and call Tina. Tina comes over. She takes one look at me and calls Dr Grossmark. Dr Grossmark comes over. He takes one look at me and calls his wife, simply to insist she never leaves him.

Life is pain. I knew that the day I was put on a train bound for Yorkshire. I knew again the day I came home to discover the terrible truth, again during an unhappy childhood with an alien family, and then once more on that fateful afternoon when on the landing I happened upon my wife kissing the penis of the late Henry Cooper.

This is different. I am old, the wrong end of the see-saw. I feel a panic attack rise up from my belly. I try to breathe it down but it forces its way up. There's no coming back from this, not at seventy-five.

How could I ignore the signs? Even Bob told me what's what and he's got senile dementia. The writing was on the wall but I chose not to read it. Worst of all it's my doing. If I wasn't so hung up on the idea of being the big hero and saving the Western world from the curse of National Socialism none of this would have happened. I could have settled into retirement and made a reasonable living on the after-dinner circuit telling stories of how I singlehandedly tracked the Ampthill Mob down to a disused toffee factory just outside Shefford.

The reason for all this? Insecurity. Feeble, pathetic, childlike insecurity. On my own I am not enough. I am impelled to prove my worth by nailing Nazis. I couldn't let it lie.

Fuck Nazis. Fuck Nazi-hunting. And fuck Potato George.

Beryl agrees to an emergency patient visit. It costs me three times the usual tariff but I don't care. I let her in and she follows me back upstairs and perches on the end of the bed. Her voice is noticeably lower than normal and she is exhibiting stubble on her face. It appears that she has embarked upon the early stages of gender reorientation but she's big on boundaries so I don't ask.

She tells me every man destroys the thing he loves most. For once I agree with her. She also says the fact I've driven my wife away shows I am unable to maintain lasting human relationships and I should consider coming four times a week. I tell her I don't want to spend what is left of my life and money sitting on a couch moaning. She says she can do me a discount if I sign up until 2022. I say I'll think about it. As she leaves she calls me Ellen.

I check my phone hoping for some kind of message from Edame. Nothing. My frustration boils over and I kick the Corby Executive Trouser Press, sending it hurtling across the bedroom floor.

Tina enters.

'I'll stay tonight,' she says.

'You're so good to me,' I tell her, stroking her face.

'What are we going to do with you, eh Dad?' she says and goes downstairs to make dinner. I hear distant sobs.

*   *   *

I awake hugging Edame's pillow. Two weeks since her departure and her aroma still lingers on the fabric. It's enough to kill a man, but also I like it.

I rise and visit the bathroom but nothing comes, not a drop. My mind is elsewhere. I turn on the tap in an effort to open the floodgates but I get stuck staring back at myself in the mirror. The longer I look the older my face seems. Behind me I think I catch a glimpse of Potato George, laughing. I collapse onto the floor and bang my head against the radiator.

Tina rushes in and holds me until I stop shaking.

'Your mother,' I say suddenly. 'Have you heard from your mother?'

A pause.

'Yes.'

'What did she say?'

'That she's had enough and has moved in with PG.'

'What else did she say?'

'That you lied to her and she couldn't take anymore. Why would you do that, Dad?'

'Because I'm a selfish, emotionally immature old prannock.'

Tina helps me to my feet.

'Have you got her new phone number?'

She fiddles with the hem of her pyjamas.

'I'm not asking you to give them all to me,' I say. 'Just a few of the digits. I can try and guess the rest.'

'It's up to her, Dad,' she replies.

Tina goes to work but promises to call later. I stare at my phone. With Edame gone the way is clear for me to listen in to Bedfordshire's premier Nazis via the shoe bug, but I don't have the heart.

Dr Grossmark pops by again. He asks me to rate my mood (-5/10), takes my blood pressure (high) and asks what animal I feel like (a mortified gnat).

'I hate to say I told you so, so I won't,' he says.

'I've never felt this bleak,' I tell him.

'Well, I did tell you to knock the hunting on the head.'

'You said you weren't going to tell me so.'

'Oh yeah, sorry about that.'

'Without Edame there's no point.'

'Nonsense,' he replied. 'Your heart may be broken but the heart mends.'

'How long does it take?'

'Seven years.'

'I don't have seven years.'

'Crying helps,' he says. 'And a pet. I'll leave you some leaflets. Mrs Albumen recently passed, leaving a hamster called Drake. No next of kin. You could have Drake if you like. That little fella could really take you out of yourself.'

Worn out by Grossmark's visit I retreat from reality into sleep. When I wake it's five. At seven I rise and head downstairs in my pyjamas to make a cup of tea.

A knock at the door. I pull my dressing gown tight and twist the handle.

'I heard.'

A blonde cloaked figure stands in the doorway. It's Deborah Meaden.

I invite her in and offer her a drink. 'Eggnog,' she says. I sit motionless in Edame's chair, sniffing the cushion. Meaden necks her eggnog then joins me. She takes the glass from my hand and places it on the table. She grabs my right hand and thrusts it into her flowery dress and onto her right breast. It's just as I remember – warm and soft with a hint of nipple.

Meaden nibbles my ear. I feel powerless to stop it. Next she stands and lets her dress fall down to her ankles. She is wearing a black bra, black knickers and black suspenders just as she did back in 1987. She has her hands on her hips in her favoured Wonder Woman stance. She looks amazing.

She straddles me, the warmth of her buttocks penetrating my thin pyjama bottoms. She kisses my face and I let her, though I do not allow our lips to touch.

'Come on, Als,' she says, leading me towards the stairs, 'Up the wooden hill to Bedfordshire.'

She starts off on Edame's side but I cannot allow this and ask her to swap. She does this with good grace, the success of *Dragon's*

Den clearly not having gone to her head. She wants lip kissing, fondling, even mouth sex. I am in no mood to deliver. We lie on the bed, her cuddling me as I stare at the wall.

I wake at 4.30am. There is a note on the pillow next to me.

Dear Alan,
    Last night when you opened the door you looked as handsome as ever, but clearly your mind is elsewhere. We had something special back in the late '80s but I was a fool to think we could just slot back into the old regime.
    And for that reason I'm out.
    Take care.
    Debs xxx

I throw the note in the bin and go back to sleep, doing my damndest to forget the whole thing.

*   *   *

I am woken by Tom and a cup of tea. It's 11am.
'How you feeling, Dad?' he says.
'Terrible,' I reply, sitting up.
'I'm not surprised,' he says. 'Susan left in 1988 and it took me twenty-five years to get over it.'
Through my cloud of desperation I wondered whether I was hearing this right, that Tom was finally over Susan?
'I'm sorry I haven't been a better father to you,' I say. 'I've been a rotten husband too, now look at me.'
'You brought me up as best you could, put a roof over my head and more recently introduced me to the internet. I can't ask for much more.'

'Meaden was here last night,' I tell him. 'You'll be pleased to hear I didn't succumb.'

'I knew you wouldn't,' he said. 'You love Mum too much.'

'Have you heard from her?'

He looks away.

'What did she say?' I ask.

'Only that she's OK and for me not to worry.'

'Have you got her phone number?'

Tom scratches himself through his Kajagoogoo T-shirt.

'I can't give that to you, Dad. I promised.'

'OK. But please, when you speak to her next, tell her I love her very much and I miss her more than hunting itself.'

'Will do,' he says, writing the message down on his hand. He kisses my cheek and shapes to go, before sitting back down on the bed.

'There is one more thing, Dad, but you have to promise never to repeat it.'

'I promise,' I say.

'Cross your heart, hope to die, stick a needle up your bum?'

'All of that. What?'

'I get the impression Mum is trying to put a brave face on things,' he whispers, conspiratorially. 'You know how proud she is. Frankly I don't believe she's enjoying herself at Potato George's. Tina told me George was already making Mum "do" things she didn't want to do. These might have been sex things or shopping at Asda, I don't know. But between you and me I reckon if you renounced all aspects of Nazi hunting and promised wholeheartedly to do so for the rest of your life she'd be back like a shot. You've got to leave her be for a few days though. She's absolutely furious with you. Remember, this is just my opinion. I could be way off the mark.'

My heart leapt. Maybe the door to my relationship with Edame wasn't closed after all. Or it was but I had the key. Or something.

Yet the question remained: could I renounce Nazi hunting? I was beside myself with grief at Edame's departure but my ego still tugged at my shirtsleeve, pestering me to continue. Why did I need to save the world simply to make my presence felt on this earth? It was crazy. I knew what to do to be happy yet couldn't quite bring myself to commit to it. Slowly I drifted back off to sleep.

And that's when it happened.

The willowy figure of Simon Wiesenthal entered the room and sat on the end of the bed.

'Alan,' it said. 'You are in a quandary. You do not know which way to turn. Let us play a game of Simon Says.'

Am I awake? Asleep? I cannot tell. I try to reach out and touch Si but my arms are fastened by my sides.

'No man likes to imagine his wife in the arms of another, let alone picture them having it off in a sweaty clinch. You must rise above these thoughts, Alan. You are the special one. No one else sees what you see, which is going some at seventy-five. I do not wish to overplay the situation but the potential to save humanity lies with you and you alone. I'd help but unfortunately I died seven years ago. Stick with it. Assistance is out there, you just need to know where to look. Online perhaps, or in Houghton Regis. Keep listening in, revelations are bound to follow. I must away. Good to chat. Stay in touch. Heaven has a fax machine.'

I came to, but didn't feel as if I'd been asleep. The bedclothes were crumpled where Wiesenthal had been sat. If he'd been sat. The man was dead for Christ's sake. Perhaps Tom crumpled the sheets. Perhaps I did. I didn't believe in ghosts.

Keep listening in, revelations are bound to follow.
Listening in?
Oh, listening *in*.

I climbed out of the bed and headed downstairs. I found my phone under a cushion on the sofa, squished in the earphones and tuned into the Kinsey Shoe Bug app. Immediately I heard the voice of The Griffin.

'. . . ich haf spoken to Josef, everysing ist in place . . . ja, ve are still on target fur ze first October . . . mit Stoob out of ze equation ve are frei to carry out our efil plan . . . let's meet Freitag midday . . . usual place . . . yes that's recht . . . number thirty-five Flitwick Avenue . . . of course no vun ist listening . . . Herb hast all bases covered . . . apparently he's on his vay zare now.'

Herb?

A knock at the door.

I refasten my dressing gown to ensure Little Alan isn't on display and undo all four bolts.

Herb Derb is on the doorstep, looking furtive.

'Hiya, Alan,' he say. 'Looks lovely and cosy in there. Can I come in?'

Behind him I notice a BMW parked up in Shirley's disabled bay.

'I prefer people to call ahead,' I say. 'I have a routine. I like to stick to it.'

'Come off it, Alan, what sort of routine involves sitting around in your dressing gown at five in the afternoon?' he replies. 'Surely you can let an old friend in for a cup of tea and a chinwag?'

I acquiesce and hold the door open. Herb passes me in a cloud of aftershave.

'What can I do for you, Herb?' I ask. 'I'm pretty busy right now.'

'Don't give me that crap, Alan,' he says. 'We both know you're mooning around, bereft at Edame's departure and your stand-down as Britain's Premier Nazi Hunter. Sorry about how your tenure ended, by the way. The whole naked willy thing must have been humiliating.'

'Fuck off, Herb,' I say. 'What do you want?'

'You've got access to the Simon Wiesenthal Centre online archives. I need the code.'

'No chance,' I tell him. 'Si gave me that code for my own personal use.'

'The British Nazi Hunting Association says it's mine to take.'

'Well the British Nazi Hunting Association can go fuck itself,' I say.

'Why are you so hostile, Alan?' says Derb. 'It can't be good for your blood pressure. I hear Dr Grossmark's worried about you.'

'I would never help out a lowlife like you, Derb,' I tell him. 'Your sort sicken me. Hunting Nazis isn't about personal gain, freebies, groupies or raising your own profile. It's not about making a fast buck; it's a vocation, a path that your heart sets you on. The late Simon Wiesenthal personally selected me to hunt down Nazis in the Bedfordshire region. He wouldn't have touched the likes of you with a barge pole or a butterfly net. You're on the make.'

'That's slander, Alan. I hope you know I'm recording this conversation.'

'So am I.'

'Well, I'm recording it better.'

'You're a fraud, Herb. Everyone knows it.'

'Shut up, Alan. No one cares what you think. You're just some washed-up has-been hunter who showed his winky to the world and now drinks whisky straight from his Britain's Premier Nazi Hunter cup.'

'How much are they paying you?'

'I beg your pardon?'

'The Nazis – how much? A thousand euros a day, isn't that the going rate? Plus other benefits including unlimited sex with some sexy German fraulein?'

'You're on very thin ice, Alan. I'm warning you.'

'Well I'm threatening you, Herb. Now if you don't mind I'd like you to shit the fuck out of my house.'

Herb squared up to me but I saw the fear in his eyes. He left.

'And you can take your stupid listening device with you,' I say, hurling back at him the tiny steel disc he had very obviously dropped into the plant pot by the front door.

I made myself a hot Ribena and sat at the kitchen table to think.

Herb was working for the Nazis.

The Nazi plan was very much alive.

Edame would still have me back but a spectral Wiesenthal was keen for me to press on.

I was torn but I knew I had to fulfil my duty. For now at least Edame would have to wait. *If* she would wait.

I rang Nigel at the BNHA and left an urgent message to call me.

I spent the remainder of the evening listening to The Griffin while half-watching *Rosemary & Thyme* on ITV2. There were few further revelations from either The Griffin or the television detectives, though I appreciated Felicity Kendal's evergreen features. At ten I headed to my empty study, dug out my ancient BBC Micro, plugged it in, turned it on and checked my emails.

Wotcha, Alan, George Michael here off of Twitter.

Listen, I know you say you've knocked the hunting on the head and that but I don't think you should. Things have been tough for you of late but retiring into your pyjamas like an old fart isn't the answer.

I'm doing some of my best work ever and I'm fifty. Seventy-five is nothing. In Nazi hunting terms you're a babe-in-arms. I believe Wiesenthal snaffled evil Jonas Schwartz when he was ninety-one.

I'd like to help. Just finished an album and I've got time on my hands. Fair's fair, in return I wouldn't mind a bit of help with tidying and that, maybe the odd lift to the Heath, but basically I'm offering my services as an assistant. I don't know much about hunting Nazis but I've got passion, staying power, a four-litre Range Rover and more pot than you could shake a microphone at.

Could also enlist Andrew Ridgeley if need be. He's definitely free.

Let me know.

George xxxxxxxxxxxxxx

PS – Boots special offer – MultiVitality 70 Plus – this week only – thought you should know.

Oct❖ber

A sense of calm greets me today. I feel refreshed and clear of thought. The uncertainty that was filling my being has departed, at least for now. I love Edame but if I am to honour the memory of the late Simon Wiesenthal I must see this through. It's only right and proper. I am both these things.

I shower for the first time in days, the sludgy water at my feet bearing testimony. After a breakfast of porridge, a small Earl Grey and a large hot Ribena I call Nigel and leave another message before heading to the study and tuning in to Nazi chatter.

There are smatterings of clarity ('ich hate ziss country!') and moments of insight ('vee should never haf allowed kleine Adolf to pursue Operation Barbarossa') but it's mostly silence against a backdrop of occasional pornography.

At 1pm the office line rings. It's Tina.

'Oi you dozy twat, it's Saturday, you forgotten you and Tom are coming for lunch?'

I fetch Tom, who is in his room breakdancing, and drive us to Tina's.

It feels strange arriving without Edame but Tina, Marco, Haden and Houdini do their best to make me feel at home. 'In The Mood' by The Glenn Miller Orchestra is a nice touch.

'Lovely tune,' I tell them. Houdini pulls a face.

'Mummy said we have to put it on to cheer you up but I think it's smelly dog's pants. Here, feel my triceps.'

Marco sheepishly enters the fray.

'How are you, Marco?' I enquire.

'OK,' he whispers, 'though I mees men.'

Over my mixed grill I ask Tina whether she's seen her mother.

'You know I can't tell you that, Dad,' she says.

'That'll be a "yes" then,' I tell her. 'I'm not a Nazi Hunter for nothing you know.'

'I think you'll find you're not a Nazi Hunter at all, Alan,' says Haden, spitefully. 'You stood down – remember?'

'It's not as black and white as that,' I say.

'Racist!' shouts Houdini.

'Tell me you're not still hunting?' says Tina. 'Mum loves you and would rather be with you than Potato George but you know she won't come back if you're hunting Hun in your dotage.'

'I think it's great Alan's still hunting,' says Haden. 'Can I come on the next one?'

'I donna think that's a good idea-uh,' says Marco.

'You're not my real dad,' replies Haden. 'You're the gay one.'

'For god's sake knock it on the bloody head, Dad!' says Tina. 'A few days ago you were in the most terrible state after Mum left. What could possibly have changed? You do know George is prepared to pay top dollar for his Viagra stash?'

'Tina!' bellows Marco.

Tina rises up to her full height. Marco looks cowed.

'Until you've earned the right to question me,' said Tina with great menace, 'you should learn to shut your FUCKING FACE.'

Marco's gulp is audible.

I visit the bathroom to cool off. I find it hard to accept Potato George has a stiffer penis than me, or that Edame might be touching it. For now I must put such thoughts to the back of my mind, which thankfully isn't hard at my age. There's always a chance I'll forget all about it.

While upstairs trying to pee I listen in to the Kinsey Shoe Bug.

'If ich had vonted runny eggs ich vood have asked for runny eggs, dumbkopf! . . . now hand me ze phone . . . Room seventy-two please . . . danke. . . Josef! . . . Ja, ich bin vell . . . how are du finding Dunstable? . . . Ze Premier Inn ist nicht ze most luxurious hotel ich agree but at least it ist central . . . und how are our little freunds coming along? . . . ve are ahead of schedule? . . . Hexcellent news! . . . Of course no one knows . . . Ja, fatty Stoob ist out of ze picture . . . Herb ist alles over it . . . OK tchuss.'

Fatty?

I head back downstairs.

'Tom, we're off.'

'Dad, I'm sorry,' says Tina. 'You know I just want you and Mum back together.'

'It's not you, it's the Nazis,' I tell her.

'The Nasties!!' giggles Houdini.

'Get a message to Edame for me, will you?' I say as we depart. 'Tell her I need to see her. Five minutes. That's all.'

Tom and I climb into the car. I remove the replica gun from the glove box.

'How do you fancy coming on an American-style stakeout, son?'

'As long as it doesn't overrun,' he says. 'Terence Trent D'Arby's doing a live Q&A on the internet at five.'

I hand Tom my phone and ask him to call directory enquiries.

'The number for the Premier Inn, Dunstable,' he says authoritatively, 'and before you ask no I do not wish to be put through.'

We park in the hotel car park, close enough to see reception. A lady taps away on a keyboard. I take out my Sunagor 18 x 21mm pocket binoculars and zoom in on her name badge.

'Name's Sandra,' I tell Tom. 'Write that down. She's pretty. You should ask her out.'

'I don't think so, Dad,' he replies. 'So, how does this hunting thing work then?'

'This isn't strictly a hunt,' I tell him, 'though there is always the possibility it could escalate.

'I'm quite excited,' he says. 'Can't wait to tell the online community about it.'

'Please, son,' I say. 'What goes on on a hunt stays on a hunt.'

He nods. I ring the number.

'You can indeed help me, Sandra,' I say. 'Could you tell Josef in room seventy-two that The Griffin is waiting outside and would like to see him as a matter of some urgency.'

We wait. A man appears in reception but only to purchase condoms from the vending machine. We sit patiently.

'Funny, isn't it, without Mum?' says Tom.

'It's terrible, old son.'

'I'm confused,' he says. 'You know she'll come home if you stop hunting Nazis, so why are we here?'

I rest my hand on his squashy shoulder.

'Sometimes you have to do things for the greater good and the benefit of humanity, not merely for the sake of your own personal happiness,' I say. 'Incidentally, you didn't happen to notice the ghost of Simon Wiesenthal in the house the other night?'

He gives me a blank look.

Movement. I train the binoculars on the doors. Slowly they open. A man of over a hundred staggers onto the pavement. I zoom in but he is cast in shadow and wearing a hat and dark glasses. I hand the binoculars to Tom.

'No pressure but take a look and see if he is familiar to you.'

The man continues to wait outside, clearly anxious not to let The Griffin down. He looks at his watch, impatient. Tom adjusts the focus.

'Who is it?' I ask. Tom doesn't reply. After a couple of minutes the man removes a pocket watch from inside his jacket before heading back inside.

'Well?' I ask.

'You're the expert in this field, not me,' he says, 'but I'm pretty sure I just caught a glimpse of Dr Josef Mengele.'

*　　*　　*

First thing I call Interpol Steve.

'Is there any chance Josef Mengele is still alive?' I ask.

A short pause.

'Yup.'

'What do you mean "yup"?'

'Just this thing we heard about him not actually dying in Paraguay but moving to Leighton Buzzard instead.'

'Leighton Buzzard? And you didn't think to mention it?'

'He'll be over 115. Didn't seem worth it.'

'The Griffin is 107, Heinrich Pump 106. Age is not the issue here, especially for an evil mastermind like Mengele. For all we know he has found the key to eternal youth or brought himself back to life.'

'Are you hunting again?' asks Steve.

'Kind of.'

'Let us know if you hear anymore and we'll pass it onto Herb.'

'Don't pass anything to Herb,' I say. 'He's dressing to the right these days.'

'No problem, Alan. Oh, and sorry to hear about Edame and George. I can't imagine what it feels like to have your wife boned by a potato.'

Next I send an email to music legend George Michael,

Dear George,

Thank you so much for your message dated 21st September.

In my line of work I come across celebrity types all the time. Few match your levels of style and longevity. My wife in particular is a big fan of your album, *The Best of George Michael*. My wife left me recently to be with her ex-boyfriend. He's such a shit, George, I can't even bring myself to write his name. But that's by-the-by.

You'll be pleased to hear I'm hunting again (though that's why she left me). There's trouble afoot. Don't tell anyone but Josef Mengele is alive and plotting something massive with The Griffin.

Your offer of help did not fall on deaf ears, despite my age. I shall be in touch in due course.

Warm regards and stay vigilant,

Alan Stoob (75)

To help order my thoughts I take to my journal:

- The Griffin is planning a major attack on the British government and Josef Mengele is involved.

- Herb Derb has gone rotten and is assisting them.

- I am no longer Britain's Premier Nazi Hunter.

- This means I can hunt in my spare time and no one will know.

- Singing legend George Michael has offered to help.

- Simon Wiesenthal's ghost appeared to me and told me to stick at it.

- That may have been a dream, not sure.

- Edame will have nothing to do with me while I hunt Nazis.

- Tom seems happier.

Understanding Mengele's role in this plot is the key to foiling it. I ring the Premier Inn.

'Hello. Premier Inn Dunstable Sandra speaking how may I help or be of assistance in any way?'

'Hi, Sandra. Could I have a room tonight please?'

'Sorry, sir, rooms all booked out.'

'On a Wednesday?'

'It's the Conservative Party Conference in Luton. We've got the entire cabinet staying here.'

'In Luton? The entire cabin—'

'Sorry caller, I've got someone on the other line, please hold.'

I googled party conferences. The Conservative Party Conference was scheduled to take place in Birmingham later in October. Sandra must have been confused. As for a Premier Inn, one might expect the Labour Party to stay there as a show of solidarity – but the Conservatives? Luton Hoo would be more their style.

I called the Simon Wiesenthal Centre but it rang out so I logged onto their system and pulled up the Mengele file. It made for grotesque reading and forced me to lie down. I hoped I might summon Si in my sleep and the promise of further instruction. Instead I am woken by a beep from my phone. The number is withheld.

OK. 3pm Thursday. Dunstable Town Hall. Edame.

Good news.

I apply a dollop of nappy rash cream, slip on my weighted pants and take a stroll to the Premier Inn.

Passing through the heart of Dunstable reminds me anew how much my life is entwined with Edame's. I stride past The Gary Cooper on Grove Park and recall our first date:

how my Max Wall impression made her cry with laughter, how I wowed her with my Morris Minor 1000 and how we parked up in a lay-by close to Ardley Hill Lower School and she did things to me that in 1958 were considered illegal outside Holland. I choke back tears of self-pity and continue on my course.

The car park of the Premier Inn is one-third full. I tuck myself at the rear behind a souped-up Vauxhall Chevette and remove my tiny binoculars.

I can just about make out Sandra on the phone, laughing and playing with her hair. She'd be perfect for Tom: a little younger than him, vivacious, pretty, kind and not living in New Zealand. Her white blouse is crisply ironed. If I were Tom I'd ask her out and give her a kiss, in that order.

No sign of any MPs. I tune into the app. My ears are filled with the industrial chugging of a diesel engine, overlaid by adults singing.

The wheels on the bus go round and round, round and round, round and round, the wheels on the bus go round and round, Deutschland Uber Alles.

A Green Line coach turns in from Dunstable Road and enters the hotel car park. The number on the front is 321, the bus that serves the Luton–St Albans route. These old Green Line vehicles had been retired a decade ago. What one of them was doing here I had no idea.

The coach comes to a halt outside the hotel entrance. The rhythmic engine dies followed by a pneumatic release of breath. A small man passes through the bus, conducting what looks like a headcount. Then one by one men in blue suits filter out of the door. There is a perfect synchronicity to their departure as if marching to a drum, but their faces are blank, glazed. Two women complete the group. They all line up beside the bus and stand stock still, awaiting further instruction.

I adjust the binoculars. At the head of the line is the Prime Minister, David Cameron. Next to him is Nick Clegg. Then George Osborne, William Hague and Theresa May. In all there are twenty-two of them. The entire coalition cabinet.

A whistle is blown – it is hard to see by whom – and they peel off into the hotel, starting with Cameron. Quickly I remove my SLR camera and attach the telephoto lens. I take seven shots before the film winds on automatically. The politicians have dispersed. The bus departs, two figures still aboard. All is quiet. Once more I call the hotel.

'Hello again, Sandra, could you put me through to Josef in room seventy-two please?'

'Sorry, sir, I think he just drove off.'

What on earth was Dr Josef Mengele doing with the British cabinet? How had he cajoled them to join him? Hypnosis? Force of personality? The promise of everlasting life?

Back home Tom makes lunch. I pour us both a Whisky Hitler (one part whisky to three parts Mountain Dew) and we clink to Nazi hunting. *Prime Minister's Question Time* is on. Ed Milliband is grilling the PM about child welfare. Cameron appears to have rediscovered his zest from this morning and is in full swing, red-faced and right wing in his efforts to drive home his point. I flick between channels but there's nothing else on.

Then it occurs to me: with Edame gone I can do anything I want. I fish out the tape of the 1987 Prudential Cup final between Hampshire and Derbyshire. I never saw it at the time and had been saving it for a rainy day.

'I remember that game,' says Tom. 'It's the one where Eddie Hemmings hits a four off the last ball to win it for Derbyshire.'

'Oh,' I say, and turn it off.

Leave yet another message for Nigel, head upstairs and start reading *Fear And Loathing in Leighton Buzzard*, the new Nazi thriller by *John le Carré*. All the while I can't help wondering what my wife is doing.

* * *

Restless night. Dream that I'd organised a Christmas game of football between the Nazis and the hunters at Bedford Rec. Klaus Von Ribbentrop gets sent off for a two-footed tackle. I myself am nutmegged by Rudolf Hess. The game ends two-two.

Nervous about seeing Edame. Already she is a partial stranger to me. How can she remain my Edame when she's spending time with Mr Potato Head?

Tom is downstairs watching my *World at War* video boxset. It's good to see his interest expanding beyond the 1980s. Perhaps he'll make a hunter yet.

'Would you like to listen in to the Nazis while I'm out?' I say. He looks up, unbelieving.

'Really, Dad?' he asks. 'You'd let me do that?'

'I think you can handle the responsibility,' I tell him. 'The time has come.'

He stands to embrace me, moist-eyed. I hand over my earpiece and phone, and lightly tap the Kinsey Shoe Bug icon on the display.

After giving myself a ruler-straight central parting I take

the car down to the town hall and park up using Bob's disabled stickers. Potato George's Jaguar XJ8 draws up. Edame leans over and gives him a peck before climbing out and walking towards me. George remains in the car, staring straight ahead.

'You've had your hair done,' I say.

'George likes it up,' she replies.

'I bet he does.'

'Come on, Alan, let's keep things civil.'

We adjourn to a nearby coffee shop where I present her with the biography of Albert Speer she mentioned last birthday. She seems nonplussed.

'How is sex on Viagra, then?' I ask, looking her in the eye.

'That's a personal matters between George and myself,' she replies, stern-faced but avoiding my gaze.

'I could give you that,' I tell her. 'I'm twice the man George is.'

'George is man enough to get a proper prescription for the Viagras,' she retorts. 'Plus he doesn't spend his whole times thinking he's the only one who can save the world from the National Socialistics.'

'But I *am* the only one wh—'

'Spare us both, Alan,' she says, playing with a sugar sachet.

'I've heard life with George is no holiday,' I venture.

'Rubbish!' she replies. 'He just isn't used to having the woman around. I'll tell you what's no holiday, being neglecting in preference for hunting hundred-year-olds. Here's £10 for the coffees, Alan. Spend the change on some Nazi hunting equipments.'

She stands and exits the café. I dash to the till hoping there's time to collect my change but am forced to leave the tenner and speed walk to catch her up. Edame is approaching George's car.

'Mengele's back,' I shout.

She stops and turns.

'No he's not,' she says.

'He is. And he's up to something – something big.'

'Then people must be told.'

'They won't listen.'

'What about Herb?'

'He's working for the Nazis.'

'Oh come off it, Alan.'

'He is! Interpol don't care. I'm the only one who can do anything about it. That's what I wanted to tell you.'

She looks towards George and holds up her palm as if to say 'wait'. With that sexy walk she strolls back over. I remove my inhaler and take a puff.

'This is why I left you, you bloody idiots!' she says, prodding my chest with her finger. 'You think it's only you what can save the world but you're wrong, Alan, especially in your seventy-sixth year. You're losing your yoyo. And if Mengele is here – so what? Someone will stop him. Or they won't. What about me and my need? What about us? I feel sorry for you, Alan. You don't know when to lets go.'

Her voice quietens, if not her intensity.

'I came here ready to forgive you. Had you shown even a tiny inking of regret or remorse I would have come back to the home with you. But I can see you are still as self-absorbent as ever. George is waiting. This really is it. Goodbye, Alan.'

There is a careful deliberation in her step as she walks back to George's Jag. He drives off at pace, waving as he goes. As they disappear round the corner Edame looks round at me one last time, her eyes full of tears.

Sitting in the Stoobmobile I pose a question on Twitter:

Is it better to seek personal happiness or save the world?
Regards, Alan.

Jeremy Clarkson is the first to respond.

'Fuck the world, Alan, look after number one.'

Geri Halliwell chimes in:

'U have look after yoself in this world, Alna.'

Then it's the turn of George Michael:

'I can feel you wavering, Alan. If you save the world
personal happiness is sure to follow. Georgexxxxxxxxxxxx'

It takes an eighties pop icon to remind me of the righteous
path. There could be little to gain from abandoning my quest
at this stage. I am on a mission and I must not stray. Saving
the world, or at least trying to, will surely bring its own
reward.

I drive home and run myself a hot bath. Reclining, I ponder
the events of the day. I'm not sure Edame will ever come back
now. She knows I'm hunting full bore, and George has got
his hands on some bona fide Viagra. It's not looking good.

Tom bursts in. Hastily I cover Little Alan with my flannel.

'You've got to hear this!' he says, handing me my phone
and the earpiece. 'Mengele and The Griffin are talking to each
other.'

I squish in the earphones and listen.

'Gut news, Herr Griffin, ze first stage ist complete.'

'Hexcellent!' replies The Griffin. 'Ve are vell under vay. Ven do du think ze task vill be complete?'

'Zat depends on ze opportunities, Herr Griffin. Ich haf many of our best mensch on ze job. Let us say drei weeks.'

'Vare are du keeping zem?'

There is a pause.

'Vare ve agreed to keep zem, Herr Griffin.'

'Double hexcellent, mein docktor. Vood du care fur eine kleine lunch?'

'Nein, Herr Griffin, ich must continue on this delicate yet top secret scientific projekt.'

'As du wish, Josef. Lovely to see du again after alles zees jahres.'

'Always ein pleasure, never ein chore,' says Mengele. The sound of a door shutting. The Griffin emits a screech-laugh.

The 'zem' in question must surely be members of the cabinet – but how could the Nazis kidnap high profile government members and not expect anyone to notice? It didn't make sense, I thought, as I dried myself thoroughly.

Since neither Tom nor myself can cook, it's Tina's again for dinner. When we arrive she's in a state. It seems Marco didn't come home again last night. He can't seem to kick the impulse for late-night cruising. Haden looks confused and upset. Houdini seems happy enough punching her Magda Goebbels doll.

Midway through pudding Marco sneaks in through the backdoor and heads straight upstairs. Tina follows him. Shouting and thumping sounds ensue so I turn on the telly to drown out the noise.

'Why are Mum and Dad arguing?' asks Houdini.

'Because Dad is a bender,' replies Haden, somewhat unhelpfully.

Tom is oblivious to the conversation and seems transfixed by the television.

'That's odd,' he says. 'Michael Gove's hands are the wrong way round. I never noticed that before.'

'What do you mean?'

'I'll show you,' he says before miraculously rewinding the news.

'Is this on video?' I say.

'No. It's modern TV. You can rewind it. I read about it on the internet. Watch this.'

I watch intently as Gove speaks from outside a school in Stoke. Tom is right. Where there should have been a right hand a left hand sprung forth, and vice versa. If that wasn't peculiar enough the rhetoric spilling forth from his gob is somewhat irregular.

'The education of this country is being held back by thickos, dunces, dolts and dimwits,' he said. 'Our schools are awash with brainless beasts. We must separate the wheat from the chav, then dispense with the chav. The last thing we need is chav mating with chav, that only creates more chav. From tomorrow those that cannot do long-division will be employed as chimney sweeps in Glasgow tenements; anyone in set five for French will be turned into glue; kids that don't know their nine times table will be skinned by members of MENSA then feasted upon by wild pigs. If we want to make Britain Great again there's no room for asshats who don't know the capital of Chile.'

'Answer's Santiago,' says Houdini.

Tina and Marco came back downstairs.

'Daddy's got something to say,' says Tina. Marco looks terrified in his short shorts. He is sporting a lump over his right eye.

'Listen up-ah, keeds. I'm-ah sorry I not get home-ah for-ah the dinner. I had to work-ah late-ah but I won't do it again, OK?'

'We all know where you've bloody been!' shouts Haden before fleeing the table and storming out of the house. Instinctively I go to chase after him but feel a twinge in my left knee and pull up like a lame racehorse.

'It's alright, Dad, he'll come back,' says Tina. Marco seats himself and makes inroads into a bowl of spotted dick, anxiously looking at his wife after each mouthful.

In the car Tom is animated on the subject of Gove.

'That is just so strange,' he says. 'The fact that his hands are the wrong way round is weird enough in the first place. That no one has noticed is bloody bizarre.'

I was more concerned about the content of his speech.

Back home Tom excuses himself to make a Skype call. I fix myself a hot Bovril and google 'Michael Gove weird hands'. Nothing comes up. I check over fifty images of the education secretary. In each his hands are normal, if a little lady-like.

I galvanised myself and headed for the basement. It was time to face my demons.

I hadn't developed a single reel of film since Whipsnade. I knew that the pictures I took outside the Premier Inn would be mixed in with those I captured on that fateful day last October. I laid out the trays of toner, developer and rapid fixer, and went to work.

Of the thirty-six shots on the film, five hadn't come out due to thumb-over-lens, two because of my nose. Four were of Edame on a day trip to Colchester. Two were pointless fuzzy long-distance views (despite my insistence they never work Edame always takes them). That left twenty-three pictures. They were developing before my eyes. I braced myself.

As the images sharpen I am transported back to the fateful day: the lions, the penguins, evil Lukas Shitte dressed as a camel. He had me running round in circles until, exhausted and wheezing, I suffered an asthma attack in the Lizard Lounge. As I lay there unable to breathe Shitte had taken my camera from me and snapped my splutterings before escaping into Sallowspring Wood. What a total bastard.

I stared at the images and revisited the humiliation, yet to my surprise I didn't feel that bad. In the end sometimes pictures are just pictures. They didn't upset me. Or perhaps I was becoming immune to hurt. After all, Edame had recently left me and I'd seen a ghost.

I shifted my attention to the Premier Inn shots. Each had come out perfectly; red-faced Cameron, quiffy Osborne, corpulent Pickles.

There were three of Michael Gove: one with his hands in his pockets, one with them behind his back and one where he's picking his nose with both hands. I squinted and raised the paper to my face. It touched my nose.

His hands were the wrong way round: right for left, left for right.

I head upstairs to see Tom, who has finished skyping.

'Gove's hands weren't always like that,' I tell him. 'In old pictures they're normal. Outside the Premier Inn they're back to front. Plus, there was no party conference in Luton. What's going on?'

'I knew this kid at school who had really weird thumbs . . .' says Tom.

'And?' I ask.

'It's probably not relevant.'

'The key to this is Mengele,' I say. 'Catch him and we save the world.'

'Isn't that a bit dramatic, Dad?'

'I don't think so,' I tell him.

*　*　*

The radio and television news was awash with talk of 'Iron Mike' Gove's speech the previous evening. Everyone seemed shocked at the hard line he was taking with respect to the under-intelligent. No one seemed to have picked up on the hand swap. They must have been distracted by his right-wing rhetoric.

I removed *The Boys From Brazil* by Ira Levin from the bookcase and leafed through the pages. Although only fiction, Mengele features. It might provide some ideas.

The landline rings. It's Haden.

'You feeling better today?' I ask.

'A bit. But it's weird having a gay for a dad.'

'He's not a gay,' I tell him. 'He's confused. Or bi-sexual. He still loves your mum. He just loves men too.'

'I know. Anyway that's not why I rang. Are you watching BBC1? Nick Clegg is backing Gove. So is Theresa May. We're lurching to the right, Granddad, just like Germany in the early thirties.'

I turn on the telly. Clegg is being interviewed by Andrew Marr. Haden is right, Clegg is blithely backing Gove. Over on ITV May is being door-stepped by reporters.

'Of course I'm in favour of Michael Gove's policy shift,' she says. 'The weak will perish, leaving the country stronger than before. As a nation we are in the doldrums. It's time for some industrial-strength governing. I would like to add that as home secretary I shall soon be outlawing immigration and in time will be scoping options for annexing Golders Green, Stamford Hill and parts of Manchester.'

I flicked back and forth. This was a truly shocking lurch to the right by the coalition. Gove didn't surprise me, nor May, but for Clegg to back Gove's strategy of extermination seemed not only out of character but also out of synch with current LibDem thinking.

It was then I noticed Clegg's ears. Or should I say ear. His right ear was where it had always been, attached to the right side of his head. The left one was entirely absent. I didn't need the internet to know that Nick Clegg was almost certainly a man in possession of a full set.

'I will do what it takes to make this country great again,' he said, 'and if that means invading Poland then so be it.'

Was this some kind of joke? Marr laughs nervously but Clegg remains straight-faced. The interview is wrapped up. I flick back to Theresa May. She too is drawing to a close before being filmed walking away from the reporters. She is a familiar enough figure but for the first time I observe something strange about her movement. Everything else seems normal but it is hard not to notice that one of her feet is on back to front.

The earpiece, which had been lying silent on the table, starts vibrating. I pick it up. There is blind fury down the line.

'ZE THIRD REICH VOZ NOT BUILT ON SUCH SLOPPINESS, HERR DOCKTOR! ZE FUHRER VOOD BE TURNING IN HIS GRAVE AT SUCH EIN CHARADE!!'

'Herr Griffin, if ich may explain . . .'

'ICH HAF NO TIME FUR EXPLANATIONS!'

'But ze procedure ich am verking on ist highly complex. Occasional mistakes are unafoidable. Ich promise to make ze necessary changes over nacht.'

'Ziss can never happen again, Herr Docktor!'

'Ich know.'

'Good. Now ich vant to hear du say sorry.'

A pause.

'Sorry, Herr Griffin.'

'LOUDER!!'

'SORRY, MEIN HERR!'

Another pause.

'Ich pardon du. Now, how many more left?'

'Ich haf just released Iain Duncan Schmidt, Justine Greening und little Kenneth von Clarke. Ich have been informed zat ze Prime Minister himself vill be abducted at seven ziss abend. Ich vill ensure ich haf ze new vun ready by zen.'

'Does it possess any physical defects?'

'Nein, Herr Griffin.'

'Und zey have alles been fully briefed?'

'Ja, Herr Griffin. Cameron in particular vill have ein lot to say during tonight's party politikal broadcast.'

'Do nicht let me down again, Herr Docktor.'

'Nein, Herr Griffin.'

The Boys From Brazil winked up at me from the sofa. How had I been so stupid?

In the novel Mengele attempts to clone Adolf Hitler.

Today the real Mengele had gone one better and cloned the entire cabinet.

How he had done it was impossible to say.

All I knew is I had to stop him.

It's not far to Houghton Regis, though the rush hour traffic didn't help. I parked up on a side road and displayed Bob's disabled stickers. I entered Charlie's Tool Depot, smiled at Charlie and made my way to the back of the shop. I pulled out the display case, located the door and opened it. The reception area had been upgraded since I was last here, as had the receptionist, who resembled Jane Russell in her pomp.

'Excuse me, sir, you can't just walk straight in,' she said, clearly unaware of who I was. I ignored her words, typed in the code (1-9-4-5) and let myself into the British Nazi Hunting Association HQ.

Everyone froze as I appeared: Nigel, Janice in accounts, Horace Billet from marketing, Jenny Hobbit and others besides. There were still three clocks on the wall: the time in England, Israel and Bedfordshire. Their little joke and a good one.

'Alan,' said Nigel in relaxed fashion. 'To what do we owe such an unexpected pleasure?'

'No pleasure in this visit, Nige,' I said. 'I came because I had to.'

'Someone get Alan a glass of water,' said Nigel. 'He looks a little wan.'

'If I'm wan it's because I bring dire news.'

'There's always the telephone, Alan. We close in fifteen minutes.'

I drank the water. All eyes were on me, each pair rife with scepticism.

'I've been calling you for days, Nige, left a dozen messages.'

'Really? Perhaps you've got the wrong number.'

'No chance,' I told him and put down my empty glass. 'One of you might want to write this down. It's quite complicated.'

I lightly mopped my brow with my handkerchief.

'Josef Mengele is alive and staying at the Premier Inn in Dunstable. Somehow he's replacing piecemeal the cabinet with a replica version, all with Nazi tendencies and minor physical defects. Meanwhile Herb Derb is working with The Griffin to undermine all Nazi-hunting activity in this country.'

I looked at their faces. None registered surprise.

A slender, well-dressed figure emerged from behind a pillar at the back of the room. Even from there his aftershave was overpowering.

'Hello, Alan,' said Herb Derb. With a swagger he walked casually in my direction. His MeisterSinger watch was expensive and noticeably German, his clothes the finest cut silks and wools from Smith & Smitherer of Savile Row.

'I've seen this so many times,' he said. 'Men, great men, who retire and misplace their bearings, lose their grip. They feel cut adrift from the life they knew and will do almost anything to get back to where they once were.'

'As with poor Peter Bone,' echoed Nigel. I look up. Where once my portrait hung there were now two of Herb.

'We are naturally pleased to see you, Alan,' said Herb, 'but perhaps you should get back to your wif— Oops, my apologies. That must be hard at your age and can only add to your sense of isolation. My thoughts are with you. When did you last see Dr Grossmark? Perhaps you should up your dose of anti-depressants, to get you through this latest bad spell.'

'You bloody bastard, Derb!' I said.

'I think you had better leave, Alan,' said Nigel.

'Oh please, Nigel, not you too.'

'I can call you a cab if you like,' he said. 'We've got an account with Addison von Lee.'

'Piss off, Nige, I'll get myself home.'

'As you wish,' said Nigel. 'Always good to see you, Alan.'

'Goodbye, Alan,' said Herb.

'Yeah, goodbye, Alan,' said Horace.

'On your way, fartbox,' said Janice.

I exit. The receptionist didn't even look up from her *OK!* magazine. In the car I tweet George Michael for help as a matter of some urgency.

That evening Bob came round to watch a party political broadcast on behalf of the Conservative Party. He arrived asleep so I guided him to the sitting room and settled him on the sofa. It was still great to see him. With Tom upstairs skyping again I appreciated the company.

I poured myself a hot Ribena, prepared a modest bowl of salted popcorn and settled down to watch. Cameron appeared. He looked normal. Bob stirred. I turned up the volume.

Hello. This is your Prime Minister speaking. As you know we are in the midst of a recession. The scope and scale of this slump is so seismic as to threaten the very fabric of our society as well as that of our friends in mainland Europe, especially Germany. If we do not act soon we risk succumbing to the tyranny of Bolshevism and international Jewry, not to mention a possible triple-dip recession. This is why I am advocating in the strongest possible terms the abolition of the democracy we have so long held dear.

Comrades, during times of great hardship democracy weakens nations. We need strong clear leadership, clarity of thought and more exports to Hamburg. What we have instead is confused, watered-down policymaking of the lowest order. As of tomorrow this country will be run as a dictatorship, with me at the helm and my cabinet providing support where necessary. This is good news and should be celebrated, ideally with a Heineken and a frankfurter butterbrot.

Silence! The international disseminators of strife are lurking in the nooks and the durchschuß, waiting to assault us with their propaganda and red terror. Do not weaken, freunds, remain resolute in the face of danger. Stay strong, and let's invade France.

Recently my colleague Herr Gove suggested the annihilation of the ignorant. Many of you were understandably concerned at this notion, believing it to be inhumane. I have sympathies with your disquiet but let us be clear: IT IS THE ONLY WAY THIS COUNTRY SHALL BE GREAT AGAIN. That, and ridding ourselves of the fatties. Fatties take up too much space, eat all the food, use all the healthcare and add disproportionately to the landfill with their coke bottles and pizza boxes. Those over 17 stone will be buried alive at sunrise.

When I was a young boy facing the slings and arrows of life at Eton I kept a diary, which I called My Struggle *by* Dave. *In it I outlined my belief that only the strong survive and rise to prominence. Those that fall by the wayside, the frail and the feeble, are an irrelevance and are to be swept under the carpet. In Margaret Thatcher I found someone with a shared viewpoint. But, comrades, we lost our way. John Major was soft like the putrid flesh of a rotting peach. Things improved a little under Tony Blair but, let us be honest, it's been a messy last few years.*

Now the mantle rests with me.

There is an old German saying: 'Shout, shout, let it all out.' We are on the precipice of change, comrades. We must shout the loudest. The wind of a thousand German bloodhounds is whistling through our teeth. Be ready. Hold firm. Stand strong.

The broadcast played out to some kind of German folk song I didn't recognise.

Twitter went berserk, overloaded, then broke down. *The Guardian* website featured the headline 'End Of Days' with blood trickling down the homepage, before it too seized up with traffic. *The Mail* led with 'PM Gets Tough On Fatties'.

A knock at the door.

'Alright, Alan?' said George Michael. 'Bloody got lost on the one-way system and had to pull over for a doze. Can I park my arse indoors or you gonna make me stand outside forever?'

I showed George Michael through to the kitchen and flicked on the kettle. It felt good to have someone that I could depend on, especially one with such an impressive back catalogue.

'That Cameron's a bloody rotten shit,' he said, sipping his camomile. 'He's talking like a bleeding Nazi. You want to have a word with him, Alan. Mind if I smoke?'

I shook my head. George pulled out a enormous hand-folded cigarette and lit up. The unmistakable aroma of pot weed filled the kitchen. I told him about The Griffin and Mengele, about the cloning, about Herb and the British Nazi Hunting Association. I also told him about Edame because it made me feel better.

'Fuck me sideways that's some serious goings on,' he said.

I called up to Tom. I didn't know how he would react to seeing George Michael in our kitchen.

'Hold up, Dad, I'm having a big shit!' he shouted back. 'Five minutes.'

When Tom finally arrived the look of shock upon his face reminded me of the time I confronted Helga the Husk in the shallow end at Pepperstock Community Baths.

'What on earth are you doing here, George Michael?' he asked, bug-eyed.

'Helping your dad chase Nazis, isn't it,' he replied. 'Here, you still pining after that girl in the New World? Your first love is rarely your last. You're a handsome lad. Get out there and live a bit. Loads of ladies would go for you.'

Tom blushed and ran off.

'Thing is, Alan,' said George Michael, 'other than singing I'm not really sure how I can help.'

'I'm sure we'll think of something,' I replied.

It was just before midnight when we came up with the plan. George Michael drove home. I felt strangely hungry and stayed up listening to Tom's Wham! records while eating all the crisps and cereal in the cupboard.

*　　*　　*

It has been nearly a week since Cameron's broadcast. The left-wing press has remained on red alert. Nearly all cabinet members have made a proclamation of right-wing adoration. Overnight William Hague tweeted something about 'broadening Britain's horizons into Belgium', while Minister of Defence Philip Hammond declared his desire to quadruple tank numbers. Iain Duncan Smith said all those on benefits will be shipped out to Anglesey, which was strange because as far as I could tell his döppelganger had yet to be unveiled.

After a breakfast of falafel and smoked salmon I drove down to the Premier Inn car park. George Michael was waiting there in his Range Rover, listening to Magic FM. He gave me a knowing wink, got out of the car and headed for the hotel entrance.

I donned my flat cap and frameless glasses and followed him. Sandra was once more on duty. I sat on the sofa in the reception area and opened up a *Financial Times* with two small holes cut out for maximum viewing. George Michael approached the desk.

'Hiya, Sandra. You look nice. Could you please tell Josef Mengele in room seventy-two that George Michael from Wham! is downstairs. I hear he's a big fan.'

Sandra made the call. George gave me a thumbs up behind his back. All we had to do was wait and hope that the Wiesenthal archives were correct about Mengele's interest in eighties pop.

Two minutes later he emerged from the lift with a huge, lopsided smile on his face. He near-galloped over to George Michael, leapt into his arms and gave him a hug.

'Vot an incredible surprise!' he said, hopping about. 'George Michael of Vam! Vot brings du to these parts? How did du know ich voz here? Und vot inspired du to write ze lyrics fur ze beautiful ditty, Careless Visper?'

'Let's take a walk, Doc,' he said, leading him outside. 'We have so much to discuss.'

I summoned the lift and selected level two. The corridor on the second floor was deserted. I walked towards room seventy-two. Out of nowhere Vince Cable appeared, walking a tiny dog. Cable was only four foot tall, yet his neck was twice as long as I'd remembered. We nodded to one another and I waited for him to catch the lift before removing the OneKey™ I purchased at the Spy Shop. With a twizzle and a shove I waited for the click. Two seconds later I was inside Mengele's hotel room.

It was too early for maid service yet his bed was made up, a classic example of Germanic discipline. Beside his bed lay a copy of the book *The Ladyboys from Brazil*, next to it the pornographic magazine *Twins Monthly*. On the desk a pad of paper with a mobile number I recognised as Herb Derb's. The room smelt of Cologne, both the city and the perfume.

I peaked through the curtains and saw GM in the car park with Mengele. Michael was animated. Mengele seemed entranced.

I opened the drawers. Inside were two-dozen eggs and an embossed sheet of instructions.

How To Clone People And Instil Them With Nazi Beliefs
By Dr Josef Mengele aged 116

1. *Take one egg (Waitrose organic preferable)*
2. *Secure blood (10ml) of subject*
3. *Add blood to yolk*
4. *Shake vigorously*
5. *Place under infra-red light for 28 days*
6. *Once 'chick' is hatched, position in shoebox alongside copy of Mein Kampf. Feed it constant diet of sauerkraut and weißbier. Bombard with the music of Richard Wagner 24/7.*
7. *After 60 days' incubation transfer it to the underground ward of Luton & Dunstable Hospital. Here it can be socialised and, if necessary, stretched.*
8. *Growth cycle should be complete after 120 days. Once it reaches full height brush hair in identical fashion to counterpart, debrief, kidnap original and retain for medical research and/or own pleasure.*
9. *Repeat as necessary.*

Also in the drawer I found a small blood-red bottle labelled 'Dr Mengele's Enhanced Life Pills – DO NOT TOUCH'. These I pocketed.

Outside, George Michael was still chatting, singing away and doing his special clapping-while-holding-the-microphone dance, but Mengele seemed distracted and kept removing his pocket watch. I didn't have long. I could of course alert the police or challenge Mengele myself but that would result in him biting down on the cyanide capsule that resides within the lower right second molar of all Nazis. Whilst it would be a great pleasure to see the evil mastermind writhing and frothing for a few short moments I needed him alive to help me locate the 'originals'.

I exited the room and made my way to the lift. Waiting by it was a man I recognised. An opportunity, perhaps, for some homespun elimination of my own.

'Iain Duncan Smith, isn't it?' I said, staring hard at the replica.

'Yes,' he replied, not bothering to look round.

'Unfortunately this lift is out of order. We have to take the fire escape.'

'Oh,' he replied.

I beckoned him towards the end of the corridor, forced open the fire escape, gestured for him to go first, then shoved him over the banisters. He plunged down the stairwell and landed with a stomach-churning thud.

'Thanks,' came a distant voice, then silence.

Satisfying though it was to murder the clone of Iain Duncan Smith I made a mental note not to perpetrate any further acts of savage brutality. As Fred Nietzsche said, the line between the hunter and the hunted can be blurred at the best of times.

Back downstairs I spoke to Sandra.

'I hope you don't mind me saying but you're a lovely-looking lady. Do you have a boyfriend or the like?'

'That's very kind of you, sir, but aren't you a little old for me?'

'Not for me!' I replied, 'For my son, Tom. He's a good-looking lad, bright too. He's recently come out of a long-term relationship and would love to step out with you.'

'Long term?'

'She left him in 1988 and he's recently come to terms with it.'

'Oh.'

'Let me write down his number. I'm sure he'd be keen to take you to a Wimpy bar or eighties revival concert.'

I left the hotel and walked towards my car. George Michael was by this time holding onto Mengele, who was struggling to escape. The moment he saw me he let go. Mengele collapsed in a heap on the tarmac. The aged Nazi dusted himself off and went inside. George Michael strode over.

'Job done, Stoob?'

'Mission complete, George Michael.'

'Glad to be of assistance.'

We high-fived.

'I may not be done with you yet, George Michael. Stand down but stay close to the phone.'

'Yes sir, Stoob sir.'

He performed a mock-Hitler salute, climbed into his Range Rover and sped off. I headed in the opposite direction – towards the Luton and Dunstable Hospital.

The radio remained alive with talk of the coalition's lurch to the right. Geoff Lime's call-in-show on Chiltern 97.6 was under siege from frenzied listeners who heard 'echoes of the Third Reich' and claimed to 'remember 1939 like it was fackin' yesterday'. His decision to interrupt the talk with the original German version of 'Ninety-Nine Red Balloons' by Nina was not well-received.

Over on Radio Four a word of calm was struck by George Monbiot, who noted that while there had indeed been a highly discernible fascist lurch by the incumbents, this would be tempered by MPs who 'wouldn't vote for such measures in a billion years'.

'Thankfully in this country we have a system that prevents the kind of frightening shifts in policy we are witnessing from becoming a reality,' he said. 'Around 625 MPs have yet to vote on such proposals. There is no chance they will be passed. And even if by some peculiar twist of fate they were, the Queen would veto them instantly. These are indeed worrying times but here in the UK we are lucky to have the dual safety net of monarchy and democracy.'

I parked up on a yellow line, placed Bob's disabled stickers on the dashboard and headed for the hospital – before returning to the car, hiding the stickers and driving to a proper parking bay. I'd already killed someone today, I didn't fancy dishonest parking on my conscience to boot.

Both Tina and Tom were born at the L&D. It brought back many memories, not least the treatment I had received for a bruised fist after I punched the side of Henry Cooper's TR7. I rubbed the knobble on my knuckle and I walked up to a stern-looking receptionist.

'Name and what's wrong innit?'

'Actually I'm looking for the old underground ward.'

'No such fing. What's the matter – you come about your breath?'

'There's nothing wrong with my breath.'

'You wouldn't say that if you was standing where I'm standing.'

I thanked her and left. I passed through the hospital, looking for a way down to the basement. Many of the departments – oncology, geriatric wards, psychiatry, physiotherapy – seemed there merely to remind me of my own mortality. I pulled my sports jacket tight.

Eventually I ended up in X-Ray. A young lady appeared in a lead apron.

'Is it your right foot, sir?' she asked.

'My foot?'

'You're limping.'

'Am I?'

'Heavily. Sprained or broken?'

'Neither. I'm looking for the basement ward.'

'To my knowledge the basement closed down in the early fifties.'

'Is it accessible?'

'There's a door next to the Munchhausen Ward but it's boarded up. Please make sure you elevate that foot later.'

I walked on and found a supply cupboard. With no one looking I used the OneKey™ to open it. I removed a set of scrubs and a surgical mask, donning both.

I reached the Munchhausen Ward. Opposite the entrance was a door, a man guarding it. He was tall, maybe seven foot three, and blond. I approached him, thrust my hand into his and administered the Nazi handshake.

'Herr Komrade,' he said, nodding and opening the door behind him. I performed a low-key Hitler salute and passed through. The door clicked behind me.

The corridor is straight but steep, sending me deep into the bowels of the hospital. After a couple of minutes there is a switchback, then another and another, until eventually I reach a set of double doors. A red light glows above – PRIVATE ACCESS ONLY. I cleanse my hands using the anti-bacterial dispenser on the wall and press the buzzer. The door clicks open.

Before me is a ward perhaps two football pitches in length. It is breathtaking to behold. Down either side are banks of beds; women to the right, men left. Yet it would be wrong to describe them as adults. As I walk gingerly down the gangway I can see the people in bed do resemble adults, but are half the size, sometimes smaller. I proceed along the divide. The further I go, the bigger the little people become. Each is talking in a squeaky voice. Each is recognisable.

Andrew Marr, Kirsty Young, Hugh Bonneville, Gary Lineker, Sir Mervyn King, Hilary Mantel, Alan Carr – Chatty Man, Fiona Bruce, Bradley Wiggins, Ant and Dec, Barbara Windsor, the Archbishop of Canterbury, Kevin Pieterson, Benedict Cumberbatch, Peter Tatchell, John Humphries, Clare Balding, Piers Morgan, Sir Alex Ferguson, JK Rowling, Shane Ritchie, Dame Helen Mirren and the man with the moustache from the GoCompare advert. Versions of Britain's most influential people, dinkified and in growbags.

Towards the back I reach an area labelled 'MPs' enclosure'. Every serving member of parliament appears to have been reproduced. Some are being briefed by men in SS attire while they are fed their lunch. Others are asleep, snuggling up to Hitler dolls.

I nod to the nurses. They nod back, whispering 'seig heil'. This nightmarish village of shrunken celebrities is complete when I am nearly knocked off my feet by a petite Bruce Forsyth dashing past me screaming 'gut game, gut game'.

At the end is a room cordoned off from the rest. The blinds are down. I try the handle.

'Can ich help?' says a voice. I spin round. A man in a white coat with a swastika lapel is standing before me.

'Ja,' I reply. 'I am checking up on ze patients, see how zay are coming along.'

'Zay are fine,' he replies coldly. 'Und who bist du?'

'Ich haf come here on behalf von Dr Mengele – to check up on all ze things.'

'A freund von Mengele?'

'Jawohl.'

'He ist quite ze genius, nicht? To create life form von only a vile of blood und an ordinary egg von Waitrose.'

'A genius, ja.'

'Vood du like to look in on his special creation?'

'Only if it is convenient, Herr Docktor.'

'Mengele ist especially proud of ziss vun,' he says before gently opening the door and letting me peek through. There, sitting up in bed reading a copy of *TV Quick* is the Queen, shrunk to two-thirds her normal size.

'Visitor, your majesty?' enquires the white-coated man.

'Not now thenk you. One is reading a mag. All the best to you. Close the door, there's a good chep.'

'Two veeks and she vill be ready for her inaugural appearance,' whispers the man, shutting the door softly behind him.

What I had seen was mind-blowing, but I needed more.

'Ze good doctor asked me to ask du vether ve should move ze bodies of ze originals to another location,' I venture.

'Bodies, komrade?'

'Ja, bodies.'

'Zare must be some confusion. Zare are no bodies. Ve are still deciding vot to do vith ze originals. Mengele vants to keep zem for further experimentation. Personally ich think ve should liqvidate zem in a liqvidiser. If zay fell into ze wrong hans it could be curtains for ze Third Reich.'

'Heil Hitler to that.'

'Quite.'

Over the doctor's shoulder I catch a glimpse of a miniature Ricky Gervais doing his shriek-laugh.

'Remind me vare zay are again?' I say.

'Sorry?'

'Ze originals – vare are zay being held?'

The doctor stands back from me, suspicious.

'You do nicht know?'

'Forgive me, Herr Docktor, ich bin getting old und forget so much . . .'

'Who bist du anvay?' he demands. 'How do du know Dr Mengele?'

'He ist ein alt family freund von ze Black Forest.'

'Vare are your papers?'

'Ich must have left zem at home . . .'

The man heads straight for the office and lifts the phone. I start to walk back through the ward to the double-doors, gradually hastening my pace. Two-thirds of the way down a piercing alarm is triggered. The lights flash on and off. The mini-celebrities either side of me scream and whoop. Newspapers, magazines, even bedpans are hurled in my direction.

I reach the doors but they are locked down. I turn round. The white-coated doctor is running towards me, flanked by nurses either side. In his right hand I make out a syringe, from which drops of clear liquid glisten in the artificial light.

Frantically I rummage through my jacket. Glucose tablets, empty inhalers, inferior quality Viagra. I knew it had to be here.

As the doctor swept through the vast ward, great swathes of the miniaturised rich and famous fell in behind him. Hundreds of them were hurtling towards me.

At last I found it.

I slotted the OneKey™ into the lock, held the button down and waited for the click.

Nothing.

I pressed again. Still nothing. Please not now. The mob was no more than a cricket strip away. I press one last time.

Click.

I flung the door open, dashed through the gap and threw the bolt. There was a thud as the doctor, nurses and small people crashed against the other side. The most terrible noise like bees could be heard. The door was bowing under the force, but holding.

I set off up the winding route back to the hospital. Then it dawned on me: a gargantuan Nazi was still guarding the entrance. He might have been tipped off. I called George Michael.

'Urgent job. Need you to chat up a tall German at the Luton and Dunstable Hospital,' I said.

'Hardly a job,' he said. 'More like a pastime.'

'He's definitely your demographic. Only thing is I need you here in the next five minutes. Munchausen Ward.'

GM was a fast driver. By the time I reached the door I could hear him coquettishly serenading the tall Teuton with a breathy acapella version of 'Last Christmas'. After two minutes he had managed to draw the German away for a coffee. I let myself out and headed straight for the car park, texting him en route to say he could stand down. I couldn't tell whether his reply – 'Not yet, Alan, this one's quite fit – FOR A NAZI!' – was a joke or not.

I sat in the car and took a puff on my blue inhaler. Maybe if Edame could see me now she'd understand how important this final hunt was. I wish she *could* see me now. I felt vaguely heroic and therefore quite sexy.

I now knew where the replicas were being kept – but what of the originals? I drew deep once more on the blue tube, slid the car into gear and drove home.

Tom was in the sitting room watching *Cheggers Plays Pop* on UK Gold. He looked pleased with himself. I asked if he'd heard from Sandra at the Premier Inn. He said he had, then rose and left the room.

I ordered myself an Indian takeaway, extra onion bhajis. There's nothing like a hot curry after a long day to relax the mind and body. Afterwards I ran myself a deep bath and plugged into The Griffin. My timing – unlike the state of my toenails – was impeccable.

'Vell get some more!'

The voice of Dr Josef Mengele.

'It ist not zat simple, Herr Griffin. Ich made zem to ein special formula. Zwei days vithout and ich bin at death's elbow.'

'How could du have lost zem?'

'Ich voz sure ich left them in ze drawer marked fur mein attention.'

'Snap out of it, doc, vee need du for ze final push. Herb Derb ist taking the president's blut next week.'

'Nicht sure ich vill make it zat far, Herr Komrade.'

'Nonsense!' said The Griffin. 'Eat ein apple, maybe some porridge, a bottle of Baden Baden spring wasser und du fill be reicht as rain. Deutschland Uber Alles – remember?'

'Ich have to rest now, Herr Griffin. Let us speak tomorrow, unless ich bin dead by zen.'

The president? Which president? President of the IOC? Of France?

Of the United States?

I clamber out of the bath, half-lobsterised but still listening. As I dry myself The Griffin pours himself a drink which makes me want one. He dials a new number.

'Derb, it's ze Griffin.'

'Griffmeister! What's up, big man?'

'Ve're losing Doc.'

'You mean you want me to finish him?'

'Nein. He's dying. Lost his pills. Ve need to bring forward ze draining of ze president's blut. Check mit Downing Street und secure ein invite to ze gala dinner in zwei days' time. Ve haf to act schnell.'

'Affirmative, Griff.'

A pause.

'Dangerous business this, isn't it?' said Derb.

'Vot?'

'I mean – what with all the risks and that . . .'

'Ja?'

'It's just, you know . . .'

'Vot?'

'Look. I mean . . . listen. All I mean I suppose is it's dangerous and risky and perhaps I should maybe be paid more than I am, that's all.'

Silence down the line.

'Du Englishmen are alles ze ficken same, grabben grabben grabben.'

'But I didn't mean—'

'If du don't vant to do it ich can easily find someone else to replace du. Permanently.'

'But Griffman . . .'

'You're lucky it's nicht 1942.'

'Please, I didn't mean it.'

'Ich can have du killed at vill.'

'Shitting hell.'

'Let me down und ich vill personally slice du into zwei.'

'I won't let you down, promise. Was only joking before. Heil Hitler and a thousand sorrys.'

A breakthrough feels close, I just wish I could share it with someone. Like my wife, for instance.

November

Start the day with a pot of coffee so strong Dr Grossmark would strike me from his books if he knew. I plonk myself in front of the BBC Micro, type in my password (ihatehenry) and start writing an e-memo to Tony Blair's former press secretary, Alastair Campbell.

Dear AC,

Alan here – how are things?

It's been ages since we last spoke. I hope life outside government is working out for you. I'm always seeing your face on the telly, promoting depression or a new novel. Incidentally I think the work you have done in raising the profile of mental illness in this country is great. As you know, I have always been a terrible worrier but have been too embarrassed to admit it. Thank god for people like you.

Enough flim flam. Back in 1999 you said that you and Tony owed me a favour for seizing evil Hans Feet, the Imp of Immenstadt. It's time to call in that favour.

I need an invitation to tomorrow's gala dinner at Number Ten. I am well aware that you are no longer part of the government or indeed politics. But your influence runs deep and you are the only person I can trust – and even then I only half-trust you after the 'sexed up' dossier. For the purpose of this request I'm letting that go.

If you swing this not only will we be quits, I'll owe YOU one. How do you like them apples?

Stay vigilant.

Alan

I press send before digging out the email address of Jon Snow at Channel Four News.

Dear Snowy,

Alan here – how are things?

Last time you saw me my penis was completely naked. Sorry about that. Frankly it wasn't ideal for me either. Such a chilly day, too.

I am now retired but have been keeping my hand in, so to speak. Basically, and in short, there is an enormous plot by the Nazis to transform the coalition into a National Socialist government by cloning all existing cabinet members and MPs, inculcating them with fascist beliefs then repeating the formula across the world starting with the President of the United States whose blood will be removed for duplication purposes at tomorrow's gala dinner inside Number Ten.

Please come to the gala dinner and train your camera on the back of the president at all times. Last time I was let down by incompetents. This time will be different. Trust me, I'm a Nazi Hunter.

Stay vigilant.

Alan.

PS – I hope you are the real Jon Snow. If you are a clone of the real Jon Snow I'm only writing this for a bet. We always do this kind of thing, me and Jon.

By the time I have sent the Snow email, Alistair Campbell has issued a one-word reply ('OK'). I slip on the weighted pants and take a stroll.

November is a tricky month, especially since the advent of 'Movember'. Everyone looks like Hitler. Though I accept that he is likely to be dead, one never knows with the likes of the Führer. That said, if he were still alive he would probably have shaved off his moustache and would be unlikely to grow a new one for charity.

I blink hard to rid myself of such thoughts and decide to get a haircut to make myself dapper for tonight. As I approach my local hairdresser's, The Grateful Head, a small boy comes towards me carrying a bag.

''Ere, mister,' he says, 'would you like a present?'

'OK,' I reply. 'But only if you tell me what it is. I don't like surprises.'

'I love 'em. It's Christmas soon and I know exactly what I'm gettin'.'

'Then how will that be a surprise?'

'Oh yeah.'

I take the bag.

'So what is it?'

'Dunno,' he says. 'These geezers parked round the corner in a blacked out beamer give me a tenner to do it.'

'Were they English?'

'Nah – their accent was foreign, like from a movie or summat.'

'A war movie?'

'Yeah that.'

Acting on instinct I hurl the bag high over my shoulder and fall onto the boy, protecting him from any impending blast.

'Get off me, you paedo,' he says.

The sound when it comes seems to obliterate my eardrums. My shoes and socks are blown off my feet, the weighted pants ripped from under my trousers, which somehow remain on. Pieces of debris rain down upon us.

I look at the boy. His eyes are shut and his face covered in blood. Nearly seventy years since the war and the Nazis are still taking out the innocent. It was then I noticed I too was bathed in red.

'Fucking nora,' says the boy, sitting up. In his hand is a dismembered paw. 'You threw the bag at a cat.'

He got up and walked into the newsagents, no doubt to spend his new-found Nazi wealth on sherbets. A huge BMW screeches round the corner. I quickly lie down again and let my tongue loll from my mouth.

The car pulls up alongside me. A window winds down. I try not to breathe. A few words uttered. Laughter. The window is raised. The car drives off.

I pick myself up and entered the hairdresser's.

'Hell's tits, Alan, you're covered in blood!' says Helen.

'I think I will have that shampoo today, Helen,' I tell her.

I do enjoy having my hair shampooed. It's like sex with your clothes on. But right now I am still shaking from nearly dying twice. My heart is thudding uncomfortably in my chest. Panic threatens to take over. I remove a glucose tablet from my pocket and feel half-calmed by the sugar.

After the shampoo I sit in the chair and am forced to stare back at my ageing face. When under stress I experience flashbacks from my early years. The cat-bomb combination was doing things to my brain chemistry.

. . . I'm up in the Yorkshire Dales. I feel the hard hands of the master of the house, Mr Meeker. He beats me for being rude, late, on time, nervous or alone. His wife Sue is standing in the corner, never intervening. I am in the front row at my mother's funeral, the tears streaming down my face. Next day the Meekers collect me, lock all the doors and pin me down in the back of their Ford Consul.

The Nazis ruined my early years. A lifetime later and I still haven't come to terms with it. Perhaps putting an end to their evil ways will lay these ghosts to rest. I blink hard to banish the thoughts and tell Helen to raise the sideburns slightly.

Back home I shower before dusting off my dinner jacket for tomorrow. I haven't worn it since winning the Simon Wiesenthal Award for Most Outstanding Gentile back in 2004. Holding the trousers up to myself I can see how much weight I have lost since Edame's departure.

Tom is out. For the first time in a while the evening stretches before me. I don't like it so I call round for Bob. He doesn't answer. I go round the back and see that he's asleep face down in a pizza. I fashion to knock at the window, then decide to leave him be. He obviously needs the rest.

Back home I cannot relax. Thoughts of the scattered cat, its paw in the boy's hand, assail me. Perhaps I'm suffering from post-traumatic stress disorder. I check the symptoms online. After some searching it seems three hours after the event is too soon to diagnose.

As so often in this situation, I ask myself: 'What would Simon Wiesenthal do?'

'Watch *Butterflies* on Yesterday +1' may not necessarily be the obvious answer, but it's certainly a comfort. Wendy Craig looks stunning with her precise features and bouncy auburn hair. She's no Edame but I'm happy to watch two episodes followed by half a *Thorn Birds*.

In bed it strikes me: nothing or no one compares to Edame. It's a mournful thought but not one I hold for long before I am lost to the night.

* * *

Wake at ten. That final hot Ribena really did zonk me. Downstairs I find a note from Tom.

Dear Dad,
    Sorry to miss you. Gone to buy a new shirt and stuff, then I've got a date! We're going to see a Smiths cover band called The Smythes then hopefully onto a lay-by somewhere off the A5.
    Best of luck tonight. Don't mess it up, you old sod.
    Much love: Tom.

A date? Good for Tom. I knew Sandra was right for him. Regardless of tonight's outcome that makes me smile.

A knock at the door.

'Good luck this evening,' says Bob. I didn't even know he knew.

'Thanks, Bob,' I say. 'Want to come in?'

'Better not,' he says. 'I've read astronauts like yourself need time to compose themselves before take-off.'

I watch through the window as he walks to the end of the drive before climbing into an untended wheelie bin.

After a silent brunch I go upstairs to change. Standing before the full-length mirror of what used to be the marital bedroom I see a gloomy-looking elderly man wearing a dinner jacket two sizes too big.

'Come on, Stoob,' I say. 'You've come a long way. Not much further to go. This is the big one. Don't mess it up, you old twit. Bedfordshire expects. Israel too. Fuck the Nazis.'

I am due in Downing Street at 5.30. As ever I've set off early. I decide to call in at Tina's.

'Fucking hell, Dad, you haven't entered *Strictly*, have you?' she says rather loudly, looking at my evening-wear. She pulls me towards her and whispers in my ear:

'Mum's here.'

I enter the house with great anxiety, flipping my inhaler over in my pocket. I feel like a teenager.

'Hello, Alan,' says Edame. She doesn't get up.

'It's so nice to see you, my love,' I reply. She smiles kindly, but her eyes are sad.

'You look smart,' she says. 'Who's the lucky lady?'

'Don't be daft. I was hoping you'd catch me on the news later. I'm meeting the president.'

'No doubt there's a hunting element to your outings, Alan.'

'No doubt,' I say.

'Another cup of tea, Mum?' says Tina.

'Not for me,' she replies. 'Best be off.'

'I love you,' I say to Edame.

'Enjoy your evening,' she replies, blinking heavily. 'Dressed like that you're bound to woop the ladies.'

She means woo. God, I love her.

'Not interested,' I reply.

'Take care,' she says and leaves, taking care not to brush my shoulder even by accident.

I slump on the sofa. Tina brings over a cup of tea and a slice of chocolate cake Houdini made in cookery. It's burnt at the edges, soggy in the middle and curiously peppery. It's disgusting.

'How is she?' I ask Tina.

'OK,' she says. 'Less herself than she used to be, but OK.'

'It's that George. He's such a bastard.'

'We don't know that. Mum says he's treating her nice.'

'Yes, well, she would say that.'

'You made your own bed with this, Dad.'

'I didn't make the bed all on my own, Simon Wiesenthal helped. Did you know he visited me in spectral form?'

'You look tired. Why don't you skip this evening? Stay here with us and have sausage and chips.'

Haden and Houdini appear from upstairs. Houdini crawls onto my lap and undoes my bowtie, which took fifteen minutes to fasten.

'Granddad, are you staying for tea?' she says, excitedly.

'Nice to see you, Alan,' says Haden. Formality has replaced low-slung jeans in his repertoire.

'May I just say how very lovely it is to see you all. I love you all so very much.'

'We love you, Granddad,' says Houdini and cuddles my neck, her corkscrew curls tickling my chin. I begin to cry.

'Jesus, what is it, Dad?' says Tina, kneeling beside me.

'Sorry,' I say, wiping my eyes. 'It's Edame, you lot, the thought of not seeing you again. I don't know.'

'What do you mean? Are you in some kind of danger?'

'Perhaps,' I say. 'But perhaps the danger will pass very soon.'

'Maybe you're just tired,' says Haden. 'That's what people say when they cry: "Oh, I'm just tired, I'll be fine in the morning".'

'Well maybe I will be,' I say to Haden. He smiles.

I rise to go. Now it's Tina's turn to cry.

'I don't want to lose my dad,' she says and hugs me hard. There is a satisfying click in my lower spine. Her strength is bordering on the Cooperesque. As she clings on I remove her phone from her pocket, find Edame's new number and memorise it before slipping it back into Tina's trousers.

'Why are you dressed up?' asks Houdini.

'I'm meeting the president.'

'That's well exciting, Granddad. Say "Hi" from me and tell him I'd like to be friends with his two girls.'

As I leave the house Marco arrives, looking sweaty and nervous.

'Ciao, Alan!' he says. 'Can't stop, need a shower.'

'Take good care of your brood,' I tell him. He winks uneasily before dashing past Tina and up the stairs.

As I climb into the car Haden taps on the window.

'Take it easy, Alan,' he says. 'If there's anything, anything at all, just call or text or tweet or Facebook or Bebo me, OK?'

I raise a thumb like a Spitfire pilot and point myself towards the M1.

Once I'm past junction 6A for St Albans I call Edame using the number from Tina's phone. It goes straight to voicemail so I leave a message telling her how much I love her and whether she'd consider meeting for another coffee with a view to moving back in.

Within minutes the clouds open and the rain falls hard and heavy. The windscreen wipers struggle to combat the deluge. I enjoy the rain, it matches my mood. What is the point of snaffling Nazis if I don't have my girl by my side? To hunt or not to hunt? That is the question. Eventually the incessant rainfall numbs my brain into a thoughtless blank.

I drive as far as Whitehall and park up. I set off towards Downing Street. As I do I find myself in the company of famous faces all doing as I am: Des Lynam, Lord Sugar and Dame Judy Dench to name but three. Sugar in particular looks tiny in person. They could all be duplicates, it's impossible to tell — though I'd be surprised he got as far as he has in business with such a diminutive stature.

Then I see someone who is clearly a miniature. The Queen, all 4'1" of her, is being ushered towards the entrance. Her integration has clearly been hastened. She should have had longer in the pot. I quicken my pace.

I move with the crowd and find myself in a queue. A woman is standing in front of Number Ten with a clipboard.

'Name?' she asks.

'Alan Stoob.'

'Stooge?'

'Stoob.'

'Boob?'

'STOOB. S-T-O-O-B.'

'Stoob . . . Stoob . . . sorry, nothing under Stoob.'

'Perhaps I'm there under my pseudonym, Michael Throat?'

'Throat . . . nope, no Throat either. Sorry.'

'But Alastair Campbell said he had arranged an invite for me.'

'The depression man?'

'Yes.'

'Let me go inside and find out.'

I stand in the rain and make small talk with a policeman. A queue is forming behind me. Elton John is becoming particularly impatient.

Eventually the door opens again and the lady appears. Behind her is the Prime Minister, David Cameron. He beckons me over and whispers in my ear. I crane to listen.

'I was told you were dead,' he says. I take a step back but he pulls me in again. 'Either way you can shit right off. We don't need a cuntweasel like you sniffing round President Big Balls from Yanksville. There are going to be some changes round here, granddad, and the last thing we want is an ageing arsehorse sticking his bollock in. Leave now or I'll have you assassinated.'

Cameron smiles to the crowd, waves to photographers and heads back inside. The clipboard lady gives me a sympathetic look before ushering in Leona Lewis.

I check my pocket for my miniature UN umbrella but I must have left it on the backseat. As I stand there in the rain the other guests filter past, some nudging me sharply with their elbows or catching me with their brollies. Rainwater trickles down the back of my shirt collar, some of it absorbed by the waistband of my underpants. I stroll aimlessly towards the Downing Street gates and back out onto Whitehall.

I have come a long way and achieved much. There is still a chance Channel Four will catch Herb in the act of siphoning blood from the buttocks of the president, though this is far from certain. My trump card turned out to be a canard. I feel lost.

Back in the car I breathe deeply and try to relax my shoulders, just like Beryl taught me. 'Clarity of thought only comes with a relaxed state of mind,' she says. 'That'll be £800 for the month.'

And then it happens; an epiphany and with it a sense of my own strength that overwhelms me. I leave the car, stride back into Downing Street and head straight for the policeman.

'Excuse me, officer, but you know that politician that allegedly called one of you a pleb?'

'You mean Conservative MP Andrew Mitchell?'

'That's him. Well he's in the queue trying to get in. I thought you should know.'

'He's a bloody bastard, I'll have 'im,' says the policeman before walking down the line in search of Mitchell.

As he does I walk away in the opposite direction, beyond the entrance to Number Ten and past numbers twelve, fourteen and sixteen before scaling a wall, landing safely in the peonies on the other side and making my way across the garden to the rear of the PM's residence.

I try the back door but find it locked. I reach for the OneKey™ before it dawns on me I must have left it in my other suit. I walk round to the kitchen but Nigel Farage is in there pilfering the lychees from the fruit salad. I find a bathroom with a crack of open window. It's small but so am I, particularly since Edame left me. Those last few weeks have worked wonders. I wriggle through and land head-first in the sink, before flipping over and landing on my feet. Perhaps this was the metaphor I had been seeking.

A toilet flushes. I freeze. George Osborne emerges. It is impossible to tell whether he is the original or a replica but I punch him in the face anyway and drag his unconscious body into a cupboard, locking the door.

I squeeze my way through the vast lobby and past very many well-known figures. Almost all are shorter than me. Clearly it is not just the Queen who has been 'released' prematurely. The entire integration programme has been fast-tracked on account of Mengele's fatigue. Deborah Meaden winks in my direction before sketching a swastika in the air. No sign of the president.

It takes ten minutes and three glasses of champagne for me to locate the dining room. There I find twenty-two tables, each headed by a cabinet minister for maximum damage. I look for Osborne on the table plan. The chancellor is to be seated between Michael Parkinson and Frank Lampard. I walk over to the table, pick up his name card, fold it back the other way and write, 'Alan Stoob, Britain's Premier Nazi Hunter' on the flap before replacing it. I then switch Parky's card with that of Ruth Madoc from *Hi-De-Hi*. Parkinson I find a terrible bore and instinct tells me Madoc will be good company and the perfect foil.

After ten minutes of small talk with the Archbishop of Canterbury who brings up the compulsory electrification of Muslims (I presume he's a clone), a gong is struck by a dwarf-sized Ken Clarke and we are requested to sit for dinner.

'Oh hallo, Alan, always been a big fan,' says Madoc as I take my seat. 'I'm Ruth but you can call me Gladys like in the show. Keep an eye on me, will you, I've already had six glasses innit!' She squeezes my upper thigh.

I introduce myself to Frank Lampard. He smiles sweetly and apologises for being a Nazi.

Parky is giving it the big I-Am as the starters are dished out – Bratwurst on a bed of sauerkraut. The Prime Minister rises.

'Ladies und Gentlemen. Thank you all for coming this evening. I hope you like my haus. We had the architects in last week. They said the building was beginning to lean too far to the right. I told them that's just how we liked it!'

The whole room is bathed in laughter. First Susan Boyle gets up to applaud, then Michael McIntyre. Pretty soon everyone bar Madoc, Lampard and myself are standing and clapping.

I look over and see Jon Snow. He winks back at me. He has a camera trained to the front.

'But enough of zees jokes. We are gathered here this evening to give a warm welcome to a man – a black man, no less – who holds . . .'

Cameron catches sight of me and loses his words.

'. . . who holds the, er, most important position in the world. Ladies and gentlemen, he may not be right-wing, he may not even be white, but will you please give a respectful welcome to the President of the United States, Barack Obama.'

The double doors open and Obama enters, emanating cool and sang-froid. A few flashlights go off. Applause is muted. Madoc releases my thigh, leaps to her feet and whistles.

'I bloody loves you I do, I bloody loves you!' she shouts.

Obama nods towards her before being seated next to the Prime Minister.

'Thank you,' he says. 'Why, this food looks good enough to eat.'

We begin our starters.

''Ere, Alan,' says Madoc, her hand re-positioned dangerously close to Little Alan. 'What you say after we go get a couple of takeouts and adjourn to my B&B?'

'Let's see how the evening pans out, Ruth,' I tell her. 'You might have gone off me by pudding.'

She hoots with laughter and sticks her tongue in my ear.

Little happens for the next hour. The main course arrives. Osborne had ordered the wiener schnitzel, which is a shame because I would have preferred the fish. Thankfully Madoc spoons morsels of trout into my mouth which I find quite erotic. The Prime Minister chats to Obama but looks uncomfortable next to a black man. I find this embarrassing and wonder what Obama could be making of it all. On the far side of the room I can see Herb and Nigel laughing with one another. Both appear to be wearing smart new Hugo Boss suits. Neither has spotted me.

As pudding arrives, Obama slowly raises himself up to his full height before tapping gently on his glass. The room falls silent.

'Ladies and gentlemen, members of the cabinet, Billy Connolly, Tony Blair and assorted British stars, thank you for gracing me with your presence this evening.'

'No worries, Bazza!' shrieks Madoc raising her glass of red, which is filled to the meniscus.

'I do hope, first of all, you will indulge me a brief story from my past,' he says. 'When I was a little boy . . .'

'A little black boy!' shouts Nick Clegg. The president continues unruffled.

'When I was a little boy, people would say to me, "Barack", they would say . . .'

'Remember the Berlin Olympics!' This time the heckler is Stephen Hawking.

'No, Stephen,' counters Obama. 'They did not say "Remember the Berlin Olympics", which incidentally was a heroic victory for African American Jesse Owens over Hitler's Third Reich. They would say to me, "Barack, if you ever become President of the United States of America you must honour the special relationship between our great nation and that of the United Kingdom. For not only are they our forefathers, the UK stands tall as one of the least bigoted, most tolerant countries in the world." And even though I was smoking a lot of dope at the time, those words stayed with me, people. I thought, "Here is a nation that displays greater tolerance even than the United States." And it's true. Or at least it was. Because you see I am sad to report that over the past few weeks my certainty about the credentials of this once great country have been tested to its limit.'

'Sit down, you black bastard,' shouts a mini Freddie Starr.

'Now, now, Freddie,' says the Prime Minister, rising. 'There's no need to be quite so rude. Mr President, please continue.'

'Thank you, Mr Prime Minister. Britain is moving to the right, of this there is little question. We are of course all aware of this painful period of economic downturn. Governments will often swing to extremes during times of great hardship. But I am concerned – deeply concerned – about the current shift in the attitudes of this coalition government. Your policies of late bear comparison to unfortunate events, events from history which surely none of us wish to revisit. If I was to – OUCH!'

The president jolts in pain and grasps his left buttock.

'What the hell,' he exclaims, his face contorted. 'I think I've just been stung by a wasp.'

'Or a W.A.S.P.!' I say, climbing to my feet and removing the replica gun from my pocket. The crowd gasps. In the blink of an eye Obama's entire staff of eight have automatic weapons trained on me.

'Tell your security to stand down!' I boom to the president. 'You have just been penetrated.'

The president looks initially bemused before recognising me and nodding to his security. One by one the men in black lower their rifles.

'Nobody move an inch!' I yell. I approach the president's table with my gun raised to the ceiling.

'You're making a prick of yourself, Stoob,' mutters Cameron.

'I think not,' I say and move cautiously towards the president.

'Easy now, Stoob,' says Obama, raising his hands, beads of sweat dotting his brow. I manoeuvre myself round the back of him and find what I am looking for. Crouching behind America's first black president is Herb Derb, clad in white coat and plastic gloves, clasping a small vile of presidential blood. I raise him up by his ear, my gun pointed at his temple.

'Are we live, Jon?' Snow pressed the earpiece to his ear before nodding. The floor was mine.

'Sorry to spoil the party, those watching at home,' I say, addressing the camera. 'I'm sure you'll see plenty more of the president during his trip to our green and currently unpleasant land. I would not choose to interrupt this great man's eloquence if I hadn't had my hand forced by the wheels of fate. Some of you will recognise the man on the end of my arm as the one who replaced me as Britain's Premier Nazi Hunter. What you won't know is that Herb Derb, for that is his name, is being paid by Dr Josef Mengele to extract blood from leading figures across the globe, enabling the evil genius to clone these great influences, mould them into Nazi sympathisers, kidnap the originals, release the duplicates and turn the world into a Nazi breeding ground.'

I grab the syringe of the president's blood from Herb's quivering hands and squirt the contents over Cameron's dinner.

'Finish him off!' shouts Madoc.

'Apart from myself, Ruth Madoc from *Hi-de-Hi*, Jon Snow and a tiny assortment of others, everyone here is a right-wing clone of their original. Some of the cabinet may have required less tampering than others but by and large they are all products of Dr Mengele's evil mind.'

'I am not a clone,' says Hawking.

'Yes you bloody are,' shouts Snow. 'You're wearing SS socks.'

'Someone else dresses me,' he replies. 'I cannot be held responsible for my nurse's political bias.' With the lack of intonation in his Vocoder it is hard to tell whether this is a joke.

'Gentlemen,' I continue, 'I think we can be sure that, with these pictures being beamed live across the country, Number Ten will shortly be surrounded. Mr President, I do hope you will accept my apologies on behalf of our nation. I am certain your trip will improve no end from here. Are you OK?'

The President rubbed his backside.

'I'm cool, Alan – it was only a little prick.'

'Quite so. Now if you'll excuse me I have some loose ends to tie up. Non-Nazis, follow me. The rest of you stay put until the police arrive – and that's an order.'

I headed for the door. Behind me President Obama, Ruth Madoc, Jon Snow, Michael Frayn and Sophie Dahl followed. I felt like the Pied Piper of Downing Street.

'YOU VON'T GET AVAY FITH ZISS!' shouted the Prime Minister.

'I already have,' I replied.

There was almost no time to react. Out of the corner of my eye something huge was hurtling towards me. I turned to see actor-comedian John Cleese flying through the air, his eyes wild with hate, his mouth all frothy. I ducked as he passed over me, one of his size-twelves clipping the top of my head. He landed in a heap on the wooden floor and hit the wall. Obama's security opened fire and unloaded a barrage of bullets into his writhing bulk. This went on for over a minute (I know because I timed it). By the end there was nothing recognisable about Cleese. I only hope it was a clone, Edame and I loved *Fawlty Towers*.

As the doors shut behind us we heard the first words of 'Deutschland Uber Alles' begin.

'I thought there was some weird shit going down here in England,' said Obama as he threw on his overcoat and straightened the collar. 'Thanks for bringing this to light, Alan. You must drop by the White House sometime. We've got plenty of wayward fuckers that could do with straightening out, Stoob-style.'

I shook the president's hand. The same policeman as before was standing by the door.

'No bloody sign of Mitchell,' he said. 'I should bloody arrest you for bloody lying.'

'You bloody do that I'll bloody scratch yer eyes out I will,' said Madoc, forcing herself in between us. The policeman frowned and opened the door. A swarm of policemen flooded in, many carrying guns. The aroma of Lynx deodorant was overwhelming.

'We'll take it from here,' said Sir Bernard Hogan-Howe, head of the Metropolitan Police.

'Help yourself,' I replied. 'I'll be in touch soon.'

The rain had stopped. Jon Snow said his goodbyes and headed for the Channel Four van. The president slapped me on the back before hailing a cab and heading into Soho. Ruth Madoc took my arm.

'I bloody fancy you like crazy I do,' she said. 'You're a bloody hero. How's about it then, you and me all snuggled up in the nuddy.'

'Ever since you first appeared on our screens back in 1980 I've found you mightily attractive, Ruth,' I told her. 'But the truth is that I must remain faithful to my wife if I am to have any chance of getting her back.'

As I spoke a familiar vehicle drew up alongside.

'Alright, Alan, fancy a lift, Alan?' It was George Michael.

'That's not yer bloody wife, is it,' said Madoc. 'That's bloody George Michael.'

Madoc stormed off into the night. I climbed into the Michaelmobile.

'Where to, Alan?'

'Premier Inn Dunstable please, George Michael. And don't spare the horsepower.'

As GM drove us up Tottenham Court Road and towards Camden in a northerly direction I let *The Very Best of Elton John Volume II* wash over me. I felt exhausted. A lack of siestas was beginning to take its toll but I had to remain vigilant until this whole caper was through.

'Like me in there was it, Alan?'

'Eh?'

'Bit hairy?'

'Not really, George,' I said. 'I had it all planned out.'

'What do you think they'll do with the clones – melt them down for glue?'

'No idea,' I said, drifting off.

I awoke at 1.05am. We were at the hotel. I told George Michael to clear some space on the back seat and wait. I headed inside.

'Hello again, Sandra.'

'Mr Stoob!' she replied. 'You're not stalking me by any chance, are you?'

'Chance would be a fine thing,' I reply. 'Is Mr Mengele still here?'

'Funny you should mention that. He's not been out for a couple of days. We were planning to call security.'

'Leave it with me,' I say and summon the lift.

Two minutes later I let myself into Mengele's room. The lights were off, the stench of farts overpowering. I flicked on the sidelight.

'Dying . . .' said Mengele in a tissue-thin voice. Even for a man of 116 he looked rough.

'What's up, doc?'

'Leave . . . me,' he replied weakly.

'Don't suppose you're looking for these?' I say, rattling his pills in front of his face.

'Please . . .'

'Want one do we?' I say, popping two in my mouth.

'Need . . .'

'What do you need?'

'Please . . .'

'Tell you what, I'll give you one now, you tell me where you're keeping the originals of the human beings you've been cloning, then I'll give you another when we get down the police station. Deal?'

'_____'

'I beg your pardon?'

'. . . OK . . .'

I placed one of the oversized red pills on his tongue and administered water. Within a minute he was sitting up on the edge of the bed. Violently I yanked back the last feathers of his hair. Instinctively he opened his mouth. I thrust a finger and thumb into his ancient gob, located the lower right second molar, wobbled it three times and tugged it free from his gum. I handed him a tissue for the blood and sat beside him on the bed, examining the tooth with its embedded cyanide capsule.

'Ziss isn't going to look gut,' he said. 'Ve Nazis do avay vith ourselves rather than being caught by ze enemy.'

'You should of thought of that before, Herr Docktor. Now where are the originals?'

Mengele checked his fingernails. He was playing for time.

'THE ORIGINALS, DOCKTOR?'

He grasped his knee and began writhing on the bed in faux-agony. I moved to the window and began pouring the pills out.

'HALTEN!' he yelled. 'OK, OK, ich tell du!'

'Well?'

He sighed.

'In zer grounds von Luton Hoo, at ze most south-easterly point, zare ist ein ancient stable. It ist being protected from ze front by zwei SS mensch. Du vill need to disarm zem to access ze building. Inside du vill find the cabinet plus ze cream of Britain's primary influencers.'

'Wasn't so hard now, was it?' I said.

'You'll never stop us though, ze president ist being cloned as ve sprechen.'

'You need to wake up and smell the coffee, old man.'

'Give me mein pills.'

'You can have more when you're getting comfy down the station.'

I lead Mengele to the lift, holding the plastic gun to his

head. He wimpers but seems resigned to his fate. It is only when we get downstairs that he reveals his true colours.

'Please help me!' he declares to Sandra. 'Ziss man broke into mein room und kidnipped me! He ist ein Nazi! Du must call ze polizei!'

'Oh really?' she replied. 'Then how come he doesn't have a German accent and you do?'

'Zat ist immaterial!' he shrieks. 'Get ziss man arrested or ich shall see du never arbeit here again!'

'That's nice talk that is,' she says. 'Mr Stoob?'

'Ignore him, Sandra,' I tell her. 'This man is evil Josef Mengele, the Angel of Death. He is the Nazi, I the Nazi Hunter.'

'You know what, I thought I recognised the name.'

Mengele begins to cry.

'Thanks for your help over these past few weeks,' I tell her. 'At the Premier Inn Dunstable nothing is too much trouble.'

'By the way, how was your date with Tom?'

'Your son?'

'Yes.'

'We never had one.'

'But I thought he took you out.'

'No.'

'But he rang you?'

'Yes.'

'And?'

'He's in a relationship.'

'A relat—'

'You should probably check your children's Facebook statuses before handing out their numbers, Mr Stoob.'

Tom in a relationship?

'Dr Josef Mengele, may I introduce eighties singer George Michael. George Michael, this is Dr Josef Mengele.'

'We've met before. Alright, Josef. Sorry about the Starbucks on the backseat, you'll have to make do.'

'How many of those pills do you have left, Mengele?' I enquired.

'Thousands, but zay are back in Deutschland.'

'Give me the address and I'll get them shipped over,' I said. 'What do they do exactly?'

'Guarantee eternal leben – or at least ein better class of living vile du ist still around. Zey give me erections von steel.'

We drop Mengele off at Dunstable Police Station. I brief the duty officer on a number of outstanding matters including locating The Griffin, finding out when Bedfordshire's Nazis are next meeting, raiding the British Nazi Hunting Association and calling in a group of world renowned scientists to analyse Mengele's pills as they could prove handy in the global battle against an ever-ageing demographic.

'Oh, and could someone please pick up my car from Whitehall and drive it back to my house for me? Ignore the disabled stickers in the window. They belong to Bob next door but this was an emergency.'

George Michael drives me home while puffing on a large reefer. The cabin is filled with smoke.

'If I recall, George, you mentioned something about helping you out round the house or taking you to the Heath in exchange for your time.'

'Don't worry about that now,' he says.

'Should I tip you?'

'It's alright, Stooby. What I've lost in time and petrol I've gained in The Bedfordshire Knowledge. Don't we need to go via Luton Hoo?'

'It's late,' I told him. 'That can wait until morning.'

At 3am I hop out of the car. George Michael gives two hoots and speeds off.

The house is dark and silent. I stand in the hallway feeling strangely peckish and grab a block of cheddar from the fridge before dragging myself upstairs, sliding into bed fully clothed and checking my phone for messages. There are literally hundreds. None are from Edame.

* * *

I am woken with a cup of tea from Tom. It's gone ten. I hope he doesn't see my powerful erection courtesy of the Mengele pills. A well-gnawed cheese sits on the bedside table.

'You're all over the papers, TV and radio,' he says. 'Plus I took a call from *Cycling Weekly*. They want to interview you about your fourth place in the 1965 Milk Race. Can we have everyone over this evening for dinner? There's someone I want to introduce to you all.'

Cycling Weekly? Bloody hell.

After a shower I call Detective Constable Mike Moomin of Bedfordshire Constabulary and ask him to meet me at Luton Hoo together with enough vehicles to return 400 politicians, entertainers, writers, sportspeople, writers and Jamie Oliver back to the real lives.

It's great to see the Stoobmobile outside the front door. It's amazing what people will do for you when you've nabbed a few Nazis. En route to Luton Hoo I call Edame yet again. The phone is switched off.

Police helicopters are swooping high above Bedfordshire's

premier stately home. As I turn into the entrance Mike is there waiting for me. I tell him to follow me down to the old stables at the bottom of the fields and if there are any Nazi henchmen outside to arrest them or chase them off.

As it turns out he does neither, choosing instead to run them over. This seems a little harsh. Sometimes it's easy to forget that when it comes to National Socialism, feelings run high in the Luton area.

For what promises to be the final time I remove my OneKey™ and pick at the lock. It is a Schadenfreude combination from the war and takes seconds to remove. The doors are stiff – a little like the German race as a whole – but with Mike's help I am able to prop them open.

The stench of urine and aftershave is overpowering. I press my leather glove to my mouth and lean up against the wall.

'You OK, Alan?' asks Mike.

'I'll take over from here,' I say, steadying myself as the nausea passes. 'If I'm not out in thirty, bang on the door.'

I enter. The barn is dim and dank. The sound of moaning echoes through the structure. I feel for switches on the wall. One by one I flick them. The space is illuminated.

It's like Madame Tussauds, only slightly more lifelike and with more dribbling. Hanging by their arms and with gags over their mouths are hundreds of Britain's richest, most famous and most successful individuals, plus Ross Kemp. The only one not bound in such a way is the Queen, who is manacled to a makeshift throne and has a hat full of water and a straw to her mouth.

'Thank you, young min,' says HRH. I hurry over and unchain her limbs. She rises, dusts herself down and heads for the exit. 'No doubt you will be hearing from us regarding the New Year's honours list,' she says, not bothering to turn.

One by one I cut down the 'influencers': Tulisa Contostavlos, A S Byatt, Richard and Judy, Des Lynam, David Beckham and his slender wife Victoria, Harry Styles, Rowan Atkinson, Peter Sissons, Anne Robinson and Mick Hucknall with his face like a punctured pumpkin. Terry Wogan's hairpiece is crooked. I straighten it before releasing him. People need their self-respect. Some kiss me and all are grateful, save for John Humphries who is in a foul mood. I ignore him.

After twenty minutes the room is nearly empty. Mouth gags litter the floor. I nearly twist my ankle on the handcuffs which only five minutes before had been used to imprison Brummie everyman, Adrian Chiles.

I saunter over to David Baddiel.

'Sorry I never responded to your tweets, Alan,' he says.

'Yes, well,' I reply and cut him down with more force than is necessary. He scurries off.

In the far corner are strung the twenty-two cabinet members. Danny Alexander has snot running down his chin. Justine Greening is crying. Nick Clegg is gasping for a cigarette. All have desperation etched upon their faces, save for Ken Clarke who is asleep. I can't see George Osborne. I must have punched the original back in Downing Street. He'll still be in a cupboard. I shall call about that later, probably.

I collect myself and summon the words I planned on the way here.

'I am deeply sorry you have all had to suffer this ordeal and I want you to know that in a few minutes' time I shall cut you down, whereupon you can leave and be reunited with your families. However, since I have a captive audience, so to speak, I feel it an opportune moment to have a chat with you about current government policy.'

There are dampened squeals. The Prime Minister tries to wriggle free but only succeeds in tightening his restraints.

'You may not know this but you have all been duplicated by Dr Josef Mengele, whom you may recall from World War Two. He cloned you by taking some of your blood, mixing it with a free-range egg and . . . I don't know the precise details of the process but he's obviously pretty clever and very evil. Crucial to the plan was to imbue the mini-yous with a Nazi sensibility before releasing you into the world. Your alter-egos have been spouting frightful Nazi nonsense for the past month, but here's a thing: many were up in arms about this shift in official policy, yet most people didn't notice the difference. And you know why? Because you lot have a reputation for harshness and cruelty towards the weak, the elderly and the infirm. Now no one, least of all me, is suggesting that you are a bunch of Nazis. I want to make that quite clear. But fascism has many faces. LOOK AT ME WHEN I'M TALKING TO YOU, GOVE!'

Michael Gove looks up.

'Introducing a bedroom tax, terrifying the mentally ill by insisting they prove their sickness in ridiculous ways, freezing benefits? I couldn't live off £71 a week if you paid me. These policies are not commensurate with a caring, sophisticated society. Half a million Britons regularly go hungry. William Beveridge must be oscillating in his grave. We judge a country by the way it treats those least able to fend for themselves. I'm afraid on that criteria you lot come up short. Very short indeed. In fact I would go as far as to say I am embarrassed to be British under such a regime. I use the word "regime" advisedly. I know the connotations. For many it has come to that. It's not such a huge step.

'"Who is this silly man?" you may be thinking. "Didn't he show the world his willy then retire?" The truth is, ladies and gentlemen, that as a result of the last twenty-four hours you will find my stature has been elevated somewhat. My guess is that in the future when I speak, people will listen. So I suggest you do the same. You lot nearly got confused for Nazis. If you're feeling peckish, that's food for thought right there. Yes Cleggnuts, well may you bow your head.

'Call this whole escapade an opportunity. The Nazis haven't taken over the world. Instead we have all been given a second chance. Especially you. I know many of you come from wealthy backgrounds. That is not your fault, but please put yourself in the position of the vulnerable, the under-privileged, the hard-up. Read around. Use your imagination. Spend less time drinking single malt in rarefied leather-bound rooms and more in the real world. Do any of you know how it feels to go hungry? Or to bring up a child on your own? Or struggle to find work? What about the torture of mental suffering? That's something I know about. I'm a worrier. A big one. I was evacuated into a beastly family during the war and it has never quite left me but I battle on with the help of anti-depressants and my therapist, even if I do feel she overcharges. Alastair Campbell is the same. I don't suppose many of you like him much. I too can find him hard going but he's doing good work. And let's face it, we are all getting old. Look at you, Ken Clarke. You're nearly my age. In fact you look older. One day, Prime Minister, that baby face will turn to wrinkles and SamCam may look elsewhere for her jollies, especially when Little Dave loses his snap. These things happen . . .'

A bang at the door.

'Alan, are you done?'

'Two minutes.'

I turn back to the coalition.

'What I'm saying is have a little compassion. Have a lot. There are people who are living or dying by your decisions. Homelessness grew by seventeen per cent last year. Suicide is on the rise. Our streets are awash with desperation. Do something about it or you'll be hearing from me, you fuckers.'

Grunts and moans fill the air as I stride away from the strung-up politicians and exit the building.

'Thanks Mike, you can cut them down now,' I say. 'Leave the Prime Minister until last. He's got the most to think about.'

As I walked across the field a wave of accomplishment washed over me. I'd done more than I could have hoped for, kyboshing the Nazi network across Bedfordshire and, most likely, the entire world. Right this second I could probably have anything I wanted: cars, clothes, a life-time subscription to *SAGA* magazine. Women over fifty will probably hurl themselves at my arthritic feet. My retirement was now set on a lucrative path.

All I wanted was my wife back.

In the car I tried calling Edame again. Once more straight through to voicemail. I left another message, this time explaining that I was now officially retired and that I couldn't live without her so give us a shout.

I located the earpiece and tapped the Kinsey Shoe Bug app. Interference, a strange fuzzing. Perhaps The Griffin had walked through a puddle, or discovered the transmitter, or given his shoes away. Whatever it was the source was dead.

I drove out of Luton Hoo along the A1081 towards Harpenden and pulled into the first layby I came to. I removed my 1967 AA map from the glovebox and checked the route to Markyate.

Eleven miles. I drove on, looked for the right turn at Kinsbourne Green and continued towards the A5.

Fifteen minutes later I parked up on The Ridings and switched off Radio Five, which was featuring rolling coverage of the unearthing of the cabinet.

Potato Cottage had changed little since I was last here in 1973. George's Jag was parked on the road. I approached the house and looked through the window. There was an eerie stillness in the living room. I tapped at the glass with my key fob. Nothing. I knocked at the door but I knew there would be no reply.

I broke in.

The first thing that struck me about George's house was the smell of chips. The second was the pictures. They were all of George: posing with Eddy Shah and Fluff Freeman, yachting with ex-cricketer Angus Fraser, mink hunting in London Colney, relaxing outside Luton Airport. There was even a coat of arms, complete with a potato in the middle.

I called out but no one answered. In the kitchen everything was cleared away. All the surfaces were polished and sparkling. There was no sign of life. I lift the bin lid: some old peelings and a note:

Darling Eds,
   I love you so bloody much.
   Back for tea (potato pie?)
   Love PG xxxxxxxxxxxxx

'I call her Eds,' I think. 'I bloody well call her Eds.'

I climb the stairs past 'humorous' pictures of misshapen spuds. At the top is a bookcase displaying copies of *The History and Social Influence of the Potato* in twenty-seven languages.

The bedroom door is open, the bed unmade. More than unmade, it's a mess. On the bedside table is a picture of George and Edame together. George is beaming. Edame flashes a smile that doesn't look real. Water on the bathroom floor. Toothbrushes, and a strip of Viagra tablets. Where six pills were once encased in the packet, only two remain.

Mortified, I close up the house and head home.

I can hardly drive into the cul-de-sac. The road is chock-a-block with reporters, news vans and local well-wishers. They see the Stoobmobile and start cheering. I drive at a pedestrian pace into the melee. People are chanting my name. Some are banging on the windows. A woman I recognise from the local WI places a sumptuous-looking fruitcake on the bonnet. I open the sunroof and on the third attempt haul myself upright and stand on the seat. Poking through the top of the car I feel like the pope that heads the church of Nazi hunting.

'Thank you so much,' I say but my words are drowned out by the throng. Someone hands me a makeshift loudspeaker fashioned from a rolled-up *Dunstable and District Observer*.

'I'd like to thank you all for your support!' I continue, now audible. Cheers go up. 'If it wasn't for your help in providing me with leads and financial backing we would be staring down the barrel of a Nazi government.'

I see Pete from Pete's Hams and catch his eye. He mouths 'sorry'. I smile back.

'I wish you all a fruitful afternoon and enjoyable evening. Now if you'll excuse me it's time for my siesta.'

Fifty minutes later I am inside the front door.

'He Stoobs to conquer!' says Tom, enveloping me in a hug. 'How about that for a homecoming! I knew you could bloody do it! By the way, you've got newsprint round your mouth.'

'Thanks, son,' I say. 'Enough about me, what's all this about introducing us to someone?'

'All will be revealed,' he says before leaping upstairs three at a time and shutting himself in his bedroom.

I lie in the bath, sipping on a port and milk. Dr Grossmark says thirty minutes max in the water but today I don't care. I have reached my professional apex, my apotheosis. That it also happens to be my personal nadir will be lost on the rest of the world. How strange to go from quietly successful man with a cosy home life to the hottest ticket in town who also has no idea where his wife is.

I made a choice, influenced in part by a ghost. I chose Nazi hunting over Edame – and now I was paying the consequences.

I dry myself with a purposeful vigour in an effort to pep myself up but to no avail so I climb into bed. On my phone there are 463 unread text messages. Shimon Peres is unduly generous ('mazel tov, honourary Jew') as is Denise Van Outen ('get in, my son') but the one I am looking for isn't there.

I try Edame's number one more time before drifting off to sleep.

I am woken three hours later by the sound of Tina and the gang arriving downstairs. I don't feel like it but I get dressed and head downstairs to greet them.

'Sorry we let ourselves in, Dad,' says Tina, embracing me. 'I can't BELIEVE what you've pulled off, you're so shitting brave!' They all look dressed up for the occasion. Clearly they are taking Tom's announcement seriously. Haden asks if he can have a word in private. I usher him into the downstairs bathroom.

'I just want you to know how proud I am of you today,

Alan,' he says, shaking my hand. 'You stuck with it and for that you should feel most satisfied. Well done.'

I am grateful for his kind words though I fear this new-found maturity is getting out of hand.

Tom has laid the table for thirteen. Tina and family plus Tom and myself makes seven. I'm confused.

I fix the drinks. Houdini lurks in the kitchen, eager to distribute them.

'Are you the most famous granddad in the world?' she asks, all shoulders and dark curls.

'I wouldn't say that, my dear,' I tell her. 'Can you take this very very large glass of Shiraz to your mother?'

'In a moment,' she says. 'Please may I have your autograph fifty times? My plan is to sell them in the playground for one pound each. By my calculations that will make me fifty pounds.'

'Only if I can have twenty-five per cent of the takings.'

'We haven't done percentages yet, Granddad.'

She picks up the wine with two hands and walks out. Marco enters.

'Heya, Alan. I heard all about-ah what-ah you-ah bin up to, eh? Tina fill-ah me in.'

'I bet she's not the only one,' says Haden, who appears at the door.

'Ma bloody san!' says Marco, punching Haden on the shoulder in a playful fashion. Haden avoids it. 'Sometime he so bloody rude, ah?'

'Yeah. And sometimes you're so bloody gay.'

'I donna need to stand-ah for thees,' he says and storms out clutching his rosé.

'Here's to you, Dad!' says Tina as I return to the dining room. She forces me to clink glasses. I'm not in the mood.

'What's up?'

'It's your mother,' I tell her. 'I know I should be celebrating but I don't have the heart. Without her everything seems empty. There are some people in our lives who are just irreplaceable.'

Tina starts fanning her face.

'Please don't, Dad,' she says. 'You'll get me fucking started.'

She takes a large swig of wine, then another.

'Where the bloody hell is my brother anyway?' she says. 'I thought he was making the dinner?'

'TOM!' I shout.

'Bloody typical,' she says. 'He's gone out, hasn't he? And what about this "announcement"? I bet there is no bloody announcement.'

'Be patient,' I say. 'Tom is used to living at his own pace. He'll be along in time.'

'He should show more respect,' says Houdini, unexpectedly. 'You're the most famous and important granddad in the world, and a potential source of future income.'

Tom appears in the doorway, beaming.

'Sorry, everyone, hope you haven't been waiting too long,' he says. 'Thanks for gathering like this. I guess it's a double celebration, what with dad's run of luck on the hunting front.'

'Stuff all that, bro!' says Tina. 'The suspense is fucking killing me!'

Tom's smile curls further upwards.

'Everyone, there's someone I'd like you to meet.'

Tom stands to one side. Behind him a radiant picture of blonde beauty emerges.

'Some of you will remember Susan from the mid-to-late-eighties.'

'Hiya everyone!' she says. 'Hi Tina, Marco. Hello Alan!' Her voice has an unmistakable Kiwi twang. 'I can't tell you how great it is to be back here, eh. These are my girls Sandy, Leighton, Buzzard and Biggleswade.'

Four little girls filter between Tom and Susan before standing in a line, fidgeting.

'Hello, I'm Houdini,' says Houdini, rising. 'I like your dresses. Let's go and play.'

My granddaughter grabs two of them by the hand and leads them all upstairs. One of them winces at the power of Houdini's grip.

'I hear you're like a total hero, Alan, eh!' says Susan.

'Forget me!' I reply. 'What a huge pleasure it is to see you. Is this a flying visit or are you staying for a while?'

'Susan's here for good, Dad,' says Tom. 'So are the girls. They're with me now.'

Tom takes a long sip of ginger ale before telling us a story. The beginning is familiar. When Susan left him back in 1988 he thought his life was over. He wasn't able to function properly and stopped making compilation tapes of the Top 40 on a Sunday afternoon.

'I knew that was a bad sign,' he says. 'Soon after Susan left I started having panic attacks, both indoors and outdoors. I was claustrophobic and agoraphobic. That's when I used to spend a lot of my time standing in doorways.'

Tina nods.

'To complicate matters Dad began his affair with leading businesswoman Deborah Meaden and home life became uncomfortable. Sorry to bring it up, Dad, but it's true. I was in a dark place. When I found out Susan had moved to New Zealand I had a kind of breakdown. People were telling me to move on but I didn't understand. I loved someone and that was never going to change. I completely lost my way. Where once I had been a decent student and accomplished juggler I became a bundle of nerves. If I bumped into anyone I knew I would blush, sweat and vomit – and not always in that order. I spent nearly twenty-five years bouncing between doctors, psychiatrists, hypnotherapists and juggling teachers. In the evenings I'd sit in my room smoking pot and listening to The Smiths, OMD, Howard Jones, Duran Duran, Kenny Loggins, Nik Kershaw, Yazoo, Shergal Farkey, The Pet Shop Boys, Vangelis, Yello, Frankie Goes To Hollywood, '19' by Paul Hardcastle, Eddie Grant, Jean Michel Jarre, Culture Club, Foreigner and Tight Fit: all the stuff that reminded me of my time with Susan. I'd make her tapes of our favourite music and send them to New Zealand in the hope she'd receive them. She never did. It didn't help that I had to guess her address.'

Susan holds Tom's hand.

'The thing is something miraculous had happened in 1982 and I didn't even know it. Tim Berners-Lee invented the world wide web. By the late nineties I had heard of the internet but felt threatened by its expanse, its potential for the unlimited. It was modern and I wasn't. I was living a very limited life, cocooned in my bedroom, wearing thin my video of *Botham's Ashes* or borrowing old episodes of *Tales of the Unexpected* from the library. I thought about killing myself when the machine chewed up the *Challenge Anneka* I recorded the day the show visited Bedford Grammar and momentarily captured Susan in the bottom right-hand corner.

'This year started badly for me. It was twenty-five years since we had split up. On the anniversary – January twenty-sixth – I went into the 99p shop and stole a plastic sword. I felt so angry and upset. I kept picturing myself in the house after Mum and Dad had died – no hurt intended, Dad – lying prostrate on the floor wondering if I'd cope. That's when Dad told me about the tweets from George Michael.'

'I ah-blaady love George Michael,' says Marco.

'Of course you do,' says Haden.

'When Dad told me George Michael had been in touch I could hardly believe it but I was too scared to try and reach out. For a time I retreated back into my eighties world of Boy George and Bill Bixby. To his credit Dad kept pestering me about going online. Eventually I caved in and borrowed his old IBM laptop, though I still didn't lob on for ages.'

'It's log on,' says Haden.

'When I did I realised the whole of the 1980s was still out there. You just had to know where to look. There were websites and fanzines and Midge Ure fora and discussion boards where people would argue the benefits of rare Japanese mono imports of early Housemartin singles. I was in heaven. Then Mum and Dad mentioned something about the Facebook.'

Susan smiled.

'I looked to see if there were any Susan Clawfoots out there. It's quite a rare name you see. The only one I could find was a fifty-year-old housewife with a foot fetish from Farnborough. I'd clearly blanked from my brain that Susan had been married. So I did something clever. Dad, you would have been proud: I searched for Susan's brother, Grant Clawfoot. From there I was able to see who his friends were. I checked through the Susans. That's when I found Susan Oxlong.'

322

'That's me!' said Susan, waving.

'I requested her friendship on the Facebook. While this was pending I looked through all her photographs, spent hours and hours poring over them. There were plenty of her with her kids in New Zealand and a few of her raising different alcoholic drinks to the camera, but surprisingly, and dare I say pleasingly, none of her with her husband.'

'Things started off OK with Mike,' said Susan. 'He was a kind man, a great father and a generous lover, eh. But he was a drinker, a real boozer. He had always drunk throughout the day, but now he was setting his alarm to neck a few in the early hours. To begin with I put up with it and even drank with him. Have you noticed how moreish alcohol can be? It's delicious, eh. But he was clearly addicted. Then one day he hit me with a toothbrush. He was sorry. As an apology he bought me an expensive bottle of wine then drank it himself. It was too much, eh. We left him in a pool of his own beer and moved to the South Island.'

'We started chatting on the instant message Facebook system,' said Tom. 'It's a free service to all users and I highly recommend it. Susan told me about her predicament. I told her I was still a virgin and that Dad had exchanged tweets with George Michael. This piqued her interest so I directed her to the appropriate forums and introduced her to Twitter. After a few weeks I asked her why she left me. She told me it was because I had taped over her favourite Nik Kershaw album, *Human Racing*. I cried that night, remembering how she had annoyed me at school that very day by flirting with Matt Weston during break time . . .'

'I had only done that so Matt would lend me *101* by Depeche Mode because I knew Tom wanted to borrow it!'

'. . . and how that night I had lodged bits of tissue into the dents at the top of the tape so I could record over her prized possession, just to get her back.'

'We were both upset by this and didn't talk for a few days,' said Susan.

'Then a couple of weeks later she changed her Facebook status to "In a relationship". I was horrified. I thought perhaps she had gone back to Maudlin Mike. It was then I checked her image gallery at some length, and discovered she had uploaded one of the two of us from 1986 . . .'

'. . . The year *The Queen Is Dead* by The Smiths was released.'

'. . . which was our favourite album.'

'IS our favourite album.'

The two of them kissed. Tina sniffed into a tissue. Marco checked his phone.

'Then she dropped the big clanger. She told me she was no longer living in New Zealand and had moved to Harpenden. "Harpenden!" I said. We met up for a drink at the Ancient Briton on the A1081 and afterwards parked up in a lay-by in Kinsbourne Green.'

'I gave him a blow job!' said Susan, triumphantly.

'We'd never done that before!' added Tom. 'It was very exciting. She said I was giving her "Come to Beds" eyes. Soon after that she moved to Pulloxhill, Central Bedfordshire. It's rented but it works for us. I'm moving my stuff in tomorrow. Thanks so much for your patience, Dad. You can let the Toddington flat go now.'

Tina hugged them both and declared romance wasn't dead, while staring at Marco. Haden shook hands with Tom before kissing Susan on the lips. He tried to slip her the tongue. I noticed but thankfully Tom didn't. Marco excused himself to make a phone call.

Dinner was a raucous affair. Much wine was drunk, particularly by Tina. Houdini ate seventeen raw chillies for our amusement. I had never imagined I would see Tom so happy. His laughter filled the room. He and Susan: young lovers back together.

It left me feeling bereft.

I made my apologies and slunk off to bed.

No message from Edame. You can have your dinners with Barack Obama and your knighthoods and whatever else lies on the horizon. You can even have your interviews with *Cycling Weekly*. I'm pleased for my son but all I want is my wife back.

* * *

A people-carrier arrives at 9am to take Tom, Susan and the kids to their new home in the village of Pulloxhill. I see them off in my dressing gown. Susan hugs me and tries to reassure me about Edame. The little girls take it in turns to cuddle my legs. Tom approaches, his eyes filled with emotion. We embrace.

'I love you so much that I've written you a jingle,' he says, thrusting a piece of paper into my hand. 'You don't need to use it but it's yours. Thanks so much for giving me time to find my feet.'

As they drive off I look at the paper.

Nazis are evil, everyone says.
Even Madonna, Shaun Ryder and Bez.
Most are called Jan, Adolf or Gunter.
My name is Alan and I am their hunter.

I head back to bed and google 'Shaun Ryder' on my phone, before tweeting, 'I don't suppose anyone has seen my wife?' There is no response. I doze off.

I wake at midday from a dreamless snooze. My head is aching, I've been asleep too long. The house is still. With Tom gone I imagine it will remain this way for some time. Possibly forever.

I head downstairs and turn on the telly. Snooker. Perhaps I can get into this year's world championships, I think. That will help pass the time. Maybe I can even start watching the soaps. They're like pals you can rely on. They never leave you.

Standing in the sitting room I stare mindlessly at the space where the *Bergerac* video box set once lived. If only I hadn't been so selfish.

The metallic springing of the letterbox followed by the tiniest thud on the mat. I go over to inspect. In my heyday as Britain's Premier Nazi Hunter I would receive upwards of 100 letters a day and that's before you even include parcels, special deliveries and confidential files biked over by Interpol.

I used to be someone. Today all I find is a letter reminding me our piano is due for re-tuning. We sold that piano in 1976 to pay for Tina's ballet lessons.

I walk through to the kitchen. There, drinking a mug of tea, her luggage covering the floor, I find my beautiful wife.

'Hello, Alan,' she says. 'I didn't want to disturbing you.'

I take one step forward. She does likewise. Another step from me, another from her. We meet in the middle and throw our arms around each other, clinging on for dear life.

'I'll never hunt Nazis again!' I tell her.

'I'll never leave your sides again!' she says.

We stay in this position until the tears streaming down both of our faces have dried. I offer her my hand and she takes it. I lead her up the stairs and into the bedroom. We lie next to each other on the bed. I loosen my dressing gown and fashion to slip out of my Y-fronts.

'We can just cuddle if you like?' she says.

'No need,' I tell her.

'Oh Alan,' she says forty minutes later, 'that was 1967 all over again!' She is still short of breath, her fringe matted flat to her forehead.

'Plenty more where that came from,' I reply. 'I've come into the possession of some special pills that should see us through.'

As she lay in my arms I see in her eyes the girl I once knew.

'I thought you weren't coming back,' I say.

'You put me in a corner, Alan,' she replies. 'Nobody puts Edame in a corner. It felt like you'd giving me no choices.'

'I know,' I say. 'And I'm sorry.'

She tells me she slept with Potato George twice because she felt she had to. I tell her that when I broke in I found four pills missing from the strip. Apparently he needed two at a time. I was heartened to hear he was prone to going off too quickly, like an excitable spud gun.

'I didn't want to be with George from the start,' she said. 'And when I see you on the news defeating all the Huns I knew I had to coming back. Have you definitely retired definitely?'

'Of course,' I tell her. 'Even if everything had backfired the only person I had in my mind was you. I realised you were the single most important thing in my life. It's difficult when the ghost of Simon Wiesenthal pops by and insists you keep fighting the scourge of National Socialism, but I should imagine he will leave me alone now.'

'So that's it, 100 per cent over?'

'That's it. No more. Nada. Le fin. Enden.'

She plants a lingering kiss on my lips.

'You will not believe what Tom has been up to!' I tell her. 'He and Susan are back together and have moved to Pulloxhill near Flitwick. Looks like we both get the girl.'

'I know all that,' she said. 'I saw it on the Facebook.'

'You're on the Facebook? How long have you been on the Facebook? Why aren't I on the Facebook?'

Momentarily I feel insecure.

'It was George's idea. I think I'll probably delete my account now.'

'What happened to George?'

Edame looks rueful and takes a swig from the bottle of Evian next to the bed.

'He didn't take it well when I told him I was doing the offski. He called me a slagger, said I was ugly and that he fancied Eva Braun. Then he started crying and didn't stop for two days. I had the sorries for him. I stayed around because I felt bad. Then just as I was leaving he declared that he suddenly felt very ancient and was moving to old people's home. I tried to talk him out of it but he put his house on the markets and moved into the Bluebell Home for crumblies on Crescent Drive. We can visit him if we like. Every day, 2–6pm. I've already got text off him. He say they don't cut his banana up the way he like. Can you imagines?'

The thought of sixty-four-year-old Potato George in an old people's home left me feeling most peculiar. Here was I, seventy-five and with renewed zest. Maybe I'll send George a few of the Mengele pills. One, anyway.

A knock at the front door. I sat up and peered out of the bedroom window. All I could see was the top of an articulated lorry.

'Go on, Als,' said Edame. 'You never know what might be being.'

I hobbled downstairs and opened the door. A young German gentleman stood before me. Behind I could see the lorry more clearly. Mengele Chemische GmbH was written on the side.

'Sign her, bitte,' said the man. 'Ve have many of ze pillz for du. Vare can ve put zem?'

This really was my lucky day.

'Please carry a few boxes upstairs, second on the right, my son's old room,' I told the man. 'The rest I would like you to deliver to the head of the Science Faculty, Cambridge University, Cambridge. Oh, and drop a couple of boxes round to Bob at number twenty-five, would you? If he doesn't answer leave them down the side.'

Edame and I lie in each other's arms. We make an occasional silly joke ('How many Nazis does it take to change a lightbulb? Nein!') but mostly we are silent, happy in each other's arms. At three I rise and shower. It's time for my appointment with Beryl.

She takes an age to come to the door. When she finally appears her face is sour like a lemon.

'Well, if it isn't Mr Big Boots,' she says. 'Go through please. I'll be in in a few minutes.'

I sit in the room on my own. I look up at the clock. It's already 3.08. This is eating into my time. Not that I care today. She's behaving weirdly. It's not going to make what I'm about to say any easier. She eventually swans in at 3.13 clutching what appears to be an extra large crème de menthe.

'Sorry I wasn't enough for you,' she says. 'What do you want anyway? I thought you'd be having tea with David Attenborough or some other media twat.'

'Why are you being so aggressive?' I ask. 'You're in a strange mood.'

'No I'm not, you are,' she says, crossing her legs and arms.

'I've got something to tell you and I'm not sure how you're going to react,' I say.

'Nothing you can say can phase me, I'm bullet-proof,' she says, taking a long sip of mint drink. 'Just remember it was me that helped you get to where you are today.'

'I'm leaving you, Beryl,' I say.

She does her best not to betray any emotion but I can see it in her micro-expressions. I've read about them.

'Good,' she replies. 'Fuck off then.'

'Don't be like that,' I say. 'You have helped me, Beryl, without question. But it feels to me like I have learnt to help myself.'

'I give you three weeks,' she says, smiling. 'Three weeks then you'll be back, begging your stupid head off to see me again. Face it, Alan, you can't cope on your own.'

'I don't need to,' I tell her. 'I've got Edame back.'

Her face falls.

'That bitch?' she says. 'It won't last you know. She's only come back for the fame and the money. When she gets bored she'll move onto some other poor sod like John Suchet or Mervyn King. She doesn't really want you, Alan. Not like I do.'

'Sorry, Beryl, but this is it for me. Thanks for your help.'

I stand and leave a bumper box of mint Matchmakers on the seat for her. She glances at them and remains seated.

'See yourself out, cunt,' she says. 'You're so fucked no one can save you.'

'I think you should get some help,' I say before exiting her consultancy room for the final time. Quietly I let myself out of the front door. As I unlock the car I hear a sickening scream.

D✤cember

A week of endless media engagements culminated in my appearance on *The Jonathan Ross Show* alongside Sir Jeffrey Archer, Diego Maradona and the ginger one from Girls Are Loud. Ross made a good joke about being glad there weren't any Rs in my name. We all laughed.

The Simon Wiesenthal Centre asked me what I wanted as a gift. I told them to send fresh flowers to Edame every day for a year. She's thrilled, though it's playing havoc with my hay fever.

Dunstable Town Council has commissioned my statue for the town centre. It is to be designed by sculptor Ron Mueck, the guy who did the massive babies. The mayor has given his word that my wilbur will not feature.

Hodder & Stoughton has approached me and asked to publish my diaries. I said I'd send them this one, the one you're reading.

On the downside my affair with Deborah Meaden has been splashed all over the tabloids and a book, *The Lone War of Alan Stoob*, hurried out in my name. It's total rubbish and full of half-truths, e.g. that Nazi babies are born with one protruding arm. The press have been camped outside the front door. We're being forced to burn our rubbish like Osama bin Laden. It's not ideal, though I can see their interest is already beginning to wane.

The Griffin has disappeared from view. He's probably camping out in the cold like Raoul Moat, waiting for Gazza to bring him some chicken. At 107 he'll not last long.

I feel happier than I've been for many years. The fact that Tom is finally settled takes a great strain off all of us. Dr Grossmark is weaning me off the anti-depressants. Not sure I need them anymore. With my dismantling of the Nazi network I was able to lay a whole host of personal demons to rest.

Perhaps predictably I am unnerved by my contentment. No doubt Beryl would tell me that I feel I don't deserve happiness. Perhaps she's right. I heard the British Association of Psychotherapists was covering her fees at The Priory. We sent her a get-well-soon card with a cat on the front.

Edame and I have booked a whole host of trips for early next year: Venice, New York, Paris, Cape Town and Melton Mowbray.

I fear the stillness. What will happen when everything goes quiet? I take the thought and squish it deep down into my stomach.

*　　*　　*

Another week, another round of media engagements. I enjoyed appearing on *The One Show*. Alex Jones reminds me of a young Edame.

Interpol is paying to have the ratline, formerly running from Bremen to Biggleswade, diverted so that the end point is now a large cell deep within the confines of Bedford police station. A stroke of genius on Mike's part. Meanwhile all other Nazis were hoovered up at the most recent monthly meeting.

Bob seems to be thriving. It could be the pills, or at least the placebo effect. He's talking again and has a new girlfriend. She's ninety-six and still sexy.

Tina and Marco have reached an understanding. He's permitted to go out once a week at night, the rest of the time he must play the loving husband. On that night she sees other men. It's a façade but one that seems to work for both of them.

Edame and I have also come to some sort of understanding: I am allowed onto the after-dinner circuit once a month, the only proviso being I must bring her with me. I'm more than happy to do this. She is after all my rock, as well as my roll.

* * *

Two weeks until Christmas and the day of my first after-dinner speech. The butterflies are back just like they always were on a hunt day. At least there's sex now to take my mind off things.

Edame prepares my pre-hunt breakfast for old-time's sake.

'This morning in the bed was amazeballs,' she says, big eyed. I don't know what 'amazeballs' means but she's started peppering her conversation with it.

'Guess what?' I reply. 'I haven't taken one of Mengele's pills since last Tuesday.'

'Does that mean the stiffenings last few days?' she asks.

'It could be. Or perhaps the burden of hunting the Nazis was weighing heavily about my penis. Maybe I don't need the pills at all.'

'DON'T GET RID OF THEM!' she says in a panic.

The speech is in Worcester, 100 miles away. The journey will be a pleasure as I've recently traded in the Omega for a Lexus. I know Lexuses are Japanese but one has to let bygones be bygones, especially when confronted with this kind of cornering. It even has heated seats. Edame loves heated seats.

But mostly it seems she loves me. Our love is burning like never before, we in the autumn of our years. It reminds me of the 1985 film *Cocoon*, directed by Ron Howard.

It's fun getting ready together at the hotel, like we are heading out to a party, which in a way we are. The speaker agency has suggested I make my address a celebration. With my sixteen miniature prompt cards and my girl by my side I feel supremely confident. Edame looks amazing in the new matching top and slacks I bought her at M&S.

It is then that I see it. Pushed under the hotel door. On the mat, staring up at me. 'Mr Stoob', it says. The handwriting is familiar. I tear it open.

> Long time no speak
> Let's cut the chase
> I know where The Griffin is hiding out.
> Sound of interest?
> Don't pretend it doesn't.
> The old reservoir at Oxley Park.
> 2pm tomorrow.
> Come alone
> A friend

No more going over Edame's head. I show her the note.

'And this same man that helped you in the before?' she asks. I nod. 'You're sure it's same man?'

'Yes,' I say. 'Same writing. Same tone. Same man.'

'Then I think you should go. Not on your solo though. Ask Mike Moomins to accompanying you.'

'But it says alone.'

'I know what is says, Alan Stoob. I'm telling you what your options are.'

She's right.

'I'll ask Mike.'

'The two of you can meet the man in the together, hopefully he can provide an addressing. Then let Mike deal with the rest. These are still Nazis we're talking about. I've got my Alan back, I don't want to lost him again.'

The thought of finding The Griffin and completing the Nazi set is an appealing one. I text Mike. He says he's up for it. The old feelings come rushing back.

My performance at the Worcester British Legion went down a storm. 'A stormtrooper!' according to Edame. I even felt comfortable enough to ad-lib the encore, during which I told a classic anecdote about Heidi Schwarzbag, the Piglet of Pappenheim. It brought the house down. Three women were outside waiting for me. Two handed me their mobile numbers. I thanked them, then threw the numbers in the bin once we had rounded the corner.

'You're amazeballs,' said Edame.

'I know,' I said.

We lay silent in the hotel bed, post-coitus. Edame was asleep. The headlights from the road darted along the wallpaper before disappearing. I turned over the day's events in my head.

'A friend.'

This friend had never let me down. The source of nothing but sound information.

I kissed Edame on all four cheeks. She stirred, smiled and muttered 'Henry'.

* * *

Drive back to Dunstable. Even Edame's somnambulant reference to the late Henry Cooper wasn't going to spoil my buoyant mood. I let her do the gears.

'This stick reminds me of your you-know,' she says giggling. I smile back at her and in my head thank Dr Josef Mengele.

We grab a sandwich at Newport Pagnell, my favourite motorway services. Roadworks on the M1 have slowed us up however, as did the sex session before breakfast. I'm in danger of being late for my appointment.

With time so tight I drop Edame off at the house. We kiss in the Lexus and she places a hand on my shoulder.

'No need to be nervous is it?' she says. 'This is not Nazis hunt and anyway Mike will be there. See you later. I'll make something special for dinner and won't be wearing any underpant.'

I turn the car round and head straight for Meppershall and Oxley Park. I was supposed to be meeting Mike at 1.30 at a nearby Pizza Express. I text him to say I'm going to be delayed. The Lexus tells me to put my seatbelt back on or it will stop the car.

I arrive in a tiz, park up and hurry to our rendezvous.

No sign of Mike. My phone beeps.

Sorry, Alan, terrible gastroenteritis. Shitting through the eye of an amoeba. Let's rearrange with your 'friend'. Don't go alone. Mike.

Why couldn't he have told me earlier? That way I could have sought a replacement. Bloody hell.

I return to the car feeling unduly deflated. Seems all I need is one whiff of Nazi and I'm back, addicted, like the ageing pugilist craving one last shot at the title. Thing is I'm already crowned heavyweight champion of the world of Nazi Hunting. This is a Commonwealth bout. In fact it's not even a bout.

This man is a friend. And you don't hit your friends, not unless they've had it off with your wife.

'Just go along and get the information,' I mumble. 'It's merely a spot of post-retirement consultancy work.' I lock the Lexus behind me. 'I've got Interpol on speed-dial.' I cross the road. 'Un-flap-uh-bull.' I head for Oxley Park.

Walking along the towpath I pass all the houseboats. 'Mayflower', 'Juniper', 'Harold', as many names as there are vessels. Most have floral decoration on the sides, plants on board and rusty bikes bolted to the handrails.

One barge caught my eye. A spotlight beamed from it, apparently illuminating my way. As I approached an elderly man appeared.

'Mr Stoob, I have been expecting you. Please – come aboard.'

I clambered up. My 'friend', 'Jimmy', was on the roof performing some kind of maintenance task that I did not understand. Unlike before he was dressed scruffily and appeared to have lost weight. I guess this is inevitable as you approach your 110s.

'Why the boat?' I ask.

'Recent development, Mr Stoob. Hard times come to us all. Gin and tonic?'

I nodded and he disappeared into the boat, only to reappear seconds later.

'Chop chop,' he says impatiently. I join him downstairs.

I am surprised at the number of technological devices around the room. The space is musty and boasts a single bed in the corner. We clink glasses.

'Depth charge going down.'

I sip, he glugs.

'So, Mr Stoob,' he says, fussing at the sideboard. 'You've

had an incredible run of success. I have little doubt Edame is pleased as punch and I bet she's showing it, eh?'

He turns to me and winks. I choose not to respond.

'I understand you have information regarding the where-abouts of The Griffin?' I say.

'Certainly,' he replies.

'Can you tell me, please?'

'All will be revealed, Mr Stoob,' he replies. 'For now we should be celebrating one of the greatest comebacks since 1963 when Ali picked himself up off the canvas and won the day against the late Henry Cooper.'

An odd thing to say given my history but I let it go. And what's with the 'Heinrich'? He pulls up a chair and sits opposite me.

'Nice place you've got here,' I say.

'Don't lie, Mr Stoob, it's a shithole.'

'I guess it is a little on the drab side in parts,' I say, choosing my words carefully. 'Forgive me, but I'm surprised to find you in such a location. I got the impression you were an eminent man of means.'

'Oh I am, Mr Stoob, I am. But there has been, shall we say, a change in circumstances.'

'Meaning?'

He leans forward.

'Between you and me,' he says, lowering his voice and checking both ways, 'I am being hunted.'

'Hunted?' I say. 'Why so?'

Once more he looks both ways.

'Long story.'

He rises to fix us both another drink. As he does the glow from the makeshift light on the ceiling catches the face of his watch as his sleeve rides up. It is gone in a flash but not before I see what I know to be true.

It's Edame's watch, the one taken from me by The Griffin next to Biggleswade reservoir.

He hands me my drink. I sip. Same as before, bitter to the taste.

'I didn't notice the name of your boat,' I say, aware for the first time of my heart hammering uncomfortably in my chest.

'Die namen, Herr Stoob?'

Where had his mellifluous English tones gone?

'Yes, the name.'

The floor was rising up towards me.

'Ve call it . . . ODESSA.'

Speaking is a struggle.

'Need to get off,' I say. 'Sea sick . . .'

Woozy.

'Nonsense!' comes the reply. 'Sea sickness ist alles in ze mind.'

The last thing I recall is checking my pocket for my inhaler only to discover I left it at home.

WHOOSH! A bucket of water is thrown over my face and torso. I come-to strapped to a chair. I quickly realise it's not water but paraffin. The man before me is clutching a lighter.

'Bit of ein lightweight, aren't ve, Herr Stoob?' he says. 'Vun trinken and you're unter das table.'

'You drugged me,' I say, shaking the liquid from my hair. I strain to wipe my nose on my shoulder.

'Nonsense!' he replies. 'Vye vood ich drug ein mensche like du, Herr Stoob?'

'You're a Nazi!' I say, surprised by my own words.

'A Nazi, Herr Stoob?'

'I don't understand why you've helped me in the past but

you are wearing Edame's watch, you're speaking German and your boat is called ODESSA which as every hunter knows stands for Organisation Der Ehemaligen SS-Angehörigen or "Organisation of Former SS Members".'

'Oh zat,' he replies, smiling. 'Zat was mein biggest clue so far. Ha! Ziss ist like *Through ze Keyhole* starring Loyd Grossman.'

'All this and you call yourself a friend?' I said.

'Oh I am ein freund, Herr Stoob. Ich always haf your best interests at heart.'

He circles me, trailing an aroma of stale sweat. I cough to indicate my disapproval.

'Pay attention, Herr Stoob,' he says, standing opposite me once more and leaning back against the sideboard. 'Here komme ze science bit.'

He tilts his head back gently until all I see is his neck and jaw line. He begins pulling at the skin, at first gently but soon with greater urgency. What appears to be latex is coming free. The real skin underneath is even more pallid and wrinkled. He lifts the plastic masking above his chin, free from his lips, up over his nose and eyes and clear of his face. Slowly he allows his head to fall back into position.

Before me, unmistakably, stood The Griffin.

'Ich haf always looked after du, Alan. Remember when ich spared du dein life by Letchworth Lake? Ich voodn't do zat mit alles ze hunters.'

'I don't understand,' I say. 'Why the elaborate disguise and impeccable English accent? Why the complex imaginings about your work as a floater? Why hand over the details of so many other Nazis? And why kill me now?'

'So many qvestion, Alan,' he says. 'Vhy must se Englishe alvays ask so many qvestions?'

'Because as a nation we seek truth and justice,' I tell him.

'How very high-minded,' he replies, picking a last scrap of latex from his neck. 'Ze sing about me, Alan, ist zat ich liebe ze chase. Ze chase ist alles fur me. Zat ist vye ich provided du mit leads, to keep sings interesting. Zat ist vye ich chose nicht to kill du. Ich enjoyed our, how du say, tussles? Ve are like Holmes und Moriarty – du know, von se Sherlock Holmes films. Unfortunately all gut films must come to ein end.'

'They were books first, Griffin,' I say, angered by his ignorance.

'Votever,' he replies before grabbing a jerry can – naturally – and sloshing more paraffin over my trousers, creating a circle of fluid around me.

'Ich like du, Alan,' he says. 'Ven du reach our level zare ist little to distinguish se hunter und se hunted, ja? Ve are both at ze top of our game. But du ruined it by destroying ze Third Reich. Unluckerlich du leave me mit keine option but to destroy du in return.'

What was left in my arsenal? No James Bond-style poison dart I could fire, no deadly spittle I could launch or knife-boot I could stab with. Words were all I had.

'I was coming with a colleague. Chief Constable Mike Moomin. You might know him. He couldn't make it for gastric reasons but is sending someone in his place. They're probably outside now.'

'Your desperation disappoints mich,' he says, drinking gin from the bottle. 'Ich thought du vood be ze kind of mensch who vood go to his agonising death mit dignity und courage. Ich can see du possess neither of zees valuable attributen.'

He took another swig. How could anyone drink neat gin?

'I'm warning you, Griffin, they know what boat you live on.'

'Boot?' he say, laughing. 'BOOT? In two minutes' time there will BE no boot, Herr Stoob!'

He removed his lighter.

'Do du haf ein dying vish? Perhaps ein message ich can pass onto your voluptuous vife?'

'Put the lighter down, you schijtlul!'

Edame was stood to my right, aiming the replica gun at The Griffin's head.

'Fell ich never!' says The Griffin. 'Sprechen von se devil und se devil appears! Vot'll it be, Frau Stoob – gin und tonic, Dubonnet or perhaps eine kleine Campari?'

'Put the lighter down and lie on the flooring with your hand behind your headbone.'

The very last thing on earth I wanted was for Edame to be mixed up in this ugly scene. I knew that the gun she held was merely an imitation, the threat of a gun, nothing more. My feelings of self-preservation had all but disappeared. All I wanted was for Edame to escape with her own life.

'Shoot me if du like!' said The Griffin, who had moved onto shots of flaming Sambucca. 'Go on!'

Edame didn't respond.

'Ach dear, vot a couple of cowards ve haf here,' he said. He stared into my eyes, flicked the lighter lid up and rolled the flint.

Each gunshot is different to the next. This one was fast and precise like a whip, with no echo. The Griffin staggered, the blood spouting from the small entry wound above his left eye, before toppling backwards, his lifeless body catching the table as he fell. Edame had shot him in the head. The Griffin was dead.

'A real gun! How did you get—' I said, stopping midsentence. The lighter was on the floor, a line of fire heading for my feet. Edame ran behind me and started untying the rope around my ankles. She was quick, her woman's nails getting under the knots. By the time she began working on my wrists we were encircled in a ring of fire, the flames licking at my legs which I held in the air.

'Please hurry,' I said.

By the time I was free we were both alight. Edame's clothes were on fire but her expression was implacable. We ran up the stairs of the boat and dived over the side. Within a few seconds we bobbed to the surface. Edame's face was black with soot.

'Are you OK?' I ask.

'Of course,' she says and kisses me. Next to us the boat is flaming like a torch. The sound of cracking glass and splintering wood fills the wintry air. We swim away from the boat and clamber onto the towpath. A man emerges from the Mayflower.

'What the shit?' he exclaims.

'Bad Nazi,' I say as we walk back towards the car.

*   *   *

A body was dragged from the River Lee. It was identified as The Griffin, aka Herbert Klopp, a low-level SS member with a history of unspeakable crimes to his name. The coroner decided it was suicide and wrapped up the case in a week.

There didn't seem much point going to the police. It would only have meant telling them Edame was in possession of an unlicensed firearm and had murdered someone with it. I in turn would have tarnished my legacy by showing myself a gullible buffoon. Thankfully my phone survived the canal plunge. When we got home I texted Mike Moomin.

Hi Mike. Sorry you're not well. Let me know when better and we can meet up with the informant. In the meantime stay vigilant. From Alan.

It seems Edame became a little frustrated following the incident at the funeral when the vicar was shot in the forehead, so she got herself a real gun. It's one of the reasons she went to visit her mother in Holland, to fetch her father's old wartime weapon. I don't know how she smuggled it back into England. Some things are better left unsaid.

I do love the run-up to Christmas. This year felt more special than most. For once I had time to do my own shopping rather than giving Edame cash and asking her to pick out something nice. This time I was buying for more than usual: Susan and the little ones.

Christmas Day round at Tina's and a Nazi-themed lunch. We had Pommes Fritz with the Turkey, Reichs pudding and Goebbelstoppers. We even had Hitler sauce with the pudding. I didn't understand this one but let it go. Houdini called it deSSert and wrote it on the tablecloth.

'I bet Hitler longed for a white Christmas,' said Haden.

Marco brought round his boyfriend. Tina said she didn't mind. She herself had a young chap in tow. What a modern family. Even Haden seemed happy. Word was he'd asked out a girl at school and she said she'd think about it, pending the outcome of his bulk-enhancing weights regime over the New Year.

Over Hun and Jerries ice cream Susan rose and tapped her glass.

'I'd like you to know that me and Tom are, like, up the duff?' she said, smiling. We were going to be grandparents again. I felt flushed with excitement and asked Edame whether it was too late for her to conceive. She said she'd already made an appointment with Dr Grossmark for the New Year.

345

That night as we lay in bed Edame spoke.

'I know we're not youngs anymore and god knows what round a corner but I do think we are lucky.'

'I know what you mean, sweetheart,' I told her.

'We do not want for the money. We have a wonderful family that cares. Most of all we have each of the other, Alan. I couldn't be happiest.'

'Even if the late Henry Cooper was in my place?' I ask.

'What a things to say!' she replies and bites me playfully on the arm. I guess there will always be a part of me lodged in the past.

*   *   *

Monday 31st December 2012

Last day of the year. Big party planned at Stoob HQ. We spend the day putting up decorations. Marco arranged a helium machine for the balloons. Edame keeps inhaling the gas and walking around talking like writer and journalist Julie Burchill. It is probably her best joke ever.

Before the guests arrive I write an introduction to the first edition of a brand new magazine entitled *Vigilance* – 'for the discerning Nazi Hunter'.

As I am adding the finishing touches to my words the phone rings downstairs.

'Alan,' shouts Edame. 'It's for you.'

I ask her to put it through to the study.

'Hello, Alan Stoob speaking.'

I recognise the piece immediately. I had heard it many times in the last eighteen years. I even liked it. But 'Ride of the Valkyries' by Richard Wagner can only mean one thing. For

346

some reason I am drawn to the window. I part the blinds. Opposite is a man in a dark suit. He looks up at me, waves, then draws his finger across his throat. He climbs into his expensive German automobile and drives off. The line goes dead.

Edame appears at the door.

'You OK, Alan?' she says. 'You look nervy.'

'Everything is fine,' I tell her. 'Wrong number.'

The End

In the best books, the ending often comes as
Not just because of that one last twist in the
but because you have been so absorbed in the
that coming back to the harsh light of reality i

If that describes you now, then perhaps you shoul
some new leads, and find new suspense in othe

Join us at www.hodder.co.uk, or follow us
Twitter @hodderbooks, and you can tap i
community of fellow thrill-seekers.

Whether you want to find out more about th
or a particular author, watch trailers and intervi
the chance to win early limited editions, or simp
our expert readers' selection of the very best
we think you'll find what you're looking

And if you don't, that's the place to tell us what

We love what we do, and we'd love you to be

www.hodder.co.uk

@hodderbooks

HodderBooks

HodderBooks

some reason I am drawn to the window. I part the blinds. Opposite is a man in a dark suit. He looks up at me, waves, then draws his finger across his throat. He climbs into his expensive German automobile and drives off. The line goes dead.

Edame appears at the door.

'You OK, Alan?' she says. 'You look nervy.'

'Everything is fine,' I tell her. 'Wrong number.'

The End